PARTING SHOT

BOOKS BY JAMES W. KUNETKA

FICTION

Warday (coauthor)
Nature's End (coauthor)
Shadow Man

NONFICTION

City of Fire: Los Alamos and the Birth of the Atomic Age
Oppenheimer: A Biography

PARTING SHOT

JAMES W. KUNETKA

ST. MARTIN'S PRESS   NEW YORK

A THOMAS DUNNE BOOK

FOR BOB AND BARBARA

The characters and events of *Parting Shot* are fictitious. The two exceptions are the characters of Robert Oppenheimer and General Leslie Groves, two men so well known to modern history that to use them as major characters with false names seemed ridiculous. The words and actions that I ascribe to them, however, are entirely mine.

PARTING SHOT. Copyright © 1991 by James W. Kunetka. All rights reserved. Printed in the United States of America. No part of this book may be used or reproduced in any manner whatsoever without written permission except in the case of brief quotations embodied in critical articles or reviews. For information, address St. Martin's Press, 175 Fifth Avenue, New York, N.Y. 10010.

Production Editor: David Stanford Burr

DESIGN BY GLEN M. EDELSTEIN

Library of Congress Cataloging-in-Publication Data

Kunetka, James W.
      Parting shot / James W. Kunetka.
         p. cm.
      ISBN 0-312-05237-5
      I. Title.
      PS3561.U448P37 1991
      813'.54—dc20
                                     90-48997
                                     CIP

First Edition: January 1991

10 9 8 7 6 5 4 3 2 1

Acknowledgment

This book is based on an idea proposed to me by my friend and motion-picture producer David Axelrod.

His interest in the scientific developments of World War II provided the basic theme of *Parting Shot*.

Prologue

APRIL 1945

THE FÜHRERBUNKER, BERLIN

History has recorded who fired the first shot. In the long run, it will be who fired the last shot that matters.
—Franklin Roosevelt, 1941

$\mathcal{T}$he man involuntarily sucked in a deep breath of air, exchanging the stale, fetid atmosphere of the underground bunker for the acrid smell of explosives and burning buildings.

The major with the Death's Head on his cap hesitated just beyond the checkpoint where visitors showed their papers and checked their pistols, still sheltered by the Chancellery's overhang. All around him, irregularly timed, were the whistling sounds of Russian artillery shells, followed quickly by the crack and thunder of explosions. The constant din of shelling that went on around the clock grew steadily louder each hour as the Russians slowly encircled the city.

Even twenty meters below, in the heart of the Führerbunker, he could hear the dull throb of the shelling.

Behind him, just in front of the guards, a small gathering of Wehrmacht officers talked in low voices and smoked their final cigarettes before descending the long staircase underground. Once in the bunker, at least on the second level, near the Führer's suite of rooms, all smoking was prohibited.

These were the *Scheissköpfe* who had lost the war!

The blond major frowned and turned disgustedly around to study the bombed courtyard with its craters and collapsed walls. A fire burned in the shell of a building a dozen meters away, large plumes of dark smoke wafting up to join the pall that hung perpetually over Berlin. In another corner, two soldiers were burying the dismembered and charred remains of several bodies.

Gott sei Dank! he was in the Waffen-SS, he thought, the elite military arm of the SS, and not the regular Army. The Waffen-SS had never faltered, never failed to fight to the finish, even when that meant sacrificing the last man. They had had glorious victories. And that was more than the traitorous leaders and halfhearted soldiers of the Wehrmacht could claim.

Somewhere beyond him a shell shrieked across the sky. Instinctively, he pulled back against the wall and waited. Seconds later there was a flash of light and a powerful explosion as the shell hit the edge of the courtyard. For an instant, all the air around him seemed to disappear. Then bits of plaster and marble flew through the cloud of dust.

Rumor had it that Zhukov's first Belorussian armies were already at the outskirts of Berlin, at the Fürstenwalde-Strausberg line. And to the south, Konev's Ukrainian armies were nearing Dresden. If this was true, then Berlin had only weeks, perhaps days, left.

The major sighed and instead thought about the last hour. Just thirty minutes ago he had been shaking the Führer's hand, something he had never dreamed he would do. The great man was frail, old-looking, and worn down by the treachery around him. But *Gott!* what inner strength. That one moment made the last few months worthwhile!

Another shell screamed by; another explosion and cloud of dust.

He had often wondered why he'd been pulled from active duty in February to train secretly at a small complex in the Hartz Mountains. Ordered—forced—to speak nothing but English and master a thousand strange technical details. And to do this while the enemies of Germany pressed closer each day.

But now it made sense. There was purpose, great purpose, explained by the Führer himself in a voice so laden with emotion that the major had struggled to hold back his own tears. *He had been chosen by the Führer himself!* Those words still rang in his ears.

A fat political official in a disheveled brown Party uniform suddenly appeared, his face filled with fear, followed by a small retinue of equally frightened aides. The major didn't bother to acknowledge them or return their salute.

Scheissköpfe!

Now he considered his options. With any luck, he'd make it through the courtyard and what was left of one wing of the Chancellery without being killed. His car and driver were on the other side, a half-block away, hopefully intact. With more luck, Potsdamer or Hauptstrasse would be clear enough to navigate and he could still make it through the Berlin suburbs to southern Germany, the only route still under German control—hopefully still under control. He needed to reach the Mediterranean in less than five days.

Five days! Then a journey of weeks, maybe more, before he could execute his Führer's orders.

Taking a deep breath, he glanced at the threatening sky and then darted out of the doorway. There was no time to look back.

Part One

We shall not capitulate—no, never! We may be
destroyed, but if we are, we shall drag a world with us—
a world in flames!

—Adolph Hitler, 1934

Chapter One

$\mathcal{T}$he man in the soiled undershirt cursed; the metal ribs of the bulldozer seat worked their way through the worn cushion into his buttock. Sweat poured down his face and clung in small beads, especially where the scar ran down the left side of his face. His chest and back were wet with perspiration.

Dinty Reeds hated digging up foundations, especially in this part of London; he never knew what he'd dig into. There were old gas mains and sewers from the last century and skeletons from the blitz. Even a bloody cave-in here and there, and he had a four-inch scar from one accident to prove it.

Today he glanced up into a rare blue sky unblemished by clouds. A lingering heat wave had pushed the temperature into the high eighties and thickened the humidity. He had no idea what the temperature was, but he knew it was bloody hot!

Nearby, the major arteries of London's South Bank—Kennington, Westminister Bridge, and St. George's Road—were clogged with cars and people. Tourists and natives reeled in the heat toward the diverse complex of museums and flats and office buildings.

"Bleedin' Christ," cursed Reeds. He was soaked through with sweat and covered in a coating of soot and dirt.

He shoved the "forward" lever again and hit the accelerator at the same time; the heavy tractor lurched forward, hesitated, then leapt, as if it were being spanked. Reeds hit the plow control, forgetting to ease it down; instead, he let all two thousand pounds of it hit the ground with a thud that drew the attention of his supervisor a dozen yards away. He gave his head a jerk to shake off the drops of sweat that had formed on the tip of his nose. He could tell without looking that the super disapproved.

Reeds lunged forward once again, this time holding back the gas just a little. As the bulldozer ground forward, he felt the foundation give way a bit; a moment later, the plow hit something heavy that echoed with a metallic ring. Reeds gave the tractor more power, but it failed to move. The cushionless seat underneath him began to vibrate as the machine struggled to break forward. From the corner of his eye he saw the super running toward him and waving his hands frantically; the man was pointing to the front of the plow. Reeds eased back and finally let the engine settle down to an idle.

"You hit a bloody pipe!" the super yelled.

Reeds lifted an eyebrow and pretended not to understand.

"A pipe!" the man shouted and pointed again to the heap in front of the bulldozer.

Reeds pointed toward the plow with a perplexed look on his face. "There?"

"Yes, goddamn it!"

He climbed down off the cab and walked to where his supervisor was standing. In the background, an empty lorry pulled up with a sign in peeling paint that read ARCHITECTURAL RESTORATIONS.

"What is it?" asked Reeds. A dark, stubby cylindrical object jutted at an angle a foot or so out of the rubble. It was less than a foot in diameter.

"How the bloody hell do I know?" barked the other man; beads of sweat dotted his expansive forehead. "Take a look!"

Reeds carefully edged his way into the pit, keeping an eye out for sharp metal pieces or unmarked electrical cables that lay like cobras in the ruins of old temples. He had lost more than one friend in this business because of the unexpected. Above him, he could hear the super mumbling something about another cock-up.

Gingerly he approached the dull black pipe, noting that much of its detail was lost under an encrustation of several decades. Whatever it was, it seemed to go down, deep into the earth. As far as he could tell, there was nothing dangerous around; just the pipe and what looked like the rotting sides of large wooden crates. And bricks and a lingering haze of fine dust.

Reeds carefully touched the pipe, then used his palm as a tool to break off some of the mud at the pipe's end. He noticed immediately that the end was rounded, and by brushing away the residual dirt with his hand he saw that the end looked as if it could be removed. There were faint markings that were visible but weren't in English. He looked closer: they were written in German. Then it hit him: the bloody thing could be a German bomb!

"Bleedin' Christ!" he shouted and jumped back so sharply that he lost his balance and fell painfully on a jumble of bricks and weathered wood.

"What?" asked the super.

Reeds pointed with a trembling finger. "A bomb! A bloody Jerry bomb!"

London at midday was all traffic: sleek sedans, imports, double-deckers, lorries, vans. And the ubiquitous motorbikes that scurried through the streets like rodents in a cellar. Or so Edmund Ramsden thought.

He often wondered how London survived the motorized age. Or, more accurately, how much longer could it survive? Ancient streets built for human feet and horses and the thin wheels of carriages were now engulfed under tons of pressurized rubber. Stones split and building facades dissolved under petrochemical effluvia. London—the city he had lived in all his life—creaked and groaned under the unrelenting stress.

He stared out the window of his car, only mildly consoled by the air-conditioning and the fact that he wasn't driving. Rupert, one of the Home Office's drivers, seemed unperturbed, however. The man calmly tapped the steering wheel in rhythm to a song that played low on the radio. They were stuck in traffic on Kennington Road, waiting to cross the Thames at Westminster Bridge. On the other side lay Whitehall and Ramsden's office at the Ministry.

Rupert rolled down his window and stuck his head out. Ramsden could feel the heat rush in. The younger man pulled back in. "They've blocked a street, sir."

Ramsden shook his head. Something like this was always happening in London. Especially during the day, when it was most inconvenient. A street closed here, diverting traffic there, clogging and jamming the narrow roads for blocks on either side. It often seemed to Ramsden that everyone with a car or lorry chose to drive it at the same precise moment. "Chaos," he mumbled.

He knew he was getting old because too often he was cranky and perturbed by small matters. Tourists. The Conservative Party. Modern architecture. That sort of thing. Certainly, the noise and traffic bothered him more than it used to. Thank God, as Deputy Home Secretary he had an official car. That was one luxury. And a corner office with a window on Whitehall was another. At sixty-two—no, he suddenly realized, sixty-three—he looked forward to retirement.

He was staring out the window when the mobile telephone rang. He was rarely assigned a car with a radiophone, so the strange high-frequency ring surprised him. For a moment he didn't know what to do.

"The telephone, sir," said Rupert.

He leaned over and picked up the receiver. "Yes?"

It was his secretary telling him a meeting had been canceled. That was good news, he thought. There were far too many of them. And something else. Ramsden had trouble hearing over the traffic outside. "What? Repeat that, please."

She did. It was something about a bomb discovery on the South Bank. German, from the last war, the authorities thought.

"Where?"

She told him. He hastily scribbled the address on the edge of his *Times*. It was on a small street off Lambeth Road, not far from where they sat paralyzed between two lorries. An unexploded bomb: that was a late-afternoon surprise. He tapped Rupert on the shoulder. "Can you pull round?"

It took them twenty minutes and two blockades before they arrived. The city police had never heard of him, of course, and stopped him at both barricades. It took a telephone call at the second to get him through.

The bomb site was apparently down a cul-de-sac, a half-block away.

6

A mixed crowd of Londoners and tourists had already gathered at the hastily erected wooden fence. Ramsden noted with disdain the number of youths with large portable tape players; he could hear their music through the windows of his car. Another unfortunate American contribution.

Ramsden got out of the car and slowly walked toward the small gathering of uniformed men and equipment several hundred yards away. He could tell by their uniforms that some were Army. Gradually, the noise from the street and the crowd faded.

Bureaucratically, the disposition of old bombs fell to the Home Office, and by some quirk, that responsibility was part of Ramsden's domain. A small office somewhere in his large department monitored these matters and sent regular reports.

There were discoveries several times a year throughout England: German aerial bombs in London; anti-personnel mines along the southern coast. An occasional live shell from artillery practice fifty years before. Ramsden rarely visited bomb sites personally, although from time to time he left the security of his office to see a particularly troublesome or unique case. Two years before, he remembered, a large German bomb had been discovered in pristine condition in the basement of a parson's home in Sussex. That, and the sight of a trembling clergyman, had been worth the trip.

Ramsden was feeling the heat and humidity now. This was what he imagined Africa to be like. Or maybe the American state of Mississippi. His suit was entirely too heavy for this sort of weather. He mopped his brow with a handkerchief and briefly debated pulling off his coat. No, that wouldn't be appropriate for a Deputy Minister.

Several dozen yards in front of him a small team of men were working in a pit. Several others stood at its edge looking down. A heavy bulldozer sat silently several feet away. Thick black cabling ran from the team of men to a van parked on the street.

Ramsden noted that several houses had recently been torn down, obviously to make way for new construction. Several other small buildings were in the process of demolition. He took a quick look around: none of the surviving buildings had any particular charm. Most, if not all of them, were new structures, probably built after the last war. If memory served him, this whole neighborhood had been heavily hit by the Luftwaffe during the blitz.

The men in the pit wore helmets with visors and were swathed in heavy padding. They appeared to be examining a dark cylindrical object, like a thick pipe, that stuck up from the ground at an angle. From were he stood, Ramsden could only see one end of it.

He waved his Home Office card to a policeman and walked closer. Just then a man in an ill-fitting blue suit turned to see him. Ramsden made a small gesture with his hand.

"Ramsden," he said calmly. And then, to clarify his position, he added, "Home Office."

The man, somewhere in his forties, with a weathered face, looked nonplussed.

"What have you got?" asked Ramsden.

The younger man hesitated for a moment, still assessing the new arrival. "We're not sure," he said. Then he extended his hand. "Flagerty. Scotland Yard."

They shook hands. Ramsden edged closer to the pit until he could see the work clearly. The black pipe jutted out of the ground some three or four feet and was seven, maybe eight inches in diameter. For a moment, both men stared at it in silence.

Sergeant Inspector Flagerty turned out to be one of the Yard's explosives experts. These days he dealt mostly with the sort of explosives terrorists and criminals were likely to use. He had been called here because the discovery didn't appear to fit any of the known profiles for World War II aerial bombs.

Flagerty stole a quick glance at the older man next to him. The fellow had said he was from the Home Ministry, which was a bit of surprise: the ministerial leadership rarely got involved, and this man looked important. He certainly sounded that way. Ramsden's accent was that of someone from a very good public school. And his clothes had that tailored look from a bespoke clothier.

"Is it German?" asked Ramsden.

Flagerty nodded. "There's information etched on it that indicates it was manufactured by the Krupps Armaments Works. But it looks more like an artillery piece than a bomb. You know explosives?"

"Not really. These things are monitored by my office, you see. But I did live out the war in London; saw quite a bit then, you know."

Flagerty smiled. One of those, he thought. An Old Boy, a man in his sixties or seventies who liked to tell yarns about the last war and how the upper class had won it.

Ramsden looked around. Odd pieces of electronic equipment sat on the edge of the pit. "What's all that?" he asked.

Flagerty pointed to a rather large box from which cables ran to the pit and also to the van a hundred feet away. "Portable X-ray machine. And electronic sensors to determine if the bomb is still live. Assuming it's a bomb, of course."

"What have they found?"

"The weapon is hollow, except for several odd pieces jammed inside. We can't tell what they are just yet."

The padded men in the pit were excavating the hardened dirt around the base of the dark cylinder. Ramsden could tell that the exposed end was capped in some fashion. Where, he wondered, were the explosives? He asked if there were any.

Flagerty shrugged. "Don't know yet. There's nothing to suggest it's live, at least from the portion we can see. A queer bird, all right."

"Yes," said Ramsden. It was not like anything he had seen before. And while he wasn't an expert, he was generally familiar with the types of bombs dropped by the Germans. And after all these years, his department had handled quite a few of them. UXBs they called them: unexploded bombs.

Whatever it was, it could still be dangerous. Assuming it was from the last war, the explosives inside—wherever they were—could be chemically unstable, merely waiting for a small tremble or vibration to detonate. Water could have rusted the fuse. Explosive gases could have built up inside. There were lots of possibilities.

The men in the pit suddenly scrambled to support the dark cylinder. Enough dirt had been excavated around its base to cause it to move. Ramsden felt his heart skip a beat.

"Step back!" someone shouted.

A man without padding and visor several feet from Ramsden jumped into the pit to lend a hand. Ramsden and Flagerty retreated several dozen yards and stood behind a pile of brick-and-stone rubble. They could hear cursing from the pit.

For a moment, neither of them spoke. Flagerty calmly took a cigarette from his pack and then offered one to Ramsden, who shook his head. Flagerty lit his and exhaled a deep cloud of smoke.

"Bloody business, isn't it?" he said.

Ramsden nodded. At the moment, he was more excited than frightened. There was something darkly captivating about the evil-looking pipe. The minutes seemed to drag by until someone shouted an "all clear."

Ramsden hurried back to the pit. The full cylinder was exposed now, lying serenely on the ground amid small rubble. He gauged it to be nearly seven feet long, with a curious bulge at one end that he couldn't be sure was part of the device or simply dirt stuck to the barrel itself.

He bent low, trying to get a better look at the strange object. For a moment, Flagerty thought the old man would fall in.

"I think you should step back, Mr. Ramsden," he said and lightly touched the other man's arm.

Ramsden ignored him. To Flagerty's amazement, the man made a small jump into the pit and landed shakily on both feet. It took him a moment to stabilize himself.

Surprised, the Army men just stared.

"What is it?" he asked.

The man with no padding leaned forward and pointed to one end.

"You see," he said, "German markings. It appears to be a one-hundred-fifty-millimeter cannon, the sort of artillery piece the Jerries used in the last war. But this cannon has been modified."

"How so?" Ramsden peered closer, lifting his glasses above his nose to get a better look.

"It's plugged on both ends. And there's some sort of metal device, like a can, on this end." He pointed to the end of the tube where it suddenly appeared to double in size. "And it seems to have been joined at the middle."

"What?"

"Yes. See here." The man ran his finger along a groove that wrapped around the circumference of the barrel.

Flagerty stayed above them. "Any explosives?" He wasn't entirely reassured by the calm discussion. He stood cautiously at the edge of the crater. Whatever it was, it could still be dangerous.

"The 'sniffer' says not. But we won't know until we take it apart."

"Here?" asked Flagerty.

The man shook his head. "At a lab. This'll take several days."

"Good work," said Ramsden. "I want very much to know what this object is."

Ramsden looked up from the pit. From where he stood, he could just make out one tower of Lambeth Palace in the distance, the home of the Archbishop of Canterbury. And although he couldn't see them, Parliament and Whitehall were just over the line of neighboring buildings and across the Thames.

He ran his hand over the cool surface of the cylinder. Inside him,

10

his sense of excitement flared. Memories from fifty years ago, from the war, suddenly flooded into his head.

He fell silent for a moment, images of searchlights, flak guns, and German bombers meshing together. Then he realized that everyone in the pit was looking at him. He smiled sheepishly.

"Ah," he said, "this reminds me of the war."

Ramsden extracted a licorice drop from the small tin and popped it into his mouth. It was one of his few remaining vices now that he had given up smoking because of his lungs and heart and drinking on behalf of his liver.

His abstemious life was the result of Edith's last campaign for him before her own death of cancer three years ago. How hard all that had been for him, fighting the urge constantly to smoke or drink, only to succeed and then lose his wife, his best friend. When she died, pitifully, begging for the suffering and pain to end, he was left truly alone. Their only child, a son, was by design an independent creature, raised by the two of them to manage by himself. He lived in America, in southern California, where he did something in the motion picture industry. Ramsden never understood entirely what, although occasionally small clippings from an American film newspaper arrived announcing his son's involvement with some movie or another.

In fact, he only saw his son when the man flitted into town as part of a film production, with either a new wife or a new girlfriend in tow. Ramsden's relatives were dead, save an elderly cousin in a nursing home in Wales. Only his housekeeper of thirty years, a woman in her seventies, provided the continuity between his former life and his present existence.

There was his club, he thought, which on the whole he detested. Certainly he disliked the food. There were a few old chums from earlier days in the Ministry, but most were retired, living outside of London, and only infrequently made themselves available in town. Ramsden could drive, of course, he still had his car, but he hated the idea of negotiating London and the maze of country roads. So he mostly stayed in town, in the same flat in Knightsbridge he had occupied for nearly a quarter of a century.

He often told himself it wasn't a bad existence; many other men his age and younger were widowers, with far less income to make their lives comfortable. He was in relatively good health, thanks to Edith, whom he had cruelly outlived. His passion these days was walking and studying architecture. His library was filled with arcane books on the subject as well as the heavily illustrated "connoisseur" volumes that cost thirty pounds and sat mostly on table ends where they could be seen by friends. Others, he knew, would envy him.

Ramsden sighed. It did no good to dwell on his condition. Instead, he was looking forward to visiting his son in America—Los Angeles in particular. That was where Roger lived. That visit was planned for October, a time, he was assured, that would be best for travel in the States. More like London in May, he was told. Well, he would see. He had never been to America before, and although he dreaded the thought of flying for so many hours, it would break the monotony of his everyday world.

He took one more licorice drop and turned back to the stack of folders on his desk. His staff had worked promptly and produced a number of ancient documents on German aerial bombs. His hope was to see if yesterday's discovery on the South Bank fit any of the known weapons the Germans had used on London and other English cities during the last war.

The device itself—the long, dark cylinder resembling a gun barrel—was already in the hands of experts. It would be another day or two before they completed their examinations. In the meantime, more out of curiosity than anything else, Ramsden had decided to do his own sleuthing.

The first folder contained a yellowed report an inch thick and entitled "German Aerial Bombs." It had been produced in 1944 by the Research and Experimental Branch, Ministry of Home Security, and was stamped on its cover with the words "Most Secret."

Ramsden smiled. For years, "Most Secret" had been the highest classification that could be given a document in England; it was the Americans who later, after the war, insisted on the words "Top Secret."

He flipped through the pages. Much of it was technical, filled with chemical equations and small, intricate sketches of fuses. One sketch of a generalized bomb had small arrows leading from different components to identifying terms in the margin. Ramsden saw terms like "gaine" and "picric acid" and "locking ring," all of which seemed to blur together in his mind after a while.

An appendix at the end interested him most. It was a forthright discussion of individual bombs with photographs of each one. They

12

ranged in scale from the smallest, holding just over one hundred pounds of explosives, to the largest, something called "Satan," that contained four thousand pounds. In between were bombs nicknamed by the Germans—"Hermann," "Esau," and "Fritz." Many of these he recognized by their size and external characteristics, like stabilizing fins or odd shapes: they were part of a collection at London's Imperial War Museum. But nothing he saw even vaguely resembled the elongated cylinder found near Lambeth Palace. It had to be an *artillery* piece of some kind.

He scanned the other documents. There was a thin booklet entitled "Defusing Manual," which was a scant ten pages long! It was written in 1941 and contained the state-of-the-art knowledge at that time for extracting fuses from a UXB. God! What kind of men did that work on a regular basis? Day in, day out, under the worst of circumstances, until they were reassigned or a bomb exploded and terminated their usefulness.

Ramsden shuddered at the thought. And yet, he could remember several occasions during the war in which he had seen these bombs being removed from the rubble of houses, or deep pits, presumably defused, and thought how marvelous it all was. Then a particular incident inexplicably came to mind.

It was 1940: he remembered it well because it was the Christmas holidays and he was home from school. He was twelve, maybe thirteen, at the time, and it was right after Christmas, just before New Year's. Despite the war, his mother had found several bouquets of Christmas roses, the white-flowered hellebore, which bloomed only during the winter.

Late one night the air-raid sirens shrieked and the German bombers came by the hundreds over London. You could hear their rumbling even before the bombs began to fall. God! it was so vivid in his mind as if it were only yesterday.

He remembered the searchlights—hundreds of them—scanning the sky, their beams of lights intersecting each other like thin sword blades in a battle between giants. Then there were the flak and antiaircraft guns, followed by the German bombs. The cacophony continued for over an hour.

Ramsden remembered darting out of his family's basement during a lull to the street, his father shouting at him to return, to get back in, the raid wasn't over yet! But he defiantly stood in the street, wrapped in a blanket, and just stared at the play of lights in the nighttime sky: it was dazzling. And just when his father reached him and grabbed his arm, there was an explosion, high above them, almost directly overhead.

It was actually two explosions: the first one was small, probably a shell or piece of flak hitting the fuel tank in the wing of a German Dornier-17 or Junkers-88 bomber. There was a streak of yellow-red as the plane suddenly began to arc erratically downward. Then the second explosion occurred, a brilliant one, that created a giant fireball in the sky. Suddenly, a thousand pieces of burning metal fell earthward, like a fireworks display. One piece wafted down not twenty yards away from where Ramsden and his father stood, and landed right in the middle of the street.

Ramsden remembered breaking free from his father and making a dash for it. That was popular then: collecting shrapnel or odd pieces of aircraft. But it wasn't until he reached it that he realized the object wasn't metal: it was a funny-looking canvas package of some kind. It turned out to be a half-burned German parachute.

Ramsden sighed and sat back in his chair. Yesterday's discovery was not in the books. It was possible, of course, that it wasn't a weapon, although he was unaware of anything made by Krupps during the 1940s that wasn't. He had to admit he was deeply intrigued by it. Perhaps it was just the boredom of his job, waiting out the remaining years until retirement. Or perhaps it was the connection with his youth in London during the war.

But as he thought about it, he realized there was something else, something more ominous. How, he wondered, had such a device made its way to London? Who had brought it? And why?

He considered another licorice drop and decided no. Edith wouldn't approve.

Chapter Two

*D*usk was beginning to creep in, and like one liquid being added slowly to another, it made the shadows blend and blur away the colors of day. The large World-War-II aerodrome stood out darkly as the single building on this end of the Army base's seldom-used runway.

Ramsden sat in the backseat, grateful once again to have a Ministry driver. He was mildly piqued at the splenetic chauffeur, however, who was obviously unhappy at working past hours; he had raced on the A-road at what Ramsden felt was an unsettling speed. At the moment at least, the man was driving with unusual caution down the airstrip.

Granted, Ramsden mused, it was an eerie setting. Darkness was settling in fast and they were virtually alone at this end of the air base. It looked like a setting for an encounter with aliens from outer space.

The base was used by the Defence Intelligence Service as part of the Defence Ministry's elaborate intelligence operation. Since it was less than thirty miles from London, Ramsden knew of its existence, but little else. But that was just as well; thank God, spies and spying and the murky works therein were neither his interest nor responsibility.

The strange object found two days ago on London's South Bank had proved more mysterious than ever; its secrets, in the beginning at least, impenetrable behind its dark metal shell. That gave it an almost sinister quality, one that until this afternoon had resisted all explanation. Apparently, the Army's bomb experts had succeeded only hours ago in unlocking part of the mystery. What they had found, however, had made them cautious enough to brief the Home Ministry only in person. Now Ramsden was at the massive doors of a vintage aircraft hangar. He was surprised to see that two somber-looking military policemen guarded the small, human-size door to the left of the building.

As daylight continued to fade, it stole all detail from the hangar. Ramsden could no longer see the faded letters above the great doors that spelled some wartime arm of the RAF. It was his understanding that, officially, the Army—the present owner—kept the building as a historical legacy of Britain's last great air war. Unofficially, the hangar served a useful purpose when a large, isolated building in a secure zone was needed for clandestine activities. Once again, Ramsden felt a sense of relief that such matters were not his concern.

As he stepped outside, Ramsden realized that the late-summer heat wave was beginning to break; the heat was rapidly dissipating as night set in, bringing with it a drop in the humidity that made London life so uncomfortable. He also noticed that each pane of glass in the huge doors—there must have been thousands altogether—had been painted a yellow-green; and neither light nor sound came from behind the doors. At that moment, the small door, its four glass panes also painted over, opened and a young man stepped through. Although Ramsden couldn't be certain at this distance, he seemed to be a captain in the Army.

"Mr. Ramsden?" the captain asked simply.

"Yes."

"You're alone?"

"Well, I have my driver."

"Cleared?"

"Ah, no, not for information of this sort." Ramsden saw one of the captain's eyebrows lift. "He'll wait in the car, of course."

The officer nodded and retreated inside without another word. For a moment, Ramsden stood there by himself, feeling a bit abandoned

16

and sensing that both guards were staring at him from the corners of their eyes. Taking a breath, he opened the weathered door and entered the hangar.

Inside, a strange panorama greeted him. Only a few of the massive lights that hung from the ceiling were on: they gave just enough light for Ramsden to make out the back walls of the single, enormous room. It was empty except for a cluster of small vans and equipment in what appeared to be the center of the hangar. Portable lights on man-high stands focused intense light on a handful of uniformed men and equipment, partially obscured by the small coterie was a worktable maybe twenty feet long. Other men, armed with rifles, stood guard at the edges. For a moment, Ramsden was confused by the surrealistic scene; then he realized that the captain was waiting for him.

"This way," the young man said, his voice correct but with an edge of brusqueness.

Ramsden followed silently as the officer walked toward the table, his Army-issue shoes making a noticeable clicking sound on the worn concrete floor. Just as they entered the field of portable lights, another officer, an older man, turned to greet them. This one had the rank of general.

"Hullo," he said, smiling slightly and extending his hand. He was a brigadier general. "Simpson, here. Army Explosives Research." His gold bridgework caught the overhead light and reflected it back in tiny gleams of yellow.

Ramsden took his hand: the man's grip was far too firm to make him a politician.

"We do apologize for bringing you here at this hour. Rather be home, I expect."

Ramsden smiled; the comment was mildly condescending, the pronunciation vaguely Etonian. "No need. The Home Secretary is anxious to know what you've learned."

"Indeed." The brigadier moved back to the table and stood at one edge. A wing commander with Royal Air Force insignia was at the other end, and officers of junior grades seemed to be engaged in activities Ramsden couldn't fathom. The brigadier introduced the wing commander, who simply nodded. "And of course you've met Captain Sulley."

Ramsden stared at the young man who had met him outside. "Yes," he said coolly, "Captain Sulley."

"I think," began the brigadier, "that you and the Minister will find

17

this, ah, rather interesting." He motioned toward the table with his hand.

Ramsden stepped cautiously forward to the edge of the large work-table. The same object he had first seen two days ago now lay horizontal on the table, cleaned and naked. Various other metal parts, bits of wire, and pieces of wood were methodically laid out at one end.

At one end was a large cylindrical object, a foot long, that looked somewhat like a bucket. Ramsden guessed it was four inches larger than the gun tube. It was dull gray and at least a foot in diameter, with walls several inches thick.

The gun barrel itself looked far larger on the table than it had protruding from the rubble of the demolished London building. And although it didn't quite shine, there was a dull, deep luster to it that seemed to Ramsden to be part of the obscene quality of most weapons. Paradoxically, he wanted both to touch it and have it covered up.

"What do we have here?" he asked, the voice odd. His words seemed to die at the edge of the temporary lights; beyond that, the half-lit empty space eerily consumed sound. There were only the muffled echoes of the men working close by at the vans, moving or adjusting their equipment. Ramsden didn't bother to look at the brigadier. Instead, he found himself hypnotized by the huge cylinder in front of him. He heard the general's words, detached and bearing that odd dead quality created by the vast empty hangar.

"Nominally, a German Wermacht one-hundred-fifty-millimeter cannon. That is, an artillery piece used during the last war that fired a six-inch shell. This one was cut in half and threaded so that it could be taken apart and reassembled." The brigadier let the words sink in for a moment before continuing.

"But in fact," he said, "we think it's a crude atomic bomb."

Ramsden was stunned. "What?" Only then did he look away from the object to focus on the senior officer.

"Yes. We think it's an atomic bomb, one utilizing a very early design. A technology from the 1940s."

Ramsden didn't know what to say. He looked back at the table. The gun barrel itself was still in good condition, although many of the smaller objects were either broken or in an advanced condition of decay.

"How can that be?"

"We don't know. But we're reasonably convinced that the cannon actors, nuclear measurements, that sort of thing. The Germans admitted they never got close to a bomb. One scientist said they were five to ten years away at best. The Allied scientific board that interviewed them agreed, too. Nothing close to a bomb."

Ramsden wasn't surprised. Any real success would be well known. "Anything else?"

"There were some reports about American activity in Germany in April and May 1945. To assess German atomic research. But nothing particularly informative. Just basically complaints about the way the Americans were operating their intelligence units."

"Anything about the South Bank?" Ramsden asked. Had anything happened in 1945 that made it into the record, any event that might explain how the German bomb got to England?

"I've searched the bombing surveys and police records for all the war years. There is quite a bit of information on the South Bank, but nothing reporting a new or different sort of German bomb."

"Anything out of the ordinary?"

"Perhaps," the man said. "There was a brief mention of a captured German officer, a member of the SS, who was interrogated in June or July of 1945."

"Why is that of interest?"

"Only that the interrogation revealed he was privy to a high-level plot to attack Allied capitals *after* the war. For revenge, as it were. Obviously, nothing came of it."

"Hmm," mumbled Ramsden. "Not terribly informative."

"No, but the odd thing was that this item on the captured German was in a section referring to something the author called the 'Lambeth Palace activities.' "

Ramsden stopped walking for a moment. "That's it? Nothing else? No mention of an investigation?"

"No." Solomon described the entry as best he could. "There is no follow-up explanation of any kind. It's rather queer. But it's only interesting because the report mentions Lambeth Palace."

"Indeed. The Archbishop's home." Ramsden thought of the pit where the bomb had been found with its partial view of one tower of the palace.

Solomon nodded.

That was interesting. Surely, any German captured in England in 1945 would have been of interest to the authorities, especially since

was converted to an elementary nuclear weapon." He moved within several feet of the cylindrical device.

"You see, both ends were capped, the breech end still utilizing a fuse. The few pieces we've been able to extract indicate that they were specially machined and placed to hold other components in place during detonation, although we can only guess at what they were to hold."

He pointed with his finger. "Here," he said, "we found traces of black powder, a propellant the Germans would have used during the war."

The brigadier moved down the table toward the smaller objects. "And while these have been heavily corroded by ground water, perhaps from the Thames, they appear to be pieces of an electrical fuse driven by a crude timer."

"But how does that make this . . ." Ramsden fumbled for words, ". . . this *thing* an atomic bomb?"

"Ah," said the brigadier, who had expected the question, "you see, there is no one conclusive element, but many small suggestive clues. For example, we found traces of beryllium inside the barrel; that is a metal commonly used to coat radioactive materials, like uranium, to make it possible to handle such substances. But the most surprising component is this." He turned and pointed to the other end of the table, where the foot-long bucket was attached. The man walked over and pushed it slightly away from the cannon barrel. "Try lifting it."

Ramsden hesitated. "Is this *thing* radioactive?"

"No. Try lifting it."

Ramsden couldn't.

"It's solid gold coated in nickel. Nearly eighty kilograms."

Ramsden was speechless. A hundred and forty, maybe fifty, pounds of gold?

The brigadier smiled. "I'm told by our weapons boys that gold makes an excellent, if costly, reflector of neutrons, a device the physicists call a tamper."

He took his hand off of it and stood back. "It fits snugly over this end of the barrel and is clearly designed to accept another cylindrical object inside." He pointed to the hole in the center. "We think uranium went here. The gold itself is probably worth half a million pounds in today's market."

Ramsden's head was swimming with questions. "How can you be sure that this is German? Or from the last war?" He didn't ask it, but he wondered where the gold had come from. All he could think of were old newsreels showing piles of gold fillings from the mouths of concentration-camp victims.

The brigadier had obviously considered this question as well. "Several reasons. First, the gun barrel; its serial numbers confirm that it was produced by the Krupps Armaments Works in 1943. Then there is the condition of the barrel and these related components. Their present state, you see, is consistent with that of other objects buried underground in the same location . . . objects that were exposed to the water and soil qualities of the South Bank. Also, shipping crates found in the proximity bear markings that appear to place their origin in 1945." The brigadier paused for a moment; he looked at the weapon and then at Ramsden.

"But there is the overall design of the weapon."

"What do you mean?" asked Ramsden. Even if everything the general had said was accurate, it still didn't mean that, ipso facto, the weapon was an atomic bomb.

"Well, you see, the bomb dropped by the Yanks on Hiroshima was remarkably like this. In fact, it was called a *gun bomb* precisely because fissionable material at one end was fired into fissionable material at the other. When they joined, they became supercritical and therefore explosive. It was crude, of course, but effective. NATO nuclear-tipped field weapons utilize the same principle, although they are far smaller and more powerful."

Ramsden's attention began to fade; the technical talk eluded him. But the brigadier had made his point: this object—this *thing*—was an early atomic bomb.

"But there's no, ah, uranium here? No fissionable material?"

"No. Nor at the site where this device was found. We searched the area thoroughly."

Ramsden frowned. The Home Secretary, the government would clearly want to know what had become of any radioactive material.

"Missing," he mumbled. It wasn't a question, just a statement of fact.

"Obviously," said the general.

But then another question occurred to Ramsden. "Was it dropped from an airplane?" How the bloody hell had the bomb gotten to within a block of the Archbishop of Canterbury's home?

"Unlikely. The firing mechanism—what we have here, anyway—is designed around a timer. There is no proximity fuse, no altitude fuse. It was obviously designed to be assembled in place."

Ramsden tried to fathom the possibilities. "But *who*?" he asked. "*Who* could have done it?"

The brigadier sighed. "That," he said, "we don't know. German saboteurs, I suppose."

He stared blankly at Ramsden and puckered his lips primly. "But I rather thought that a matter for your Ministry."

It seemed as if the weather was breaking. It was still hot, but less humid; only the sky threatened rain. Well, that was something, mused Ramsden.

"Let's head for Trafalgar Square," he said to Solomon, his gaunt and balding younger companion, "that should be a nice walk."

Walter Solomon was in his mid-forties; he said nothing but stiffly kept pace. He had just emerged from a day-and-a-half in the archives, sitting in uncomfortable chairs and reading old reports for hours at a stretch.

"I found little that was concrete," Solomon said finally. He kept hoping that Ramsden would turn back. Looking at the darkening clouds, he regretted not carrying his umbrella. He was well aware that the Deputy Minister liked to conduct informal meetings on what the man called his "little health walks." Under most circumstances, Solomon was prepared for the weather; it was the sort of thing he prided himself on. But today he was fatigued; naturally he'd forgotten his umbrella.

He kept pace with Ramsden, thinking how agile the older man seemed to be. But then something was on Ramsden's mind, something that made him more energetic than usual. Solomon checked the sky again; at least it seemed no darker than before.

Both of them were flanked on either side by the graceful government buildings that dominated Whitehall Street. In the distance, just barely visible from where they walked, was the top of the memorial column to Lord Nelson.

"I unearthed some material on wartime German atomic research," said Solomon. "A collection of interviews, really, with captured scientists. It all dates from 1945. It's waiting for you."

"Anything in it?"

"Not really. A description of what had been done in Germany,

there was still a fear that die-hard Nazis would seek vengeance against the Allies. Somewhere, years ago, in some old intelligence report, Ramsden had read that.

"You checked with the Yard?"

"Yes. No follow-up there, either. But then, I don't have access to their archives."

"No," said Ramsden. Every bureaucracy had its secret files, of course; each agency jealously guarded its treasures like the Crown Jewels.

"There are several other things. I just don't know how relevant, though."

"Like what?"

"There was a memo, an official intergovernment thing, requesting a file called 'Archbishop.' The memo, you see, not only asked for the file, but return of the requesting memo itself. As if someone was trying to cover his tracks. I guess they got one but not the other."

"Who asked for it?"

Trafalgar Square was within easy sight now. Ramsden could see the tourist buses encamped at one end, disgorging wilted passengers in synthetic clothes and carrying cameras of all descriptions.

"British intelligence. MI5, in fact."

"MI5?" asked Ramsden. That was an interesting twist.

MI5, like its counterpart, MI6, had been created before World War II and operated until their respective responsibilities were absorbed by larger organizational entities in the 1950s: MI5 became the Security Service in Ramsden's own Home Office; MI6, the Secret Service in the Foreign Ministry. During the war, MI5 would have had responsibility for monitoring Nazi activity within Great Britain.

"Yes," said Solomon simply. He stopped when Ramsden abruptly halted at the corner of Whitehall and Northumberland Avenue. Nelson's memorial dominated the square, his pigeon-festooned figure staring down from a 170-foot-high column.

"Was there a name on the memo? Any kind of identification?" Perhaps that would lead them somewhere else.

"No name. It was a 'return' sheet, the kind that routinely covers a classified-document request. The only piece of identifying data was the requesting agency: MI5. Perhaps that's why it was left in the file."

Ramsden considered all of this for a moment. Something nettled him, something he couldn't quite put his finger on.

"The other thing is, I found a mention, a reference, really, to the so-called Archbishop file in our *own* records. You know, in the papers transferred to the Home Office by MI5 after its, ah, reorganization."

The "reorganization" needed no explanation. Soviet penetration of British intelligence during the late thirties and forties and revealed in the fifties had made headlines around the world. A massive intergovernmental reorganization had followed.

"A reference?"

"A specific one, to a report of continuing German resistance after the war. But when I went to find the file, which by our own records we're supposed to have, it was, ah, missing."

"Missing?"

"Yes. But undoubtedly it once existed. But again, I don't know if there's a connection."

"Intriguing," said Ramsden. He looked at Solomon, who was watching the tourists photograph Lord Nelson. The man seemed nervous to get back. Ramsden glanced at the sky and realized that it would rain soon; if they hurried, they would just have enough time to make their offices. Then he would have to decide how much further to press this little investigation.

Someone was covering his tracks; Ramsden felt it. But who? And why?

From where he stood, the window offered a rather nice view of the Old Admiralty Building diagonally across Whitehall Street. If he remembered correctly, the overall style was Palladian Revival; in any case, he remembered that it was built in 1725, although the stone screen in front, in a style called Adam, was completed nearly forty years later.

Ramsden knew these things because London's architecture was his passion; how easily he could have become an Oxford don, lecturing with his plates and innumerable slides on the variations and vicissitudes of architectural styles. What postage stamps were to some, the claddings and flutes and undercrofts of buildings were to him.

And to think, he mused, that many of London's architectural treasures had been threatened by a Nazi atomic bomb that no one had known about for almost fifty years!

Suddenly an image of himself and his son, his only child, came to him. It was there, at the Old Admiralty Building, where one day he'd taken Roger at age six or seven to see its wonders for the first time,

24

quoting the odd bits of history and gossip that he had garnered over the years on all of London's major buildings.

It was here in the Admiralty Building, he remembered saying that Lord Nelson had received his orders, and here, where tradition lives as long as stone, that even Winston Churchill had refrained from smoking his cigars. Roger had looked at him with wonderment, and then asked with a child's innocence, "Father? Will you be Prime Minister one day too?"

Today, as a Deputy Minister in the Home Office with two years until a much-desired retirement, he stood wistfully at a window in the Defence Ministry waiting for a meeting to start. Of course, he was early—he had been early to everything all of his life. He looked at his watch; the minute hand was edging ever so slowly toward ten o'clock. As far as he knew, there would be only three of them—his boss, the Home Minister, and a representative from Defence.

For a moment, Ramsden looked around the office. It was small but luxuriously paneled in walnut; the dark, rich finish seemed to absorb light. The great conference table was oak, too large for the room really, but a masterpiece of craftsmanship from the last century. The room had the lingering smell of tobacco, and Ramsden wondered if it had always been a meeting room. Or had it been someone's office, another Deputy Minister's, perhaps, who had died or fallen from grace and thus been forgotten or relegated to a lesser room? Just then, one of the double doors opened and both Sir George Hastings and a man named Allensby entered, both looking rather somber. Or was it, Ramsden guessed, that they were merely bored?

"Ah, Ramsden," said Sir George. Allensby from Defence nodded perfunctorily. Ramsden nodded in return and all three sat down, careful to put generous space between themselves.

Sir George, the Home Secretary, was younger than Ramsden, perhaps in his middle fifties. Knighted several years ago, he was in the Prime Minister's inner circle. In the "fast track," as the Americans would say. Of course, thought Ramsden, his family wealth was a useful asset. Allensby, in his forties, was similarly well thought of. He was younger, brasher, more obviously ambitious. And one of the most visible Members of Parliament.

An attractive young woman entered and took a seat behind Sir George with a notepad. A second young woman put a tray with a coffee service on the table and withdrew. The door was soundless as it closed.

"Well, now, Ramsden," said Sir George, "what is this business about a Nazi bomb?" He seemed to prefer the Churchillian pronounciation of "Nah-zee." He drew himself close to the table and rested his pudgy arms on the polished surface. From Ramsden's position, there was a reflection of light off the table that gave the Secretary a momentary but artificial glow.

Ramsden had anticipated skepticism. "Yes, that seems to be the case."

"A gift for the Archbishop, perhaps?" said Sir George with a wry smile.

"What's that?" asked Allensby.

"The bomb, or whatever it is," said Sir George, "was apparently found a block or two from Lambeth Palace, the home of our distinguished senior prelate."

In Ramsden's mind, the palace with its Romanesque and Gothic buildings assembled itself into an architectural image. There were wonderful examples of Perpendicular and English Renaissance characteristics in the towers, the great hall, and chapel. If the Nazi bomb had exploded, it certainly would have reduced to dust both the Archbishop and his palace.

The loss of the first might have been borne, perhaps, but not, he thought, the other.

"From all the facts, yes, a Nazi atomic bomb. The evidence seems undeniable."

Sir George lifted an eyebrow. "How so?"

"Mr. Allensby was good enough to put at our disposal some of his most knowledgeable weapons people. Although the device utilizes a conventional gun barrel manufactured by the Germans during the war, the overall configuration is that of an elementary fission bomb, one that would have used large but impure quantities of uranium alloy. The experts say it was crude, but theoretically workable."

"Definitely from the last war? Not some bloody Iranian or Irish muck?"

Ramsden shook his head and explained about the corrosion and the microscopic examinations undertaken by the weapons experts.

"And assembled there, on the South Bank? During the war?" Allensby evidenced a new interest. He seemed to Ramsden to be keen on establishing that it had not been brought to London during the term of the present Prime Minister.

"No. It was designed to be assembled and detonated on the ground."

All of this was in his report prepared and distributed yesterday to Sir George. Had no copy gone to Allensby?

Allensby shifted in his seat and leaned forward. "And German?"

Ramsden nodded and patiently explained. All the components were genuine and typical of German materials of the forties. Even the corroded metal alloys checked out. He mentioned the gold wrapper.

Allensby raised his eyebrows. "Solid gold?"

The older man nodded. "We can only assume that it was somehow spirited into London sometime in 1945. We know from captured war records that metallic uranium wouldn't have been available to the Germans in any reasonable quantity until that time, although production of uranium was always kept separate from nuclear research in wartime Germany. That might explain why Nazi physicists captured after the war had no idea of how much uranium was actually available."

No one stirred; Ramsden could hear the stenographer's pencil scratching on her pad. Were they wondering about the gold? Had it crossed their minds, as it had his, that it probably came from the mouths of slaughtered Jews?

Finally, Sir George broke the silence. "But no uranium?"

Ramsden shook his head. "No. The uranium would have been in the shape of large cylindrical slugs. They were missing from both the bomb and the site where it was found."

"So we have several stone of radioactive uranium hiding somewhere in dear Old England?" asked Sir George.

"We have to assume that." If the Germans could bring a large weapon in by stealth, they could certainly bring several small metal cylinders.

"And still dangerous?" asked Allensby.

"Yes." Ramsden decided to forgo telling what little he had learned about radioactive decay.

Allensby took a different course. "What about the building the bomb was found in? Who owns it?"

"According to records we studied yesterday, the neighborhood was first hit in the heavy Luftwaffe raid of December 29, 1940. There were periodic hits during the blitz and several during V-2 rocket attacks in early 1945. We don't know precisely when the building itself was hit—it consisted of a series of shops, actually—but the 1946 London Survey indicates the structure was unsalvageable and put it on the list to be razed. A new structure, a series of flats, was built in 1949 and stood until earlier this year, when the owners sold the building and land under a ninety-nine-year lease to a foreign company which received a permit to demolish it and build another."

Ramsden cleared his throat. "It was, you see, deemed of no historical or architectural value."

"And who was the owner for the last forty years? Didn't they have to have a permit or something when they first laid the foundation for their building? What's the bloody procedure?"

Ramsden hesitated and stared at the surface of the table.

"Well?" insisted Sir George.

"It belongs to the Crown." Ramsden's voice was little more than a whisper.

"What?"

"Yes. Since it was a Crown property, some of the, ah, normal procedures were waved and a new building permit was issued in 1949 without the usual reviews." Ramsden cleared his throat again. "Or whatever. I'm not familiar with the details of the process."

Sir George made what sounded to Ramsden like a sigh of resignation. "*That's* the sort of bloody news that Fleet Street loves."

Allensby seemed not to care. "Well, gentlemen," he said. "so we have a Nazi A-bomb. That's a jolly twist for the historians, of course, but hardly anything for the present government to be embarrassed about. And as for the South Bank property, well, I daresay that we can keep the Crown out of this. Should any of this be made public, that is."

Ramsden looked up from the table. "I should think it would be difficult to keep it quiet."

Sir George lifted his imperious eyebrows. "Why?"

"There are now a number of people who know about the discovery." He cleared his throat.

Allensby relaxed in his chair. "I think we can legitimately declare this an issue of national security. True, we may have uranium sitting about, but then, we can't be sure about that, can we?"

The tall, slender man waved one hand as if to dismiss the problem. There was a similar sense of amiable relief from Sir George, who nodded his agreement with Allensby's analysis. Unfortunately, Ramsden knew it wasn't all that simple. And there was still the historical issue.

"Well," he began tentatively, "there is another dimension for us to consider."

Both men stared at him; the stenographer lifted her pen.

"You see, it's one thing to discover the bomb for the first time after more than four decades." Ramsden glanced around the table; all eyes were fixed on him. "But it's quite another kettle of fish if the government knew about it in 1945."

There was absolute silence in the room; only the faint rumble of traffic outside on Whitehall Place could be heard. Finally, Sir George broke the uneasy quiet. "What do you mean, Edmund?"

Ramsden clasped his hands together and leaned forward on the table. The atmosphere had suddenly become charged, as if the four of them were conspirators trapped in an electrical field.

"Two days ago, I decided to have our records searched for any historical material that might be relevant. Largely to anticipate the question of how the bomb got where it was. It was during that search that we found specific and intriguing references to post-war German reprisal efforts. In the annexes of MI5. Unfortunately, those particular reports could not be located, at least not during the brief search we conducted. And it's possible that they were deliberately pulled." Ramsden sensed that he had failed to make his case.

"There are discrepancies, you see, in the records." As thoroughly as he could, he attempted to explain what his assistant Solomon had found. He told them about "Archbishop" and the capture of the German SS Officer near Lambeth Palace. And the missing files. The more he said, however, the less meaningful it sounded.

When he'd finished, Sir George sat back in his chair and visibly relaxed. "Well, is that all? The whole business sounds specious to me. Allensby?"

The younger man nodded. "Hardly firm information, Ramsden. Haven't you blown it out of proportion? I mean, the Government does have the right to protect its secrets. What would be gained by going public on this matter?"

"Perhaps," said Ramsden. He had failed. "But I'd like to check it out further."

"Of course, of course," responded Sir George. "Though I don't know how much time it's worth."

"Just the same," said Ramsden slowly. His colleagues started to get up. The meeting was over.

"Yes," said Sir George, "I'll inform the Prime Minister. A decision can be made regarding a public announcement, although I think one can argue strongly it would serve no purpose. Certainly, we can't frighten the good public with news of radioactive material unless we're certain it exists."

Ramsden was surprised. "I should think the public would want to know all it could about this weapon."

Allensby snorted; he saw no point. "Why should we tell them about it?"

"It's a matter of history. Posterity. The role of Great Britain after the war." Ramsden suddenly caught himself; he was waxing on to a disinterested audience.

"Well," said Sir George with a smile, "we'll see about that. At least we have the gold," he joked.

Part Two

JUNE 1945

LOS ALAMOS, NEW MEXICO

An atomic bomb, even of small dimensions, if it can be realized, can easily annihilate a great capital city having a few million inhabitants.
    —Dr. Peter Kapitza, Address to the Soviet Academy, 1940

Chapter Three

*T*he morning was crisp, with an edge that even in June made Cavanaugh shiver. He had on a light jacket, a corduroy affair he'd bought in college, that he could still fit into. It was just cold enough to make him put his hands in the pockets.

For a moment he studied the rim of the Jemez Mountains: all the winter snow was gone and replaced by a line of dark trees. Below that line, like a mottled canvas tarp, were clusters of dark-green fir and spruce trees intermingled with aspen.

Phil Cavanaugh knew that it would warm up later in the day. Living in Los Alamos for a over a year had taught him that. June was a time in northern New Mexico when the early morning carried the scent of new spring foliage but with a hint of the previous winter. At an altitude of 7,500 feet, the nighttime temperatures lingered well into the morning.

It was seven o'clock, a time that even a year and a half ago Cavanaugh would have considered impossible for human beings to survive

33

on a daily basis. But then, that was when his graduate laboratory experiments took all day to set up and most of the night to get to work. In those days, Cavanaugh was accustomed to falling into bed at four or five in the morning and sleeping until noon. That left just a little time to shower, grab a bite, and get back to the lab to fix whatever was wrong from the night before.

Cavanaugh thought about it. A year and a half ago he'd just finished his doctorate in physics at the University of Michigan. Finally, after a college career that spanned almost ten years. It had taken him a decade and every student job he could find to finish college. Not bad, his mother was fond of saying, for a poor Catholic kid from Detroit.

Cavanaugh walked briskly, something he had always done, and watched his breath form small clouds each time it hit the cold morning air. He had always walked fast, starting back when he was ten or eleven. That was when he was an altar boy, and he served at Mass at six-thirty in the morning twice a week, including winter.

His life in those days was simple: he got up at the last possible moment, letting the warmth of the bed coddle him for a few minutes. Then he jumped up and dressed and left the house at twenty minutes after six. That gave him seven minutes to get to St. Michael's Church, and three minutes to tumble into the black cassock and white surplice that was the official costume of the altar boy. Then, flushed with the cold, he would appear bright-eyed and ready for Father Joe. God! what a long time ago that seemed.

This morning he was walking from one of two bachelor dormitories that were half a mile away from the central laboratory complex called the Technical Area. He was walking west, along the unpaved road that ran beside a large pond. Ahead of him was the eight-foot-high fence that enclosed the Tech Area; beyond that, on the right, was Gamma Building, where he and his team had their offices and laboratories.

All the laboratory buildings in Los Alamos had letter or scientific designations. Robert Oppenheimer, the Director of the laboratory, had his offices in A Building; chemistry laboratories were in U; metal fabrication was in Sigma. There was a conference room in Delta. All together, there were a couple dozen buildings like this with names that took newcomers a week or so to memorize, since no one had ever bothered to draw a map.

The single main street in Los Alamos ran east-west through the

34

Tech Area, dividing it unequally in two sections. Both areas were surrounded by high security fences and guard towers. There were several security gates and two elevated walkways over the road that connected both sides, so that if you were inside one area, you could walk into the other without having to clear a security checkpoint. Most of the buildings on the main road were two stories high and, like the rest of the Tech Area, built of wood with green shingled roofs. The most prominent structure in town was the five-story-high water tower at the north end of the Tech Area.

Cavanaugh smiled to himself. No one in Detroit could possibly imagine where he was and what life was like in this place called Los Alamos. As a wartime security precaution, he was prohibited from describing where he lived and what he did; all mail was censored, and incoming mail arrived at an innocuous post-office box in Santa Fe, thirty miles away. His parents only knew that he was working on an important defense project in New Mexico. They knew it was important because he had received a draft deferment for two years in a row. In a country at war, that was almost unheard of.

As he walked, he dodged puddles of water and mud in the street. With a few exceptions, there wasn't a paved road in Los Alamos. When the snow melted in the spring, the roads became deep pits of mud in the heavy traffic; it was usually easier to walk somewhere, even in the cold, than to try to drive. Most of the scientific buildings and laboratories were near his dormitory anyway, except for the explosives and weapons-assembly people, who dwelt in the canyons below the mesa. In any case, it didn't bother Cavanaugh because he didn't have a car; it *did* bother the older folks who frequently had to rely on the Army to pull their Oldsmobiles and Packards from the mire.

As Cavanaugh approached the main entrance and guard gate to the Tech Area, he unconsciously began to fumble in his pockets for his white security badge. Without that, he couldn't enter the mesa's holiest of holies.

He often wondered how he would explain what he did here. Assuming someone gave him permission, of course. How would he describe the wizardry that went on behind the barbed-wire fences? Would even his fellow graduate students in Michigan understand how far nuclear physics had come in just the last eighteen months? And how in the hell do you explain an atomic bomb?

Cavanaugh fell in behind several others at the security gatehouse.

He looked at his watch: it was barely five after seven, and the Tech Area was buzzing with people. He nodded several times and said good morning. Most of them he knew only by their last name.

One of them was a small, gaunt man named Korshak who was reputedly a genius in mathematics. In Los Alamos, his walk was as famous as his intelligence; he scurried everywhere, like a miniature Groucho Marx, perpetually stooped forward with both hands thrust rigidly behind him. For Cavanaugh he was the daily source of news on the war.

"Heard the latest?" asked Korshak.

Cavanaugh shook his head. "No. What?"

"The Marines took Sugar Loaf. Okinawa." His eyes roamed the crowd as he spoke. He did a curious little dance as he waited in line to be cleared. "Japs won't give up."

Korshak always spoke like that: in short, brief phrases or sentences. He was the only bachelor who could be relied upon to stay up all night catching radio broadcasts from the Pacific. For some reason, his passion was memorizing troop movements and the intricacies of tactical assaults. With the war in Europe over, the funny little man threw all of his energies into analyzing nuclear cross-sections during the day and the successes or failures of the American Pacific forces at night. No one knew when he slept.

A heavyset guard waved Cavanaugh through the gate. He turned the corner and headed for his office in Gamma Building. In the distance, the diesel generators in the power plant rumbled noisily; in fact, you could hear the sound from almost anywhere on the mesa. It seemed to travel just below the ground, like the low, trembling noise near a subway or train station.

There was a sense of excitement all around him, a feeling that was almost dizzying in its effect. Everyone knew the work of Los Alamos was moving toward a finale of some kind. There was activity around the clock.

Two different types of atomic bombs had been built, one of uranium, the other of plutonium. The uranium bomb was going through a round of final checks before being shipped to the Pacific. Cavanaugh knew this one very well, because he had spent the last year and a half working on it. The other one was being prepared for a secret experimental test in the desert of southern New Mexico.

Almost everyone, including himself, had been drafted into preparations for what people were simply calling "the Test." Several hundred people were already living in temporary buildings and tents at a place Oppenheimer had nicknamed Trinity, 175 miles south of Los Alamos.

For the moment, that was all that mattered to any of them. When the war ended, Cavanaugh and the others would decide what to do with the rest of their lives. But this morning, that concern seemed far away.

Cavanaugh was just about to enter Gamma when he looked across the street and saw Oppenheimer emerging from A Building. Oppenheimer: the god-king of Los Alamos. Cavanaugh had never met anyone like him. Brilliant, a genius, really, he ran Los Alamos like a private graduate school. He had talked everyone with a reputation in physics into coming to teach here; the "faculty" of Los Alamos was the best in the world. And somehow, in two years, his top-secret school had produced two atomic bombs.

Cavanaugh watched for a moment. There was a small group with Oppenheimer, including two men in Army uniforms. One of the two was heavyset and Cavanaugh wondered if this was the infamous General Groves, the overall commander of the Manhattan Project.

This man was as legendary as Oppenheimer himself. Efficient and organized, the General reputedly managed his nationwide collection of secret laboratories and industrial plants with a ruthless energy. Most scientists disliked him, thinking him dense and insensitive. Behind his back, they called him "goo-goo eyes," and a host of other less pleasant names, although Cavanaugh had no idea why. For him, the General was just a shadowy figure that operated on the fringes of his life.

There was another man with Oppenheimer, a civilian whom Cavanaugh recognized instantly. This man was one of the "Immortals," as Cavanaugh liked to call them: one of those individuals who had a recognizable textbook name from before the war. Most often they were foreigners, and they had made the monumental breakthroughs in physics: they had visualized in their heads and worked out on paper the calculations and the nuclear theories that people like Cavanaugh took for granted as "given."

This particular man, a Hungarian, also was as well known for his brilliance as for his difficult personality. Cavanaugh could see him animatedly waving his hands. The accented voice didn't carry across the street, but he could bet it was charged with emotion. Oppenheimer stopped dead in his tracks; the General and his aide stopped. They all seemed to talk at once.

Cavanaugh chuckled. Thank God he didn't have to deal with that!

Right now, his job was inside Gamma and at a remote site a few miles away where the uranium bomb was undergoing its final inspection. A few more days and it would be disassembled and crated for delivery to a small island in the Pacific called Tinian, one of the Marianas.

Then Cavanaugh would turn his full attention to the test at Trinity.

To his staff it was a work of beauty. With a tinge of the macabre, Cavanaugh realized, but certainly an incredible piece of technology. And they had conceived it and built it lovingly with their own hands.

The uranium bomb lay exposed on a long table on a special wooden cradle. The steel outer shell hung on a hoist a dozen feet behind him.

Cavanaugh and a small team of men were in a prefab building at S Site, a few miles away from the Tech Area on another mesa, and connected by one of the few paved roads. S Site was deliberately remote because the laboratory did explosives research here.

The bomb mechanism itself was deceptively simple. A specially modified howitzer cannon barrel formed the basis for the bomb, which they had nicknamed Little Boy. It was slightly over six feet long. At one end, flaring slightly like a chopped-off and rounded pyramid, was a heavy mass of uranium-235 bored out in the center to receive a matching cylinder of uranium. That cylinder, called the projectile, was at the opposite end of the barrel, along with cordite explosives and a fuse.

The bomb would produce a nuclear explosion only when the small uranium cylinder was fired at great speed into the larger mass of uranium. For that reason, they called it the gun bomb.

Its secret was twofold. First, you had to know how much uranium it took to make a bomb. And second, you had to have a special isotope of uranium called U235. Right now, only Los Alamos knew the first secret, and it possessed all the enriched uranium-235 in the world.

There was uranium in other parts of the world, of course; there were big mines in Czechoslovakia and the Belgian Congo. The Germans certainly knew about them. But most uranium you dug out of the ground was an isotope called U238 and not particularly usable in a bomb. The trick was to take the plentiful U238 and transform it to U235. The government had already spent millions of dollars on huge secret plants in Tennessee to produce the valuable U235.

Cavanaugh studied the assembly for a moment. Every time he saw it, he felt a slight rush of excitement and a great deal of pride. This bomb was his group's baby. Other men had come up with the theoretical basis for it, and still others had toiled to refine the uranium or mold it into the right shape, but it was his men who had put the whole thing together. No wonder they hung around it, cooing and awing, as if it were a child.

They had perfected a checklist that covered each step of the assembly, from attaching the breech plug to connecting each cable. Each step had been checked and rechecked. When the guys at Tinian put it together for the last time, there would be no question but that it was ready to do its job. They had to be sure. There would be no second chance.

Behind him was the shell casing, a gleaming black cylinder with tail fins, nearly seventeen feet long. It hung perfectly still on two chains from the roof of the corrugated-metal building.

It was warm inside the room. The afternoon sun had already heated the metal shell of the building; the only breeze came through the half-opened door and windows. Cavanaugh watched as members of his team ran through their checklist one more time.

Cavanaugh couldn't suppress a smile. He had been intimately involved in the bomb's design. He'd spent most of the last year conducting measurements of what physicists called critical mass. That meant taking measurements of the U235 as it came from the plants at Oak Ridge.

Los Alamos had another type of atomic bomb, one that utilized plutonium instead of uranium and was nicknamed Fat Man. The trouble was, its concept was so new that no one, not even the Immortals, knew—really knew—if the blasted thing would work. That was the reason for the test at Trinity. That, and one other reason. All of them wanted to see with their own eyes if the bomb worked. It would be their payoff for two years of hard and often frustrating work.

His staff made a few jokes as they ran through the checklist. One of them was scribbling a note on the steel-bomb casing. Everyone had been invited to write something on the shell before it left for Tinian. A message. His name. A greeting for Hirohito. Most of what Cavanaugh had seen so far fell into the range of the scatological. Everyone agreed that it was a pity that Tojo and the Emperor—the two names most frequently mentioned—would never have a chance to read the messages.

After checking the last item, the men relaxed and lit cigarettes. One began to hum and then broke out into a slightly off-key song.

With Little Boy I do declare,
Hirohito ain't got no heir.

The men laughed and Cavanaugh smiled.

Jesus! he'd been lucky. All of his life. Falling in love with science as a child. Choosing physics instead of mechanical engineering. Ending up here in Los Alamos, during the war, rather than in the Pacific. All luck, he knew. Or God's will, his mother would probably argue.

The men on the other side of the table suddenly froze. The humming stopped. For a moment, there was only an uncomfortable silence, the kind you get just after being caught doing something bad by the teacher but just before you're punished.

"Ah, sorry," said a voice behind Cavanaugh. It was Oppenheimer's.

Cavanaugh turned around and saw Oppenheimer and the two Army men from this morning. The larger of the two had a sour look on his face.

Oppenheimer sensed their surprise. "Didn't they call? To tell you we were coming?"

"Who?" asked Cavanaugh.

"My office."

Cavanaugh shook his head. General Groves was far more impressive close up than he had imagined. He was a large man, with an elegant head full of silver hair. His uniform was meticulously starched. The man next to him was thinner, his uniform less starched, and he had the look of an individual who always had to run to catch up.

"Well," said Oppenheimer, "here we are. General Groves wanted to see Little Boy before it's shipped out. Have you met?"

"Uh, no," said Cavanaugh.

Oppenheimer introduced everyone, dredging from his memory the name of every individual in the room. It was a remarkable feat and part of his unquestioned charm.

"Tell us about Little Boy, Dr. Cavanaugh." Oppenheimer lit a cigarette and motioned toward the table with his hand.

Cavanaugh did. With just enough information to sound expert and just smoothly enough to make it sound easy. The look on Groves's face softened.

Unfortunately, the sour look returned when the General examined the seventeen-foot-long bomb casing. The collection of expletives made his mouth drop; he turned away with a frown. Just then Cavanaugh remembered the General was known to dislike intensely the sort of humor scrawled over most of the steel shell.

When he turned back to Cavanaugh he fired off a volley of questions, surprisingly technical, which suggested he had read the reports Oppenheimer no doubt sent him: projectile speed; assembly at Tinian; possibilities of failure.

Cavanaugh answered all of them, as calmly and succinctly as he could. He had never been grilled by a general before. Especially by one as powerful as Groves.

The General stared directly at him, a tactic that made Cavanaugh uncomfortable.

"What can we expect?" he asked. "From the explosion."

"You mean blast? Fireball? That sort of thing?"

The General nodded.

Cavanaugh rapidly assembled what he knew in his head; at this point, until the New Mexico test next month, a lot of what they expected was pure guesswork.

He began slowly. "We expect both Little Boy and Fat Man to produce an explosive force somewhere between ten- and fifteen thousand tons. That's equivalent, maybe, to fifteen hundred of the British blockbuster bombs dropped at once, each of which generates a ton of explosive power. At detonation, there will be light and heat, followed by the shock wave itself; and radiation, of course."

Groves turned his stare away from Cavanaugh to the bomb. "And what if the bomb fails to detonate?"

"What?"

"What if it doesn't work?" If the General meant to be skeptical, his voice betrayed nothing.

"Well, I suppose it would hit the earth at considerable speed. There is the chance the conventional explosives would go off in the process, but there wouldn't be an atomic explosion, if that's what you mean."

"Could it be used after that?"

Cavanaugh shook his head. "Doubtful. The uranium could be reused, of course, in another weapon. Assuming the Japs knew what they had."

"And what if it fell in the water?"

"Most likely a dud. With the present designs for both weapons, water would soak the high explosives and make them difficult or impossible to detonate."

"And the uranium?"

"What about it?"

"How would the, ah, enemy know what it was?"

Cavanaugh thought about it a moment. "A good scientist, a chemist or physicist, could probably figure it out pretty easily."

"What would they look for?"

"Weight. Spectrographic analysis. Chemical tests. That sort of thing. And if they had a neutron counter, they would know right away that they had something radioactive."

Groves turned to the colonel next to him. "Make a note of that," he said.

Then the General paused and stared at Cavanaugh, as if he were looking deep into his head, rooting around for something long hidden. Even Oppenheimer caught the look and glanced nervously at Cavanaugh, then at Groves, then back at Cavanaugh.

Suddenly Groves asked, "Do you speak German?"

Cavanaugh was taken aback. For the first time in thirty minutes he stammered. "Well," he said finally, "I studied it in college. A doctoral requirement."

Groves's face was unfathomable. "You're single?"

Cavanaugh nodded.

The General looked at his watch, then at Oppenheimer. Without saying a word, Groves limply shook Cavanaugh's hand and then walked out, with Oppenheimer and the colonel in tow.

One of Cavanaugh's team finally broke the awkward silence. "What the hell was all that about?" he asked.

Cavanaugh shook his head. He didn't have the faintest idea.

Later in the day, Cavanaugh was back in the Tech Area scrounging around for coaxial cable. The guys in Supply had none at the moment, so the next best solution was to steal it from someone else's office or lab. Cavanaugh thought he knew just where he could find some.

Blinking in the bright sunlight, and fumbling for cigarettes, he had just stepped outside of the Metals Fabrication Building. By now, the temperature had to be in the high seventies. Then he heard his name.

"Phil?"

Cavanaugh turned around and saw the lanky form of Oppenheimer, surrounded by a small group of young men. The memory of this morning's spur-of-the-moment briefing came immediately back to him.

Oppenheimer excused himself from the group and walked toward Cavanaugh. The Director usually had a group of men in tow, most often young. Older men found the image amusing since it looked like a mother hen and her chicks. Cavanaugh wondered if Oppenheimer was going to bring up this morning's event.

Instead, he said, "Walk with me back to the office." It was part of the Director's considerable charm—when he wished to exercise it— that commands sounded like requests. He had what older men Oppenheimer's equal called "practiced charm." It meant he could deftly chair meetings, say No to the Immortals, and occasionally snap at lowlies like Cavanaugh and get away with it.

The man was complex, full of seeming contradictions, and elicited universal admiration in Los Alamos. But he was not necessarily universally loved. Cavanaugh knew that some men here held back on that, never certain how Oppy felt about them. Really felt. As Cavanaugh heard someone say about Oppenheimer, he practiced a philosophy of "I keep your secrets but I don't tell you mine."

But he was charming, and the charm began with the Director's admonition to call him "Oppy."

"The General was impressed with you," Oppenheimer said through puffs on his pipe.

Cavanaugh picked up his pace to keep up with Oppy's broad stride. "I can't imagine why. We weren't really expecting visitors."

The Director smiled. "Well, the General fancies himself a quick judge of character." There was an edge of sarcasm in his voice, although the two men were known to get along well together. Oppenheimer alternately spoke, puffed on his pipe, and spoke again.

"How involved are you with preparations for the Test?" he asked. Small clouds of blue-gray smoke churned from the pipe and became thin, disappearing wisps in the air.

"It takes about half my time."

"And the gun bomb? Can you pull away?"

Cavanaugh wasn't sure what Oppenheimer meant. "Why?" he asked.

The Director took three deep puffs on his pipe before he spoke. The effort mimicked his conversational pattern, which was often punctuated by a "nim-nim-nim" sound between sentences.

"There might be something else you could do. Something very important."

"What?"

"I can't say just yet. But it would be something you're particularly qualified to handle."

"The General thinks this?"

The Director smiled again, this time with an enigmatic curve at the edge of his lips. "He asked me specifically about your part in the development of the gun bomb. And I told him."

"But what would I do?"

"That I can't say. Not yet." The Director waved at an older man walking on the other side of the dirt street. Cavanaugh recognized him instantly as another one of the foreign Immortals.

"You know," he said, "we have a team in Europe right now. Evaluating the German atomic-bomb effort."

Cavanaugh remembered staff briefings on something called ALSOS. It was a special group of scientists sent by the Manhattan Project to follow advancing Allied armies into Europe to look for German atomic scientists and their laboratories. "I didn't think the Germans had done much," he said.

"So it would seem," said the Director. They were at the corner of A Building. "We'll talk later," he added, and disappeared into the two-story structure.

Cavanaugh stood by himself and wondered what the hell all this was about. Mystery upon mystery. Then a thought hit him: could this have something to do with speaking German?

Cavanaugh stepped outside Gamma Building to find the sun low on the horizon. For him, it was the most magical part of the New Mexico day. Filtered by the high altitude, the light had a rich, golden quality, sometimes so thick that it seemed you could reach out and feel it like a mist on your hand.

He looked up into the sky and saw the tiny, barely visible dot of Venus, the evening star, just emerging over the mountain ridge. Within an hour it would be pitch-black except for whatever light Los Alamos created.

Tonight, he had an hour to clean up and grab a bite at the commissary. Then he planned to return to Gamma Building and work. Tomorrow, the schedule would be the same. So would the day after.

There wasn't much of a social life in Los Alamos these days, not with all the work everyone had to do. Certainly not with the Test of Fat Man scheduled for next month.

44

The lack of a social life, the lack of women, really, was something all the guys complained about. In fact, they griped about it all the time. There were some single nurses on the Hill, and the WACs, who mainly hung around with the enlisted men. He'd been told the WACs liked a good time, but then, he had no personal experience to confirm the rumor. In fact, his last sexual encounters had been with two girls at the University of Michigan: one took his virginity along with his record collection; the other one, his first true love, still had his heart, although she was now married to someone else. Cavanaugh sighed and thought of Merry, the one who always said, "As in Christmas, dear."

Things had gone so well between them, almost up to the last day. Then suddenly he'd gotten cold feet, which at the time he felt as the urge to slow down, to consider the next step carefully. He'd told Merry there was a war on, that he didn't know what was going to happen to him, to any of them. And just then, the offer from Los Alamos came and with it a chance, an excuse, to breathe. He'd taken six months.

That had been too long. Merry had fallen for another man, an Army captain now serving somewhere in the Pacific. The last word from his mother had brought the big news: Merry had a son. For some inexplicable reason, his mother kept in contact with Merry, or Merry with her, but in any case little pieces of news always seemed to drift down to him in his mother's letters.

Okay, there were no women, no available women, to speak of. But other than that, Cavanaugh liked Los Alamos. He loved his work. He was addicted to the mesa top, to the clean air.

He had special memories from the last eighteen months he knew he would never forget. There was the great Danish physicist who loved American comic books and chuckled every time Superman defeated the Nazis. There was the thrill of setting off high explosives as if they were firecrackers. There was the sound of a dozen foreign languages being spoken over dinner at the mess hall. There was the sensation of holding a beautifully machined slug of uranium in your hand, marveling at its subtle warmth. There were the discoveries, almost daily, that took you from one scientific frontier to another.

Cavanaugh loved all of it. It often struck him that this last year and a half would probably turn out to be the most exciting in his life.

That thought made it easier to bear the moments of loneliness. Like tonight, when he realized Merry wasn't his any more and no one was going to go back to his room with him.

Chapter Four

*H*e was deep in sleep, lost in a dream where he is a boy of nine or ten again.

He is playing baseball, his team, all guys from the same Catholic school, are playing kids from another school in Detroit. He's at bat, tensing to swing, when someone—sometimes in his dreams the catcher or maybe the umpire—mutters loudly, "Goddamn Mick." Then he says it again, louder. Suddenly everyone is silent, staring at Cavanaugh, waiting for him to react. Beat the hell out of whoever said "Goddamn Mick." Defend himself. His church.

Suddenly, the dream was interrupted by a loud pounding sound. Only after a long moment did Cavanaugh realize there was someone at the door of his room.

"What?" he shouted, only half awake. "What?" The dream was so real, always is so real.

A deep voice, vaguely familiar, said, "Cavanaugh?"

"Yeah?" He tried desperately to wipe away the cloud of sleep from his eyes and face. The thought hit him that someone has sprayed him with sleeping gas.

The voice said, "Telephone. For you."

"Oh shit," he mumbled, and dug around for his ratty bathrobe, another college possession. "What the goddamn hell?" he said to no one in particular.

When he opened his door, the dimly lit hallway was empty. For a moment, he considered the possibility that the knock had been part of the dream. Then he looked down the hall and saw the receiver off the hook. Still dazed from sleep, he padded down the hall to the phone.

"Hello?" Was this bad news? he suddenly asked himself. What else calls in the middle of the night?

"Cavanaugh? Phil?"

He couldn't quite recognize the voice. It was familiar, but—

"Phil, sorry. This is Oppy."

Oh shit! he thought, the Director. "Hullo." He tried to sound awake. Suddenly he wondered what time it was. He looked at his watch: only midnight. He'd been asleep no more than two hours.

"Listen, I know it's late, but can you come to the office? I, uh, want to talk to you about something." Then the Director made his nim-nim sound.

Cavanaugh shook his head as if to shake the last of sleep from his brain. "Sure. Give me a few minutes. I'll be right there." Slowly he returned the receiver to its cradle. Was he still dreaming?

As he walked back to his room and began to dress, he remembered he had been up since five and returned only a couple of hours ago. He had fallen asleep without eating; the only thing he had managed to do was undress down to his shorts. Somewhere during the day he had attended several meetings and personally constructed a prototype of a neutron detector that he had in mind for the July test. And he'd consumed maybe fifteen cups of coffee and a stale sandwich.

When he was dressed, he brushed his teeth and studied himself for a moment in the mirror. He didn't need a shave, or if he did, he didn't have the energy to do it right now. With the exception of his bloodshot eyes, he figured he looked okay.

At twenty-eight, his face was still lean but had lost the pale coloring of Michigan under the intense New Mexico sun. His blue eyes were still blue. His older sister always swore that she knew when he was lying or sick because his eyes turned clear; she said it was like looking into a bowl of colorless Jell-O.

When he stepped outside the dorm, wrapped in his corduroy coat, he felt the cold night air hit him like a slap in the face. It was wet, as if it had rained, and the dampness penetrated easily through the light jacket. He started toward the Tech Area, numbed by the cold, and speculating on what the Director could possibly want that couldn't wait until morning.

A few blocks away he saw the bright lights of the Tech Area breaking the darker gloom of the mesa top. There was a sort of pulsating glow that emanated from behind the eight-foot-high security fence; in turn, it formed a bowl of misty-yellow light that rose several hundred feet into the dark sky. There were no streetlights to speak of, just the harsh security lights from the tall poles scattered among the buildings.

Once through the security gate he could see the lights burning in Oppenheimer's office. When Cavanaugh first arrived eighteen months ago, the lab had been on a six-day work week. For the last six months, it had been operating around the clock.

He was still shivering when he climbed the few steps into the entrance of A Building. He took the stairs to the second floor three at a time, shedding his coat as he did so. The hall had people in it, a few in uniform, although as of late that wasn't so unusual. The security was really tight now. Oppenheimer had personal guards assigned to him twenty-four hours a day.

The door to Oppy's suite was open; he entered and knocked on the door to the inner office. There was no answer.

Just as he was moving to knock again, the door opened. An unsmiling Army colonel greeted him. Sitting on the edge of the desk was Oppenheimer, smoking his pipe and motioning animatedly with one hand as he spoke in a low voice, his speech punctuated with the ubiquitous pauses. An Army major he had never seen before sat in a chair by the conference table.

"Ah, Dr. Cavanaugh," said the Director. "Come in. Sit down."

So now it was *Doctor*, thought Cavanaugh. More formal than usual, perhaps to impress the Army? Or to put some distance between himself and Oppy?

"This is Colonel Milo. And Major Franklyn."

Cavanaugh nodded; suddenly he recognized Milo as the hapless aide to General Groves during the unexpected visit to S site last week.

"The colonel would like to ask you a few things."

The man cleared his throat. "We have some questions, Dr. Cavanaugh, about the gun bomb." For an instant, the colonel glanced at

48

Major Franklyn. Then he turned to look at Cavanaugh with limpid eyes. "For example, the artillery barrel you use in the gun bomb."

"The barrel?" asked Cavanaugh. "You mean the howitzer?"

"Yes. Is it necessary?"

"Asolutely. The uranium can't be made supercritical without it."

"And what about the casing? The shell?"

Cavanaugh pictured the seventeen-foot behemoth down at S Site. It weighed about two thousand pounds. "Necessary if you air-drop the bomb. Protects the mechanism during transportation and the descent."

"What if the bomb isn't air-dropped?"

Cavanaugh raised one eyebrow. What were they getting at? Were they even cleared to know this? He grappled for a safe answer. "Then it wouldn't be necessary."

Milo looked at the major with the pudgy, nondescript face and wire-rim glasses. "Just how portable are these gun bombs, Doctor?" he asked.

"Not very." Cavanaugh looked at Oppenheimer for guidance. How much was he supposed to say?

"What do you mean?" Milo shifted in his chair; the major's eyes darted back and forth across the room.

Somehow, Cavanaugh sensed that Franklyn was orchestrating the questioning, or at least had an agenda that wasn't all on the table. Cavanaugh wondered if the pale major was someone with a scientific background.

"I mean," began Cavanaugh, "that the bomb itself weighs a thousand pounds or more, fully assembled and loaded. The shell, however, weighs considerably more. At best, the bomb is *transportable*, but hardly something you could carry around in the backseat of a car."

"Could it be constructed in such a way as to be made more portable?" Franklyn asked.

"I suppose."

"What if the gun barrel were made in two parts that could be screwed together? In the field, maybe."

Cavanaugh turned searchingly to Oppenheimer.

"It's okay, Phil. They work for the General." He took several puffs on his pipe. "They're cleared."

Cavanaugh considered Franklyn's question for a moment. "That would probably work. There are lots of questions about such a design, however. Frankly, we've never considered anything but an air-dropped atomic bomb before."

For a moment the major's gaze drifted toward the window and the dark images outside. "I wasn't thinking about our side, Doctor."

He turned back to the colonel. "Show him."

The colonel reached over and picked up a briefcase which he snapped open. Extracting a large brown envelope, he pulled out a photograph and handed it to Cavanaugh.

He looked at it for a moment, trying to understand what he was looking at. There was a fuzzy image in the upper left-hand corner that looked like a smiling American GI. But it was the pile of objects in the foreground that was confusing.

"What are they?" he asked.

"German gun barrels," said the colonel. "Manufactured by Krupps in '43 or '44."

Cavanaugh looked at the photo again: three, maybe four, long dark cylinders lay in a pile in a small earthen pit. Judging from the GI standing next to the pit, the barrels had to be six, maybe seven feet long.

"So?" he said.

"So these are special," replied Franklyn. "They've been cut in half, but connected somehow to form a single barrel. You can't tell from the photograph, but there are caps on either end."

"I still don't understand."

The major shook his head. "Could these gun barrels be used in an atomic bomb?"

Then it hit him. Weapons. *That's* what they were getting at. Stunned, he looked again at the photograph. The barrels were generally the right dimensions, maybe a little too large in diameter, at least compared with Los Alamos' Little Boy.

"Yes," he said slowly, "under the right circumstances. I think so."

"That was my guess," said Oppenheimer, "but we wanted to hear it from someone who knew the gun bomb very well."

"Where were the photos taken?" asked Cavanaugh, pointing at the photo. He was still trying to fathom the implications.

"In Germany. It means the Nazis might have been closer to an atomic bomb than we thought," said the Director. "Dangerously close."

"But," stammered Cavanaugh, "but I thought that our intelligence guys told us that Heisenberg and Hahn and the others had come no closer than making a small reactor? That's a long way from constructing a workable bomb."

50

Right now, it was tucked into his beat-up suitcase. It'd almost been an afterthought: an item he'd remembered as he was rushing out the door of his dormitory room to catch the car down to Albuquerque.

In front of him, one engine of the mottled-green C-47 was just beginning to crank over, the metal propeller turning slowly amid bursts of dense black smoke and backfires. The black smoke matched perfectly with the camouflage paint. There was the smell of aviation fuel everywhere.

Someone in a uniform waved from the open door of the airplane and shouted, "Let's go!" He had a cigar in his mouth.

The last thing Cavanaugh saw before he walked up the metal steps was the name of the airplane: *Lucky Duck*.

"That's as far as *they* got. But apparently there was another group and they got a hell of a lot farther."

"Germans?" asked Cavanaugh incredulously.

"Yes."

"But what makes you think these barrels have anything to do with an atomic bomb? I mean, they could just be gun barrels."

Everyone was silent for a moment. "We'd like to believe that," said Milo. "But we can't be sure." He looked at Oppenheimer.

Oppy lowered his head and stared at the floor.

"I'm not following," said Cavanaugh. He had only pieces of a puzzle and he guessed that these guys knew more than they were saying.

"That's all I can tell you at the moment," said Milo.

"But—" began Cavanaugh.

Oppenheimer interrupted. "There's something you can do, Phil. Something important. But I can't force you to do it."

"What?" he asked quietly.

The Director said nothing for a moment and then looked over at Milo. "I think you should tell him."

"We need your expertise, Doctor. We need to have you check these things out. Personally."

For a moment, Cavanaugh couldn't think of anything to say. "Well, what about our intelligence people? The ALSOS team?"

"Can't use them," said Milo calmly. "There are reasons. A lot is going on right now."

"But why me?"

"Your expertise on the gun bomb," said Oppenheimer. He lit his pipe again and puffed heavily on it.

"Oppy, I've got so much to do. Trinity. Shipping out Little Boy." Like everyone else in Los Alamos, Cavanaugh felt the pressure to finish the work on the bombs and prepare for the Test. And like everyone else, he was looking forward to the explosion: to see if the device worked. To witness something never seen before. Maybe.

"Where are these gun barrels, anyway?"

"Germany," said Franklyn.

Cavanaugh did a double take. "Where?"

"Southern Germany, near Garmisch on the Austrian border."

Oppenheimer smiled; his face seemed to say that he understood. "Don't worry. We'll have you back in time for Trinity." He looked over at Milo and Franklyn. "Are you still talking about ten days? Two weeks?" He looked at the calendar on the wall. "It's June twenty-ninth."

"Sure. No problem. We think seven to nine days, maybe a few more at most. And you get to go by plane."

Cavanaugh was still trying to understand what was happening when the mention of an airplane trip added another dimension: since he was a child he had had a fear of flying. Now these guys were talking about flying overseas!

Milo pulled a military map from his briefcase and spread it open on the Director's conference table. With his finger, he pointed to a small dot on Germany's border with Austria.

"Here," he said.

Cavanaugh walked over and studied it for a moment. The dot read "Garmisch-Partenkirchen" and looked as if it were maybe ten miles from the Austrian border. There were all sorts of unintelligible red and blue and black pencil marks on the map. It didn't seem to Cavanaugh that they could be troop movements, not with the war over for more than a month.

"You'll fly to Washington, get briefed, and then catch a transport to London." The colonel's finger moved northwest on the map. "From there, we'll fly you to Stuttgart; you'll have to drive from there."

Suddenly, another thought hit Cavanaugh. He blurted it out without thinking. "Is it safe?"

Then instantly he regretted saying it. Good God! He'd been in Los Alamos for almost two years when every guy his age was in uniform.

The colonel didn't seem to be offended. Instead, Franklyn shrugged. "I think all resistance is over," he said simply. "Maybe some scattered snipers. Nazi holdouts, you know."

"You'll be in uniform, of course," added Franklyn. He was gathering up a pile of papers on the opposite end of the table.

"What?"

Milo smiled. "Yes. You'll be given a temporary commission as captain."

"First lieutenant," said Franklyn.

"In uniform?" Cavanaugh tried to picture himself in khakis.

"You'll be less conspicuous that way," said Milo.

"It's only for a few weeks," added Oppenheimer. He laid down his pipe and lit a cigarette instead. Two years ago he had fought a major battle with Groves to keep Los Alamos a civilian laboratory instead of a military base.

"When do I go?" asked Cavanaugh.

"Something has come up that has pushed up the schedule," said Franklyn.

"Well, when?"

"Tomorrow morning. At 0700, from Kirtland field in Albuquerque."

"Holy shit!" muttered Cavanaugh. He looked at his watch. "That's just a couple of hours from now." He waved his hands wildly. "And it takes almost four goddamn hours to get to Albuquerque."

Colonel Milo nodded. "You've got two hours to get ready."

Franklyn held out a stack of papers to Cavanaugh. "Read these on the way down. Don't show them to anyone and don't talk about what you've read. We'll collect them in Albuquerque."

A few minutes later, Cavanaugh stood on the outside steps of A Building, looking through the security fence across the road. His dormitory was lost in darkness a half mile away. What the hell had just happened upstairs? Clutching the papers with one hand, he gripped his coat collar with the other and started walking back to his dorm room. He had little more than an hour to pack for a two-week trip.

Then he realized that he had never said he would go.

At 7 A.M. Cavanaugh waited on the tarmac of Kirtland Army Air Force Base for the crew of the C-47 to give the okay to board. In his hand was an Army envelope with enough paperwork in it to fill a small book. Some piece of paper inside made him a captain, although he wouldn't be given a uniform until he got to Washington. One of seven million presently in uniform, the clerk at Kirtland cheerily told him.

Being in the Army was probably the least of his problems, although he knew very little about military behavior. Hell! he didn't even know how to salute. And all he did know came from watching movies like *Thirty Seconds Over Tokyo* and *The Fighting Seabees*. And the last, of course, was about the Navy.

Dealing with all that would come later. Right now he stared C-47 and felt his stomach tighten. It was the same feeling he had time he climbed on a roller coaster. Only now, he'd be thou feet off the ground for most of a day.

The only other thing he had with him, other than a few his shaving kit, was a small portable Geiger counter radioactivity. He had designed it himself a few months of a small gas-filled electrode, a resistor, and some 3 All of this fit into a narrow metal box nine inches lo

Part Three

JUNE–JULY 1945

WASHINGTON, D. C.

He stood upon that fateful ground,
Cast his lethargic eye around,
And said beneath his breath:
Whatever happens,
We have got
The Maxim gun
And they have not.

—Hilaire Belloc,
The Modern Traveller, 1898

Chapter Five

Lucky Duck landed in Washington following a thunderstorm. They picked up the edge of the storm a hundred miles out, just west of the Blue Ridge Mountains, and a few hours from their last stop, Scott Field in Illinois.

What had been a reasonably smooth series of flights for most of the day now turned into a turbulent final act that left Cavanaugh feeling like a small bird in a storm.

"Gonna be a rough one," said the Army colonel sitting across from Cavanaugh. His cigar smoke had filled most of the rear of the airplane since Scott Field.

Cavanaugh nodded and tightened his seat belt, although he had no idea why. Somewhere inside of him a voice said that he needed to be able to jump out of his seat if something happened. He couldn't imagine anything worse than burning to death because he couldn't get out of his seat.

The airplane continued to shake, dropping suddenly every now and then as it hit small pockets of air. Lightning flashed in the distance, obscured and diffused by the clouds, although to Cavanaugh it seemed more like a car headlamp turning toward him in the fog. The Army guys in front of him kept up a cheerful conversation throughout the descent.

Finally, with a series of powerful heaves, *Lucky Duck* broke through the last layer of dark clouds.

When Cavanaugh screwed up his courage to look outside, he saw that they were only a couple of thousand feet above the ground: it was almost dark and a light but steady rain was falling. Beaded rivulets ran diagonally across the airplane's windows.

As the plane began to bank steeply to the right, he had his first sight of the District of Columbia. Unfolded before him like a three-dimensional map were the Capitol, the Washington Monument, and the plethora of low white buildings that formed official Washington. Suddenly he forgot everything about the previous twelve hours and stared wide-eyed at the beautiful city below. The dark-indigo Potomac cut like a wavy highway between the city and the green wooded countryside. Like a misplaced brooch, the five-sided figure of the Pentagon drifted into view.

"Where do we land?" he asked the colonel.

"Bolling Field. Right next to Washington National."

Moments later, the C-47 seemed to lose power, fall slightly forward, and then drop from the sky. Cavanaugh gripped the armrests. A few moments later, the plane was on the ground, taxiing to a large aircraft hangar.

He could see a small party of men in uniform waiting at the edge of the hangar. He had been told that he would be met; were these men waiting for him?

Lucky Duck rolled to a stop and cut its engines. It took a minute for him to realize just how much noise the engines made; suddenly he could hear voices talking on the tarmac outside the airplane. He straightened his tie and gathered his one suitcase. Gripping the handrail, he slowly made his way down the metal steps and put both feet on the ground. Silently he thanked God he was safe—for the moment; he put the prospect of flying to England out of his mind. It was enough to be in Washington in one piece.

He stood still, expecting one of the milling NCOs to come over and introduce himself. Instead, one by one, the corporals and first sergeants saluted the majors and colonels stumbling out of the *Lucky*

Duck. Even the crew exited, talking indifferently about the weather, the landing, and, with even less enthusiasm, the turn-around the next day, back to Albuquerque. With the exception of the ground crew, Cavanaugh was left standing by himself.

The aircraft hangar was brightly lit from within, as was the public terminal building a block away; little of the light filtered out to the field, however, and Cavanaugh found himself standing dumbly in the darkening night air. Where in the hell was the person who was going to meet him?

"You expecting somebody?" It was a young man in mechanic's coveralls; in his hand he carried a large wrench. He had the remnants of a wooden match in his teeth.

"Yeah."

"They gonna meet you?"

"Supposed to."

The young man spat the gnawed match from his mouth and glanced around. "You staying in D.C.?"

Cavanaugh nodded. He didn't know where; in the frenzy of departure this morning, he had failed to ask what hotel he would be staying at.

"Motor pool kin take you into town, if you need it." He pointed to another small building not far from the hangar. "What hotel you at?"

Cavanaugh shook his head. "I don't know. I haven't been told."

The mechanic stared at him for a moment. "Jesus. Hotel space is worth more than a whore here in D.C."

Grabbing his bag, Cavanaugh walked toward the hangar building; perhaps there was someone inside who could call the Manhattan Project offices for him. Someone had to know what was going on, for Christ's sake.

Just then, a dark four-door car slowly turned around from the side of the hangar onto the tarmac. The headlights blinded Cavanaugh and obscured what he could see of the car and its occupants. For a moment the car seemed to hesitate a dozen yards away, then rolled forward again. When it finally stopped, the rear door opened and a man wearing an Army uniform stepped out. That was as much detail as he could make out.

"Dr. Cavanaugh?" The headlights erased any detail from the speaker's face.

"Yes." Cavanaugh squinted into the two beams of light; it looked as if the driver had his high beams on.

"Sorry we're late," said the voice; the Army man stepped away from the door and stood in front of the car. Through the double shafts of headlights he became an actor walking through a break in the stage curtains. Cavanaugh found himself looking into the pleasant, full face of someone he thought he dimly recognized.

"Do I know you?" The more he looked, the more Cavanaugh thought he knew the face.

The Army captain smiled and extended his hand. "Jack Gilbert. We were at Michigan State together." He smiled again "Undergraduates. Mechanical engineering, remember?"

Something inside of Cavanaugh clicked. "Yeah," he said, "it's been—what?—six, seven years?"

The captain nodded. "A long time, but I've had the chance to follow you and some others through the office here in D.C."

This was a hell of a coincidence. "You're with the Project?" Cavanaugh meant the Manhattan Project.

"You got it. An assistant to the assistant to the General. You know, the Army way." Gilbert held open the door for Cavanaugh, then climbed in himself. He tapped the driver's shoulder. "Hit it."

Unlike the approach, the car jerked forward, throwing Cavanaugh and Gilbert back into the seat. The car spun around and headed around the side of the aircraft hangar.

"Hey, slow down, buddy," shouted Gilbert. He turned to Cavanaugh. "Sorry about being late. I was told to hold off until everybody else was picked up."

Cavanaugh shrugged. "Why? Who the hell knows who I am anyway?"

Gilbert smiled. "Maybe no one. Maybe someone. It's hard to keep a secret in Washington."

Cavanaugh still didn't understand. "So what?"

Gilbert turned around to face Cavanaugh. He motioned with his head toward the driver. "A lot of people like to know what's going on. That's especially true about the guys at the Pentagon." He lowered his voice even further. "A lot of people know that there's something called the Manhattan Project, but that's about it. They'd like to know more."

"Spies?" asked Cavanaugh.

Gilbert laughed. "No. Our side. But nosy sons of bitches." He continued to grin. It was the sort of broad, innocent smile that Cavanaugh sensed had charmed many people. In fact, his only memory of Gilbert from Michigan State was that of a congenial, jolly good fellow—the all-American kind that did his work, played the game, and got along with everyone. He guessed it was a skill that was particularly useful here in Washington.

"You have to understand," said Gilbert, "that the war isn't being *fought* in D.C. It's being planned here; it's being talked about here. The goddamn action is somewhere else. Everybody feels bad about that, so they play war here by knowing as much as possible about everyone and everything else. That's the battleground here." He slapped Cavanaugh on the back. "That's why we're trying to keep your arrival secret, buddy."

Cavanaugh thought of something. "Did you arrange for the plane to land at Bolling?"

"Yeah. Less conspicuous. Why?"

Cavanaugh shook his head and looked out the window. The white facade of the Pentagon was fading from view on the left side of the car. As they began to cross a bridge, a gleaming circular building came into view. Behind it was the tall, slender obelisk that even he recognized as the Washington Monument. Gilbert leaned toward him.

"Over there, that's the Jefferson Memorial," he said. "They turned the lights back on a few months ago."

"What?"

"Blackout," Gilbert said. "Most of official Washington was blacked out during the European war. They've just turned the juice on." He laughed. "I guess no one's worried about the Japs anymore."

The car entered the downtown area, just passing the block-long Commerce Department Building. Cavanaugh suddenly realized something: Washington was alive with people! This was the first big city he had been in since leaving Michigan in what seemed a lifetime ago.

It was just after seven-thirty, and even now men and women walked the sidewalks; cars and taxis honked; storefronts were lit. The city seemed to breathe motion and exhale light. For the moment, he forget entirely about who he was and what he was doing here and simply stared out the window. The women—there seemed to be young, beautiful women everywhere—seemed so stylish and elegant, so like the images from *Life* or *Collier's*. Los Alamos looked smaller and more parochial every moment.

After a series of turns, completely disorienting him, Cavanaugh saw a street sign that said "Connecticut Avenue." The car slowed down in front of a building with a marquee that read MAYFLOWER HOTEL.

"This is it?" asked Cavanaugh.

"Yeah. This is the good news. A room at the hottest hotel in D.C."

"Oh? So what's the bad news?" The car stopped and a doorman opened the door from Gilbert's side.

"You've got a meeting with the General at 0700 in the morning." He reached down and pulled a large brown parcel from the floor of the car. Then he stepped out, pausing under the glare of the marquee lights. "I'll see you up. Got something for you."

Both of them walked through a polished brass door held by a black man in a red jacket. The lobby seemed to run for a mile and was jammed with people, mostly in uniform. Cavanaugh couldn't tell a colonel from a major, but he guessed that most of these were high-ranking men. And the women—the WACs and WAVEs—were stunning.

"I thought you didn't want to draw attention to me?" he asked.

"We didn't. That's why you're here. Who the hell would look for Philip Cavanaugh at the Mayflower?"

Somewhere, music played, something lively, a tune he knew but couldn't quite remember. Then he guessed it: it was "Tangerine," and it was being sung by a woman with a beautiful voice.

"They've got a band here?" He had never been in a hotel with a band before. No, that wasn't quite true. The La Fonda Hotel in Santa Fe sometimes had a local cowboy band in their bar. But nothing that sounded like this.

"Yeah, I think so. In the bar. Check it out." Gilbert looked into the lobby and its occupants. "You might get lucky."

Cavanaugh just stared. "You're paying, right?"

Gilbert nodded. "Well, the Army is. But you can't imagine how hard it is to get a hotel room in Washington, let alone at the Mayflower. You owe me for this one, pal."

Gilbert pulled a key out of his pocket and handed it to Cavanaugh. "You're already checked in. And out. Tomorrow. One night only. Live it up."

A small, ratlike man operated the elevator. He mumbled a greeting and eyed both Gilbert and Cavanaugh as he pumped the lever that moved the small brass box they stood in. He looked about sixty, with a face and eyes that suggested he had seen everything come and go in his elevator at one time or another.

Cavanaugh unlocked the door to his room and flipped the light switch. The room was the opposite of his dorm in Los Alamos: it had furniture, real wood furniture, soft-looking chairs, and a flowery bed-spread. Even curtains.

Gilbert walked past him and dropped his package on the bed. Then he flopped down in one of the easy chairs.

"You ever met Groves before?"

"Just once. A couple of weeks ago. He was in Los Alamos. I told him about my work." *That,* undoubtedly, had been his downfall, he thought.

"He's tough. Very smart. Accustomed to getting his way. He's run the whole show himself so that he knows everything that's going on."

"A son of a bitch?"

Gilbert waved one hand. "Some think so. I'm not sure, though. I think he just wants results. Big ones. But then, consider what he's been asked to do."

"The word at Los Alamos is that he doesn't like scientists." Cavanaugh thought about all the rumors and stories about the General. Almost everything that went wrong was blamed on the portly man: the lack of toilet paper, bad housing, censorship of mail; you name it and the General was responsible.

"Hmm," said Gilbert, "I don't think that's true. It's true that he's career Army; I know he thinks everyone fighting the war should be in uniform."

Cavanaugh laughed. Suddenly he thought about his mother: she was fond of saying that the world would be a lot better place to live in if everyone were Catholic.

"Whatever he is, he's sharp. I wouldn't bullshit him."

Cavanaugh unlocked his suitcase and pulled out his one other suit; it was wrinkled. He hung it in the bathroom, hoping that the heat from the shower would smooth it out. That was a trick that his college roommate had once taught him. He stepped back out and saw Gilbert unwrapping the parcel.

"These are your uniforms. Which you are to wear starting tomorrow." He pulled out a neatly folded khaki shirt and a pair of pants. Underneath was a small brown bag and under that something dark green. "You have been issued one summer khaki uniform and one Army green. For Europe. Also belt, insignia, underwear, and socks. Cotton. And one pair black leather shoes. I had to guess your size."

Cavanaugh stared at the bed; it looked as if he had been shopping at an Army PX. The khaki pants and shirt were heavily starched; the folding had created a checkerboard of creases. He thought of Groves and his immaculate uniform.

"Tomorrow, I'll get you a duffel bag. No suitcase. That'll mark you as a civilian. I'll hold on to the suitcase until you get back. Leave everything in your room and wait in the lobby for your driver. Not in front of the hotel."

Cavanaugh shook his head. "What about my shaving kit? Prophylactics? Things like that."

Gilbert laughed. "No problem. You probably won't need the rubbers anyway. You know what all this is about?"

Cavanaugh smiled. He had been told to talk with no one, no matter what. "Don't you?"

The man turned and looked at Cavanaugh; there was a wariness in his face. Something about his expression made Cavanaugh think he knew more than he was saying.

"It has something to do with ALSOS. I suppose you know about them?" His voice carried the smallest tinge of sarcasm. He sat down in the overstuffed chair next to the bed and put his feet up on the edge.

"A little. We got their reports in Los Alamos."

"Well, cables have been sent to ALSOS headquarters in London notifying them of your arrival. I sent them myself. That's how I made the connection." Gilbert smiled a knowing smile. In high school, it would have been called a shit-eating grin. "I guess you'll find out more tomorrow, huh?" He brought his feet off the bed and stood up. "And remember, tomorrow you wear khakis. In the meantime, sweet dreams."

For the first time all day—and it seemed like the day had started yesterday—Cavanaugh was alone. He sat down in one chair and just stared at the room for a minute. This was how civilized people lived, he thought. He took off his shoes and socks and let his feet sink into the deep wool pile. The thousands of small fibers seemed to massage his feet as he worked them into the rug.

Then he stared at his feet: they were as pale as an old sheet. He suddenly realized that he hadn't been in a bathing suit since graduate school. He had a tan, all right, but only on his face, hands, and arms—all the places the intense New Mexico sun hit when he walked or worked outside. The rest of him was a pasty white. In school, he used to go swimming in the lake, in the cold Michigan water, or naked at the YMCA.

64

He thought of Merry and their daring midnight swim at the small lake on the edge of Lansing. Just the two of them, giggling, a little high from the beer, and sensing that at last the time had come for them to go all the way. They had shed their clothes, awkwardly at first, then hurriedly, since, even in summer, the night air was cold. Then they'd walked into the water, which was still and silken, trembling from the cold and the expectation of sex at the same time.

Cavanaugh closed his eyes. The hotel room was so lovely, so elegant, and yet he was in it by himself. The image of all the attractive young women he had seen earlier in the evening walking on the sidewalks came back to him. They'd been so close that he could almost smell them.

Then he laughed. He was horny and exhausted at the same time. More accurately, he thought, he was horny, exhausted, and alone.

Chapter Six

*E*verything started badly his first morning in Washington.

Cavanaugh was awakened by the sharp, piercing ring of the telephone next to his bed. He shot up, dazed and confused, and heard a woman's voice on the other end of the line tell him it was 6 A.M. Holy Christ.

He groggily got out of bed, luxuriated under the hot shower until he felt he was sufficiently awake, then stood staring at himself in the fogged mirror until a deep breath propelled him to lather his face and shave.

Wearing only his new GI shorts, he stared at the uniforms Gilbert had given him the night before. He had no idea where to put the small pile of insignia he held in his hand. Gilbert had also forgotten to tell him whether he should wear the green coat with the khaki shirt or what. He guessed it was warm outside, so why wear a coat at all? The hell with it! He put on his suit, then slipped into the pair of stiff, Army-issue black shoes, his only concession to military code.

Then, with only minutes to spare, he caught the elevator downstairs and waited in the lobby for his driver. Gilbert had been specific about that: wait in the lobby.

He waited. And looked at the collection of military uniforms and civilian clothing milling around. His suit *was* frumpy. As discreetly as he could, he straightened his collar and tried to smooth the remaining wrinkles from his jacket. From somewhere behind him, he heard, or thought he heard, his name. He turned around.

A half dozen yards away stood a confused young GI, looking even more out of place than Cavanaugh did in his out-of-date suit.

"Captain Cavanaugh?" the young man repeated.

Cavanaugh walked up. "You looking for me?"

The GI stared blankly for a moment. "You Captain Cavanaugh?"

"Yeah, I'm Cavanaugh."

"Where's your uniform?"

"Upstairs. Should we go?"

The man nodded. "They said you'd be wearing a uniform. That's what they said."

"Well, I'm not. Let's go."

They made it in twenty minutes. The offices of the Manhattan Project were in the New War Department Building on Virginia Avenue, just a few blocks from the White House. It wasn't particularly far from the hotel, but the traffic was heavy and the GI spent most of the time cursing the delay and fretting over his fate.

"If you're late, my ass is gonna be in a sling," he whined. "The General don't like delays."

Cavanaugh tried to reassure him. "It's not your fault," he said calmly. "The traffic's heavy, that's all."

The driver seemed to relax only when he pulled up in front of the War Department and let his rider out.

Cavanaugh's stack of military orders got him through the guards at the front entrance, but it took another ten minutes of waiting at the information desk before an escort could be found to lead him to the third floor.

Walking through the labyrinthine complex of hallways and stairwells, he was reassured to see as many civilians in suits as men in uniform. He didn't look particularly out of place.

"This is it," said the nameless lieutenant. He pointed toward a plain door with no description other than the number "5120" painted on it. There was nothing that identified it as the personal headquarters of the officer in charge of the multibillion-dollar Manhattan Project. In that sense, both Oppenheimer and Groves shared something: they both seemed to lack any pretensions about their offices.

The lieutenant knocked on the door and an electric lock clicked and buzzed.

Inside, in a surprisingly small room, an attractive middle-aged woman sat at a wooden desk. She looked up from her Remington typewriter and smiled. She could easily be a secretary to a lawyer or accountant; there wasn't the faintest hint of Los Alamos, or Oak Ridge, or Hanford in the room.

"Dr. Cavanaugh?" she asked.

Oh, thank God, he thought, a friendly face and voice. He nodded and walked toward her desk.

"The General will be with you in just a minute." She looked at her watch. "You're five minutes early." She picked up her phone and spoke softly into it.

Cavanaugh smiled and looked for a chair. His driver's ass was safe.

The office was furnished in an unremarkable decor that included green carpet, gray file cabinets, and metal-frame furniture with green plastic coverings. The walls were completely bare. The only softening effect came from the curtains on the window. Cavanaugh noticed the heavy-duty lock on the door and the fact that the ventilating duct was sealed over.

The phone on the secretary's desk rang; a moment later the woman looked up at Cavanaugh.

"General Groves will see you now." She pointed toward the door on her left.

"Thanks," said Cavanaugh, although he wasn't sure for what. Maybe just for smiling when he had no idea what lay in store for him on the other side of the door.

When he entered, he stepped into another unremarkable room with one exception: the General's desk. It was large and carved in florid detail; it looked as if it belonged in the office of a European ambassador. Groves sat motionless behind it for a moment and only then rose, majestically, a single gold star glittering from each of his lapels. The look on his face said that the one star should really be two. Standing next to the desk was the red-faced Major Franklyn.

Cavanaugh stared, speechless. The son of a bitch must have taken his own plane!

Groves stared at him and frowned. "Where's your uniform?"

68

"There was no time to put it on this morning." That was partially true anyway.

The General continued to frown. "The uniform is not for your convenience, Dr. Cavanaugh. It's to make you less conspicuous here in Washington."

Cavanaugh said nothing. He remembered Gilbert's explanation about the power of information in Washington. And the all-consuming game of obtaining it.

"Well, sit down, we don't have much time." The General nodded toward the table. "You know Major Franklyn from G-2?"

"We met last night." Or was it the night before? The last few days were a blur in his head.

As he sat down, Cavanaugh heard his stomach growl; there had been no time this morning to catch a bite. Unconsciously, he pulled out his pack of cigarettes and took one. He was fumbling in his coat pockets for his Zippo when he realized there was no ashtray on the table. A quick glance at the General's face made him quickly reinsert the cigarette in the pack and put it away. He centered himself in his chair and put both arms on the table, hands clasped.

"Dr. Cavanaugh," began the General, "I've asked you here on a matter of the greatest importance. And also the greatest secrecy." He peered gravely at Cavanaugh, his large, well-shaped head slightly cocked back; the silver hair gave him an air of distinction. The General was utterly different in look and demeanor from Oppenheimer, but there was no doubt that both men knew how to wield power. Only right now, Cavanaugh knew that it was the General who controlled his fate.

"As you know, we are concerned about the recent discovery in Germany. Would you get the files, Major."

Cavanaugh stared at Franklyn as the man arranged some papers on the table. This morning, the wire-rim glasses gave him an academic look. Cavanaugh wondered what the man had done before the war. His uniform was neat, but not impeccable, not at all like the General's. He guessed that Franklyn was not a lifer, a professional Army man, but rather someone whose prewar experience had naturally landed him a job in intelligence.

If he had to, Cavanaugh would bet money that Franklyn had been a college professor, maybe of European history. And just for the hell of it, if he could, he would try to find out later. Maybe Gilbert would know.

"I must emphasize again the importance of what we're telling you, and the absolute need to say nothing about it. To anyone, under any circumstances. Is that clear?" The General had leaned forward on the table as if to emphasize his words with an aggressive posturing of his body.

"Yes." What else he could say? Or what would happen if he disagreed?

From one folder, Franklyn pulled a small stack of photographs and a map. Cavanaugh's curiosity was growing. There had to be more to this business than a collection of strange gun barrels to bring him to Washington.

"Review what we know, Major." The General relaxed somewhat and sat back in the chair.

"Oh, yes, two weeks ago, on, ah . . ." The major thumbed through his stack of papers looking for a date. He was considerably less poised in front of Groves than he had been two nights ago in Los Alamos.

"Yes, yes, that's all right. Just get to the facts."

Franklyn straightened his papers. "Approximately two weeks ago, a unit of the U.S. First Army was outside of Mühlhausen, in central Germany. Ah, that's some sixty kilometers from Nordhausen. Are you familiar with it?" He looked at Cavanaugh.

He shook his head. "Never heard of it."

"The Germans maintained a huge underground factory outside of Nordhausen for the assembly of V-2 rockets. In a series of tunnels in a mountain. It was called the Mittelwerk." The major unfolded a map and pointed to a small dot diagonally between Frankfurt and Berlin. Then he studied Cavanaugh for a reaction.

"I'm familiar with the V-2, but I've never heard of Nordhausen. Or the Mittelwerk."

News in 1944 of the V-2 had caused a sensation at Los Alamos. If such a rocket could be made large enough, it could theoretically carry an atomic bomb. The larger the rocket, the larger the bomb. And the larger the bomb, the greater the destruction. That realization had caused most people in Los Alamos to think about the atomic bomb in a new way; more than ever before they had come to believe that only America should have the new weapon.

"Major, this isn't about rockets," interjected the General. "Get to the point."

"Yes, well, in Mühlhausen—I mean outside of the town—the First

70

Army unit made an unusual discovery. They found a scientific laboratory, a rather sophisticated one, we understand. Much of the equipment had been removed, taken somewhere else, we presume, but the complex was wired for heavy electrical use."

"What sort of laboratory?"

"We aren't certain; it contained equipment for machining metals. There was evidence of metallurgical and chemical processing equipment as well. Most of it disassembled. And a supply of black powder."

"Explosives?"

"No. The propellant for a cannon probably."

"Were they doing research?" asked Cavanaugh.

"Possibly. But again we don't know with certainty. They did find several large weapons there, however."

"The gun barrels?"

"Yes. The ones specially produced by the Krupps Armament Works. You'll remember these, I presume?" Franklyn handed Cavanaugh several photographs.

Cavanaugh took them and recognized one of them as the photograph he had been shown in Los Alamos. The grinning face of the American GI stared at him once again.

"I've seen this one," he said, flipping through the small collection. They were all of the same scene, but taken from slightly different angles.

But then a thought hit him. Something *was* different, but it wasn't the photographs. It was in the name of the town Franklyn was talking about: Colonel Milo had never mentioned a German town called Mühlhausen. It was some other name. Cavanaugh started to inquire about the discrepancy but changed his mind. Instead, he asked if the GIs had found any fissionable material; that, after all, would confirm that the gun barrels had been intended as an atomic bomb.

"We don't know. That's been part of the problem in confirming the precise intent of the gun barrels."

"Did they find anything else? Detonators? Electronics?"

"It hasn't been possible to do a thorough investigation. Under the circumstances," said Groves. The General leaned forward again on the table. This time, the expression on his face was serious but not angry. There was a look of genuine concern that ran across the handsome face. "We haven't been able to get in our own team yet."

Cavanaugh was confused. What was the problem? "I don't understand."

Groves stared down at the table. "I really can't use ALSOS for this, ah, special project."

Cavanaugh felt the confusion was growing. What the hell did they have an intelligence group for if they couldn't use it?

"Why not? I thought that's what they were in Europe for—to check out German scientific research." He had, after all, read dozens of pages of secret ALSOS reports in the car ride to Albuquerque. All of them by flashlight.

Groves pursed his lips. "We made a deliberate decision not to," he said. Cavanaugh knew enough to know that the "we" was actually an "I."

"Intelligence data comes from a variety of sources: Army G-2, Naval Intelligence, Office of Strategic Services, even British Intelligence. We have our own sources, such as ALSOS. We work every day with the intelligence people, in fact. But information can go both ways. I don't want news of what's been found in Mühlhausen to go anywhere but here."

Cavanaugh's suspicion was correct. Something else was at play, something much larger than the gun barrels and the containers of black powder. A skeleton in a closet somewhere rattled uneasily.

"But why should we assume these gun barrels are actually atomic bombs? There seems very little evidence of that." Cavanaugh cleared his throat. "At least from what you've told me," he added.

"We assume nothing," said Groves brusquely. "That is why we need to investigate Mühlhausen. To be certain."

Then Cavanaugh remembered the name of the German town identified by Milo in Los Alamos. "I thought this laboratory, or whatever it is, was located outside of a village called Garmisch? Near the Austrian border? No one mentioned, uh, Mühlhausen."

He recalled something else. "And I thought that the Germans came no closer to an atomic bomb than making a crude reactor. Isn't that what ALSOS concluded?" He shook his head. "I mean, your people interrogated Werner Heisenberg himself, didn't they? Wasn't he the leader of the wartime program?"

"True. ALSOS found a crude reactor and some unprocessed uranium. And they interrogated Heisenberg. But they've never seen the laboratory at Mühlhausen. They don't even know about it. We've deliberately withheld its existence from ALSOS. To protect it."

To protect it from what? wondered Cavanaugh. Or from whom? The whole business seemed more about spies than atomic bombs.

"You see," said Franklyn, "no one but us suspects these gun barrels might be parts for atomic bombs. The ALSOS teams are looking for broad developments in nuclear physics, not the actual mechanisms for weapons. But more important, ALSOS is presently working with members of British Intelligence. We want this, ah, 'discovery' to stay in the family."

"That's why you're being sent, Cavanaugh," said Groves. "To check this out independently. And quietly."

Cavanaugh thought about it for a moment. "I'm still confused why you need me."

Groves tapped his hand on the tabletop. He seemed out of patience. "We want you to confirm if those gun barrels are indeed atomic bombs. We need to know precisely what the GIs found." The General relaxed somewhat. "You see, no one in Europe knows what you know about atomic bombs. Not how they're made or how they work. And we want to keep it that way." The General leaned back from the table and resumed his imperious pose.

"General Marshall has created a joint American-British team to assess German scientific and technological developments. This is not something I approve of, but it seems to be something he and the President agree on. For the moment, I want to keep this new discovery an American matter. And in our own office."

"Why don't we bring the equipment and the gun barrels here?" Cavanaugh asked. "After all, we'd have better facilities to evaluate them here."

"There's a difficulty with that." The General straightened in his chair. "You see, Mühlhausen is in the Soviet Occupation Zone."

Cavanaugh felt as if someone had landed an unexpected punch on his chin. "What?"

"Yes. It became part of the Soviet Zone in June. It wouldn't be easy—impossible, probably—to get a full team in." He looked hard at Cavanaugh. "But we can insert a small team of two or three."

The Soviet Zone? The thought chilled Cavanaugh. All he could think of were photographs he had seen in *Life:* fierce-looking Russians in bloodstained uniforms holding out at Stalingrad; hardened, war-weary men hoisting the Red flag over Hitler's Reich Chancellery.

"Wouldn't the Russians know about these gun barrels by now?"

"Our information says no. Apparently, their big concern right now is in stripping German industry and sending it piece by piece back to Russia. But we can't be sure."

A hundred questions flooded Cavanaugh's mind. "What about fissionable material? Uranium, plutonium? There can't be a bomb without that. I thought the Germans had only a small amount of crude uranium." He searched the General's face.

"We have new evidence that the Germans were able to obtain a supply of uranium, in secret, of course, and to have it refined to some degree. All without the knowledge of Heisenberg and his people. The ALSOS team never picked it up."

Franklyn spoke up. "Apparently, there were many efforts within the German war machinery that were virtually unknown. Small efforts that were the pet project of one Nazi bigwig or another. We think they were able to get uranium ore from mines in Czechoslovakia. It was shipped to Germany, where it was purified and sent to Mühlhausen. Or maybe somewhere else for storage."

Franklyn waved one hand. His voice was laconic. "This shouldn't surprise you. Look at their rocket development. Other than a few public 'announcements' from Hitler about secret vengeance weapons, the V-1's and V-2's were unknown to most of the German Army. If our intelligence is right, this laboratory at Mühlhausen was supersecret, a small program known only to a few highly placed men."

Cavanaugh shook his head slowly. "I don't know anything about undercover operations. Nothing about spying."

"You don't need to," said Franklyn. "We have people who do. Special people who will help you."

"You can understand our concern, Dr. Cavanaugh," said the General. "If the work at Mühlhausen is indeed what we think it is, then we need to know how far the Nazis got in making a bomb. We need to know what might have already fallen into Russian hands. Or British."

Had he heard right? "British?"

"The Brits have their own scientific people over there, you know, scouring the countryside, and they're not terribly interested in sharing what they find. They've got a team they call the Red Indians."

Groves waited for the irony to sink in. "Yes. That's what their intelligence people call this special scientific attack force. And they're grabbing whatever they can get their hands on: reports, equipment, jet-powered aircraft, midget submarines. Even personnel."

Groves leaned forward in his chair again. Cavanaugh could tell he wasn't a man who liked meetings; he certainly didn't like sitting for very long. "We have to move fast. G-2 tells me that it won't be possible to get a team into Mühlhausen much longer. The Soviets are moving troops in to solidify their border. We've got to act while we still have a chance to slip through."

Cavanaugh sighed. This was much more than Milo and Franklyn had talked about in Los Alamos. And Oppenheimer? Was he aware of all these developments?

Groves stood up. The meeting was over.

"Captain Gilbert will brief you further on what you'll need to know and do. We're sending you over as a captain in the Army Corps of Engineers; that should give you some flexibility to operate without drawing an unusual amount of attention. If asked, you are to say that you've been sent to look at German atomic work. To confirm the AL-SOS findings, that sort of thing. But under no circumstances are you to say why you're really there."

Cavanaugh nodded weakly. He started to rise, but the General raised his hand.

"There's something else, Cavanaugh. Something, uh, disturbing. The same Army team that found the gun barrels in Mühlhausen also made another discovery. A shocking one."

"Something else?"

"Yes. A mass grave. Twenty, maybe thirty bodies, all shot in the back of the head. Obviously executed."

Cavanaugh didn't know what to think. "By whom?"

"Germans probably. But then, the victims were German too."

Cavanaugh was stunned. "Why?"

Groves shook his head. "We don't know. The bodies were dumped into a pit and halfheartedly covered up. It must have happened during the last days of the war. The victims had no identification papers, but there were enough personal items to identify the group as German citizens. Well dressed, too, maybe technicians or workers at the laboratory. We have to assume that the Nazi leadership wanted to cover something up. Trouble is, we don't know what."

For a moment, no one spoke. Then, quietly, the General added, "We can only assume that Hitler placed the highest importance on this project. That's why we have to be sure."

Franklyn stood up. "I'll get the rest of the paperwork going," he said. Cavanaugh felt weak but he wanted to leave; he just didn't want to hear any more.

Groves put up his hand again. "I want a private word with you, Doctor." He looked at Franklyn. "I want Cavanaugh out of Washington tonight. This afternoon, if possible."

75

The major nodded and left the room.

Groves moved away from the table to the window. He seemed interested in something outside that Cavanaugh couldn't see.

"I know this is a lot to throw at you at one sitting, Philip," he said, never turning from the window. Cavanaugh straightened in his chair; the man had used his Christian name.

"But I can't tell you how important this is to the security of the country." He looked at the door and then at the window before continuing. Cavanaugh just sat where he was, fearing to utter even a sound. He just prayed that Groves couldn't hear his stomach rumbling or his heart beating.

"Dr. Oppenheimer doesn't know what you do. I am deliberately sending you because I don't trust the ALSOS people. I mean, I don't doubt for a second their loyalty or the integrity of their work, but I worry that they might be careless with news of this, ah, new development. There's the chance that the British, perhaps even the Soviets, have sources of information within our military services. All good-natured 'victory' stuff, and all that, but still a threat to *American* security." He turned and stared directly at Cavanaugh.

"Frankly, I want the secret of the atomic bomb to stay in America. We're the only ones who can be trusted with it. I don't like the idea that the President and some of his advisers want to share it, even with the British. We can only trust our own people."

Cavanaugh thought about his British friends at the laboratory. They knew as much as anybody, and most of them were talking about going home after the war. But this didn't seem the time to bring it up.

Groves turned and looked outside the window again. Cavanaugh could only see the branches of a tree. "The real threat is the Russians. *They're* the enemy now."

He said it softly, but Cavanaugh heard each word as if it had been spoken through a public-address system. Groves made the possibility sound frightening, obviously the effect he intended.

"But what can we do about Mühlhausen? It's in the Soviet Zone. Even if I get there and check it out, I can't bring anything home."

"We can take care of that. Later. But right now, first things first." The General studied Cavanaugh with his large, serious eyes. "I want you to report what you find only to me. Is that understood? Not to Major Franklyn. Not to anyone else on my staff. Not even to Dr. Oppenheimer."

Cavanaugh started to speak but was interrupted.

"Is that understood?"

Cavanaugh nodded. "Yes."

"Remember, you're doing something for your country that no one else can do." The General stuck out his hand and shook Cavanaugh's. It was solid and sharing. And conspiratorial.

He started to walk out of the office when the General's powerful voice boomed from behind him.

"And Cavanaugh, get into uniform."

Groves watched the door close and shook his head. Cavanaugh might be bright, but he was like all scientists: naive about security, maybe even deliberately so.

He rang his secretary and asked for Franklyn to be brought back in. A few minutes later the major reappeared. "Put a tail on him," said Groves. "I want to know where he goes. Who he sees and talks to."

"He's leaving tonight," reminded Franklyn.

"Even so. I want him watched at all times when he's here in the States."

Franklyn nodded. He shared the General's view about scientists, especially one this young.

"You've arranged for similar coverage overseas?"

"As much as we can."

"Good."

Franklyn thought a moment. "Do you think Cavanaugh will cause problems?"

"Not necessarily Cavanaugh," mumbled Groves. He knew better than anyone how hard it had been to come this far, how extraordinarily difficult it had been to restrict knowledge of the Manhattan Project to as few people as possible. And yet, he knew that the worst was yet to come: *keeping* the secret of the atomic bomb was going to be the next great challenge.

He turned to Franklyn. "But I don't trust anyone Cavanaugh comes into contact with," he added gravely.

Chapter Seven

*L*unch was the Blue Plate Special: lamb chops for ninety cents, and that included two vegetables. Cavanaugh ate ravenously, as if he hadn't eaten for days. Actually, that was largely true: the last real meal had been two scrambled eggs, bacon and toast in Los Alamos. Everything else had been U.S. Army sandwiches served in transit on airplanes and stale candy bars at fuel stops.

He and Gilbert were eating in the War Department cafeteria, located somewhere in the bowels of the great building. It was a vast, cavernous room, with what looked like hundreds of tables and thousands of noontime diners. Almost all of them were in uniform. To Cavanaugh it looked like a military field parade. There were uniforms of all varieties and colors: blues, grays, greens, and the ubiquitous khaki. And decorations: shirts with epaulets; coats with gold and silver braids; medals and horizontal bars divided into tiny multicolored bands that looked like a chemist's spectra.

The noise was deafening: voices, laughter, the clatter of dishes and the scraping of chairs on the floor. And the conversations ranged from news from the Pacific to jokes and tall tales, including one about a box of Army prophylactics shipped by accident to an orphanage in France; from winners and losers in bureaucratic battles and inter-office struggles to the latest gossip about who was sleeping with whom.

"I gotta have one more piece of pie," Cavanaugh said. The wedge of apple pie he'd just finished hadn't been half bad and only cost fifteen cents.

"Sure," said Gilbert. "Help yourself."

Cavanaugh got up and walked back to the end of the cafeteria line. He quickly navigated around the late noon diners who were trying to decide between entrees. Haggard-looking black men dripping with perspiration continually exchanged vast tubs nearly empty of mashed potatoes or red beets for full ones. No one would ever guess that the United States had been at war for three and a half years.

Out of the corner of his eye he caught sight of Gilbert sitting at their table talking with another man. A man in a khaki uniform.

In turn, Gilbert watched Cavanaugh make his way through the cafeteria line, deliberately holding off conversation with the lieutenant colonel who had just sat down.

"Who is he?" asked the colonel.

"Name's Cavanaugh," replied Gilbert.

"Works with you guys?" The man lit a cigarette.

Gilbert smiled. "Sort of."

The lieutenant colonel took a deep drag on his cigarette and exhaled. He waited patiently for Gilbert to explain.

"Groves brought him in from New Mexico."

One thin eyebrow lifted. "Los Alamos?"

Gilbert nodded, then glanced around him as he leaned toward the colonel. "Groves is sending him to Europe. Germany."

Another deep drag. Pause. Protracted exhale. "You know why?"

Gilbert shrugged. "I just learned he was coming to D.C. yesterday; picked him up last night."

The lieutenant colonel stamped out his cigarette, inadvertently snapping it in two as he did so. "We hear the General is up to something. Something big. There's been a lot of traffic between him and London, I understand."

Gilbert assumed he referred to the cable traffic between the central Manhattan Project offices in Washington and its European office in London. Mostly the cables concerned intelligence matters. The lieutenant colonel on the other side of the table was high up in Naval Intelligence; in fact, the man's boss reported directly to General Marshall.

"We'd like to know more," the colonel said softly. He pushed his chair away from the table. "You know how much we always appreciate your help." He smiled. "Catch you later."

Gilbert pointed a finger at him. "Right," he said.

Just then Cavanaugh walked back with his second piece of pie. "Who was that?" he asked.

"A friend at the Pentagon. Whaty'a get? Apple again?"

After lunch they took a walk. Cavanaugh said he needed cigarettes and Gilbert said he knew the best place in town to get them.

The source was a small newsstand operated by an Italian with a wooden leg. A carton of Lucky Strikes cost fifty cents.

"How so cheap?" asked Cavanaugh.

"Black market. Probably lifted from an Army-supply center. You can get all kinds of stuff like that."

Cavanaugh was surprised. "Stolen?"

"Liberated." Gilbert watched the Italian pivot on his bad leg and hand Cavanaugh his carton of cigarettes and some change. At the same time, he glanced at the cover of *Time* and noticed that Donald O'Connor was on the cover in an Army uniform.

"Ready?" he asked.

"Sure. Where to?"

Gilbert nodded with his head. "Back to the office."

They walked in silence for a few minutes until Cavanaugh asked a question. "You can get anything?"

Gilbert smiled. "Just about. I found four new tires the other day for a colonel friend of mine. *That* was a coup."

Cavanaugh smiled and noticed that it was a cloudy day, hot and humid enough to make him feel sticky. They had walked about six blocks, just far enough for him to remember what humidity was like; this was something he'd been unaccustomed to in Los Alamos.

There was also that smell again, he thought, the one from last night, which he'd noticed on the drive from the airfield. It was the pungent, contradictory mixture of odors that only a large city possesses: automobiles, human breath, rot, the remnants of rain on a wool jacket. Even the faint hint of cinnamon from a bakery somewhere. A vast, stewing caldron of smells.

"Where does the stuff come from? Tires, things like that?"

"Everywhere. People hoard stuff, then unload it at ridiculous prices. Make a killing, you know? Sometimes you can buy directly from the manufacturer. Sammy probably gets his cigarettes from a GI with connections in the Quartermaster Corps. They rip off a couple boxes, sell the cartons for ten, maybe fifteen cents, and the GI in turn doubles the price to his contacts. Everyone makes a profit. It's the American way."

Gilbert grabbed Cavanaugh's arm. "Let's cut through the park, okay?" He pointed down the street.

Cavanaugh nodded. Right now, despite the fact that it was muggy, he was enjoying the walk. The overcast sky created a filtering effect on the city: the color of everything he saw seemed deeper and richer, as if he were looking through a pair of Kodachrome glasses.

More than anything he was struck by the people on the streets: there were so many of them. And how they were dressed: women in chic outfits like those worn by the models in *Ladies Home Journal* and men in stylish suits. At least, they looked stylish to him. He felt a little shabby in his rumpled brown wool suit.

The park was filled with people eating lunch or just sitting outside. Gilbert seemed to take great care to avoid clusters of people. Cavanaugh sensed that he wanted to talk but not where they could be overheard. When they were on the other side of the small park, Gilbert deliberately took a narrow street that had few pedestrians.

"You know you're going over as part of the Corps of Engineers?" Gilbert dropped his pace even more so that they were out of step with the few individuals on the street.

"So I was told."

They stopped to look into the window of a small bookstore. Edna Ferber's book, *Great Son*, was featured on a small wooden stand. It had been so long since Cavanaugh had been able to wander around in a real bookstore. That was something he and Merry had liked to do on Saturdays.

Gilbert suddenly laughed. "He said to give you a fake name. Down to dog tags."

"Who did?" Cavanaugh asked.

"Groves. He wanted us to create a bogus person; you know, with parents, family, college, jobs, the works."

"Why?" Before this morning, secrecy meant telling no one about his work and always being sure that his notes and papers were locked in a safe overnight. He hadn't had a false name since the third grade when the kids in his neighborhood organized a "secret" club and everyone was given a code name: his had been Falcon.

"Safety. Just in case."

"Just in case of what?" There had been a disquieting edge of uncertainty, of things that could go wrong, throughout all of the morning.

Gilbert shrugged. "Something bad, I guess."

Once again, Cavanaugh had a feeling that Gilbert knew more than he was telling. He sensed the joviality and good-old-boy behavior was just a mask for a more manipulative person underneath.

"I think it's crazy. It's bullshit."

"Maybe, maybe not. But Franklyn and I managed to persuade Groves that we didn't have enough time for fake names. Besides, it *could* backfire. After all, it is possible that someone at ALSOS might recognize you." He smiled. "That would create a problem, you know."

"What kind of problem?"

"Your face but a different name. It might cause someone to ask the sort of questions we don't want asked."

"So I'm going as Philip Cavanaugh."

Gilbert looked at him. "Philip Andrew Cavanaugh. With the Army Corps of Engineers. Therefore your background fits nicely. There's no cover to be maintained other than why you're there."

Cavanaugh thought about it a moment. He couldn't tell Gilbert what he was going for—he had sworn that to Groves—but then he had damn little information about how he was supposed to accomplish his job. Damn little. A thousand things *could* go wrong. And there was the maxim, the saying every GI knew by heart: if something could go wrong, it would.

"So I go as myself and I'm with the Corps. Then what?"

Gilbert looked over his shoulder. The street was empty. It was nearly one-thirty and most people had gone back to work. "You're checking out the ALSOS stuff, right?" He continued to stare into the display of books; the glass pane in front of them acted as a mirror to reflect images from the street.

"Right," said Cavanaugh. Gilbert sounded sincere, but Cavanaugh couldn't be sure. After this morning's briefings, he didn't trust anyone. He couldn't afford to.

"Let's head back," said Gilbert. He started down the street and effortlessly regained his good humor. He told jokes. He talked about

82

women. He gave a running commentary on life in wartime Washington.

"It's a great place," he said. "I'm gonna try to stay here after the war."

"In the Army?"

Gilbert laughed. "Maybe. But you never know. Seems to me that we're gonna need intelligence people after the war, though. Maybe I can find a slot there. I hear the OSS is looking for men with technical backgrounds."

That sounded reasonable, thought Cavanaugh. Plus the man had an easy skill with people that made him work well within the system. It was difficult to think of Gilbert outside a system where he couldn't negotiate black-market tires and nylons. But would he make a good spy? For some reason, Cavanaugh saw Gilbert ending up in Congress. Lots of voters would like nylons and tires.

Twenty minutes later they were in Gilbert's small office, the smallest that Cavanaugh had been in that day. Gilbert retrieved a box from a locked cabinet and placed it on his desk. He pulled a file folder from the box and pushed it toward Cavanaugh. "Read this," he said. His voice and manner had changed again: he was serious now.

Cavanaugh opened the folder and began to look through the contents.

There were multiple copies of a form that permitted him to travel to Europe; other forms clarified his assignment to the Corps of Engineers. But it was the single sheet of paper stamped "Secret" that caught his attention: a series of instructions—proceed to Stuttgart; wait to be contacted; wait for final orders. The names and locations meant nothing to him.

"What does all this mean? What do I do with this?"

"Memorize it. You'll be given further instructions when you're in Germany. Right now, you just need to know where you're going and who you need to talk to when you're there."

"Who'll contact me in London? Someone from the Army?"

"Well," said Gilbert, "sort of."

"What do you mean, 'sort of'?"

"I mean, our man will be in uniform, but he's with Strategic Services, not the Manhattan Project. He's the one that'll arrange for you to get around."

Cavanaugh felt his heart beating faster again. There was nothing about any of this that he liked.

"And then?"

"And then they'll get you out and on a plane back to England. You're on your own there. But your orders take you back to D.C. and then to Albuquerque."

Cavanaugh could imagine a dozen bad possibilities. "What if I get lost?" That fear was near the top, right under being shot by a Nazi sniper.

Gilbert smiled. "You got your dog tags. Find someone and tell them you're lost." He glanced out the small window in his office. Above both their heads was a cloud of smoke from Cavanaugh's cigarettes.

"Look, getting lost is the least of your problems." With that, he pushed the box across to Cavanaugh.

"What's this?"

"Things you'll need."

Cavanaugh lifted one flap, then the other. The first item he saw was an envelope. As soon as he picked it up he knew what was inside. "Money?"

"Yeah. One thousand smackeroos. American. In tens and twenties."

Cavanaugh thumbed through the stack of ten- and twenty-dollar bills. "For me?"

"Yep. Try not to spend it if you can. We expect it back."

Cavanaugh laughed. "What do I need this much money for?"

Gilbert thought a moment. "You might need to buy your way out of something. There's also Army scrip. The currency of the Occupation. Use that if you can."

Cavanaugh dug through the box some more; he suddenly felt something cold and hard. Gently he lifted out a pistol.

"It's a thirty-eight," said Gilbert. "Standard issue for spies."

Cavanaugh didn't like the look or the feel. His father had always made a big deal about how deadly guns could be; as a kid, he never even owned a BB gun. "What do I do with it?"

"Wear it. Don't lose it. It's on loan too."

"Holy shit!" muttered Cavanaugh. "What *can* I keep?"

"Your dog tags. They have your name on them."

"Great," said Cavanaugh. Holding the gun, he felt like an Old West gambler. "What next?"

"That's about it, as far as I'm concerned," said Gilbert. "Later, we'll get you in uniform—I've already caught shit on that—and give you some pointers on how to act like a captain."

"Then it's bye-bye?"

"Right. You're on a flight for London tonight. You'll be there to-morrow afternoon. But right now, Lieutenant Leiter is going to tell you more about Nazi research and help you sharpen your German."

Cavanaugh shook his head. "I don't speak German," he said. Why in the hell had he ever said anything? "I read it. Or I did. Sort of."

Gilbert looked puzzled. "I thought you did! It was on a report some-where, I think. Well, it doesn't matter. You'll enjoy the session any-way."

"Why?"

"You'll see." He picked up his phone and told a secretary to find Lieutenant Leiter. "Tell her that Captain Cavanaugh is ready for his briefing."

He gently put the receiver back into its cradle. "Look, I know all this is very different from what you were doing in Los Alamos, but don't worry. Just play along. You'll be back in a week or so and you can tell all your friends you've been to war." For a brief moment a frown crossed his unlined face. "It's better than anything I've done."

"Tell me one thing," said Cavanaugh.

Gilbert looked up from the table. "What?" He was checking to be sure nothing was left in the box.

"About Major Franklyn. What's his background?"

Gilbert looked puzzled. "Why do you ask? I think he was a teacher."

"What kind of teacher?"

"In a college somewhere. I don't remember which one. I think he taught history." He tossed the empty box into the trash can by the side of his desk.

Lieutenant Leiter was a young woman in her middle twenties. At-tractive, but not stunningly beautiful. But still, when she first walked in the room, Cavanaugh just stared at her.

She was very self-possessed and didn't stare back, two facts that Cavanaugh tried to fit with her face. He relaxed when she spoke. Her voice was pleasant and unthreatening. She nodded at him, then smiled at Gilbert and said hello. For a moment he wondered if she had a thing going with Gilbert, but it was only a smile. The hello was civil, nothing more. Cavanaugh put the idea out of his mind.

"I'll leave you two alone," said Gilbert. Cavanaugh wasn't certain, but he thought he caught the man winking at him.

Leiter casually sat down and laid a stack of folders in front of her. It wasn't until she looked up and looked at him that he saw her face clearly. It was pretty, though with features that would appeal to one man but not necessarily to another. Her light-brown hair was cut on the short side, perhaps to conform to military code. Her skin was fair and very clear; he could tell she didn't stay in the sun a lot. She bore no resemblance to the WACs or nurses Cavanaugh knew back in Los Alamos. This was a very feminine, big-city girl.

"Well," he said, not knowing what else to say.

"Well," she repeated, "you're from Los Alamos?" She obviously didn't know what to say either. Her voice was pleasant, but again neither friendly nor unfriendly.

"Yeah. New Mexico. You're familiar with it?" Then he realized that of course she would know who he was and what he did. There was no way she would be trusted with ALSOS intelligence data if she didn't know what the Manhattan Project was up to. Leiter would have a security clearance that would give her access to all sorts of intelligence data. Certainly data about the men who were building the bombs.

She nodded. "I was even in Santa Fe once, before the war."

"Really. What for?"

"I was a tourist. With my parents. My father had a strong interest in archaeology."

"Was he an archaeologist?"

"No. A mathematician, actually."

"And you? Where are you from?"

"Well, originally from Chicago. It's where my father was teaching when I was born. But since then, lots of places."

Cavanaugh smiled. "And you're a mathematician?"

"No," she said, "a chemist. I'm going for my doctorate after the war." She began to organize her papers. The small talk was apparently over.

"I understand you've been briefed on ALSOS?" She gently touched her hair as if to be sure it was in place. "And the special task force called T-Force?"

Cavanaugh nodded. T-Force had been created to enter the Württemberg region of Germany as the German armies pulled back but before the French armies entered.

"I've read some of their reports."

"Then you know about the German reactor work at Haigerloch? The interviews with Heisenberg and the others?"

"Right." She appeared to him to be very comfortable in what she was doing. There was an ease in her manner, a composure that could stem from competence as much as from having grown up around educated people. She was also accustomed to having men stare at her; that much was obvious to Cavanaugh. Of course, wartime Washington would have provided plenty of opportunities for that.

She pushed some papers across the table to him. "You can read these later, but I'll give you a summary now."

She talked for over an hour, covering the last year of ALSOS sleuthing in a precise, almost melodic voice.

As he had been told, the German atomic-bomb effort had not progressed beyond making a crude reactor. They had used heavy water and developed a general theoretical sense of what it would take to make a weapon, but that was as far as they got. They knew nothing of implosion, of nuclear dynamics like cross-sections and neutron sources—the real secrets of a bomb.

There was a lot they *had* done, however. The Nazis had made substantial advances in aeronautics and chemical warfare. Of course, as Leiter pointed out, they had used human guinea pigs in a number of their experiments.

"You've heard of the gases tabun and sarin?"

He shook his head.

"Nazi doctors developed these gases and used them on concentration-camp inmates. Both are deadly." She frowned as she talked.

He watched her face closely, marveling how her features reflected what she said. "How deadly?"

"Tabun kills in about twenty minutes; sarin in four."

"Jesus," he murmured. Why did the Germans want atomic bombs when they had chemical weapons like these? Either one could easily kill every human being in a city and yet leave every structure intact.

"Just how good is your German?" she asked.

Cavanaugh waffled his hand. "Not that good. It was only a graduate course, you see. A reading course, really."

"Well, I have a list of terms here that might be helpful." She dug through her papers and found a sheet. She glanced at it for a moment and then handed it to him. "Will this help?" she asked.

He looked at it; the mimeographed page consisted of two columns, the first with a word or phrase in English, the second with the corresponding word in German. Some of the terms were footnoted.

The list contained maybe a hundred words and occupied both sides of the paper. He recognized a few dozen of them, although a few were obscure chemical or engineering words unknown to him; others, like *Uran* for Uranium and *Stampfer* for tamper, he recognized at once.

They talked for another hour. Cavanaugh's head was swimming. He rubbed his eyes.

"You're tired?" she asked. Her voice sounded solicitous.

"Yeah. I've been on the road for two days. Or two weeks; I don't really know."

She smiled. "How about some coffee?" She took off her glasses and touched her hair as if to straighten it.

"That would be great," he said.

She called for a secretary, who delivered two cups a few minutes later. They continued to sit at the conference table, still opposite one another. The late-afternoon sun had shifted to the other side of the building and Cavanaugh could see deep shadows forming on the outside walls. Though Leiter didn't smoke, she didn't frown when he lit up. His upper back and shoulders throbbed from hunching over the table; he sat back in his chair and tried to find a comfortable position. These chairs were no more comfortable than the ones in Los Alamos.

"What's Los Alamos like?" she asked.

He thought for a moment. "It's a community of secrets. Odd but exciting." He thought of Korshak and the others. "Crazy. And temporary. We're all wondering what we're going to be doing after the war."

For a while, they exchanged bits of personal history, the kind one might share with someone you sat next to on a long train journey. They talked about schools, where they had grown up, how they had come to the Manhattan Project. Just as he thought, she had grown up among her father's academic colleagues and had traveled extensively; if anything, her life was as cosmopolitan as his was parochial.

"Where did you learn your German?" he asked. Perhaps this would take them away from the differences in their backgrounds.

"My parents spoke it at home; my father was German, you see, and came to the United States to teach before the last war. He became a citizen, but both of my parents insisted that I learn more than one language."

"How many do you speak? Besides English?"

"French and German. But I'm studying Russian. I think there'll be a great need for Russian speakers after the war, don't you?"

"Probably." Right now, he was painfully aware of his pathetic attempts to learn foreign languages at school. He had come closest with Latin, but that was because his parochial school taught it to ease their students through the Catholic Mass. He had tried French in high school, but had barely passed and remembered nothing. And German—well, what he didn't know was obvious from the earlier conversations with Leiter.

"What about you? Anything besides English? And some German?" she added mischievously.

Cavanaugh winced. "Oh, none, really. I've tried a few." He noticed that she had a devilish look in her eyes as well.

"I thought you had to master German in order to get a doctorate in physics?"

"That's probably true," he said finally. "But I was a special student."

"Was that because you're Irish?"

He laughed. "No, I don't think that was the reason." He studied her for a moment. She seemed to like this sort of verbal play. He decided to try something, although he remembered his father once cautioning him to be wary of clever women. "Do you have a first name?" he asked.

"Yes. Don't you?"

But of course she would know from his file. "It's Philip. Phil."

"Christine. Not Chris."

"You don't look like a Chris."

She smiled. "You don't look like a Philip."

That surprised him. "Oh? Why?"

"Too English. You're Irish, aren't you? And besides, you look all-American to me."

"You don't look German."

"Ah," she said, smiling, "that's because I'm only half-German. Scottish on the other side."

"Well, tell me," he said as easily as he could, "do half-Germans, or half-Scots, eat dinner here in Washington?" Somehow, he drew on a forwardness he didn't know he possessed.

She studied him for a moment, her face inscrutable. "Do you mean, do we eat dinner at all? Or just today?"

He couldn't help it; he laughed. Inside, he worried that he had moved too quickly, too crudely for what she was probably accustomed to with the men here in Washington.

"I mean, I haven't had a good fish dinner since I left Ann Arbor two years ago, and I have to leave Washington tonight at ten o'clock. I mean, 2200 hours. Will you, or could you, have dinner with me?" At least he had asked it. At the worst, he would end up with a hot dog by himself at the delicatessen down the street from the hotel.

For a moment she said nothing, worrying Cavanaugh even more. Finally she spoke. "That's strange," she said, "I was thinking of eating seafood tonight."

Chapter Eight

*T*heir corner of the dining room was dimly lit. They were in a booth, far away from the central overhead light, and bathed in shadows except for the small lamp fixed to the wall next to them. The beaten-brass shade had a colonial motif with minutemen etched on it that reminded Cavanaugh of something you'd find in a young boy's room.

The lamp, which was at the level of their heads, shot light through the top of the shade to hit the ceiling, and down, in a spreading cone, to cover the table. Both of them sat close to the table, their hands sometimes resting on it, and their faces darting in and out of the light when they moved or laughed.

Christine was laughing now over a story Cavanaugh had told about an incident in Los Alamos, one about mud coming out of the water pipes. Over dinner, they had told each other stories from their wartime lives. As Christine laughed now, Cavanauagh noticed that her head shifted back slightly, out of the light, so that her eyes disappeared; for a moment, he only saw her smile.

"Is life there really that rustic?" she asked, still smiling. She, like him, never referred to Los Alamos or New Mexico by name in public.

"Worse," he replied. "I've only told you the good things."

She laughed again. "It's hard to describe Washington," she began, "the war has had its effect here, too, but in different ways. We still have to save our ration coupons; gas is hard to get sometimes. And it's almost impossible to get good stockings. But there's more liquor now, I'm told, than before the war. And the food at the commissary sometimes has fresh fruit just in by train from California. And people dress up when they go out, like to an embassy party or something. The black market here is unbelievable! But the war also has given us a sense of"—she searched for words—"a sense of impermanence, I think. It shares that with your home."

She looked dreamily away from the table for a moment. Through the open doorway was the first dining room with its cashier's desk and large aquarium where supposedly you could handpick the evening's dinner. For a moment, when she turned, her face disappeared from the light of the table lamp. Only her light-brown hair was highlighted, leaving Cavanaugh to remember the details of her eyes and nose and mouth.

"So many young men come here on their way to somewhere else. Women, too. Some come to get married and move away; then there are those who find life here too difficult or too lonely, they move on as well. But mostly it's men like you. You're only here for the day before you leave; others come for a few months, maybe a year, and then the war takes them somewhere else."

She turned back to look at Cavanaugh. He wondered what thoughts were really behind those luminous eyes.

"I've only known Washington during the war. I can't imagine what it will be like when the war is over."

For a moment he studied her. Was it possible, he thought, that a woman as attractive as this was actually lonely? There were so many people in Washington, so much life and energy. How was it possible that someone could be lonely in the midst of all this?

"Well, can you imagine my little corner of the world after the war? All of the wooden buildings, the Quonset huts and dirt roads built overnight by the Army? I sometimes think that when the war is over, the whole damn place will fall down flat. Then the Indians and Spanish people from the valley will come and haul it away and have one big bonfire." He took a sip of his wine. Somewhere, a jukebox was playing a Dorsey tune.

"What will you do then?" he asked. He deliberately picked at what was left of his food with his fork in order to prevent the waitress from taking his plate away. He didn't want dinner to end. Not yet, anyway. He was enjoying Christine's company too much.

"Oh, I told you. I want to get my doctorate in chemistry. I want to perfect my Russian. Get ready for the future, you know, that sort of thing."

"With your German and Russian, shouldn't you be in Europe? I mean, what could be a more lucrative place for intelligence these days than Germany?" To hear Groves and Franklyn, someone with Christine's background would be terribly useful overseas.

Christine sighed. "I'd love to be there. We lived in Germany when I was young, you know. That's where my mother and I learned the language. And I'm better qualified than most to be there."

"Why aren't you?" She was, however, just attractive enough to make some general keep her assigned to the office next door.

She laughed, although it lacked warmth. "Women don't get the best assignments in this man's Army. At least, on the basis of merit. I've asked, but they always find a reason to say no."

Cavanaugh thought he'd better change the subject. "Are you studying chemistry because of your father?" He caught her looking up at him with a change of expression: quizzical, not unfriendly. He worried that he might have offended her. Instead, she seemed to want to talk about her father.

"In part. I was an only child, you see, and my father spent lots of time with me, explaining things, taking me places. But above all, he introduced me to the idea of asking why things are the way they are. My interest in chemistry stems from all of that. And you? Why did you study physics?"

Cavanaugh thought for a moment. "I guess . . . because I couldn't become a priest."

Christine smiled. "And why was that?"

"I couldn't learn Latin," he said.

They both laughed. "Like your German?"

"I suppose. But like you, I was always fascinated with how things worked. At first it was clocks and toasters, but then, when I had taken everything at home apart and left it in a mess, I graduated to bigger things. Cars. Telescopes. I was a mechanical engineer first, then I finally moved up to cloud chambers and Van de Graaff machines. So you see, here I am."

Cavanaugh turned suddenly to see the waitress standing by the edge of the table.

"Finished?" she asked. Her voice was throaty and deep. She pointed with one finger at his plate. She wore a little white hat that sat slightly askew on a great bun of hair. Her face was young and old at the same time and Cavanaugh wondered if she was one of the lonely women Christine had talked about. The kind that came to Washington to find a man.

He nodded. "I guess so." As the waitress bent down to clear the table, he caught a full view of her face: the wrinkles were more severe in the light and the bright-red lipstick was larger than her lips.

Christine looked at her watch. "You don't have much time," she said.

Cavanaugh's heart fell. Everything was moving so quickly that he felt out of control again. Soon he would be on a plane flying three thousand miles over the ocean at night. For all he cared, England and Germany were on the other side of the world.

"What about coffee?" he suggested. "I have time for that, don't I?"

Christine smiled. "Oh, probably. But I promised Captain Gilbert that I would get you to the airfield two hours before departure. I'm responsible for you, you see."

"Of course. But surely the captain would want me to enjoy my last meal. And what is a last meal without coffee?"

"Well, what about it?" asked the waitress. "Coffee. Yes or no?"

"Yes," he said.

The heavyset woman rolled her eyes.

Cavanaugh thought briefly about Gilbert. Earlier, the man had gone with him to the hotel to pick up his suitcase and instruct him on uniforms. When he told Gilbert he was having dinner with Christine, he had only winked and said, "Good work." Then came a highly accelerated training program in which Cavanaugh was told where to put his captain's insignia and act like an officer: rank on the right, the Engineer's "fort" on the left. Or was it the other way around? As casually as he could, he looked down at his lapels. Rank was on the right.

"You look good in a uniform," said Christine. "Most men do. But you'd look even better in a tuxedo."

"I'm doing well to have this uniform," said Cavanaugh. "The tux will have to wait until after the war. Or at least, until I get back."

"You remember how to salute?" she asked. She had drilled him on this earlier in the evening when he'd met her outside the Mayflower with a salute. As a lieutenant, she said pointedly, it was her responsibility to salute first.

"Like this," he said, moving his right hand smartly.

"Keep your hand a little flatter. Right. And whom do you salute?"

"Ah, all persons, that is, officers, of a higher rank. And I return salutes from those of lesser ranks, including you." He thought about it for a moment. "Or don't I?"

"Right. Unless you're put out or bored, in which case a sloppy jerk of the right hand will probably do. Except for those of higher rank." She smiled.

"I don't feel comfortable in this damn uniform. I like ordinary clothes." He faked a frown.

"If you were a priest, you'd be wearing a dress."

"A cassock, please, and then only during official priestly duties."

"Well, I told you, you look good. Someone might even mistake you for a West Point graduate."

Cavanaugh smiled. "I doubt that, but it's worth a try."

Christine looked at her watch again. "We have to go. Really."

He looked at her, studied her eyes for as long as he thought he could without unnerving her, trying to memorize everything he thought he saw in them. That might help during the next eighteen hours on the plane.

"Thanks for coming," he said.

"I enjoyed it."

"Can we do it again? When I come back, that is, if I have a chance?"

"It's a date."

Cavanaugh smiled. Full of the best food he'd known in years, and easy from the wine, he never noticed the thick, featureless man who had been across the room all evening and left only when he and Christine walked out of the restaurant.

Base Operations at Bolling Field was a two-story brick building with windows on all sides. Through the alternating strokes of the windshield wiper, Cavanaugh could see the small building a half-block away. Dense, yellow light seemed to pour out of the windows.

Christine stopped at the guard gate. A tall, lanky GI with a rifle and an armband that said "MP" walked over and peered in. The guardhouse and streetlights brightly lit the gate area.

"Howdy, Lieutenant," the man said with a drawl. "You going somewhere tonight?" He pronounced the last word "too nat."

She said, "No, Corporal, but the captain is," and nodded toward Cavanaugh. He leaned toward her so that the MP could see him.

"Good luck," the young man said, and waved them through.

Trucks and jeeps cluttered the parking lot. Even from the car, Cavanaugh could tell the ground floor was filled with people. They parked the car and got out.

Cavanaugh kicked open the operations door with his foot, clutching his bag with one hand and a folder of papers in the other. Christine took the wooden steps two at a time and came in behind him. Both of them were met by a din of ringing telephones and animated conversations. At the far end was a wooden counter much like those Cavanaugh had seen at country grocery stores. On the rear wall was a giant blackboard divided into dozens of columns crisscrossed by horizontal lines, forming rectangular cells. In the first column, scrawled in chalk, were destinations—mostly American cities like St. Louis, San Antonio, Denver—followed in succeeding columns by dates and times, load capacities, and the like.

On another wall, nailed between two large windows, was a map of the United States with hundreds of small red pins stuck in it. Scattered throughout the room were chairs and sofas, on many of which the dull black cushions were torn or split from use and age. One man, his face hidden by a newspaper, lay asleep on a couch. Behind the desk were two young NCOs arguing with a half dozen men standing in front of the counter. A battery of telephones rang unanswered behind the NCOs. A thick cloud of cigarette smoke hung just below the ceiling.

Cavanaugh just stood there, his face wet with mist. He dropped his suitcase and fumbled for a handkerchief. Christine opened her purse and handed him hers. When he wiped his face, he smelled her perfume.

"Good God," mumbled Cavanaugh. What in the hell was supposed to happen here? He took it as a sort of omen that a six-foot-long sign, hung on the wall behind the counter and reading WE FLY THE WORLD, was hanging about six inches off-center.

Behind the counter, a short, wiry man with kinky black hair had his hands in the air, palms up, repeating in an east Jersey accent, "What can I do? What can I do?" Cavanaugh noticed that he had three stripes on his sleeve. He was talking to a heavyset major with a cigarette in his mouth.

"I gotta be there tomorrow. No fail, understand?"

"No one ain't going nowhere in this weather. Nothing's taking off. That's what I've been telling you." The wiry man's eyes were wild. Both men were close to shouting.

"Well, what the hell am I gonna do? I gotta be there." Ash fell from the major's cigarette as he shook his head.

"What can I do?" repeated the man behind the counter. He threw up his hands again in exasperation.

Cavanaugh made his way to the desk. The weather had obviously delayed departures. The question was, had it delayed his flight to London? Had God heard him?

For a moment, he just watched. The two men behind the counter were responsible for getting the people in the room somewhere else. They looked harried but confident. Maybe they knew someone in the Pentagon who would keep them from being sent to Alaska if they offended an officer. The small wiry man in particular looked as if he would stand up to anyone and win. His voice carried above everyone else's.

"What? What?" he shouted to someone. "What am I gonna do?"

"Got a minute?" asked Cavanaugh. He waved his hand to get attention.

"What?" said the short man.

"The flight to London?"

"Which flight?" He pointed to the blackboard. "I got a dozen."

"Ah," floundered Cavanaugh, "let's see." He fumbled around in his folder of papers looking for something called "travel orders." Gilbert had said something about a flight. But then he had said a lot of things that Cavanaugh could no longer remember. He turned to Christine.

She shrugged. "Let's check your orders." She calmly took the stack of papers and began to leaf through them.

"Wait," said the wiry man, looking at Cavanaugh, "what's your name?" He pointed a hand with a lighted cigarette at Cavanaugh.

"Me?"

"Yeah, you. Who else?"

Cavanaugh looked around. He was the only one at this end of the counter.

"Cavanaugh."

"Captain Cavanaugh?"

97

"Yeah, that's me."

"I was told to expect you. Call from downtown."

"So?"

"So your flight's postponed. Weather. Same shit as screwing up all these guys' flights. Sorry."

"Postponed to when?" Cavanaugh didn't know if he should be upset or not.

"Tomorrow. At 0600 hours earliest. Whenever this shit lifts."

"Jesus." Cavanaugh turned to Christine. "I leave tomorrow morning."

A few people melted away from the counter, leaving it relatively quiet. "You must be someone important," the NCO said matter-of-factly.

Cavanaugh just shrugged. "Why?"

"I don't get many calls from War telling me to be sure someone gets on a plane. What kind of doctor are you?"

"How'd you know that?"

"The guy at War called you Dr. Cavanaugh. Said it was damn important that you made your plane and that I was to hold it no matter what if you was late. I'd say that makes you pretty damn important to someone. So what do ya do?"

"What do you mean?"

The NCO rolled his eyes. "What kind of doctor, all right?"

"I do gallstones," said Cavanaugh.

The NCO laughed. "Right. And I do goddamn hemorrhoids." He whirled around and grabbed a piece of paper and scribbled something down on it. "Look, here's my name and the telephone number here. Call me in a couple hours. Maybe I'll know more then."

Cavanaugh looked at the paper. There was the word "Polo" and a phone number. "Polo?" he asked.

"Yeah. It's my nickname. Polo Beckerman. Of Trenton, New Jersey." He grinned a broad, toothy smile and then laughed until he coughed. The cigarette never left one corner of his lips.

Cavanaugh turned around to find Christine; she wasn't there. When he looked around the room, he found her at the rear using a pay telephone. He turned back to see Beckerman watching him.

"Well, Polo, what the hell should I do between now and whenever?"

Beckerman looked at Cavanaugh, then at Christine, then back at Cavanaugh. "I'd just go back out and try to have some fun," he said with a wink.

98

Cavanaugh shook his head. That was asking for too much. "What about a hotel room?"

Beckerman laughed. "This is D.C., Doc. The nation's capital, remember? Finding a hotel room here is like finding a whore who'll tell you she's got the clap." He waved his hand around the rest of the room. "These guys want rooms too. What can I do? Check with the Commander."

Christine came softly up and put her hand on his shoulder. "Delayed, right?" she asked.

"Yeah. Till tomorrow. Maybe six o'clock, maybe later. I don't know what I'm gonna do for a hotel."

"Stay at my place." She said it straightforwardly; Cavanaugh could read nothing into it but a kind offer to help out.

"Thanks, but—"

"I mean it. Someone's always sleeping on the couch. Half of Washington probably sleeps on couches. I called Helena, my roommate; she's planning to be out late. So you're welcome to it."

Cavanaugh studied her face for a moment, trying to read it. Anywhere else, the offer would be a double invitation, even in Los Alamos. But here, in Washington, he didn't know what to make of it. He sighed. It was her couch or the couch here.

"I'd appreciate it. Really."

She nodded toward the door. Outside the mist seemed thicker, as if it were turning to fog. "Let's go," she said. "I think we'll have time for a drink before Helena gets back."

Cavanaugh looked at the piece of paper Beckerman had given him with his name and telephone. "I'll call," he said, holding up the torn piece of paper.

"Yeah," said Polo with another wink. "Do that."

It took only a single glance to know this was Christine's apartment. The colors soft and pleasant, the furniture sparse but comfortable. The few paintings and knickknacks were selective and expensive. On a wall table there was an old Russian icon carefully placed on a brass metal stand. Chinese cloisonné vases sat on another table, filled with yesterday's flowers, drooping now but still colorful.

Her apartment was in Georgetown, just across the invisible line that divided the District from Maryland. The building was old, showing signs of needing paint, but still surrounded by gracious trees and flower beds.

"I found this through a friend," said Christine from the tiny kitchen. "It's too expensive for me to keep by myself, so I have roommates. Helena's the latest."

"And the others?"

"Part of that sorrowful lot I was telling you about." She walked back into the combined living and dining room. "She's nice, really, but she's dead set on finding a husband before the war ends."

"Shouldn't she hurry?" Cavanaugh took the glass of Scotch and thanked her.

"That's what I told her. And that could be a matter of months. But I think she has a captain she's interested in. He's stationed at the Pentagon."

"Why doesn't she grab him?"

"She will if she can. But I think there's a problem."

"What?"

"I'm convinced he's married and just stringing her along. I can't prove it, but I just feel it."

"What makes you suspect him?"

"The way he acts. What he says to her in front of me. What she claims he says to her in private. That sort of thing." She took a deep sip of her own drink. When she set the glass down on the end table, the tiny ice cubes clinked together. In the stillness of the room, they sounded like crystal glasses touching.

"Can you always read people that well?" he asked. Can you read me? he said to himself.

She laughed softly. "Not always. I make mistakes sometimes."

Cavanaugh tried to relax in his chair. Nothing in his past had prepared him for a setting like this. Somehow, in college, and again in graduate school, his few adventures of the heart had worked themselves out without any particular effort. They just happened. But what about now? Was it the couch or something else? Sitting opposite him, Christine gave no clue.

"Are you tired?" she suddenly asked.

He was, but he lied. "No, not really."

They talked pleasantly for a while, this time about their families and their childhoods. Then she stood up. "I'm going to freshen up. Why don't you make us another drink?" She pointed to the kitchen.

Cavanaugh got up and stumbled into the tiny room. He found the ice and dropped new cubes into their glasses with a sharp clinking sound. In doing so, he spashed water on his khaki trousers. "Shit!" he mumbled to himself. He probably looked like a clown anyway in this uniform. Just as he was brushing his pants with a small towel, he felt Christine's hand on his shoulder. He turned around; she had taken off her uniform and wore a dress, something loose and comfortable. He didn't know what to do. Then she acted for him. Very slowly she stepped forward and up slightly and kissed him. He kissed back.

After a moment, he broke away and stared at her. "What about your roommate?"

"She'll be out late."

He kissed her again. "But what if she comes back?"

"We have separate bedrooms," she said and took his hand.

Later, after they had made love and fallen asleep, Cavanaugh suddenly woke up, briefly wondering where he was. Then he knew and smiled.

As quietly as he could, he reached over to the nightstand and lifted his watch to check the time; soon, he would have to call Base Operations about his flight. For the moment, he languorously turned over and lay still in the bed. Christine's scent permeated everything around him; he felt her heat a foot away. For some reason he couldn't quite grasp, he felt like a mixture of schoolboy and married man.

She stirred and turned to face him. "You're awake?" she asked.

He said nothing, but touched her arm. As gently as he could, fearing to move suddenly and break the dream, he leaned forward and kissed her.

"I have to go," he said, knowing that that must be something often said in a city like Washington.

She kissed him back. "Be careful," she said. "Remember, we're having dinner again when you come back. You're wearing a tux, right?"

Just then, outside their room, he heard a noise and soft voices. Cavanaugh tensed.

"My roommate," she said softly, taking his hand.

There were bumping noises, like bodies knocking against furniture; muffled laughter. Cavanaugh started to get out of bed but Christine grabbed his arm. "No, wait," she whispered, starting to laugh. "It must be the man from the Pentagon."

The blurred voices outside continued, legs banged against furniture. Then a door closed.

Both Cavanaugh and Christine smiled, their faces barely visible in the darkness. After a long while, she said quietly, "The plane."

"Yes," he replied. "Soon."

Christine watched the airplane take off, disappearing rapidly into the cloud-filled sky. She drove home slowly, tired and feeling an odd mixture of euphoria and depression. Somehow, she had let herself have one of those sordid little affairs that she always warned her girlfriends about: the kind with lonely men passing through the city. And yet?

And yet she liked this Philip Cavanaugh. He was three years older than she, marriageable, but still a schoolboy. She smiled. More like an altar boy with a Ph.D.

Her apartment was empty when she came back. Helena and her boyfriend were both gone. She looked at her watch: seven-ten. She had less than thirty minutes to shower and change for work.

On her way to the bathroom she passed by the telephone in the hallway, hesitated, then dialed a number. She didn't like doing this.

"Captain Gilbert," the voice said.

"He's off," she said simply. Nothing else.

"So our boy's on his way?"

Quietly. "Yes."

"Good work. See you in a bit."

"Gilbert?"

"Yeah?"

"You didn't have to send a goon to watch us at dinner."

Gilbert laughed. "Sorry. Orders." He hung up.

None of this was what she had intended.

Part Four

AUGUST 1991

LONDON, ENGLAND

Pyrrhus, when his friends congratulated to him his
victory over the Romans under Fabricius, but with great
slaughter of his own side, said to them, "Yes; but if we
have such another victory, we are undone."

—Francis Bacon

Chapter Nine

The room was lit by a single naked bulb that was protected by a small wire cage like a miniature device for torture. The light was so dim that Edmund Ramsden had to request a small table lamp be brought in from someone's office.

The files he was looking at were faded, their contents stale with age. Each time he opened or closed a folder, a small cloud of dust and flecks of desiccated paper drifted over the table.

The table itself was low and uncomfortable; Ramsden kept hitting his knees on the edge each time he shifted in the wooden chair. And every movement caused the wood to creak and echo in the deadness of the room.

He was surrounded by metal shelves crammed with history. Paper records, yellow and decaying, were slowly revealing a foggy, dark world that had been hidden for nearly a half century by the National Secrets Act. Piled on the table and jammed on the shelves around him were the written records of MI5, Britain's wartime intelligence arm.

Only by using his position and invoking the name of his Minister had he been given access to this aging collection of state secrets. Even Solomon couldn't be cleared for the materials on this floor. But the story Ramsden was searching for—if there was one—was still vague, shifting like light and shadows playing on the ground.

He studied the list of small notes he had made for himself. They covered the minutes of committee meetings, weekly intelligence summaries, enemy communications traffic—in short, a summary of two tedious days of eye-straining work. The few bits of useful information were hardly what he wanted or needed: obscure, incomplete references to the mysterious "Archbishop," notations of missing files. Nothing that would convince the Home Minister that there was more to the discovery in the South Bank than a crude German atomic bomb.

He pulled a file from a small stack on the table, one that he had read before. This contained the first reference he had found to the mysterious 1945 effort called Archbishop.

Two-thirds down the page was the phrase: ". . . and the extraordinary events at Archbishop." But there was no explanation, no clarification, nothing more than those words. The memo originated out of MI5b, a division concerned with counterespionage. Ramsden considered the phrase again: "at Archbishop." That seemed to suggest a location. Could that mean Lambeth Palace, the home of the Archbishop of Canterbury? He put the folder down and picked up another.

This one was undated and headed "Security." Inside were memoranda on the "Protection of Government Officials in Occupied Germany" and the "Repatriation of Foreign Nationals on the Cessation of Hostilities." In the latter file were the curious sentences that read,

> The exception would be the so-called Special Foreign Detainee Class, whose activities and background warrant specialized concern under wartime security provisions. Their detention involves the Archbishop Programme, the events of which have been reported under Security Review, Special Events, 25.6.45.

This memo was stamped "E"; presumably, that meant it had been written by someone in E Division.

Ramsden considered this. Despite all his searching, he couldn't find the report entitled "Security Review, Special Events." Even more disturbing, the report was listed as part of a weekly index prepared for the wartime Director-General of MI5. He reread the brief memorandum, most of which was irrelevant so long after the war. But the phrases "Special Foreign Detainee Class" and "Archbishop Programme" continued to intrigue him. The first could connect with the arrests of the German national in London in June 1945, the curious reference Solomon had located the week before; the second suggested that "Archbishop" was a program a special secret activity of some kind, and not necessarily a location.

There were two intriguing finds in files marked "Weekly Summary." Evidently, these summaries were regularly prepared by the assistant director who ran counterespionage. One was for the last week of June; the other for July 1945. Ramsden found them by chance, since they were misfiled in an unrelated folder.

The first file was a lengthy collection of intelligence reports of possible German retaliation activities, apparently intended against the Allies after the end of the war in Europe. Within it, there were numerous pieces of intelligence garnered from German prisoners, spies within the collapsed Nazi system, and a dozen other sources. The general assessment, as far as Ramsden could tell, was that field reports greatly exaggerated the threat. But what caught Ramsden's attention was what was *missing* from the file!

Maddeningly, the Table of Contents had been torn out—part of the jagged paper remained—and twenty pages at the end had also been pulled. It seemed as deliberate an attempt to purge the record as any he had seen. But whoever had pulled the pages had failed to catch a brief reference in the first innocuous section, an introduction to the report. That reference, which cited "full status" at the end of the compilation, mentioned the "dramatic events of Archbishop," and how, under the circumstances, they must be treated with the "utmost discretion and secrecy according to internal directives." Once again, the report had been prepared for the Director General of MI5.

Alas, thought Ramsden, that man was honorably dead. Beyond the pale, as his great-aunt used to say, and certainly beyond his—or anyone else's—power to bring him back to explain. And perhaps to account.

The second file reviewed activities for the first two weeks of July. The contents were similar to the previous file, with the exception of several references to intelligence traffic between MI5 and various British field agents in Germany. Each of the queries—they all originated out of London—mentioned the same name: Philip Cavanaugh. The explanation that accompanied each notation was brief, but Ramsden was able to learn that Cavanaugh was an American and his travels in Germany were being closely monitored by British agents. There was no further explanation.

Ramsden made a note of the American's name. It could mean nothing, or it could be related in some way to the events recorded in the first file. These two files, after all, were found together.

On his list he scratched off two possible leads he had been investigating. With his pen he circled another item, "internal directives?" and added the word "investigate."

Ramsden glanced at the table and the messy stacks of decaying paper. The small pile of folders in front of him contained the only tangible evidence he had found that in any way related to something called Archbishop. But tangible as it was, it was hardly evidence of government knowledge in 1945 of a German atomic bomb in London.

He sat up straight and tried to relax the muscles in his back and neck. Surely this was work for younger men, and younger men would be doing it if the security level weren't so high. He wondered how Solomon was faring upstairs, where he was studying materials with a lower classification. Their dinner-time note-swapping seemed to be producing the same inconclusive results.

Ramsden wanted to use the bathroom but decided to wait: that required checking out of the reading area and then back in. The old buzzard who ran the archives was, well, uncooperative to say the least.

Ramsden studied the small, almost airless room he was in. It was part of the government's historical archives, the ones that historians and ordinary human beings were forbidden by law to see until sometime in the next century. He was in a nameless building not far from the Home Office, on the third floor; all of the windows had been sealed shut from the inside. Not to prevent the deterioration of material—that process went on inexorably—but to keep the unwanted out. The racks and racks of gray metal shelving ran from floor to ceiling as far as he could see, the ancient paint peeling and falling to the floor in lifeless piles of chips. And each shelf was lined with innumerable files and deteriorating boxes.

The gnome who governed this particular floor had been singularly unhelpful, even curt. It had taken several telephone calls and several signed authorizations to get Ramsden in here; more pleading, even threats, to let him see what was on the shelves. He had choosen to do this search himself, with the help of Solomon, the only aide he trusted.

108

The Nazi bomb had dictated that. Only the greatest care could be taken to root around for information that possessed the potential for an explosion of a different kind: a political one that could embarrass the Nation. Something inside of him said to dig, however, whatever the cost.

But, as he had quickly discovered, the task of digging wasn't easy. The process was complicated by a lack of an index and cross-referencing system. There was no way to know what to look for until he had some idea of what existed.

Ramsden had been forced to begin with the time period—mid-1945—as a global starting point. When he had some sense of what was available—it was substantial—he broadened his requests for material. The gnome shuffled and hesitated, grumbled and only reluctantly acquiesced. He acted, Ramsden thought, as if he were guarding vestal virgins.

He picked up a file he hadn't read before and quickly began to thumb through the contents. What he saw was mostly interdepartmental memoranda, again made moot by the passage of time. But variously stuck between one sheet and another were pages of handwritten notations, some brief, others extensive, the kind one would make while attending meetings or working through a large project. The writing never varied; Ramsden could only guess that it was from the same hand. Undoubtedly, it had been a practice to classify even personal notes as "Most Secret."

The information itself seemed useless, and Ramsden found himself hurrying through the scribbled notes in an effort to finish scanning the folder. Then a phrase leapt out at him from one of the handwritten note sheets: "Lambeth Palace."

Holding the sheet as gently as he could to prevent damage, he put it under the small table lamp. The ink had faded to pale blue, and with age the paper had become almost translucent. At the top was a simple calendar note of "25.6." There was a small list of seven items, perhaps from the agenda of a meeting, and nothing else. The phrases that electrified Ramsden were two: "Arrests/Lambeth Palace," and "Southend—Metal Alloy." The last item, almost as intriguing, read, "Implement High Security—No Advisory." But the line immediately underneath contained a name!

It read simply, "Wm. Canning—Liaison?" The list ended with that line, penned in a neat, studied calligraphic style almost forty-five years before. The author no doubt never intended his notes to survive. This single sheet could well exist because, in someone's haste to cover up, it was lost or accidentally misplaced.

"Metal Alloy . . ." Could that possibly mean uranium? Surely if it had been lead or zinc, for, example, those specific words would have been used.

The file folder read "Internal/June." Everything else in the folder was mundane, relating to the daily operations of an unspecified division of MI5.

And "Southend"? What did one of England's seaports have to do with uranium? Was this how the gun bomb had entered the country?

Ramsden took a deep breath. He had to get Solomon on this right away. The record could be scanned for any intelligence from or about the port at Southend. And the name William Canning could be checked out, run through the records for identification. There were multiple sources for that. Perhaps the man was still alive, or at least more could be learned about him and with whom he had worked. The records could now be cross-checked for any mention of Lambeth Palace. That too, could lead somewhere, perhaps to another box in this room. And the handwriting on this memorandum could be examined, compared with handwriting samples from known wartime staff of MI5. That could be still another direction.

But right now, he had a name. And a city and a potential reference to uranium. And a reason to keep going.

He pushed the last of the dusty folders away and stood up. Like the paper around him, he thought, the air was dead in here.

He always felt better outdoors. And more sprightly today. Part of it was the sun, which had broken out for the first time since morning. And besides, Ramsden was enjoying his "little project," as he liked to call it.

Solomon, who carried his umbrella despite the sun, seemed more concerned with the heat. With his free hand, he frequently mopped his brow with a handkerchief. For him, this was another "little walk" for a "little chat" on the Deputy Minister's "little project." But then, he had to admit that the events of the last few days were compelling indeed.

"So he's alive," said Ramsden, taking a deep breath despite the exhaust fumes from traffic. Today, they were walking south, down

Whitehall Street, across Parliament Square and along St. Margaret Street. The Houses of Parliament dominated the left side.

"Yes," said Solomon tersely, "he retired to Ipswich."

"Ipswich?" Ramsden could think of a dozen better choices for retirement.

"Yes. To 1209 Swallow-on-Sea."

"Well, who is this William Canning?" Ramsden picked up his pace and tapped the metal tip of his umbrella on the cobblestones.

"The records list him simply as a retired civil assistant."

"What did he do during the war?"

"He was attached to the War Office until 1953. But of course, he was with MI5 during that time."

"And he retired in '53? Wasn't he comparatively young then?" In fact, he would have been a man in his prime.

Solomon looked through the small pile of notes in his hand and at the same time maneuvered his way through the slight crowd on the street. "He was a captain in the Royal Artillery until 1942; that was when he was seconded to MI5. Apparently he was wounded during the retreat from France in May 1940." Solomon flipped another page. "He has double pensions: civil service and military."

"Convenient," said Ramsden. The tip of his umbrella made a metallic click each time it hit a cobblestone.

Solomon continued. "It's difficult to tell precisely what he did at MI5. Apparently, he was in B Division for a while. That was counterespionage. But then in D as part of the War Office liaison with the military. It's possible he had something to do with field security. The records on this are obscure, you know."

Ramsden nodded. The last few days had taught him a great deal about obscurity.

"But he was part of MI5?"

"Yes."

"And his early retirement?"

"Medical reasons, apparently."

Ramsden kept his eyes straight ahead, on the trio of teenagers dressed in punk clothes with bright-orange and blue hair. They were standing on the street corner handing out flyers announcing a rock concert.

"Will he talk to us?" Ramsden asked.

"We've asked him to," replied Solomon.

"And?"

"And his wife tells us he's too ill right now."

"How did you approach him?"

"We asked if he could help clear up a certain matter. An issue from the last war."

"And?"

"He said he would get back to us. But then his wife called a day later and said he had taken ill rather suddenly."

Ramsden smiled. Certain memories from the past often had that effect.

"And what about the American? Philip Cavanaugh?"

"I've put in an official request to the CIA. Background and all that."

Ramsden considered it all. "I think I need to visit Mr. Canning. Personally."

He stopped looking at the punks and turned toward Solomon. "I want to talk to him before he takes a turn for the worse."

Ramsden had his coffee brought in and asked not to be disturbed for the next quarter hour or so. Except for an emergency, of course, which was a small, old joke between himself and Mrs. Throcksley, his secretary. Fortunately, for the life of the joke at least, no emergency had ever arisen to interrupt his afternoon coffee.

He wanted the time this afternoon to collect his thoughts. Much had happened this last week, turning the rather odd discovery on the South Bank into something far more sinister than an old Jerry bomb. The proverbial tip of the iceberg, as it were. The full story still eluded him, though for the first time he believed he was on the edge of uncovering some major thread, some core fact or event that would begin to unite all the disparate pieces. He had pieces: Canning; the American named Cavanaugh; the possible reference to uranium alloy; the existence of a file called Archbishop; and, not least, the recovered Nazi atomic bomb itself.

A request had already gone into the American CIA. A discreet inquiry that would take a day or two for an answer. In the meantime, they were using their own resources to check the name out, including anything that might be on the government's computers.

They had started with the infamous "Registry" files of MI5, part of which were now computerized and integrated into the government's larger intelligence collection. The old Registry, however, which reached its zenith during the last war, consisted of millions of small index cards, some with a single name or place or event on them, all cross-indexed and filed. It was an early if not cumbersome attempt at systematizing information. A sort of "pre-computer," as Ramsden saw it.

The Registry files had indeed revealed several entries on one Philip A. Cavanaugh. Though some of the cross-references were missing—Ramsden was hardly surprised—there were at least two references. One for Philip Cavanaugh, the subject of several reports prepared and sent from occupied Germany; they were missing, too. The other entry for the same name was as a member of something called "ALSOS" and attached in some way to the SHAEF Command during World War II. The same entry mentioned Los Alamos, New Mexico.

That was a name that surprised Ramsden. He knew that Los Alamos was one of America's major laboratories for nuclear weapons; he also knew that it had been created during the last war to design and build the first atomic bombs used on Japan. So what, he wondered, was the connection between Philip Cavanaugh and Los Alamos? And, more important, what was the connection between this man and the bomb discovered near Lambeth Palace?

He took a sip of coffee and sat back in his chair. Somehow it was all going to fall into place. He *sensed* it.

Chapter Ten

*S*ir George fumbled around in his desk drawer and retrieved a crumpled box of cigarettes. Alfred Dunhill Menthol. Publicly, he pretended to have kicked the habit: privately, he smoked. Everyone in his office knew it, smelled the tobacco on his breath and clothes, but politely pretended otherwise. Especially in front of the Home Minister's wife.

"You don't mind, Edmund, do you?" he asked. The cigarette was already lit.

Ramsden politely shook his head.

"Now then, I gather you have something else? Something even more, ah, surprising?" He inhaled deeply, lifting his bushy eyebrows as he did so.

Sir George appeared to be in a good mood. The capture yesterday of a pair of IRA terrorists probably helped, Ramsden thought.

He had spent all morning preparing for this. He knew he had to perform better than last time. To present the new evidence succinctly and compellingly.

"Yes, I do," he said. "Rather surprising."

Using his notes, he went item by item through the last few days of work. Through each of the discoveries, such as they were. He was calm, dispassionate, and, he hoped, brief. He emphasized what he thought were the most important elements: the existence of a wartime special project called Archbishop; the curious voids in the records; the names of Canning and Cavanaugh; the reference to uranium.

The Home Secretary's cheerful mood ebbed as Ramsden talked. At last he interrupted. "Are you certain that's a reference to *uranium*? Not something else?"

"Not certain, no. But likely." But both he and Solomon agreed among themselves: what other metal "alloy" would be worth mentioning in such a context?

Sir George shook his head. "Rather a leap, I should think. And these missing files. Shouldn't we *expect* the records to be incomplete? After all, these events took place nearly fifty years ago."

"Perhaps," said Ramsden. "But nonetheless, each piece supports the larger interpretation."

"Or it's made to do so."

"I don't think we've done that, sir. I really don't."

"Well then," said Sir George, his exasperation growing, "just what do we have here? Really?" He pulled another cigarette from his crumpled box and then peered inside.

From where he sat, on the opposite side of the desk, Ramsden could tell that it was the last one. The Home Secretary frowned. He began to dig around in the desk drawer with his free hand.

"I think that we have justification for continuing this investigation into the, ah, record. I think we owe ourselves that."

Sir George said nothing. Ramsden knew enough about the man to know that he wasn't one to dig any deeper than absolutely necessary. He was fond of saying, "Dig a little and you find a worm; dig a lot and you find many." Ramsden guessed that literary allusions were not the man's strong point.

"Indeed?" asked Sir George gruffly.

"If there was knowledge of this weapon in 1945 by our government, and if it was subsequently suppressed, then we should know the circumstances." Ramsden tried to remember to keep his voice the same

115

tone and level. He could not afford to have the Minister reject his request because he was perceived as emotionally involved.

"Beyond the obvious historical questions, I think we must be prepared for, ah, more interest."

"Interest by whom?"

"Other elements of the government, the PM perhaps—"

"Hah!" Sir George slapped his hand on his desk. "I do not think the PM is interested in any revelation, no matter how sensational, that will throw the present diplomatic climate into chaos." He struck an imperious pose, one that caused him to put his head at an angle but enabled him to peer down at Ramsden.

Ramsden nodded. "I am also thinking we must be prepared for a possible break of the story to the press."

The Secretary's face softened. "I do not want that, Ramsden."

"No, sir. Of course. But should it happen, should some hint of 'missing Nazi uranium' hit the front pages, we must be prepared to put the whole business into the proper historical context." He paused. "And besides, I think we're quite at the end of the search."

Sir George sighed. "You think we can't contain this?"

Ramsden chose not to answer directly. "I think we must be prepared. But of course, there are levels of revelation. There is always a question of how much the public should know when there are other, ah"—he searched for the right word—"other national *priorities* at stake." Ramsden thought that sounded sufficiently vague.

"Yes, I suppose."

Ramsden waited a moment. "I can proceed?"

"Yes, yes. But wrap it up. Who is this chap you propose to talk to?"

"His name is Canning. He worked closely with the Deputy Director General of MI5 during the war."

"He must be eighty. Where is he? London?"

"No. Ipswich."

"Ipswich? God."

Ipswich lay seventy miles northeast of London. It wasn't directly on the Coast, but inward ten miles on the river Orwell.

It was not, as Ramsden well knew, a particularly beautiful town. It was, at best, typical of that part of England: cold, wet, and generally shrouded in fog and dreary weather. Ramsden remembered one ancient guide to English towns that described it as "picturesque," a word he would never use for it.

116

He drove himself in his vintage Jaguar, the twenty-year-old car that Edith had loved so. Sentiment was the only reason he kept it, in fact. The bloody thing cost him thirty pounds a month to park and another five hundred a year in odd repairs. His son wanted it, God knew why, since there were so many fine American cars the boy could choose from.

He had to admit he liked the occasional drive, however. The A-12 Road was good and took him through Chelmsford and left of Colchester straight into Ipswich.

It took him half an hour to locate the small river road, Swallow-on-Sea, where the mysterious Mr. William Canning lived. It was a nice cottage-style house, however, set back from the road, with a front garden that suggested careful tending. Ramsden particularly liked the roses, which for some reason seemed to thrive in this wet climate.

He was received grudgingly. No, that wasn't quite right. He was received under considerable protest.

William Canning, or his wife, or both, had made complaints directly to the Home Minister. Reasons of grave health, and all that. Fortunately, Sir George had not been persuaded; partly, no doubt, to satisfy Ramsden, and most certainly to get him off the Minister's back.

Ramsden knocked gently on the door. Out of propriety. Silence. He knocked louder. There were footsteps and the door opened halfway. On the other side was a woman in her late sixties, or maybe early seventies. Attractive, however, and wearing the sort of loose, dumpy clothing that genteel country folk seemed to favor.

"Mr. Ramsden?" she asked.

He nodded. "Yes. Good morning." He doffed his hat.

"My husband isn't well, I hope you know that."

Ramsden was prepared. "Yes. Quite sorry. But it's rather important."

The woman sighed and opened the door full-way. "Yes, well, come in. Warm up. Tea?"

"Yes, thank you." He wiped his feet and stepped in. It *was* chilly. A large arrangement of fresh roses filled an antique vase on a table opposite the door. It was exactly the sort of display Edith would have done.

"My husband's in the study. In there. Through the door. I'll bring the tea."

Ramsden nodded. Mrs. Canning was very businesslike. Obviously disapproving, but still civil. Ramsden rather liked that. He only hoped Mr. Canning would be the same.

Mr. Canning was not. For the first minute the elderly man just sat unspeaking in his wheelchair by the fireplace. His legs were wrapped in a shawl of some kind. His chair was set at an angle, to allow him to look into the fire rather than out the window to the trees behind the house. His head hung low, as if the muscles of the neck had deteriorated with age, leaving him unable to lift it.

Ramsden repeated his greeting. "Mr. Canning?"

Finally the old man spoke up. "I'm quite ill, you know," he said in a faint, distant sort of voice.

"Yes. Quite sorry."

"I regard this as an intrusion."

"Yes. An intrusion. But it's rather important."

Canning cleared his throat, which came out as a combination of hacking and snorting.

"Well, get on with it." He shuffled his hands underneath the shawl.

Ramsden moved to an empty chair opposite Canning and sat down. The old man was no more than six feet away. He had a small, nearly bald head with skin that appeared drawn back to some invisible point that Ramsden couldn't see. Blue veins ran from his temples along the sides. His eyes, which were clouded with cataracts, still seemed lively, and Ramsden suddenly wondered just how ill the man really was.

"We have recently made some discoveries that we believe you might be particularly helpful in explaining."

There was a silence before Canning spoke. "Discoveries?"

"Yes. From 1945." Ramsden watched the man's face for any unusual sign.

Canning coughed again. "Ah, that was a long time ago. I've been retired for many years now."

"Yes. Since 1953, I believe?"

Canning was silent. Ramsden realized this was going to be more difficult than he'd thought.

"I have been given permission to speak to you frankly, Mr. Canning. About matters that are, well, still rather sensitive. I trust that you'll speak to me in the same way."

"What matters?" Canning shot back. He removed one hand from underneath the cover and with it a rumpled handkerchief. He coughed several times rather loudly into it.

118

"Do you remember anything about a project, a very secret project in 1945, called Archbishop?"

For the first time, Canning lifted his head and looked in Ramsden's direction. Ramsden couldn't be sure just how much the man could see with those clouded eyes, but his question had obviously struck some ancient memory in the old fellow.

Then Canning turned and looked back into the fire.

"Archbishop? No. Not really."

It *was* going to be cat and mouse, thought Ramsden. That sort of game could take all day.

"Mr. Canning, we have memoranda and reports with your name connected to this project." That was an exaggeration, but not one that he could be easily called on. "Are you sure you don't remember something?"

"You're asking about a time long ago. A great deal happened during the war. I can't be expected to remember every detail." He coughed again, spitting some murky fluid into his handkerchief.

" 'Archbishop' hardly appears to have been a detail, sir." Then Ramsden had an idea. Perhaps Canning needed to be reassured about his culpability.

"You understand, Mr. Canning, the past is done and over. The Home Ministry is interested in these events because of their historical interest. We're *not* interested in sending a pack of solicitors or newsmen to your door." There seemed no need to mention the atomic bomb—not just yet, anyway.

Canning produced what looked like a small smile. "Historical interest. Really? And historical interest brings you to Ipswich?"

Now Ramsden smiled. Canning might be ill, but he wasn't senile.

"Well, there are developments that have precipitated this interest."

"Ahh," murmured Canning.

"Tea?" It was Mrs. Canning with a tea tray. Ramsden noticed that the teapot had no cozy on it. Mrs. Canning wasn't planning for a long visit.

Canning took his cup and saucer and set it on his lap. "Historical interest, indeed," he repeated. He looked up at his wife, who was standing solicitously nearby. "I think you'd better let us talk alone, dear."

She hesitated but then walked out of the room. "I'll check on you in a bit," she said in passing. At the same time, she threw a heavy look in Ramsden's direction.

Ramsden swirled the milk in his tea and decided to press his luck. Otherwise, he could be here all day and come up with nothing. He had to be careful, however, and not feed more to Canning than Canning would volunteer.

"Look here, we're confused. We don't know if 'Archbishop' refers to a location, or a series of events. Or perhaps a special project of some kind."

Canning slowly sipped his tea. "No. Not a location. This is hard for me to remember—it was a long time ago—but I think it was a code name for a series of events. Special activities, as you say."

"What were they?"

Despite the internal clouds, Canning's eyes began to dart nervously. The old goat damn well remembered! thought Ramsden.

"I was an assistant to the Deputy Director General of M15 at the time. Lytton-Harte. Do you know his name?"

"I've seen it written." Ramsden had looked over a list prepared by Solomon of key wartime figures in both M15 and M16. The name rang a bell but that was all.

"A brilliant man. A genius, really. Damn good luck to have worked for him then." He took a sip of his tea and seemed to collect his thoughts. "I worked closely with the man, but obviously the Deputy Director possessed more information than I did. It was common practice, of course, to compartmentalize intelligence. And he had access to the ULTRA intercepts."

Ramsden nodded, although he knew that Canning wasn't looking at him.

"So much happened. Especially at the end of the war." He fell silent again and seemed to drift away.

"Yes. And 'Archbishop'?"

"Ahh. I remember we received intelligence about a discovery in Southampton. No, Southend, I think. It was a spectacular discovery. Fascinating."

A connection! Ramsden remembered seeing Southend mentioned. His interest soared: he involuntarily moved to the edge of his chair and gripped his tea saucer to keep from accidentally dropping it on the floor. Inexplicably, he felt he knew what Canning was going to say next.

"Our men found several, ah—" He searched for the word and gesticulated emptily with one thin, translucent hand. "Several containers of purified uranium. German, of course."

Ramsden knew it! He and Solomon had guessed correctly. "Metal alloy" indeed meant uranium. No doubt about it now.

"It was a rather unexpected find. After the war and all. No one was able to account for its origin. Or why it was in Southend. It seems to me it was found on a captured German boat. A small seacraft of some kind."

"Uranium for a weapon? An atomic bomb?"

"Undoubtedly."

"But you never found a weapon? A device, I mean, something for the uranium to fit in?"

"No. But it was clear even then that such a large amount of uranium, purified uranium, was intended for only one purpose. That was clear."

Ramsden was listening and considering the possibilities at the same time.

"Extraordinary," he murmured.

"Indeed. It reversed the picture we had of German atomic work that we had assembled from interrogations." He started to cough again, and brought his handkerchief up to his mouth. The hacking sound reverberated in the small room.

Ramsden had so many questions. But uppermost was the question of why it had been kept a secret. He asked Canning about it.

"The Americans" was the simple reply.

Ramsden didn't understand. "What?"

"The Americans. They had armies of men wandering throughout Germany seizing German technology. We feared that to reveal this discovery would be to draw their attention to the existence of a special, though obviously very secret, Nazi atomic program. Quite beyond what was discovered and publicly reported."

"The discovery was never reported to the government?"

Canning produced another faint, almost imperceptible smile. "I was only an assistant," he said, choosing his words carefully. "I have to assume it was reported. That would have been the normal procedure."

"Yes. Quite." Ramsden quessed the man to be in his late seventies. Old. Sickly. But smart as a fox. Nothing would be laid at this old man's door.

"We have references to a number of reports on this matter, none of which can be located. Do you have any idea where they might be?"

Another faint smile. More coughing. This time Ramsden could see sputum on the handkerchief. He turned politely away to look into the fire.

"The Deputy Director was a cautious man. He might have gathered these reports together. There's no telling what might have become of them in fifty years."

Ramsden thought a moment. "Was there any reason for the code name? 'Archbishop?' "

Canning didn't answer for a long while. Ramsden was almost ready to repeat the question when the man spoke up. His face seemed genuinely to reflect an inner lack of certainty.

"There was another event. About the same time, I think. Something that made us believe there was a connection between the containers of uranium and this other, ah, circumstance. I don't quite remember, but I think it gave rise to the use of the name 'Archbishop.' " His voice drifted off for a moment.

"Or . . ." Canning said suddenly.

"Or what?"

The old man smiled weakly. "It might have been a private joke. The Deputy Director was like that, very wry."

"A joke?" Ramsden couldn't believe that an atomic bomb would have been regarded as a joke.

"Lytton-Harte and the Archbishop were old friends, you see. School chums. The event, whatever it was, near Lambeth might have given rise to the code name. The Deputy Director's private joke."

Ramsden thought of Lambeth Palace. Apparently MI5 never discovered a gun barrel of the type recently found on the South Bank. Had they found one, they no doubt would have matched the uranium with the weapon. The government would not have left it lying in the cellar of a Crown property. So perhaps the name was no more than a joke.

Canning stirred in his wheelchair. "There was so much going on then, so much for us to consider. The Americans. The Soviets." He broke into another fit of coughing. And then, in a faint voice, he added, "England."

Yes, England, thought Ramsden. In possession of German uranium. And with the Americans working on an atomic bomb.

"Did you know that the Americans were working on an atomic bomb?" he asked. "During the war?"

"Oh, yes," said Canning. His voice had grown hoarse from the strain of talking. "We had men there, you know. In America. But even in the summer of '45 we knew the Americans weren't likely to share their successes. Or do so readily. Lytton-Harte thought that even then. It

122

was one of his great concerns." Canning leaned his head back against the chair. Even this brief conversation had taxed him. Suddenly, he struggled a moment and sat up straight. "And he was proven right, you know. And still they pushed him aside."

Oh, loyalty, thought Ramsden, even after all these years. Such a time, though: the war, the sweet afterglow of victory dissolving so rapidly into a realization that England was no longer a great power. Even with victory, the war had robbed her of that.

"Dear?" Mrs. Canning had appeared at the doorway.

"Yes," said Ramsden. "I must be going. You've been most helpful." He stood up. If he needed to, he could come back. Canning was cautious, but not unwilling to talk. If he lived, that was.

Then Ramsden thought of something he had almost forgotten. A name. Cavanaugh.

"One last thing. Do you remember a name from that period? Philip Cavanaugh? An American, I think."

Canning's gaunt head turned sharply to look at Ramsden. For a long moment he just stared. There was no smile this time, but his eyes moved nervously in their worn sockets.

"There were many Americans we were interested in at that time. But this name? Cavanaugh. I—I don't remember. So long ago."

Ramsden watched the old man's face. Something told him that Canning was lying, that he knew damn well who Cavanaugh was. And why he had been important to MI5. But there was no way of proving otherwise. And this wasn't the time to press the matter.

"Yes," repeated Ramsden. "So long ago."

Ramsden thought of little else on the way home. The conversation unfortunately had been short. Too short to answer the many questions that Ramsden had in his head.

But a major piece of the puzzle had fallen into place.

The government—or some part of it—had known about a German atomic bomb. They had guessed that fact from the discovery of several containers of purified uranium. There was no weapon, no mechanism to go with it, but enough evidence to grasp the implication of the uranium itself.

God! thought Ramsden. What a shock that must have been. Atomic bombs were old hat now, but in June or July of 1945? No wonder Lytton-Harte and MI5 had guarded the secret so closely.

And the other event—the one Canning couldn't remember but which

123

might have given rise to the code name "Archbishop"—could have been linked to the odd reports that he and Solomon had discovered in the old records of MI5. Their sleuthing hadn't been a waste of time after all!

But now what?

The missing reports would fill in the gaps. Might even explain the full story. *If* they could be found.

Ramsden tried to consider the possibilities. Lytton-Harte—or Canning, for that matter—might have destroyed them. They could have been sent to the Prime Minister or other members of the government, although Ramsden guessed they had not. Information like this would have produced a sensation and almost certainly would have involved others. That meant more paper somewhere else. And more chance of discovery.

No, reasoned Ramsden, the Archbishop files had been either destroyed or hidden away somewhere. But where?

If they still existed, the key to their discovery, if there was one, seemed to lie in the name "Archbishop."

He remembered the small fact Canning had mentioned, the one about Lytton-Harte and the Archbishop of Canterbury being old friends.

Perhaps that was the place to start.

Part Five

JULY 1945

LONDON, ENGLAND

There is perhaps in everything of consequence, a secret history which it would be amusing to know, could we have it authentically communicated.
　　　　　　　—John Boswell, *The Duke of Wellington*

Chapter Eleven

$\mathcal{E}$ngland appeared abruptly, out of the clouds, in the form of mist-covered green fields. For Cavanaugh, it was like turning a corner after a long journey to find, unexpectedly, the place he'd been searching for all along.

The flight over the Atlantic had been over clouds. A solid, unbroken blanket of them. When at last the co-pilot announced they were landing, Cavanaugh looked out the small window and saw rolling green fields. There was no London, just a small, haphazard city made up of aircraft hangars, Quonset huts, tents, and odd buildings.

The C-47 named *Deuces* touched down on a long concrete strip, surrounded on either side by hundreds of parked B-17's, the larger B-24's, and a host of smaller planes, both American and British. The planes were painted dull green, or camouflage colors, or left unpainted, their bright aluminum skins shining in the sunlight.

Base Ops was more like a terminal, far larger than the single room in Washington. It was also far busier: men in military uniforms gathered in small clusters, as did individuals in suits and ties. There were the same large blackboards against the wall with flight numbers and destinations sketched in chalk. On one blackboard, Cavanaugh caught several city names that gave him a chill: Berlin, Nuremberg, Dresden.

He was tired—exhausted, really—from the long flight and the uncertain future he faced. He stretched and bent over, trying to free the cramped, tight feeling in his muscles. His uniform was wrinkled, and for the first time since putting it on he felt the subtle discrimination that his rank evoked from both senior officers and the NCOs who apparently ran the Army. Thank God he had an envelope full of papers; somehow, shoved into the hands of a sergeant, he was able to arrange for transportation into London where supposedly a hotel room awaited him.

The city was thirty miles away, he was told: an hour's drive if he was lucky. Cavanaugh fell into a chair and lit a cigarette. There was no sense of being in England: with one or two exceptions, the uniforms were U.S. Army or Navy, the language and accents pure American; a man from Detroit stood out as clearly when he talked as did someone from Brooklyn. And the atmosphere seemed more convivial than that in Washington; these men knew that they had just won the war and they were damn proud of it. And perhaps more important, they were going home. Their enthusiasm was infectious; he found himself buoyed despite his exhaustion.

When at last a car was called up, Cavanaugh found himself sharing the backseat with a young major named Hartman who chewed Blackjack gum and chain-smoked. As he quickly learned, the major was a twenty-six-year-old bomber pilot who had completed thirty-one missions over Germany, including the last bombing mission over Berlin the previous March. The man had those all-American looks that Cavanaugh sensed girls liked: blond hair, blue eyes, athletic build, but with a face that looked forty-five. Or maybe it was just his eyes that seemed older.

Hartman, however, talked cheerfully about his exploits, as if nothing bad had ever happened to him. He had bailed out twice, he said, once in the Channel, and lost a dozen crewman and even seen friends in other planes go down to the ground in flames.

"Look!" shouted Hartman, pointing to the nose of a B-24. Several dozen small swastikas were painted underneath the pilot's canopy. "Goddamn, he must have fifty, sixty missions under his belt."

Cavanaugh split his attention between listening to Hartman and

128

glancing out the window of the car. They were in the countryside now, where the landscape was flat and green; it reminded him of Michigan. They passed through one village, then a succession of them, all grim and neglected.

But the real shock hit Cavanaugh when the car entered the suburbs of outer London. Suddenly they were driving down streets banked on either side by huge piles of rubble.

"The blitz," said Hartman casually, flicking his Zippo. "This part of London took it heavy."

"Jesus," murmured Cavanaugh. He had never seen anything like it before, except in magazine photographs. And none of those really captured the effect of empty blocks of rubble a dozen feet high, or the shells of blackened one- and two-story buildings. As they stopped to let a line of young children cross the road, he caught sight of a faded poster stuck to a half-standing wall. It was of a woman wearing a scarf and the message read: COVER YOUR HAIR FOR SAFETY: YOUR RUSSIAN SISTER DOES. A small gold hammer-and-sickle sign was in the upper-left-hand corner.

Hartman took a deep drag on his Old Gold. "This area was mostly houses. Family neighborhoods, you know."

Cavanaugh stared silently, unaware that he was gawking with his mouth open. London looked like a cross between a giant garbage dump and a Hollywood movie set.

Hartman alternated between talking animatedly and staring silently at the floor. When he was up, he joked about British girls with the driver, who couldn't have been more than eighteen or nineteen years old. When he was down, he seemed not to want to see what was outside.

Then, inexplicably, he said, "You can't see anything from up there, you know. Not really."

Cavanaugh looked at the man's face and thought he understood. "Yeah," he replied.

Hartman's mood then swung back. "You just come from the States?"

Cavanaugh nodded. "Just an hour ago. By way of Newfoundland and Iceland."

"What's it like there? In the States, I mean. I've almost forgotten what it's like."

Cavanaugh tried desperately to think what he could tell this man. How could he explain the curious isolation of Los Alamos? Or his all-consuming work on the atomic bomb? "Well," he said, "we're anxious to finish the war. Get it over with."

129

"Yeah. What about the broads?"

"Waiting for the guys to get back." Cavanaugh thought of Christine. What would her intuition tell her about a man like Hartman?

Hartman laughed. "I'll bet." His laugh had a hollow ring. Then he studied Cavanaugh's insignia for a moment. "Corps of Engineers? What the hell are you doing here?"

Cavanaugh shrugged. "I'm in the Army," he said, forcing a smile. "What can I tell you?"

Hartman smiled back and slid down in the seat, his hat moving forward so it almost covered his eyes. He lit his last Old Gold, crumpled the pack and threw it on the floor of the car. "Ain't we all," he said, "ain't we all."

Cavanaugh's hotel was the Dorchester. It was a name he knew from English movies of the thirties but had never imagined he would ever see, let alone stay in. For some reason, he hadn't bothered to ask the billeting officer where he was staying; he had only been told that the driver would take him directly. When the car pulled off Park Lane into the drive-through, Cavanaugh was once again struck by his good fortune.

Had the Manhattan Project pulled this off? Maybe Gilbert, bless his soul? Or was it just blind luck? Hartman, who waved him good-bye, apparently thought it was the latter. He shouted, with good feeling, "Shit! What luck, asshole."

But a feeling of inferiority hit him again in the lobby; it was filled with high-level brass from the American, British, even French armies. The civilians, including the women, looked and were dressed like diplomats. A porter took his bag—his new duffel bag from Gilbert—and silently walked him to the check-in desk, where he was carefully inspected by the clerk.

Cavanaugh felt as if his captain's insignia were burning through the collar of his shirt. In a thoroughly correct, but hardly solicitous voice, the man asked Cavanaugh's name. He gave it, and for a moment it seemed as if there had been a mistake, or worse, that a bad joke was being played and Cavanaugh was the butt.

And yet, after a long and studied moment, the distinguished-looking man in the cutaway coat nodded and said, indeed, his room was ready. And welcome to London.

Cavanaugh nodded and signed the register, then waited for another porter to escort him to his room.

130

It was almost eight o'clock; all he wanted to do was brush his teeth—something he hadn't been able to do on board the *Deuces*—and go to sleep.

An elderly porter touched his sleeve. "Ready, sir?" He had Cavanaugh's duffel bag in his hand.

Cavanaugh nodded and followed him to the elevator.

"This way, sir," the porter intoned, in a voice that told Cavanaugh he had said it a million times.

When at last he was alone in his room, he flopped down on the large bed and sank swiftly into the middle. On a level of discomfort, it ranked closely with his Army-issue mattress in Los Alamos.

I'll just take a nap, he thought, and noticed a small vase of fresh flowers on a nearby table. He fell asleep thinking about the flowers in Christine's living room.

At some point during his dream, Cavanaugh thought he was being choked by someone. He still had that impression when he was awakened by a ringing telephone. Only then did he realize that his dog tags were wrapped tightly around his throat.

"Captain Cavanaugh?" The voice was American.

"Yeah?" He struggled to pull out of the soft center of the bed and looked at his watch: it read ten-thirty. He'd only been asleep a couple of hours.

"This is Captain Hardy."

The name meant something to Cavanaugh. But what? Then it hit him: it was the Manhattan Project liaison in London.

"Yes. Hardy. What is it?"

The voice on the line hesitated for a moment. "Ah, were you asleep?"

"No. Yes. Well, just a little. I just arrived."

"Sorry," said the voice. "but I need to tell you about tomorrow."

Cavanaugh rubbed his eyes. "Yes. What about it?"

"I'll pick you up at 0800; we have a meeting at ten."

"Right," mumbled Cavanaugh, "I'll be ready. Downstairs, okay?"

"Fine."

Cavanaugh heard the receiver click. The call sounded like long distance, although he surmised that Hardy was calling from somewhere in London. The background noise on the line, however, reminded him of talking long distance from Los Alamos: all calls from the mesa went on a Ú.S. Forest Service telephone line first down to Espanola and then to Santa Fe before they went anywhere else. Even on good days, you had to shout and the call still sounded like two tin cans and a string.

Cavanaugh wondered when he would be contacted by the OSS. A man called "Reginald." Where in the hell would the two of them make connections? Gilbert had been very clear: the OSS would contact *him*. Not the other way around. Everything seemed so uncertain. Except for being in bed in a London hotel. And then—

For the second time that evening, he fell asleep in an English bed and in the same uniform he'd worn for two days.

This end of the dock smelled like dead fish. As far as he was concerned, all of Southend smelled bad, but this area was the bloody worst he'd ever been in! Not only that, but there wasn't a piece of metal that wasn't rusted or a pier that didn't have something slimy and encrusted on it.

Or so Sergeant Churchman thought. But then, he had been a farmer before the war and had been raised naturally to prefer the green lands of Devonshire. And *clean* and *aromatic* they were, compared to this.

He stood with two of his men on a concrete embankment while a third walked down the swaying wooden pier to a lonely and dilapidated fishing trawler. What bloody work for the Army!

He and his squad had been stationed in Southend a month now, awaiting deactivation. Before that, they had been part of an Army antiaircraft battalion that had seen a lot of action back in '40 and '41.

Southend itself was a small port, serving mostly industrial needs, on the north side of the Thames before the river opened into the Channel. With any luck, this would be his last assignment before getting out. With any luck, in fact, he'd rejoin his wife at their small farm in less than a month. Or maybe two.

Six bleedin' years in the Army. Christ!

"Aw, 'ere it is," shouted Lance Corporal Jerkins, pointing to the hold of the old fishing boat. The wooden cover was still dislodged from his earlier visit. Jerkins, who still had adolescent acne, stood unsteadily on the slowly rocking boat ramp, which was lifted up and down with the motion of the water.

Churchman stared at the boat. The faded name on the bow read *Mystic Home*. Reluctantly, he started down the bobbing wooden deck.

Earlier, he had been given its history, or what there was of it. Apparently the old tub had been docked here for a over a week, which wasn't anything out of the ordinary, since this was the part of the docks at Southend where small commercial boats often berthed. Except that the captain of this boat had disappeared shortly after docking. The single crewman—a drunk old sot who still thought it was the Great War—didn't have the faintest idea where the man had gone. And there were fees to be paid.

The Harbormaster's records listed the captain as a Dutch citizen, although the boat was registered to an English firm in Southampton. Somehow, the local official responsible for collecting the fees—and who had failed to do so—had managed to pass the matter on to the Army, largely based on the fact that the boat had spent most of the war in Antwerp under German control. It had therefore fallen to Sergeant Churchman to investigate.

And Sergeant Churchman, who had unfortunately missed his afternoon tea, wanted above all to be somewhere where it didn't bloody stink!

He joined Jerkins on the rear deck of the boat. "Aw right," he said, "go on. Show me." In his pocket were papers provided by the Harbormaster that showed *Mystic Home* had been seized by the British when they liberated the port at Antwerp. The boat had been formally released back to its British owners in April.

Somewhere between Antwerp and Southend the old boat had picked up a small cargo of tea. A dozen or so large crates of it, in fact. That was a bit unusual, since the boat was outfitted for coastal fishing; but then, the war had screwed up a lot of things.

Jerkins and another soldier lifted the heavy wood cover and laid it on the deck. From where he stood, Churchman could see a large box with the lettering, "Typhoo Tea" stenciled on it.

He looked at his watch. Wouldn't you know it? It was now an hour past tea.

"Wha' the hell's this old scow doing with cargo?" he asked. "Looks like it's still bloody rigged for fishing."

It was a silly question to ask, of course, since most of the men in his squad knew less about the boat than he did. The only exception was Jerkins, who had been detailed to check the boat out before Churchman would agree to come this close to water. And the only thing Jerkins had learned was that not all the cargo was tea.

"Bloody smell!" he mumbled. It was particularly strong on the boat. No one had bothered to wash the deck down and Churchman could see the residue of rotting fish and mildewed rope lying about.

"Aw right, where is it?"

Jerkins pointed to two smaller boxes next to the one marked "Typhoo Tea."

"Well, 'aul 'em up," Churchman barked.

Ten minutes later, his sweaty crew had the boxes on deck, the wooden lids fully off, and wood shavings removed and scattered all around them. Inside both were smaller boxes of black metal, perhaps two feet square. They had been outfitted with latches and a handle.

"Bloody contraband," someone said.

Churchman nodded. It sure as hell wasn't tea.

Like everything else around them, the latches were rusted and immobile. One of his men began to pry the first box open with a large screwdriver. Only when it popped off and the man opened the lid did Churchman think that it could be booby-trapped.

It wasn't. Inside, lying tranquilly on some sort of support lay what looked like a thick metal cylinder, maybe eight inches thick with a hole in the center six inches in diameter. The cylinder was a foot high.

"Wha'?" He reached over and tried to pick it up but found he couldn't lift it with one hand. It was solid metal and heavy as hell.

The thought crossed his mind that it might be gold—what else could weigh so damn much?—that perhaps he had stumbled onto a cylinder of solid gold! From the German Reichsbank, maybe. The bleedin' Nazis had tons of it, and this was was heavy and gold was heavy. But it didn't shine; it was a dull-gray color.

Then it occurred to him that maybe it had been painted. To camouflage the gold, of course.

He grabbed the screwdriver and made a deep scratch in it and then looked closely. Unfortunately, it appeared to be the same color underneath. "Damn it!" he cursed to himself. Of all the bleedin' luck.

"Aw right, wha' else?" he asked.

The latch was popped on the second metal box. Inside was a smaller cylinder, solid, and looked as if it fit into the hole in the other metal ring. Nothing else.

No tea, no gold, Churchman thought. Just like the bleedin' Army.

Chapter Twelve

*A*long night passed in which Cavanaugh seemed not to dream. The persistent and unique *ring-ring* of the bedside telephone brought him groggily from sleep before dawn, his head thick and confused from the long journey and his neck and back sore from the formless mattress.

He gobbled a so-called English breakfast stylishly delivered by room service on a silver cart with linens and fresh flowers—oh, Christine!—and then showered under a cranky nozzle that alternated between delivering hot and cold water. At precisely 0800 he was picked up by a driver and a rotund, merry major named Hardy with some unspecified connection to ALSOS.

Hardy wasn't much older than Cavanaugh. He was friendly and chatty, and—he said with a wink—a former linebacker for Notre Dame with a degree in chemistry. It took Cavanaugh only a few minutes to realize that Hardy didn't know much about him, no doubt didn't even care except to replay how the Dodgers and Yankees had played their last season. They were driving to SHAEF Headquarters, the Supreme

Headquarters Allied Expeditionary Force, where Eisenhower still presided.

SHAEF, Cavanaugh learned from Hardy, who seemed to collect small facts like some did stamps, was located outside of London at Bushy Park in Middlesex; not far away was Henry VIII's old palace at Hampton Court on the River Thames.

"God has an office in London, too," said Hardy.

"Who?"

Hardy laughed. "God. Eisenhower. We don't see him too much these days out here. He's either in London or on the Continent. He's the grand pooh-bah, you know."

The car stopped at a security gatehouse where an MP looked seriously at Hardy, then at Cavanaugh, then waved the car through.

Cavanaugh fiddled with his shirt and jacket as the car drove on, suddenly aware that the MP, like his driver, wore an insignia patch with a flaming sword on the left shoulder. Cavanaugh remembered, as did probably every boy over six in America, that the emblem represented the liberation of Europe; he guessed that anyone working with General Eisenhower wore one.

The car drove into a large encampment, with hundreds of men and cars, tents and temporary buildings. Oddly, it reminded him of Los Alamos: haphazard and temporary.

Hardy leaned over and began talking in a low voice. "This isn't an ALSOS briefing," he warned. "It's an inter-allied briefing on German science and technology. Strictly lower-level stuff."

"What's the purpose?"

"Don't know. Politics, I guess. British and French reps are invited. But we don't mention ALSOS a lot around this group."

"Why?"

"Bad feelings. ALSOS went in with the U.S. forces when they took Germany. Grabbed a lot of scientists and things. Our Allies complained."

"Oh. But why am I here?"

Hardy shrugged. "Don't know that either, except that we got word to involve you."

Cavanaugh thought about it a moment. What the hell was he supposed to say around these guys? How should he act?

"Well, what am I supposed to say? I mean, what if someone asks me what I'm doing here?"

136

"Tell 'em the truth: that you're with the Sixth Army Group, 1269th Engineer Combat Battalion, Corps of Engineers. And that you don't know what the hell you're doing here. They'll believe that." Hardy laughed; and as he did, his large, friendly face turned red.

"Hell," he said, "they know what we're doing here. The Brits. The French. We're doing the same thing they are: scrambling around trying to grab whatever the goddamn Nazis left behind that's worth a damn. Rockets. Wind tunnels. Chemical formulas. You name it."

Cavanaugh smiled. A game. The game. Groves was right.

"So why the meeting? The facade of cooperation?"

"Eisenhower thinks it makes for good relations with the Allies. Partners in vict-o-ry and all that. So-o, SHAEF's sponsoring this little cartoon."

They parked and walked down a dirt road with curved metal buildings, called Nissen huts, on either side, sometimes no more than three or four feet apart. They looked like half-moons dropped on their flat sides and reminded Cavanaugh of the huts in Los Alamos. The roofs and sides were made of corrugated iron sheets, the end walls of wood, with windows on either side of a single door. Wooden signs nailed to doorjambs or on small stakes identified the occupants: the 807th Laundry Group, for example, was right next to a building identified as Conference, Sixth Army. He and Hardy headed for that one.

"This is it," said Hardy.

"Thanks," replied Cavanaugh, and opened the door. There were voices on the other side. For a moment he hesitated; he knew that when he stepped in, his secret assignment would begin. He took a deep breath.

"Hullo?" said a voice from within.

Cavanaugh opened the door all the way and stood in the threshold.

"Come in, come in," said the same voice.

There were maybe a dozen men in the room, all standing in small groups; a man in the nearest group stared at him. Most were smoking cigarettes, but there was the faint overlay of a pipe or two. Everyone was in military uniform, mostly American, but some British and French.

"Captain Cavanaugh?" The same voice.

"Yes." He stepped in, aware that everyone was staring.

"Good," said the voice, "we've been waiting for you." The voice belonged to a tall, thin man with an American major's insignia. He motioned to the others and made his way to the front, where there was a small table next to a map of Germany tacked to a board. "We can start now. Introduce yourselves, please."

Cavanaugh stepped in and shook hands. In between hellos, he suddenly wondered if he should salute those with higher ranks than his. Oh, what the hell? he thought. He probably looked green as could be anyway.

No one seemed to mind. Everyone was pleasant, the British officers, with one exception, polite but cool, the French aloof.

The one exception was a young British captain named Christopher Brooke, who, as it turned out, had studied at Harvard before the war.

"Physics?" asked Cavanaugh.

"Yes," Brooke replied, "I had wanted to continue at Cal Tech but ran out of time." He smiled generously.

"Time?"

"Yes. The war brought everything to a halt."

Cavanaugh studied him for a moment. They were about the same age, even the same build. Brooke, however, looked very English to him: pale-blue eyes, fair skin, and blond, faintly strawberry hair. His round gold-rim glasses gave him an academic look.

"Too bad," said Cavanaugh.

"Yes, the war rearranged a lot of lives over here." He smiled again. "First trip to England?"

Cavanaugh nodded.

"I expect you find it rather dreary," said Brooke.

"Well," stumbled Cavanaugh, "not dreary, exactly. But I hadn't expected all the bombing."

Brooke smiled sadly. "This has been a long war for us; it's taken its toll everywhere, especially in London." He dropped his cigarette butt and stamped it out on the wooden floor. "Thank God the war ended when it did; I don't think this great old city could have taken much more. It'll need a few years to get back to its former glory." Brooke smiled again. "How was Washington?"

"Ah, Washington?" Cavanaugh quickly tried to change gears.

"Yes, aren't you stationed there? Attached to the Corps of Engineers?"

"Well, yes." Cavanaugh hastily reassembled his new job in his mind. "That is," he said, "I've only been there a short while."

"I liked Washington," said Brooke, "it's European in many respects.

138

Very unlike the rest of America." The word "America" tripped briskly off his tongue, like a burst from a machine gun.

Cavanaugh nodded. As little as he had seen or knew of Washington, he agreed. Around him, the small groups of men were slowly breaking up and taking seats in several rows of metal folding chairs.

"And before?" asked Brooke.

"Before what?"

Brooke laughed. "Before the Engineers. What did you do?"

Cavanaugh thought quickly. "A defense project."

Brooke looked at him for a moment, giving Cavanaugh a chance to explain. When he didn't, Brooke smiled slightly and chose not to pursue the issue. Instead, he suggested they take a seat.

"And where have they billeted you?" he asked as they moved toward the last row of chairs.

"A hotel in London. The Dorchester."

"My God, that's fabulous. How'd you pull that off?"

Cavanaugh shook his head. So far, he had had nothing but first-class treatment. "Luck of the Irish, I guess."

A strange, amused look crossed Brooke's face. "No doubt," he said simply, "no doubt. Wish I had that sort of luck, old man."

The major wrapped his knuckles on the table to get attention. "Shall we begin?" he said, shouting slightly to be heard over the many small conversations in the audience. Chairs squeaked as bodies adjusted in them. Cigarette lighters clicked open. A round of coughing spread through the audience. Smoke began to drift up toward the curved reaches of the Nissen hut. Except for the participants, Cavanaugh thought it could be a meeting in Los Alamos.

There was a different smell, however. Intermingled with the cigarettes and pipes was something else. Starched khaki. Wool. Sweat. Wood. Oil.

"We're covering a lot today," said the major; "we have status reports on all current activities and investigations in Europe." He glanced around the room. "We'll break at 1200 hours for lunch, then continue until we finish."

The audience shifted, settling in, as it were, for the long haul. Cavanaugh felt the metal rib of the chair press into his back.

"Before I begin," continued the major, "I want to introduce Captain Cavanaugh, who's just been assigned to the Sixth Army Group. For those of you who haven't already met him." He held out his hand and

139

pointed to the back of the hut. "Phil's been transferred here from the project at Los Alamos."

Cavanaugh stiffened and felt his face flush at the same time. He wasn't supposed to mention Los Alamos. No one was. But this jerk had just blurted it out! He felt several pairs of eyes turn on him, including Brooke's, who sat next to him. So much for his cover.

The major smiled and continued with his agenda without missing a beat. He introduced the first speaker, who clumsily tried to attach a crudely drawn chart of German research organizations to the existing map of Germany; it kept falling down. Cavanaugh sighed and tried to find a comfortable position in the tiny chair.

He wondered just how much these men, including the Brits, knew about Los Alamos. Most—no, probably all of them—knew that America was working on a new type of weapon, an atomic one, but did they understand what that meant? Fission? Supercriticality?

Cavanaugh tried to focus on the speakers. Through a series of presentations, the broad, often fantastic, range of Nazi scientific research and development unfolded, from rockets to synthetic fuels.

"Clever bastards," Cavanaugh heard someone say. Then he realized it was Brooke talking out loud. The man was shaking his head as he said it.

It was after lunch when the major himself spoke about German atomic research. By then, Cavanaugh knew that his name was Lansing. The man recounted the activities of the last four months.

In March, Lansing said, an American team—he made no specific mention of anything called ALSOS—captured both scientists and a cyclotron in Heidelberg; in April, they investigated potential sites in west and southwest Germany. Northeast of Frankfurt they found a low-temperature atomic pile, heavy-water equipment, and nearly eight tons of uranium oxide. Cavanaugh sat up straight in his chair. Northeast of Hannover, the British had discovered an experimental centrifuge for separating uranium isotopes. That particularly interested Cavanaugh, since some isotopes of uranium—like U235—were more useful than others in bombs.

Lansing then recounted his own experiences as part of a special team that followed the American Army's advance into southern Germany. Lansing didn't say it, but Cavanaugh knew from his briefings that General Groves had nicknamed this particular effort Operation Harborage; it had been a major undertaking of ALSOS.

Lansing's team had visited the small Württemberg villages of Haig-

140

erloch, Hechingen, Bissingen, and Tailfingen. These communities had been the center of German nuclear research, although the central group of laboratories consisted of a cave, part of an old textile factory, and several rooms in an abandoned brewery.

Of interest to Cavanaugh were the supplies found: heavy water, several tons of metallic uranium cubes, and ten tons of carbon pellets. These were the essential materials for a nuclear reactor.

Lansing talked quite freely about their discoveries. Apparently, this level of information could be shared. Either that, or Lansing didn't know what the hell he was doing. There was no mention, however, about the discovery at Mühlhausen. If Groves was right, only a handful of men knew about *that*.

At the end of the day, when everyone stood around smoking cigarettes and drinking bitter coffee, Cavanaugh found himself sought out.

"Los Alamos, huh?" said an American captain. "I got a friend there." He mentioned the name. "You know him?"

"Sure. Great guy." Did the man know anything else? Just how secret was Los Alamos anyway?

"I don't believe I've heard of it," said a British major. "Anything like our Tube Alloys program?"

He referred to the early British atomic-bomb program, which for some reason had been code-named Tube Alloys.

"I don't think so," said Cavanaugh.

"Can't say, old boy?"

"Not really. My work is pretty mundane." Cavanaugh forced a smile.

Lansing waved at him from across the room.

"Excuse me." He joined Lansing, who was gathering up his papers.

"So you're coming with us to Germany?" he asked.

Cavanaugh was confused. "Am I?"

"Well, that's what I was told. You, me, and some others. Including some Brits. A special SHAEF team. You didn't know?"

Cavanaugh didn't, not really. He knew he was joining a special team that was going into Germany, but that was it. And as far as he knew, it was something arranged solely to cover his real purpose for being on the Continent.

"Well, I knew I was joining someone. Just not who. I was waiting for orders."

"We're leaving tomorrow. I'll see you when I see you."

Cavanaugh was left standing by himself wondering what the hell was going to happen next. It was then that Brooke joined him.

"You're in London for a while?" asked Brooke pleasantly.

"Unfortunately not. I'm shipping out tomorrow."

"Germany?"

Cavanaugh nodded.

"Too bad," said Brooke.

"Why?"

"Well, London's a great old place to visit. There's still a bit of life in the old girl yet." He winked and smiled without any trace of ambiguity.

Cavanaugh smiled back. Brooke was a likable-enough guy. He had an easygoing personality that vaguely reminded Cavanaugh of Gilbert.

"I'll be back eventually."

"Good," said Brooke, "I'll buy you a drink. Even dinner. Then you can tell everyone about our famous English food."

The street noise drifted through the third-story window, turning muffled once it entered the still room. Christopher Brooke could tell the traffic was building outside on St. James Street.

He took a drag on his cigarette and watched the smoke curl lazily upward to the high ceiling. It would take an hour and a half, maybe two, before he could make his way through London traffic to Blenheim Palace, where most of MI5's Administrative Division had its offices. Then back to the city this evening in time to take Augusta, his girlfriend, to the theater.

Behind him, an older man's voice coughed and then sputtered. Marion Lytton-Harte, the Deputy Director General of MI5, sat hunched over his great oaken desk slowly reading a long wireless from their embassy in Washington. Most of the time he was referred to as the DDG, but without affection, Brooke noted.

"Do you know him?" mumbled Lytton-Harte. His voice was deep and thick, as if he were in a perpetual drunk. Sometimes Brooke had to strain to understand what the man said.

"We met this morning," he said simply. It was just that: a couple of hours shared at a Yank briefing. A brief conversation afterward. That was it. But something told him he was going to regret even acknowledging the two of them had met. He had been called before the DDG because of a casual mention of the new American arrival.

Brooke stared down at the street and watched the traffic. Busy. From somewhere came the sound of jackhammers. Almost like before the war. From the third floor at least, the street gave every appearance of being back to normal. Almost.

He knew it was only an illusion. From the window, London surged with people and activity, most with a look on their faces that said the war was over. And yet it wasn't: there were still the Japanese to finish off. It might be another year before the war really ended and everyone came home. His father, his elder brother; they were Navy men, serving in India and Burma.

Brooke sighed. It had been five years since he had seen his father. No, six. And three years since he had seen his brother. Well, at least they were alive. That was more than many families could say.

From the window he could see small groups of American GIs wandering the streets, probably looking for somewhere to spend their money before being shipped home.

That made him think about Philip Cavanaugh, the subject, after all, of this meeting between himself and the DDG.

Brooke judged that the American was in his late twenties, putting them both at about the same age. Cavanaugh was reportedly a physicist and worked for the Americans' highly secret atomic-bomb project. That much he had learned this morning at SHAEF; the telegram Lytton-Harte was reading said substantially the same thing. It was from an M16 agent in Washington, D.C.

Brooke guessed that Cavanaugh had worked himself through college. In his experience, most Americans did that. How different from England, where the university was still largely the province of the upper classes.

The Deputy Director mumbled something.

"Sorry?"

"Is this all we know about him?"

"Cavanaugh?"

The heavyset man with the thick voice paused for a moment. "Who else would we be talking about?"

Brooke cleared his throat. "Yes, well, that's about it. He's a physicist assigned to what the Americans call Project Y. It's part of their Manhattan Project. Their code name for atomic-bomb work. It's the equivalent of our old Tube Alloys Project."

"What's he doing here?"

Brooke shook his head. "Officially, he's to join an American and British task force going into Germany. Something pulled together by

143

SHAEF. But judging from this morning, I'd say he was really here for something else. Something he can't talk about. Or won't."

"Hah!" snorted Lytton-Harte. "Most probably a cover for American Intelligence." Lytton-Harte smoothly closed his reading file with the thin fingers of one hand. Despite his low, heavy body, he moved his delicate hands gracefully, almost like a woman.

The older man mumbled something else that Brooke couldn't understand.

"Sorry?" Brooke asked again. He quietly took a seat in the over-stuffed chair in front of the Deputy's desk. Light from the window gave the older man's frizzy hair the look of a silver halo.

"I said, I don't understand them. These new atomic bombs." The *a* in "atomic" became a long, drawn-out "ahhh." He looked across to Brooke. "Do you?"

"Only the fundamentals, sir," replied Brooke. He was a physicist, yes, but much had happened since he'd left Harvard. He understood fission and supercriticality. But a bomb was more complex than that.

Lytton-Harte wasn't a scientist; in fact, his only interest in science lay in discovering its potential for politics. If Brooke remembered correctly, the DDG had read history at Cambridge. Unconsciously, Brooke smiled.

"You find this discussion amusing?" The Deputy Director had a sour look on his face.

"No, sir, not really. Just a stray thought."

The DDG just stared at him. "I am concerned about the Americans," he said. "Frankly, they're an unscrupulous lot. They come bloody late to the war and then act as if they've won it single-handed."

Brooke sat there and took a deep breath; he had heard this talk before. Lytton-Harte's dislike of Americans bordered on loathing.

"And, ahh, now they're scavenging the Continent for Hun secrets. Bloody bastards!"

With some difficulty, Lytton-Harte pushed himself up from his mammoth chair and then steadied himself before walking to a map on an easel in one corner. In his hand, he gripped one of his many pipes; this one was of yellowed ivory with a bowl carved in the shape of a woman's head. Reputedly, it dated from his early career in China when he was a young officer in the Foreign Service.

"You see," he said, tapping the map vigorously with the stem of his pipe, "the Americans found the manufacturing source of the V-2 rocket here." He tapped the small dot called Nordhausen. "Without telling

144

us, they removed everything they could crate up and sent it back home. Rockets, machinery, archives. Everything." He waved his pipe toward Brooke.

"And they have the leading rocket scientists in custody. Von Braun. Dornberger. The lot of them!"

Brooke knew this story as well. The Americans had successfully plundered the vast underground caves where the Nazis had manufactured the V-2. In June, it had become part of the Soviet Zone. Hundreds of crates from Nordhausen ready for shipment to the States had been discovered by British Intelligence officers in Antwerp. Urgent appeals to General Eisenhower to stop the shipments had been ignored.

Lytton-Harte suddenly shifted and thrust his pipe at northern Germany. "In the north," he said, his voice a low rumble, "the Americans have stripped Germany of its aeronautical research. In the south they've captured the atomic scientists. And what of Anglo-American cooperation? We have been left the leavings."

Brooke was just about to say something when Lytton-Harte started again. "And here," he said dramatically, waving his hand in a vertical sweep, "the Soviets have taken over entire aircraft factories, the best electronic and scientific factories, including Telefunken, Blaupunkt, and Zeiss! And we are scrambling for what's left. We'll be lucky to find a sausage stuffer intact!"

Brooke chose to remain quiet. There was no arguing with the DDG when he was in this mood. England under attack by her Allies: that was the gist of it.

"I want to know more about this American. Who he is and why he's here. They're up to something; I can smell it." He turned and studied his map again, then shook his head. "Look him up," Lytton-Harte said, "befriend him. Talk to him. Tonight. I want to know why he's here."

Brooke saw his chances for the play and dinner suddenly evaporate.

"How close should I get?" he asked.

Lytton-Harte wrinkled his brow. "We're not talking buggery, Brooke. Just close enough so that he trusts you. And perhaps talks a little."

"I'll do what I can." He tried to conceal his distaste. This was not the sort of work he liked, especially since Cavanaugh seemed like a good enough fellow.

Lytton-Harte watched Brooke go out the door. He dug around in his drawer for his tobacco pouch and filled his maidenhead pipe. Brooke

145

wasn't a bad chap, he thought, although a bit lazy. Or perhaps he didn't have much of a stomach for the real work of intelligence. But so many of these younger men failed to see that the war wasn't really over, not by a long shot. True, it wasn't the Germans anymore; but it was all those who would deprive England of her rightful share of the spoils. And her role in the postwar world. And that included the bloody Americans!

Reports from their sister organization, MI6, revealed a blatant pattern of American plunder in Germany. Men and material. Scientific discoveries. Technological breakthroughs. The Soviets, at least, were open in their pillaging: they simply took whatever they could lift or pry off and sent it back to Russia. All under the aegis of "reparations."

But what about England? Her misery and suffering and economic burden? And America was virtually unscathed. It galled him; no, it angered him.

And now, even more appalling, were indicators from the highest levels that the Americans, especially under their new President, were rethinking postwar sharing of the atomic bomb. England, despite her early work in the Tube Alloys program—which she had shared willingly with the Americans, he knew—might now be left out. Or treated as less than a full partner.

No, he thought, the war wasn't over yet.

Chapter Thirteen

Cavanaugh had just returned to the hotel, turned the lock on his door, when he heard the telephone ring next to his bed: two brief staccato rings, then a pause, then two more.

As he dashed for the side of the bed he briefly noticed that the hotel had placed fresh flowers in the vase on his small desk. For the first time all day, he thought of Christine.

"Hello?"

"Captain Cavanaugh?"

"Yes?" The voice was American, but not one he recognized.

"This is Reginald. We need to meet."

Reginald? At first, Cavanaugh was confused; he wasn't sure what he'd heard. Then the name clicked in his head: Reginald! That was the name for his contact with the Office of Strategic Services. But weren't they supposed to meet up in Germany? A rush of adrenaline hit him and his heart suddenly began to beat faster.

"Now? Meet now?"

"Yes."

Cavanaugh's mind was still racing to put everything together. Was there something else he was supposed to say? Some other code word? Jesus! he must sound like a fool.

There was a clicking on the line that sounded like someone else was trying to cut in. In fact, it sounded like the party line his folks had back home in Detroit.

"Hello?" he asked.

"Yeah, I'm here."

"Uh, where do we meet?" Clutching the phone between his cheek and shoulder, he scrambled for a piece of paper and a pen. On the other end of the line Cavanaugh heard voices, lots of them talking all at once. It sounded like a hotel lobby.

"Walk north on Park Lane to Oxford Street," the voice said, "and find the Marble Arch tube stop. You got that?"

"Marble Arch tube stop?"

"The underground. You know, the subway."

Cavanaugh made a note on the small pad provided by the hotel. At the very top of each page was the elaborate crest of the Dorchester Hotel. "Oh."

More clicking on the line.

"Catch the train to Queensway Station. It's the Central Line. The only one you can take. But check the list of stops so you don't go the wrong way. And you'll need change. Then exit at Queensway and walk out to the street. It's called Bayswater Road. You got that?"

Cavanaugh was scribbling furiously. "Yeah."

"Walk across the street. Wait at the Black Lion Gate. It's one of the entrances to Kensington Gardens. You can't miss it. Understand?"

"Yeah. But why?" The more he heard of the background noise, the more he was convinced that the man on the other end was calling from a hotel lobby. Could he be calling from a house phone downstairs?

"Why what?"

"Why all this trouble? Why don't you come here, to my hotel? Or I'll come to your office tomorrow."

There was silence on the other end. Cavanaugh couldn't be sure, but he thought he heard the man sigh.

"Just come. Now. You'll be met in thirty minutes. You got that?" The line clicked dead.

For a moment, Cavanaugh held the telephone receiver in his hand, the disengaged sound humming relentlessly. Why all the subterfuge?

148

He looked at his scribbled notes: the tube. Black Lion Gate. Thirty minutes.

Cavanaugh staggered to the bathroom and turned the cold-water faucet on. Air bubbles gaseously exploded several times until the line was clear and the water poured continuously. He splashed some on his face and stared into the mirror. Circles under the eyes. Not enough sleep. A biological clock that still read American time. After dousing his face several times, he dried his hands and straightened his tie. God! he didn't want to do this. He just wanted to sleep.

Reluctantly, he put his coat back on and went downstairs. For a moment he stood to one side and scanned the crowd milling in the lobby; could the man who called him be one of them?

With the directions stuffed in his coat, Cavanaugh walked out of the hotel and took a left on Park Lane toward Oxford Street, a handful of coins from the hotel cashier clinking in his pocket. He found the entrance to the underground and followed the crowd through a tunnel under the street to the subway entrance. Then he realized that he had never been on a subway before and had no idea where or how you paid. His problem was solved when he saw a small booth where people were buying what looked like paper tickets. He stood in line and asked for one, his hand full of odd change.

"Destination?"

"Uh, Queensway Station."

The man tore off a small ticket, the size of a theater ticket back home in Detroit, and then grabbed a few small coins.

Cavanaugh arrived at the platform just as the train arrived. He rushed on board and took a seat, mentally reconstructing the subway map in his head. A few stops later and he saw the word "Queensway" on the wall in blue tile. This was it.

When he was outside again, smelling the fresh air, he noticed that the air had begun to cool. For the first time since he had arrived, the sky was completely free of clouds.

More or less across the street was Black Lion Gate. Beyond the fence, Cavanaugh could see a large park. From somewhere in his memory, he remembered that Kensington Gardens contained a statue of Peter Pan, one of his favorite storybook characters from childhood.

When at last he was able to cross the road and walk to the gate, he was the only one there. Standing by the entrance, feeling a bit foolish, he lit a cigarette and waited. Five minutes passed and still he was the only one except for the occasional passerby.

It wasn't until ten minutes later that he saw a man in a simple blue suit approach the gate from the park side. The man had no hat on—which seemed a bit strange to Cavanaugh, since every man in London in and out of uniform seemed to wear one—and had both hands in his pockets. He looked neither left nor right but seemed to be heading directly for Oxford Street, as if he were going to dart across at any second. But then he slowed down and looked around him. Cavanaugh knew this was the man.

He had short hair and was bald on the top of his head; he wasn't old—Cavanaugh judged him to be in his mid-thirties—and his face was fairly youthful. He had a clean, well-scrubbed look. More American- than British-looking; at least in Cavanaugh's brief experience.

The man looked at Cavanaugh and nodded. "You're waiting for Reginald?" he asked. It wasn't the same voice Cavanaugh had heard on the telephone less than an hour ago.

"You're not the man I talked to," he said. Had something gone wrong? Suddenly, he felt a bit frightened.

"No," the man said. "That was just one of our men at the hotel. His job was to contact you in your room."

Cavanaugh wasn't entirely convinced. "How do I know that you're Reginald? Or whoever I'm supposed to meet with?"

The man stared at Cavanaugh for a moment. "You're Philip Andrew Cavanaugh, right?"

Cavanaugh just stared.

"And you've just arrived from Washington, D.C. Before that, you were in Los Alamos for almost a year and a half. You have a doctorate in physics. Wanna know more?"

Cavanaugh shook his head. "I already know it." He guessed this was how they played the game. "So what do we do now?"

"Take a walk," said the man. He was shorter than Cavanaugh by maybe two or three inches, and at least twenty pounds heavier. "Through the Gardens."

Cavanaugh looked at the sky; there wasn't much light left. "So is your name really Reginald?" he asked.

The man smiled slightly. "Does it matter?" He pointed down the gravel path. "We'll walk this way."

Cavanaugh shook his head and sighed. "Why the subway? Waiting at the gate and all that?"

The man stared straight ahead. He had a very distinctive mole on the right side of his face, just above the lip. Cavanaugh wondered how he could be a spy with a prominent facial feature like that.

"We needed to see if anyone was following you."

"Why would anyone follow me? The war's over."

"It's not the Germans we're worried about." He turned and looked at Cavanaugh.

Cavanaugh heard Groves talking three thousand miles away.

"We know the Brits are interested in you. You see, they know you're from Los Alamos."

Cavanaugh thought about the introduction this morning in the Nissen hut at SHAEF Headquarters. Damn right, they knew about him! And it was an American major who'd told them. "I was introduced this morning as someone from Los Alamos."

"I know. It shouldn't have happened. But we think British Intelligence already knew."

"How?" Cavanaugh still found it difficult to believe that he could be the center of so much interest.

"One of their agents was asking about you in Washington. We picked it up immediately, of course."

"So, what do we do?"

"Nothing. Stick to the plan. We'll go into Germany as scheduled and then break away. We'll get you back to London and home again without letting anyone know you've been. At least, until it's too late for them to do anything about it."

"Why can't we trust the British?"

The man didn't answer right away. When he did, the explanation was vague. "There's lots going on right now. And we have to protect our interests." That was all he said.

Suddenly, Cavanaugh remembered Peter Pan. "Isn't there a statue of Peter Pan in the park? In the Gardens, I mean."

"Yeah. We'll walk by it. You like the book?"

Cavanaugh nodded. "One of my favorites as a kid. Along with Tom Swift and the Hardy Boys."

"Yeah," said the man, "Tom Swift. I read him."

The sun was below the horizon of trees and buildings. They were in a period of half-light where the colors of the lawn and vegetation turned darker and richer; the greens looked almost black. The street lamps along Oxford Street were beginning to go on.

"You'll leave tomorrow afternoon for Germany. It's all arranged."

"I know. A major named Lansing told me. Apparently I'm going with him and some others."

"Lansing, yeah. A bigmouth. I don't like men like that, but it's too late to do anything about it."

"How come I wasn't told that I was going with him when I first got here? Or back in Washington? I sounded like a fool."

The man shrugged. "We had to set it up. Run the operation through SHAEF to avoid attention. Look, Lansing is gonna want to know what's going on. Just play dumb, okay? Blame it on the Army."

"That's what I've been doing."

The man smiled. "It works, doesn't it?"

They walked in silence for a while, Cavanaugh following the strange man's lead.

"I'll meet up with you in two days. Maybe three. In Germany. You shouldn't tell anyone that you've been with me tonight."

"Who would I tell?" asked Cavanaugh.

"Someone was asking for you at the hotel. A British officer."

"Who?" asked Cavanaugh. Who in the hell did he know here in London that could be calling on him?

The man shrugged. "Don't know. But when we meet again, you need to act as if it's the first time."

"But what do I do in the meantime? I mean, for two days, for God's sake."

"Stick to the plan. You're attached to the Sixth Army Group, but traveling with a special SHAEF scientific team. Do what they do. As far as anyone knows, you've been sent on a scientific mission. That's all."

"But where will you contact me? I might be traveling, or out of touch." Did this guy even know about Mühlhausen? How in the hell was he going to get there?

"Don't worry. You won't be out of our sight. It's just that we have to *arrange* things for you."

"Arrange what?"

"We have to set it up so that we can break you off from the group without drawing a lot of attention. You'll be with British, maybe even French officers from time to time. We gotta be careful. Low profile, you know?"

"Right." Cavanaugh had learned just enough in life to guess that little went as you planned. Trouble was, a bad plan in Germany could cost him his life. "And the Soviet Zone?"

152

"What about it?"

"Well, I mean, what'll we do there?"

"You'll be briefed. Later. It's being arranged."

About twenty feet off the path Cavanaugah caught sight of a large crater maybe fifty or sixty feet across: trees on its perimeter had been uprooted and thrown to the ground as if smashed by a giant hand. Although he couldn't see all of it clearly—it was night now—the crater looked as if it had been created by an explosion.

"What's that?" he asked. He pointed.

The shorter man stopped for a moment and peered into the darkness. "Oh," he said, "a V-2 did that. One of the last to fall."

Cavanaugh studied it for a moment and tried to imagine a thirty-foot metal monster and a ton of explosives hitting the ground. For a moment, he tried to compare it to what Los Alamos expected of Little Boy. He wasn't sure; if Little Boy worked at all, it would at least incinerate Kensington Gardens. And probably a mile of the city in all directions. And if it worked *big*, well—

Suddenly, out of the darkness, a small statue six or seven feet high loomed into view. It was of a young boy playing a pipe. It was unmistakably Peter Pan.

"Here he is," said the man. "Most people wanna see the Tower of London," said the man. "The Crown Jewels. Big Ben."

"I don't think I'll have time this trip," replied Cavanaugh. Peter Pan would have to do. Then a thought hit him. "What do I do if I need to get hold of you? You know, something happens, goes wrong, that sort of thing."

"You can't. We can't afford to have you linked with us. Even the smallest connection could be, well, unhelpful."

"Us? You mean Strategic Services?"

"Right. No connection. But don't worry."

"Why not?"

"We'll be looking after you. Piece of cake."

"And when we cross into the Russian Zone?"

The man said nothing for a moment. "That's different."

"No piece of cake, huh?"

"No. But you'll be with good men. The best we have."

"What if we get caught? What then?"

"It won't happen. But if it does, say you're lost."

"And the Russians will fall for that?" Cavanaugh was skeptical.

"Probably not. But it won't matter. You're not the enemy, you know.

At least, not yet. They'll hold you for a while, question you, probably register a complaint with someone. But you'll get sent back. You understand, if that happens, you must not, under any circumstances, tell them what you were there for."

"And what about the men I'm with? What do they say?"

"Same thing. Lie. Tell the Russians they're lost. And they have no idea what you're after."

Cavanaugh thought for a moment. They were approaching Bayswater Road again and he could hear the traffic noise quite clearly. It had turned chilly now, and damp. He hoped the meeting was nearly over, although there were a million questions he would like to ask. But the big question was what the man walking next to him really knew about his mission. How could Cavanaugh keep from letting something slip in Mühlhausen? Some small word or clue that would reveal he was looking for an atomic bomb.

Ahead of them was a large gate, similar to Black Lion Gate. On the other side, the evening's traffic bustled up and down Bayswater Road. People hurried down the broad sidewalks on both sides of the road.

"That's Marlborough Gate," the man said. "Cross the street and you'll find a tube station called Lancaster Gate. You can catch the Central Underground line back to Marble Arch. It's the next stop. You know the way from there?"

Cavanaugh nodded. He had one more question. "Your name," he said, "it's not really Reginald, is it?"

The man laughed. "No. That's just the code name we have for contacting one another. My name is Conti. Bob Conti of Spokane, Washington."

For the first time in almost an hour, they shook hands. The man seemed a little reluctant to let Cavanaugh go. For a long moment, they just stood within fifty feet of Malborough Gate and watched the traffic.

It was Cavanaugh who spoke up. "You've been in London long?"

"About a year. I haven't been able to do any field work until now."

That was either good news or bad, thought Cavanaugh. Good, if you assumed he was too valuable to send out where he might be caught; bad, if he wasn't good enough to be trusted with an assignment in the field. Until now, that is. And where did that put Cavanaugh?

Conti suddenly straightened up and looked at his fellow American. "Well, we'll all be home soon," he said. He held up two fingers. "Two

154

days. Contact in two days." And then, abruptly, he turned and started to walk back into the darkness of the park.

"Right," said Cavanaugh. He wasn't sure that Conti had heard him.

Cavanaugh walked back into the hotel resolved to go straight to bed. But barely into the lobby he heard his name being called.

"Cavanaugh!"

He turned around to see Christopher Brooke smiling at him.

"Where've you been, old boy? I stopped by earlier."

Cavanaugh shook hands. "Just out for a walk. I wanted to stretch." Was Brooke the man Conti had referred to? The one who'd asked for him at the hotel? "What are you doing here?"

"I met some chums here for a drink." He nodded toward two men in uniforms walking out the door. "The Dorchester has one of my favorite bars. Great postprandial spot."

Cavanaugh smiled. So far, he had seen the lobby and his room.

Brooke feigned a serious face. "You look like you could use a drink."

"I'm beat," said Cavanaugh.

"Come on," Brooke said, grabbing Cavanaugh's arm. "I'll buy you the best whiskey this battered island has to offer."

"Gee, thanks, but I'm really tired." Conti, Groves, everyone, it seemed, was wary of the British.

"Oh, come on," repeated Brooke. "Just one drink. You'll sleep like a lamb."

Cavanuagh hestitated, then sighed. "Okay. One drink."

"Right. One drink."

"Have you been in the bar yet?" asked Brooke.

Cavanaugh shook his head. "My room and the lobby. That's it."

"Good Lord, we've got to get you out more. At least the hotel bar. All of London parades through here at one time or another."

Like the lobby, the bar was decorated in a combination of deco and classic styles, and it was quieter. Only a half dozen small tables were occupied.

"Doesn't look popular tonight," he said.

"Ah," replied Brooke, "this is the lull before the storm. It'll pick up with the after-dinner crowd."

Brooke motioned to the bartender as they took a table. "Two," he said simply. The bald-headed man just nodded. Brooke was obviously a regular.

"I like the Dorchester," he said quietly. "My family used to take rooms here before the war." He smiled.

"And now?"

Brooke shook his head. "No. My father's in India; my mother stays in the country. She has vowed not to return to the City until the war is over. Ah, Charles, thank you," he said, when the bartender put down two iceless drinks in small glasses. Cavanaugh couldn't be sure, but the Scotch looked darker than he was accustomed to.

"Chin-chin." Brooke clinked his glass against Cavanaugh's.

Cavanaugh took a swallow and nearly gagged. The Scotch—if that was what it was—had a burned, almost rancid, taste. Brooke caught his reaction and smiled.

"It's malted Scotch. An acquired taste. This one's quite rare, really."

Cavanaugh nodded. Acquired, indeed. He took a second sip; it was only slightly less overwhelming.

"Like most things," said Brooke, "this has been hard to get in England during the war." He held the glass up and studied it against the light from the bar. "We've become a penurious nation, you see, and it's my considered opinion that the state of a nation can be measured by the quality of the liquor it drinks. As this Scotch has become endangered, so has our civilization."

He laughed. "Or maybe you think that this particular Scotch endangers our nation?"

Cavanaugh laughed too. "You're right: it's an acquired taste."

"Is there rationing in the States?"

"Some things. Everything you want, that is. Gasoline. Tires. Meat. Those sorts of things." But as he said it, Cavanaugh knew that America had suffered very little compared to Britain. He thought of Gilbert and his set of four black-market tires.

"Ah," said Brooke. His voice suddenly sounded tired, or maybe he was only remembering the war. "It's hard to tell about America," he said softly, "since what we see here of your country appears endless: tanks; airplanes; petrol; food. Even your military wages. It's hard to imagine one nation able to build and supply so much."

Brooke leaned back in his chair and lit a cigarette. He smiled mischievously. "You know," he began, "our officers at the front receive a weekly ration of gin or whiskey. Or they're supposed to. Your boys don't. So our men often pool their liquor and barter for your meat. Ironic, isn't it?"

Cavanaugh nodded. He wondered what Brooke would think of Los

Alamos with its triple-A rating that allowed the laboratory to order and get anything in America on a priority basis. Suddenly he remembered those gallon tins of brandied peaches that showed up one day at the PX in Los Alamos. They would bring a fortune here on the black market.

"How long have you been stationed in London?" he asked. It seemed time to change the subject.

"Since '41."

"And with SHAEF?"

"I'm not with SHAEF, actually. Simply attached for the moment while we investigate German scientific developments."

"And before that?" Cavanaugh was curious about what a man like Brooke had done during most of the war. He didn't quite *look* like a scientist or engineer; he was, well, too polished for that. In the United States, Cavanaugh thought, the man would have been a lawyer or politician.

Brooke smiled. "Like in your country," he said in easy but knowing tones, "there was a need in England to have a portion of the armed forces coordinate scientific developments. Both here and abroad," he added cryptically. "And you? Have you been at Los Alamos from the beginning?"

Cavanaugh winced at the public mention of Los Alamos. He could hardly deny he worked there; Lansing had revealed that today. Still, secrecy had been drilled into him since his first day at the lab there.

He shook his head. "Only for a year and a half. Before that, it was a defense project at the University of Michigan."

"But you're in uniform," said Brooke.

"Not uncommon," replied Cavanaugh. Actually, he had no idea how common it was. Hopefully, Brooke wouldn't pursue it. He changed the subject again. "Do you know many Americans?"

Brooke smiled again. "Quite a few, really. And I have friends from Harvard before the war. Actually, it's hard not to know some here. England, you see, is flooded with Americans." Brooke gesticulated grandly. "You know, we have a saying that England's an occupied country. Occupied by Americans!" He laughed loudly.

Cavanaugh smiled.

Brooke eased back in the tiny chair. "How long will you be over here?"

Play dumb? Cavanaugh asked himself. He shook his head. "You got me," he said. "However long they think they want me."

"Well, we must get you a first-class dinner here in London before you return."

"I'd like that. But I haven't heard encouraging things about English food."

"Nazi propaganda," smirked Brooke. "It's just that we don't often advertise it. Keeps the good spots in the family, so to speak. Maybe tomorrow."

"No," said Cavanaugh. "I'm leaving tomorrow."

"Oh, yes. SHAEF's fact-finding mission to the Land of the Huns. Jolly good that'll do."

"You sound skeptical?"

Brooke smiled. Half-smiled, really. "A little. It does strike me that Eisenhower and his boys may be pushing the old 'We're all equals' a bit too much."

"What do you mean?"

"Just that the spoils of war haven't exactly been divided equally. But you'll see. Dinner then? When you get back?"

"Yeah. Great." Cavanaugh felt uncomfortable; Brooke's comments had hit home, but what could he do about it?

They shook hands in the lobby. Cavanaugh watched Brooke walk out the doors to the street and pause under the awning to light a cigarette. For a moment, he wondered where the man lived—a house? an apartment? He didn't seem like the dormitory type.

Then Brooke turned and walked toward Oxford Street.

Part Six

JULY 1945

OCCUPIED GERMANY

We shall fight on till midnight—Till five past midnight.
—Adolph Hitler. 1945

Chapter Fourteen

*T*he earth disappeared beneath a layer of clouds as England and re-emerged hours later as Germany. It was a half day's roller-coaster ride through heavy clouds and turbulence.

The choppy ride left Cavanaugh with an uneasy, churning sensation in his stomach, which, in some vague, uncomfortable way, he sensed was setting the stage for what was coming.

He nervously clutched the strap above his head with first one hand, then the other, until both were aching and leaden and he was forced to let them drop by his side. He sat uncomfortably with his butt on a canvas seat stretched over a metal frame that jutted out from the interior of the fuselage. He and a dozen others were in a B-25 Mitchell bomber converted to a transport.

Across the aisle was a young man, a former bomber pilot, who periodically issued weather and flying reports.

"Too much moisture in the clouds . . . gonna be rough like this all the way . . . lightning sometimes hits you midair, you know, throws out the electrical gear . . . we ain't topped ten thousand yet . . ."

Cavanaugh didn't know how much was true except that they weren't much higher than ten thousand feet; if so, they'd be wearing oxygen masks.

When at last Germany appeared, it was through a break in the clouds.

"Je-sus Christ," shouted a portly Texas GI, "lo-ook at that!" He pointed to something outside the small Plexiglas window of the B-25.

What he pointed to was a city of several hundred thousand inhabitants reduced to rubble.

Intrigued, Cavanaugh unsteadily made his way to the small window and looked down. "Oh my God," he murmured.

Beneath him was a city leveled on both sides of a snaking river, block after block, mile after mile, with only a few streets, like veins on a leaf, cleared between half-shells of buildings and total ruins. Only the tall, blackened spire of a Gothic cathedral stood defiantly untouched.

Cavanaugh suddenly thought of an image that a nun in his third-grade religion class had once conjured up: that of Jerusalem—the city that rejected Christ, the nun emphasized—destroyed by the Romans so that not one stone was left upon the other. Cologne was the Jerusalem of 1945, he thought, the feeling in his stomach even less easy than before.

Working his way from strap to strap, he lumbered back to his place near the rear of the bomber and sat down, shaken by the images.

Oddly, what in reflection struck him now was the utter lack of color. Cologne was a city where war had preemptied summer green with perpetual gloom. It was as if an artist had been ordered to paint the city with only two tubes of paint: black and gray.

The pilot across the aisle was talking again.

"Yeah, we bombed the hell out of it . . . one raid, we had a thousand planes, imagine, a sky from horizon to horizon filled with everything that would fly . . . afterward, you could see the goddamn place burning a hundred and fifty miles away . . ."

Cavanaugh tried to imagine a thousand planes. Los Alamos was planning to use only three planes: one to carry the bomb, two to observe and photograph the results. One plane, one bomb, one city like Cologne wiped off the map.

Cavanaugh closed his eyes and tried to put all of this out of his mind.

162

He forced himself to think of Christine, wondered what she was doing now, what time it might be in Washington, day or night? But his thoughts, no matter how hard he tried to concentrate, were always a mixture of Christine and Los Alamos and what he had just seen. Then he felt someone tapping his shoulder. It was Major Lansing.

"Let's talk, okay?" said the man.

Cavanaugh nodded. Lansing had accompanied him from London, both meeting at Base Operations. Despite some off-color remarks about the Army's lack of intelligence, Lansing seemed to enjoy his rank as designated officer in charge of the special SHAEF expedition into southern Germany.

The two of them were virtually alone now in the back of the B-25. The pilot across from them had joined some others in the forward part of the plane. They were smoking cigarettes and laughing.

"There'll be five others in Stuttgart," Lansing said in his usual ebullient voice, "two of us and three Brits."

"What about the French? They had guys at the SHAEF briefing, didn't they?"

"Yeah, but they declined, who knows why. So it's the seven of us. Plan on six, maybe seven days among the Krauts."

Lansing lit his own cigarette and took a few drags before he continued talking.

"You know what this is all about?" he asked.

Cavanaugh thought quickly. "You mean the trip?" he responded cryptically.

"Yeah, what the hell else?"

"Only that we're going to follow up on the ALSOS sweep through southern Germany two months ago. Except that I gather we're not supposed to mention ALSOS."

Lansing looked at him hard for a moment, then took several drags on his cigarette.

"All right, we'll play it your way. We're doing a repeat performance."

Cavanaugh sensed the man's irritation. "Look," he lied, "I don't know what the hell I'm doing here. Someone, Groves probably, thought that someone from the States needed to see first-hand what you guys found at Haigerloch and places like that. And, hell, I'm that someone. That's all I know."

Lansing crushed his cigarette butt with his boot on the metal-and-wood floor of the plane.

"Okay, but you need to know that people are talking."

"About me?" asked Cavanaugh.

"Who else? I got my ass chewed out for mentioning that you came from Los Alamos. Sorry, but hell, I didn't know that just to mention the goddamn place was a big no-no. No one told me. But anyway, I got a dozen people asking me about you. And what you're doing here."

Cavanaugh thought a moment. "Well, it's like I said. As far as I know, I'm along for the ride. And that's the official story, at least that's what I was told." He prayed he sounded convincing.

Lansing lit another cigarette. The only man Cavanaugh had seen chain-smoke more was Oppenheimer.

"This detachment's official task is to re-investigate Nazi atomic work in southern Germany. To give our allies a chance to see what we found in April. That's the public story, anyway."

For a moment, Lansing studied the small group in the front of the plane. They seemed oblivious to him and Cavanaugh.

"The unofficial reason is to see if we missed any German reserves of uranium. But our British friends waiting for us in Stuttgart don't know that."

"What if we find some? Uranium?" asked Cavanaugh.

"Make a note. Get word pronto to the Sixth Army Group. And then push on like that was all we had to do."

"Could be difficult. Especially with the others around."

"Yeah. We'll split up, though, send the Brits one way while we go another. That'll help."

Both men fell silent for a few minutes. Cavanaugh listened to the pitch of the motors change, then settle down again. For the moment at least, the ride was smooth. He relaxed a little and tried to find a comfortable spot against the hard metal of the fuselage.

Lansing cleared his throat. "Hey, look," he said, "can you at least tell me what you do? You know, back there in hush-hush land?"

Cavanaugh hesitated. "Not really." He could tell, however, that Lansing was disappointed in his response, as if he had failed to honor some trust between them, between men at war.

"Well," Lansing said brightly, "it's probably a safe bet that you're working on a bomb, ain't it?"

Cavanaugh nodded. "Yeah, that's a safe bet."

Chapter Fifteen

The next twenty-four hours were a blur for Cavanaugh. A painful, sometimes nightmarish collection of images.

Stuttgart was almost as devastated as Cologne. They landed at night, so Cavanaugh saw the city for the first time in the light of early morning. Gray and black were still the predominant colors.

The shells of buildings, the piles of rubble loomed larger, were more shocking, from eye level. The city—what was left of it—was shrouded in gloom and filled with the pervasive smell of smoke and charred buildings.

They had met up with the rest of their team at the U.S. Army's airfield outside of town and spent the night at a small hotel whose bombed-out roof had been hastily repaired by the Corps of Engineers. The entire building had been requisitioned as an officer's billet.

After a surprisingly good breakfast of bacon and eggs, the seven of them left in a small convoy of three jeeps. Cavanaugh rode with Lansing and a first lieutenant in the lead, in a jeep with sandbags on the floor. At the hotel he had asked about the sandbags.

"Land mines," said the first lieutenant, who was the driver. "I don't want my balls blown off."

A few minutes later, Cavanaugh privately queried Lansing about the land mines. "Are they still around?"

"Nah," said Lansing. "We're more likely to get shot by snipers than blown up by a goddamn mine."

Lansing then unfolded a map on the hood of the jeep and briefed the others about the journey.

"If we get separated," he said, "we'll meet up in Haigerloch." He pointed to a small dot on the map.

"Let's hit it!" he ordered. "Take it slow through the city. Don't mix with the Krauts. Stay together."

And off they went. Through one of the few streets free of rubble, cleared by elderly Germans working laboriously passing stones to one another, stone by stone, in a long human chain. Small packs of children ran by the sides of their jeeps shouting, "GI, GI," or "Zigarettes."

Cavanaugh was relieved when they finally left Stuttgart and headed south through countryside. Miraculously, like a curtain suddenly pulled aside, they left winter and entered summer.

The fields were green, the trees in bloom. Each village they passed through seemed to take them farther and farther away from the war. There were signs of bombing here and there, and of small battles, and frequently lines of refugees, including ragged and weary soldiers along the roads. But the war seemed to retreat behind them, mile by mile, on the small roads.

In mid-afternoon they reached Haigerloch, the small village in southern Germany where only a few months ago Lansing and his men had located the Nazi atomic reactor.

Haigerloch was another surprise: the village was as beautiful as Stuttgart was ugly. It lay nestled in a steep valley on the Eyach River, just where the river snaked through a dramatic series of turns, forming a tight S. The sides of the valley were heavily wooded and halfway down the descent Cavanaugh picked out something in the air, a strange but pleasant scent.

"What's that?" he shouted to Lansing. "That smell?"

"Lilacs. They must still be in bloom."

It was like a dream. The village had been spared the war entirely;

there was no trace of the horror Cavanaugh had seen in Cologne or Stuttgart. There were several churches, all perfectly intact, including a large, castlelike monastery that dominated the top of a hill. The houses, with their exposed wooden beams, were out of *Hänsel und Gretel*. There was even a Roman tower that sat on the bank of the river.

"This is beautiful," Cavanaugh gushed. It was just like a photograph in a travel magazine.

Lansing took out his camera and took a picture from the moving jeep. "Yeah, real storybook stuff."

Ironic, thought Cavanaugh. The Nazis chose to build their atomic laboratory away from the cities, in a picturesque setting. Oppenheimer and Groves had made the same decision for Los Alamos.

"There it is!" shouted Lansing to the driver. "There. Right there! Behind that building."

The driver crossed the stone bridge and made a sharp turn to the left down the narrow cobblestone street. The second jeep followed behind. Lansing motioned to pull over and park.

"What is it?"

"The cave," said Lansing. "Where we found the reactor. Come on, you'll like this."

Cavanaugh got out stiffly and stretched his legs for a moment. It was cramped and uncomfortable as hell riding around in the back of the jeep. Not to mention the loose sand that seeped from the sandbags and flew around him.

Down a narrow street that looked more like an alley was the almost vertical face of a 200-foot limestone cliff. Directly above, with dozens of rococo touches, was the monastery. Lansing ignored the church; he headed straight for a large, dark, rectangular patch at the base of the cliff. This was the entrance to the famous cave Cavanaugh had heard so much about.

Cavanaugh picked up his pace to catch up with Lansing, who had stopped briefly to take another photograph.

"Didn't have my camera last time," he said animatedly. He had the look of a schoolboy in a candy store. It seemed to be as exciting for him this time as the last, even though Cavanaugh knew that everything of value had been hauled away months ago by Army engineers.

"Goddamn it! Look at that," shouted Lansing angrily. He was standing in front of a wall of vertical timber twice the height of a man. On one end, several boards had been pulled down.

Cavanaugh walked up next to him.

"Someone's broken in." He pointed to a space that would easily accommodate several men side by side.

"We boarded this damn thing up. Tight as hell, too. Look at that."

Cavanaugh glanced around. Several of the houses obviously had been used as offices or laboratories. But the reactor itself had been hidden deep inside the cave. The Germans probably had twenty or thirty scientists and technicians here at any one time. But even if they had had only two, the whole village would have known about it. Everything was so close together, it would have been impossible to do anything without attracting attention.

Suddenly, he noticed something on the ground. Tire tracks. From several trucks, in fact, since the tire patterns varied.

"Look," he said to Lansing. By now, the rest of the men had joined them.

"Goddamn French," murmured Lansing. "Got to be them."

Then Cavanaugh remembered that they were officially in the French Zone of Occupation. They had crossed the "border," such as it was, right out of Stuttgart. The line was marked only by a hastily painted sign in French, Russian, German, and English.

Lansing pulled out his flashlight and stepped through the entrance. Cavanaugh cautiously followed.

Fortunately, the floor was level. There were odd pieces of equipment—he couldn't tell what—scattered around, but Lansing's flashlight provided just enough light for them to make their way. Several shafts of light played at their feet from the flashlights behind them.

Cavanaugh's excitement was growing. He knew that everything had been removed, but he couldn't suppress the thought of the possibility that something might have been left behind, something telling, that would help fill in the puzzle that lay waiting for him in the Soviet Zone.

There was just enough light to see that the tunnel was large enough for a small truck to drive through. That would explain how the Germans had brought in the steel reactor—in pieces—as well as metal tubing and all the other equipment. Several thick electrical cables ran the length of the tunnel just at shoulder height.

There was a fetid smell that lingered heavily in the air. Pools of dank liquid gathered along the floor. There were several empty chambers to the right and left that had been cut off the main tunnel where

168

the smell was even less pleasant; it was a mixture of decay and urine. In the subterranean quiet, Cavanaugh could hear the steady *drip-drip* of water falling from the ceiling.

A few minutes later they were in the main room. A large hole had been dug into the ground and lined in concrete; just a few months ago it had housed the Nazis' atomic reactor.

In several spots Cavanaugh found fresh footprints that couldn't have been made by any of his group. He touched Lansing's shoulder and pointed.

"Goddamn Frogs," said Lansing. "They musta just been here."

"Do they know what they're looking for?"

Lansing shook his head. Cavanaugh could barely make out the motion in the dim light. "I doubt it. They have scientific teams in here looking for stuff, like jet-aircraft factories, but I don't think they know what the Krauts were doing here."

The room was large; Cavanaugh could tell that by the way the voices echoed. Lansing sounded close up and far away at the same time.

Well, why not? wondered Cavanaugh. Why wouldn't the French be here? Everyone else was in Germany looking for scientific booty, and at least it wasn't the Russians.

"Let's go," said Lansing. He whistled sharply; the sound echoed again and again. "Let's move it."

Slowly they made their way out. Cavanaugh had to stop at the entrance for a moment, shielding his eyes and blinking rapidly, trying to adjust to the sunlight.

He took a deep breath. It was good to be outside again. There was something about caves and dark places that he'd never liked.

He lit a cigarette and waited for the others to make their way out. The reports had been right: the German atomic effort had been small. The remains of the reactor were sufficient to tell him that it was experimental at best; it was *not* a device to produce bomb-grade plutonium, for example. In contrast, he knew that the American reactors in Hanford, Washington, were huge and far more sophisticated.

So was it possible—really possible—that the Germans had somehow figured out *how* to make an atomic weapon? A gun-type bomb like Little Boy? It just didn't seem likely, not given what he'd seen in the cave. The feeling was growing that this whole trip was a colossal waste of time. And—Jesus!—with so much for him to do back home in Los Alamos.

"Uh-oh," said Lansing softly. "Company."

Cavanaugh looked down the road and saw a jeep driving slowly toward them. It was impossible to tell who was in it.

"Us or them?" he asked Lansing.

"Frogs, I'll bet." The jeep drew closer. "Yep. Our fellow victors." He waved solicitously.

The jeep stopped and two men in green uniforms stepped out. Cavanaugh didn't know that much about uniforms, but he guessed Lansing was right.

"*Bonjour!*" shouted one.

"*Bonjour,*" repeated Lansing. He broke into a smile and pitched his cigarette. A minute later, he was speaking passable French with the two officers.

Cavanaugh was amazed. That made two languages—German and French—plus English. Lansing's three to his one. Christine would be impressed.

Lansing turned around and waved at Cavanaugh. He had a smile on his face. "Hey!" he shouted, "come on, get the rest. We've been invited to dinner."

The French, as it turned out, were billeted in Haigerloch. In the town hall, which had been requisitioned and turned into a small billet for three officers and a dozen enlisted men.

"They've been here a couple days," explained Lansing in a quiet moment; he seemed to find the circumstances extremely amusing. "They're here as military support to a scientific team, all right, but the technical guys are snooping around somewhere else."

"What did you tell them about us?"

"I told them we were doing pretty much the same thing, looking for German poison-gas factories, but that we'd gotten lost. Outside of Stuttgart. They've agreed to let us spend the night."

"Great," mumbled Cavanaugh. They were supposed to billet in a town thirty kilometers from here. This unscheduled stop could well throw them off by a day. Then how in the hell would Conti know where he was?

His face must have reflected the concern. Lansing slapped him on the back. "So what the hell, fella? It's a meal, right? French cuisine."

Cavanaugh nodded. "So where did you learn French?"

"In school. I got a knack for languages, see. Look. Wine." He pointed to the table. There were a dozen bottles on it.

170

Dinner was excellent. Some of the best food Cavanaugh had eaten since Los Alamos. It was chicken—*poulet* something or other, one of the French officers explained—cooked in wine and tantalizing sauces. And fresh vegetables and baked bread. Where in the hell had they gotten the chicken? Most of Germany seemed to be starving.

And the wine! Each bottle was spectacular. A mix of French and German. A French major named Passon laughingly told a tale about "liberating" a German hotel of its remarkable wine cellar.

"Repayment," Passon said, smiling, and in very good English. "For the honor of France, of course."

Later, over a stiff brandy, Passon turned to Cavanaugh. "The major says you are looking for poison gases."

Cavanaugh nodded. He remembered Lansing's admonition to them all: absolutely no mention of atomic research. If pressed, say you were looking for secret nerve-gas factories hidden in southern Germany.

"I have seen reports," the major said. "Horrible."

"Yes," said Cavanaugh. "Horrible."

"They kill in minutes, I understand."

Cavanaugh nodded again.

"How do they work?"

"They attack the nervous system." Cavanaugh explained briefly, hoping the major would change the subject; what he knew about nerve gases might take two or three minutes at best to tell.

"Barbarians," Passon said angrily. He made a deep frown. "The next war will not be like this one," he added. "More terrible than we can imagine. No, I am not a scientist, but I know that scientists have brought us to this."

Cavanaugh said nothing. But then, what *could* he say? He was, after all, one of the men who had helped build Little Boy. And that would either change war forever, as the major said, or—as Cavanaugh and the others at Los Alamos hoped—it would end it forever.

Passon hit his hand hard on the table. Conversation stopped and all eyes turned toward him.

Very slowly, the major lifted his wineglass. "Let us drink to victory, eh?" He paused for a moment. "While we still have it."

They arrived back in Stuttgart three days later, tired and cramped and covered with dust and grime.

In the tiny lobby of the officer's billet, Cavanaugh noticed Lansing talking with a young Army sergeant and examining some papers. Both men turned his way and then Lansing motioned him over.

Oh, shit! thought Cavanaugh. This looked like trouble.

"We'll, you're a lucky son of a bitch," said Lansing loudly. It was loud enough for several others to turn and stare. The room they all stood in wasn't even the size of the rec room back home in the Bachelors' Dorm in Los Alamos.

"What?" he asked.

"You're being sent back." Lansing handed Cavanaugh several sheets of official-looking paper. He had a curious look on his face that seemed to say, *I knew it all along.*

Cavanaugh glanced at the papers, uncertain if this was good news. What had happened to his secret mission?

"You're being sent back to London. Back to the Sixth Army. Maybe it's back to the States." Lansing was all smiles.

Slowly, Cavanaugh let himself believe it was good news. Maybe Groves had changed his mind and was bringing him home. His "assignment" to the Sixth Army could be a cover.

All he could think of was, when? "When do I leave?" he asked.

"Immediately," said the sergeant.

"What? I just got here." Cavanaugh motioned with the hand holding his orders. He was thinking of his shower.

"Well, you're just leaving. Get your gear together. This man will take you to the airfield for a night flight." Lansing seemed amused: a wry smile crept across his face. "Tell 'em we did our job, okay?"

Cavanaugh nodded. He had nothing to pack. Everything he owned was in the duffel bag on the floor next to him. Almost unconsciously, he shook Lansing's hand.

"Don't do anything I wouldn't do," he said.

Cavanaugh couldn't believe what was happening to him. With a little luck he'd be back in Los Alamos in a few days.

"We're going straight to the airfield?" he asked the sergeant. So far, the man had said nothing.

He shook his head. "Stopping at Headquarters first. Picking up another guy."

Cavanaugh nodded and lit a cigarette; he offered one to the sergeant, who took it and mumbled thanks.

It was dark now, the night sky still filled with the afternoon's clouds. Once more, the city drifted into darkness, the buildings resuming the eerie, abandoned look Cavanaugh had first seen five days ago.

172

Headquarters, hidden behind a wall, was protected by armed guards. Behind the walls, the buildings—there seemed to be a small complex of them—blazed with light. Just seeing the buildings lit up brightly made him feel good. Cavanaugh felt himself beginning to relax; he even began to think about a hotel room in London and a long, hot bath.

That vague thought was in his head when he walked through the doors of the Headquarters building. Someone saluted him and he saluted back. Then he heard his name being called.

"Captain Cavanaugh?" the voice said. It was vaguely familiar.

He turned around and looked into the quiet face of Bob Conti.

"I'm Major Novello," the man said, extending his hand.

"Sorry for the surprise," said Conti. "Really couldn't contact you directly." He nervously fingered his mustache. The mole on his lip was as prominent as ever.

"Uh, huh." Cavanaugh tried to conceal his disappointment. "Am I supposed to keep calling you Novello?"

"No, I'm Conti now. That was just so word wouldn't get back to any of your buddies that you hooked up with me."

Cavanaugh wondered whether Lansing or any of the others cared.

"How many fake names you got, anyway?"

Conti sort of half-laughed. "However many it takes."

Cavanaugh waited for Conti to explain, but he didn't. "What's the plan, then?" he asked. There had been no discussion at Army Headquarters; the sergeant had been dismissed and he and Conti climbed into another car, this one a Ford sedan with no official markings on it.

"Spend the night here and drive to Munich tomorrow."

"Munich? And then?"

"We catch a special flight to Hannover. Then we get you across." Conti calmly inhaled a cigarette, slowly exhaling the smoke so that it seemed to linger around them in the dark car.

"You're coming?" Cavanaugh remembered Conti saying others would take him into the Soviet Zone.

"You bet."

Another surprise. What else? "Where are we going now?"

"A private house. It's safer than Headquarters."

"Why?"

Conti never answered; instead he talked about the next few days.

"If everything goes well, we'll be at the border of the Soviet Zone tomorrow night. We should reach Mühlhausen fairly quickly, let you look around, and return within a couple of hours."

"We have to go at night?"

"It's difficult to travel during the day; our information is that the Soviets have moved several battalions into the area. Obviously, we want to avoid them."

Conti made a series of turns down dark streets that eventually put them in a neighborhood where the damage was far less severe. Complete houses were still standing.

"We're going to try to cross at Wanfried, if we can. It's on the American-Soviet line, about twenty kilometers from Mühlhausen."

"And if we can't?"

"There are other possibilities. Wanfried is the most direct, though."

"Is it just us? Just you and me, I mean?"

"No."

"Someone else?"

"Yes. A third person. Someone who knows the area."

Cavanaugh wondered who in the hell it could be. "Who?" he asked.

"A German."

Conti slowed down, then suddenly pulled the car into a driveway. "This is it!" In the distance was a large two-story house.

Conti abruptly stopped the car in front of the house and jerked up the brake handle. "You'll like it here. It's real comfortable. Even has a wine cellar. It belonged to a Nazi honcho during the war."

Chapter Sixteen

*T*he luminous half-moon was high in the sky, almost directly overhead. It cut in and out of view as clouds drifted somnambulantly across, alternately lighting and darkening the landscape like a flashlight turned on and off in a dark room.

Cavanaugh stood outside in the chilly night air, smoking a cigarette and staring at the half-disk as it played its light through the stormy sky. There was no sense of imminent rain, just winds that shook the tops of trees. What a hell of a time to play spy, he thought.

Soon they would cross into the Soviet Zone. It had taken all day and a successsion of jeeps and an airplane to arrive at nightfall at a Seventh Army encampment outside of Wanfried, apparently just walking distance from the border.

Now he was waiting for Conti to arrive with an unknown third man who would accompany them into Mühlhausen. Conti had left over an hour ago, saying he would be back in thirty minutes; now Cavanaugh wondered if something had gone wrong.

Earlier in the day, over a long jeep ride, they had discussed the "foray"—as Conti called it—into the Russian Zone. And what would happen. And what would happen if they were caught.

The worst, Cavanaugh was told, was that they would be held for a few days before being returned to the American Zone. After all, the so-called demarcation line was an arbitrary creation, barely two months old. It wouldn't be unlikely for GIs to wander accidentally across the border on a back road or something. Probably happened all the time. That sounded like Lansing talking.

Cavanaugh still worried. And now that he had been alone for an hour, he had had plenty of time to think about the possibilities.

A few dozen yards away the bivouacked GIs were laughing and talking, their voices audible but indistinct through the sound of wind-buffeted trees. Cavanaugh noticed that his cigarette glowed continually, as if the wind itself were inhaling it. From the opposite direction he heard a jeep approach: two headlights bounced like yellow balls on the rough dirt road. Another band of clouds cleared the moon, and he could see Conti and two other men. Seconds later, the jeep pulled up and abruptly stopped before the tent they had been assigned.

"We're back," said Conti. He gave no explanation for the delay.

Cavanaugh flipped what was left of his cigarette into the dark; it made a dying red arc. He looked at the two men with Conti: one wore a U.S. Army uniform, the other was dressed as a civilian. He knew neither of them.

"Will there be four of us?" he asked.

"Just three. This is Captain Vaclav," he said, pointing to the man in the Army uniform. "He's one of us."

The man nodded and shuffled slightly in the loose dirt by the jeep.

"And this is Rudi. He's the one I told you about. He'll help us make the crossing."

Cavanaugh looked at Rudi, who stared back unblinkingly. The German was tall and slender, and even in the darkness he could tell that his clothes were slightly too large for his body.

"I've got something to show you," said Conti. "Let's step inside." He motioned toward the tent.

Cavanaugh followed along in silence. So far, only he and Conti had said anything. Somehow, the evening seemed chillier now.

Conti flipped on the single unprotected light bulb that hung from the rod across the ceiling of the tent; far away, Cavanaugh could hear the steady drone of the electrical generator.

"You got those photos, Captain?"

From a beaten leather valise, the man named Vaclav withdrew a tan Army envelope and handed it to Conti. Cavanaugh briefly studied the man's face, which was pleasant but expressionless. He seemed to be the very epitome of the type who could never be outbluffed at a poker game; his face conveyed a simple congeniality, nothing more.

"I've had these made for us by the reconnaissance people in London. I had them ordered through another detachment, to kill any connection with us." He looked at the photographs briefly and then handed them to Cavanaugh one by one.

Each photo was of a cluster of buildings taken from different positions, all obviously from aircraft, but at low, oblique angles. Whoever had taken them had done so by nosing down in a plane and making low passes. At the bottom of each photograph was a small box with typed information inside: unit, target, map series, date, name. The only piece of information that meant anything to Cavanaugh was opposite the word "name": the single word "Mühlhausen."

"This is where we're going?" he asked.

"Yes. Aerial-reconnaissance photos," said Vaclav. "All of your target area."

The expression "target area" made Mühlhausen sound as if it were being prepared for bombing.

"They're different angles, or what?" The same cluster of buildings was in each shot, sometimes larger or smaller, and from different directions, depending upon the altitude and direction of the airplane. In one photo, the cluster of buildings was very small and sat at the edge of a town.

"Different dates too," said Vaclav. "Look there." He pointed to the data box on the lower-right-hand corner of each photo.

"Tell us what you've found," said Conti, motioning to Vaclav. He sat down on one of the cots set up inside the tent. The man named Rudi sat down on another one.

Vaclav nodded. "This shot," he said, selecting a particular photograph, "was taken in early April 1945. See the activity? Trucks, jeeps. Same thing in this photo taken three days later."

Cavanaugh studied them closely. Suddenly the details in the photographs came to life. Not only did he see vehicles outside the cluster of buildings, but small antlike creatures around them. They were human figures, a dozen of them!

"Now look at this photo," said Vaclav. He handed Cavanaugh one in which the same buildings were nearly at the top of the image.

"The pilot wasn't particularly looking for those buildings in this pass. They appeared near the edge of a negative, so I had the photo enlarged and cropped to center on them. But see how the trucks are gone now? And this photo was taken only two days after the last one. That makes a five-day history. And during that time the Germans came in and hauled a shitload of stuff away."

Cavanaugh looked at the slightly blurred images. It was true: in the last shot, the trucks and jeeps were gone, and even from an altitude of several hundred feet the buildings looked abandoned. But then he noticed something else. Almost at the upper edge of the photo was a crude circular indentation in the earth, just outside of one of the buildings. And inside the circular ring were several faint but still recognizable straight lines, barely an eighth of an inch long. There was no doubt in his mind: they were the infamous "gun barrels" that he had been sent to examine!

He got up and moved the photo underneath the light bulb to see the images more clearly. The pit and its contents were visible, but barely. To someone else, they would only be small streaks of white, maybe defects on the negative, hardly anything to get excited about. He was still staring at the blurs of light when he heard Vaclav talking again.

"Now look at this one." He handed the last photograph to Cavanaugh.

This one was similar to the others, except that there were several open-bed trucks and a jeep parked near the buildings. Small dots were scattered among the buildings.

"Germans?" he asked.

"No," said Vaclav. "Russians."

The word had an electrical effect on Cavanaugh. "When was it taken?" he asked. His voice was almost a whisper.

"Two days ago," said Conti calmly from his seat on the bed. "I arranged for it, just to be sure there was something left to visit."

Cavanaugh focused on the buildings, then at the pit: the faint images of the gun barrels were still there. "Do you think they took anything?" It suddenly dawned on him that Conti and the others might not know

178

what he was looking for. Only that it was worth risking trouble with the Russians.

"Can't say," said Conti. "But at least now we're certain that they know about the laboratory."

The laboratory? What *did* Conti know? Cavanaugh sensed the man knew more than he was telling.

"Will they be back?" The bad feeling in his stomach was growing.

"Probably. That's why we have to get in and get out real quick."

"We're still going?" Cavanaugh could think of a million reasons not to go. Not now, for God's sake!

"No choice, fella. That's what we've come for."

Cavanaugh nodded weakly and sat back down on one of the cots.

Conti meanwhile pulled out a map and spread it out on his cot. "Okay," he said, "take a look." With his finger, he pointed to their present position, then moved it east four or five inches to a large dot marked "Mühlhausen."

"This is eighteen kilometers, give or take one. But we may or may not be able to use the road. Rudi knows the territory and says there's a dirt road, unmarked, that loops north and then enters Mühlhausen from the east side of the town. We'll take that as a second option."

Cavanaugh looked at the map and then up at Conti. Despite their conversations, the actual details of the trip had never been mentioned. "Do we just drive across the border? I mean, aren't there Russians posted there?"

Conti nodded. "We have a truck on the other side waiting for us. Rudi arranged it."

Cavanaugh looked at Rudi, who said nothing. His face, which was expressionless, looked as if it had been deadened with some kind of drug: only the eyelids blinked rhythmically, moving not out of will, but to some genetic programming.

"We'll cross on foot, north of Wanfried, and meet our contact on the other side. That's at three?" he asked, turning to look at Rudi.

The man nodded slowly. "Yah," he said.

"We'll drive, if we can, without headlights, and park off the road at the edge of Mühlhausen. Fortunately, the lab is on the west side as well." He tapped his finger gently on the map. "You'll have a couple of hours to poke around at night; maybe thirty minutes at dawn. After that, it won't be safe to hang around."

"What if the Russians are still there?"

"We have to risk it. Rudi? How long to drive it?"

He thought for a moment. "Twenty minutes, maybe, if we go direct. Otherwise, an hour. We must go slow." His English was good but heavily accented.

"What if we're stopped?" No one yet had talked about the risks.

Conti was unemotional. "We don't plan to be."

"But if we are?"

Conti reached inside a canvas bag and pulled out a small bottle of American bourbon. "We pretend to be drunk," he said.

Cavanaugh gave a small laugh. "Do you think they'll fall for that?"

Conti shrugged. "Maybe. But remember, you and I are American GIs. Drunk and lost. Rudi is the one with the problem. He's German. If he's caught, he'll be arrested and interned."

Cavanaugh's eyebrows lifted. There seemed about a hundred holes in the plan. "And what if the truck isn't there? The one the contact is supposed to have for us."

Conti smiled. "Then we hoof it. Eighteen kilometers? That's ten, eleven miles at most. We could make it in a couple of hours."

"A couple?" asked Cavanaugh. He had hiked enough in Los Alamos to know that four hours could be more like it. "And if there are Russians everywhere? What do we do then?"

"We wait it out. Until tomorrow night. Rudi knows where we can hide. Right now, we should change."

"Change what?"

"Our clothes. We can't go in uniforms. From a distance, we need to look like Germans." He pointed toward the same canvas bag that contained the bourbon. "I've got us some old clothes."

"But what if they catch us? How can we prove we're Americans?"

"Wear these clothes *over* your uniform. Take your dog tags, ID papers. American money. That sort thing. If we need to, we'll ditch the local finery."

Cavanaugh thought about it for a moment. A dozen miles didn't seem so far unless you had to worry about being caught every step of the way. And about finding your way at night. Which was what they'd be doing at four o'clock in the morning. And what about Rudi? What would he do if he was caught? Turn them all in to save his own neck?

Cavanaugh looked the man over again. In the glare of the light there was more detail. He had a heavily bearded face that could easily need shaving twice a day. Without his coat, the man was thin, rather than

180

slender; like most Germans, he probably survived on half of what it took to live healthfully each day.

But more than anything, Cavanaugh was struck by the hard look in the man's eyes and the perpetual frown, almost a grimace, that dominated the mouth. He had the look of a survivor all right, but something else as well.

"And Rudi? What if he's caught?"

"He can't afford to let that happen," said Conti calmly. "If necessary, he'll make a run for it. He knows that, and he's prepared." He turned and stared at Cavanaugh. "You got your pistol?"

Cavanaugh nodded. It had never left his duffel bag since London.

"Well, be sure and bring it along. You never know."

"I thought we weren't in any danger?"

"You never know," repeated Conti. He stood up. "I've got some things to work out with Vaclav. Why don't you catch some shut-eye? We won't be leaving here until after midnight. I'll wake you in plenty of time."

Cavanaugh wondered if he could sleep after everything he had gone through today. Or worrying about everything that was going to happen in the next twenty-four hours?

"Yeah, maybe," he said, and stood up himself. "I think I'll take a little walk first. Get some air, okay?"

Conti nodded and Cavanaugh walked out of the tent, struck again by how chilly the nights were here in northern Europe. It would be cool in Los Alamos too, he thought, but the mesa was at 7500 feet. He had no idea what the altitude was here.

Cavanaugh walked toward the jeep and lit a cigarette and stood there quietly looking at the night sky; the clouds obscured the stars. Only the half-moon, when not hidden by the clouds, could be seen.

A moment later he heard someone walking toward him. He tensed and quickly turned around; it was Conti.

"Easy," the man assured him. "Just me."

Cavanaugh just stood there for a moment, the cigarette frozen between his lips.

"Hey, relax. This is no big deal," said Conti.

"I just wish it was over," said Cavanaugh. Despite all the easy talk, he knew that the trip to Mühlhausen wasn't going to be a lark. They weren't a bunch of Boy Scouts on an overnight camp-out. There was a lot at stake and the risks weren't small. "What about Rudi? Who is he, anyway?"

Conti was quiet for a moment. "Someone who's been helpful to us. A former SS officer."

"No doubt." Cavanaugh took a deep drag on his cigarette. Images of Dachau and Auschwitz rushed into his head.

"Jesus, Conti, I thought they were rounding up these goddamn storm troopers? Putting them in jail, for God's sake."

"Most, yes. Some are, well, being given a chance to help the Allied cause. Rudi's one of them."

"Why? Because he knows the road to Mühlhausen?"

"No. Not just that. He was assigned to Hans Kammler, the SS Obergruppenführer in charge of manufacturing V-2 rockets. Rudi commanded an SS garrison at Nordhausen. He has a technical background. And there are other things that make him valuable. You just have to trust me. We need him for this."

"Yeah, sure," mumbled Cavanaugh.

"Look at it this way," said Conti cheerily. His tone was flippant. "He's being given a chance to redeem himself."

Cavanaugh woke up on his own. Sometime after ten he had fallen asleep, barely conscious of Conti a few feet away. It was pitch-black in the tent and he could easily read the luminescent dial of his watch: it was a quarter after two.

"Conti?" he whispered.

There was no response.

He sat up in bed and realized that he had fallen asleep in his uniform. He found his lighter and used the flame to look around the tent. He was the only one there.

Suddenly he was wide awake. He stood up awkwardly, teetering for a moment, trying to decide what to do. From the gentle movement of the tent flaps he could tell that the wind was still blowing, although not as hard as earlier. Cavanaugh stepped into his shoes and stumbled outside.

It was still cloudy and dark, although the moon had drifted to another part of the sky. The wet night air had a bracing effect against Cavanaugh's face; slowly he realized that he was cold. He looked around. The camp was asleep; even the generator had been shut down. There was only the sound of the wind blowing eerily in the trees.

"Ready, Cavanaugh?"

He jerked instinctively, as if he had been given an electrical shock.

"Jesus Christ!" he stammered; Conti had startled the hell out of him. "Where were you?"

"Taking a leak; why?" Conti appeared as calm as ever.

"God, you scared me."

"Sorry. Take it easy," he intoned reassuringly. "Let's get ready. It's almost time."

He studied Cavanaugh for a moment. "Where are your clothes?"

"In the tent."

"Time to change. Take only what I told you," said Conti. "Vaclav will take care of the rest. We'll pick everything up tomorrow."

Cavanaugh nodded. He slipped the oversized civilian clothes over his Army uniform. It made him look bulky, but he guessed that it didn't matter what he looked like; who in the hell was going to see him, anyway? He reached back into his duffel bag and pulled out the black Geiger counter from Los Alamos; then he inserted the two 300-volt batteries and stuffed the rectangular metal box into one of his pockets. He was ready.

"And your pistol. Don't forget that."

Cavanaugh reached back into his bag and pulled it out. He wasn't even sure it was loaded.

"I think it's empty."

Conti reached over and grabbed it, then flipped open the chamber. A .38 shell fell into his hand.

He calmly reinserted it and shook his head. "You're okay." He handed it back to Cavanaugh. "Next time, be sure the safety is on when you're traveling, okay?"

He seemed to take a deep breath, then said quietly, "Time to go." Cavanaugh hesitated, uncertain of precisely where they were going. He had seen the map, all right, and he knew they were headed due east, but that was about it. He had no choice but to stick closely to Conti and the German, wherever the hell they went.

"You won't be able to bring anything back with you. Nothing big, anyway. It's too dangerous if we're caught."

Cavanaugh fingered the Geiger counter in his pocket.

Conti saw him do it and offered some advice. "Drop that if you have to. It could tell the Russians more than they need to know, okay?"

Cavanaugh nodded. How in the hell did Conti even know what a Geiger counter was? Now he was convinced that the man knew much more than he was telling.

"I've got a camera," Conti said, "for documentation." He took a last look around.

"Okay, this way," he said. "Talk only when it's necessary, and then only in whispers. And stick close by; if we separate over there"—he pointed with his hand toward the Soviet Zone—"you're on your own."

On his own! The words frightened him. He felt himself trembling inside. "If that happens," he asked, "if we get separated, what do I do?"

"You're on a direct line with Wanfried. Follow the road back—you'll see which one—and travel at night if you can. If it looks like you're gonna get caught, dump the old clothes. Remember, pretend you got lost."

"Right," said Cavanaugh; he felt that his voice was lost in the wind.

They walked for ten minutes along a dirt road with deep ruts that ran like a railroad track into the darkness. It was remarkably quiet except for the occasional rustle of the wind. Intermittently, Conti used his flashlight for brief moments when the clouds covered the half-moon. It went on and off like a flashbulb, its beam always pointed downward.

A large, bulky shape loomed in front of them. Conti grabbed his arm and pulled him near. "This is it," he whispered. He gently tugged Cavanaugh off the road.

The dark shape was a house. At first, Cavanaugh worried that it might be inhabited, but then, as they got closer, he could see that its roof and windows were missing. Blown away in an explosion. Conti crept along the wall of the building until they reached the side that couldn't be seen from the road. He motioned for Cavanaugh to stop.

"We're on the Soviet side," he said softly. "Rudi's gonna go ahead and check out the truck."

Cavanaugh suddenly realized that he hadn't seen Rudi for five or ten minutes.

It was cold, and for the first time he was grateful for the extra layer of clothes. When the clouds were right, there was just enough moonlight to make out ghostly images. He could see Conti next to him, and a partially destroyed wooden fence a few feet away. He could tell that Conti was looking at his watch dial from the position of his hand.

The man stood up. Cavanaugh started to rise, but then felt Conti's hand on his shoulder; he stopped and froze in a half-squat. Suddenly, shafts of light shot out of Conti's hand, then stopped, then started again, three times. He was obviously signaling someone with his flashlight. From somewhere in the distance, a circle of light flashed back three times.

"It's okay," whispered Conti. "Come on."

Cavanaugh quietly stood up and followed Conti as he moved toward the source of the light. Moments later he could make out the shape of a truck and then a man, standing near the hood. Cavanaugh held back and let Conti go first; there was an exchange in German. It was Rudi.

"In the truck. Hurry," said Conti. He grabbed Cavanaugh's arm. "Rudi says the Russians have a night patrol in the area. We ain't got time to kill."

Cavanaugh got into the cab of an ancient truck whose seat had long ago been replaced with simple wooden slats. The entire back of the truck had been removed, so that there was only a flatbed. Rudi got in the driver's side and Conti sat on the other. Cavanaugh was sandwiched in between the two men. The motor choked and stalled, and then started noisily. They took off, bouncing and shaking as they hit rocks and holes in the road. The headlights were hooded and partially covered so that only a downward slit of light escaped to illuminate a dozen or so feet in front of them. Cavanaugh's heart was beating hard; the engine noise seemed incredibly loud. How could anyone nearby not hear it?

Rudi and Conti didn't seem concerned. "We must stay on this road," whispered Rudi in his German-accented English.

"It now will take longer."

Cavanaugh gripped the edge of the wooden slat to steady himself as they bounced around over the back road. Conti and Rudi talked softly in German, both men instinctively speaking in tones just loud enough to be heard across the cabin.

"What are you talking about?" asked Cavanaugh.

"The Russians," said Conti. "They've blocked off the main road into Wanfried, but it's only a small contingent of men."

"There are others," said Rudi without further explanation.

"Where?" asked Conti.

"A small force is in Mühlhausen. But it is expected that they will reinforce the border very soon."

185

"Are they closing the border?" asked Cavanaugh. The newspapers had talked about the division of Germany for administrative purposes only.

"Consolidation," said Conti. "They are controlling access to and from their Zone."

Cavanaugh had turned his head halfway to see Conti, but out of the corner of his eye he caught a form, a flicker of a shape, like an animal, dart in front of the headlights. Suddenly there was a loud thump and the truck bounced slightly. Rudi instantly pulled his foot off the accelerator and slowed down.

"What in the hell was that?" said Cavanaugh excitedly. "An animal?"

Rudi pulled over and stopped the truck by the side of the road. He glanced over at Conti, who opened the door and, like Rudi, got out. Cavanaugh got out as well; he didn't want to be left alone. When he reached the others, he asked again, "What was it?"

Conti flicked on his flashlight for an instant. In that brief moment, the light fell on the writhing figure of an old man. Blood was oozing from the side of his head.

"Oh, Jesus," whispered Cavanaugh. They had hit an old man!

Without saying a word, Rudi lifted the man up and placed one arm under his chin and the other behind his head. Then, with a violent twist, he snapped the old man's neck. There was a discernable crack that could be heard over the dull sound of the truck motor.

Cavanaugh was so shocked that he just stared as Rudi pulled the body into the trees.

Conti rushed up and grabbed his arm. "Come on!"

Rudi re-emerged, looking calm and in control. "He was drinking," he said simply. "He felt nothing."

Cavanaugh had never seen anything like this before. He jerked himself free of Conti's grip and started for the trees.

"Get back in the truck," ordered Conti.

Cavanaugh shook his head. "No. That man . . . ?"

"He's dead," said Conti, "and we're losing time. Get in the goddamn truck!"

"I don't believe this," Cavanaugh mumbled. There was nothing he could do. He started to get in the cab of the truck, then hesitated.

Conti literally pushed him in. Hard. Cavanaugh knocked his knee on the gearshift; he struggled to straighten himself on the wooden seat. Conti got in next to him and slammed the door shut.

Cavanaugh started to say something, to protest, but Conti interrupted him. "Forget about the old man. It's too bad, but at least now he can't talk. It's over, understand?"

All Cavanaugh could think about was the old man, squirming in pain on the ground, blood coming out of his head. And the sound of the neck breaking, like the crack of a broken twig.

"It is near," said Rudi.

Conti sat up on the rough wooden seat and felt the inside of his jacket. Cavanaugh could tell his was checking for his gun.

"We'll park and hide the truck," he whispered, "then hike the rest of the way."

Chapter Seventeen

The forest was dark but loosely wooded. It thinned even further and at last they broke through the trees to the edge; Conti held up his hand to stop. Ahead of them was a large clearing and, within it, vague, boxlike shapes that alternately appeared and disappeared as the clouds passed over the moon. It was the Nazi laboratory.

Cavanaugh was still trembling, not from the cold, but from the shock of the accident and the murder of the old man. His stomach churned.

He knew he had to pull himself together long enough to do what he had come to do and get back home. To Los Alamos. To Christine. His friends.

The cluster of buildings was in a broad clearing, not far from a low ridge that jutted out of the otherwise level ground. Cavanaugh tried to orient the buildings according to the aerial photographs he had seen earlier in the evening but got confused. There wasn't enough moonlight to make out clearly each of the buildings. He saw Conti motioning to the German to circle around.

"Come on," he said softly in Cavanaugh's ear, "we'll go this way."

Conti took the lead, always staying slightly within the rim of forest trees, and stepping carefully to avoid small bushes and rocks. The buildings looked deserted, although in the darkness it was impossible to be certain; at least there were no lights and no trucks or jeeps. Cavanaugh turned around once to check on Rudi, but the man had disappeared.

Slowly, they edged their way to the outermost building. Several times Conti quickly flicked his flashlight on and off in order to check something in their path. When they reached the exterior wall, Conti stopped and pulled Cavanaugh close to him.

"Be careful," he whispered, "and be prepared to run like hell."

Cavanaugh could feel the man's warm breath on his face. Where was he supposed to run? Back into the forest, to the truck? But before he could ask, Conti moved away, creeping along the wall toward the corner of the building. The clouds cleared momentarily and the shape of other buildings coalesced into view in the cool blue-gray light of the moon.

Cavanaugh cursed silently. Conti was moving quickly now, almost darting; in a flash, he disappeared around the corner. From somewhere nearby there was a soft grating sound, like an old door hinge. Cavanaugh held his breath and peered carefully around the corner: Conti wasn't there. He stepped around and saw a window and a partially opened door. Beyond that were more windows that ran the length of the structure. The wooden building, still new-smelling, was much larger than Cavanaugh had first thought.

He made his way to the door, hesitated, then peered in: a dark shape was shifting in the interior shadows, making small crunches on the wooden plank floor as it moved.

"Conti?" he whispered.

The moving stopped, then started again. Suddenly someone grabbed his arm hard.

"Shut the hell up!" hissed Conti. Then closer, in his ear: "Don't talk until we're sure we're alone." Carefully, the small man relaxed his tight grip. Cavanaugh could still feel his skin burning through the layers of clothing.

Cavanaugh stood dumbly by the doorway, feeling himself sweating inexplicably in the cold night air. Twice he saw Conti's flashlight click on, the angle of the beam always low, toward the floor. Then he heard the man walk slowly back to the doorway.

"This place is empty. Nothing," he said. "Let's check the next one."

Cavanaugh felt his anxiety rise again. "When do I get to look around?" he asked quietly.

"When we know we're alone" was the reply.

They found a second building, a smaller one, that was also empty. They were on their way to a third when Conti suddenly stopped and pulled Cavanaugh roughly against the wall of the building. It was amazing how much strength the smaller man had.

Cavanaugh strained but at first couldn't see or hear anything but the distant rustling of wind in the trees. Then he heard it: footsteps on newly turned earth. It was a soft, snapping sound. His heart started to race and he sucked his breath in sharply, holding it so he wouldn't make a noise.

Conti pulled his gun and held it against his chest.

"Conti?"

Cavanaugh relaxed; it was Rudi.

Before either man knew it, the German was standing next to them. "We are alone," he said simply. "But nearby there are Russians."

"Where?" asked Conti.

Cavanaugh could see Rudi point toward the ridge.

"Perhaps half a kilometer away. I think several trucks. And the tire marks on the ground here are very fresh. From yesterday maybe."

Conti turned to Cavanaugh. "How fast can you work?"

"As fast as I can. But I need to see what's inside these buildings, what kind of equipment. And the pit. I need to see that, too."

"Okay," Conti said. "Let's move it. Rudi, keep watch."

Cavanaugh looked toward the horizon, which was still dark; dawn, at least, was not imminent.

He and Conti headed for the third building, which, like the first they had seen, was long and narrow, although taller than the others. Conti entered first and reconnoitered. Then he signaled with his flashlight that it was safe for Cavanaugh to look around.

The building apparently had served as a chemistry laboratory; there was just enough glass reagent and piping equipment to suggest that. There was, however, no particular clue to the purpose of the lab, just a hodgepodge of hurriedly abandoned equipment.

Cavanaugh moved slowly through the building, letting his light play on the tables and equipment. Suddenly, in a second, larger room, it revealed a series of metal frames, as tall as himself, and several large

190

metal pipes standing vertically within the racks. Dozens of other similar pipes lay clustered on the ground.

There was a different smell in this room, not chemical like the last, but more industrial. For one thing, Cavanaugh could tell that the room had been heavily heated: there was that lingering smell of high temperatures operating for many hours, or days.

He was studying the industrial-grade pipes when a thought hit him. With his free hand he extricated his Geiger counter from his pocket and put on the headset. It was just a thought, but it was worth checking out. He flipped the switch on the counter.

It went wild in his ear!

For a moment he didn't move. Then he played the counter along the standing pipes: the clicking intensified. The sound lessened as he moved over to the stacks of horizontal pipes, when it shot up again.

He focused his flashlight on a pipe that had been cut in half lengthways. Inside was an electrical wire of some kind.

There was only one explanation. These pipes—there had to be hundreds of them—were a crude plant for enriching uranium. The process was known as thermal diffusion, and the lingering radioactivity indicated by his Geiger counter meant that the pipes had been used!

Could he believe what he was hearing? His Geiger counter told him these pipes were radioactive, but not to what degree. It could be dangerous here. Very dangerous!

Cavanaugh searched his memory. Thermal diffusion had been discovered by a Swede around the turn of the century; but German scientists had greatly improved the process before the war. Cavanaugh even remembered the names of the scientists: Clusius and Dickel. And now he was looking at a direct application of that pre-war process.

Numbed by his discoveries, he hurried outside to join Conti; he knew he could say nothing about this to him or to anyone else. The specter of the German atomic bomb suddenly loomed very large.

The fourth building contained heavy-metal-working equipment, including lathes and presses. The rear half of the two-story room contained a large brick oven that could have been used for small smelting jobs. A pile of coal seemed to confirm that. And dumped on the floor were heavy cast-iron molds.

Some of the machinery was partially disassembled and stacked on the concrete floor, as if someone intended to come back and pick it up.

Sometime soon. A half-eaten apple, not more than a day old, lay nearby. Conti saw it too.

"Russians?" whispered Cavanaugh.

"Probably."

Cavanaugh played his flashlight around. There was no doubt that this equipment had been used. There was grease on the machines and the floor was scarred where equipment had been moved and singed black where hot or burning objects had lain.

He studied the molds, which were attached to long handles. They also showed use.

Cavanaugh quickly pulled out his Geiger counter again and held one of the earphone speakers to his ear. Then he flipped the switch and moved toward the mold. Once again, the clicking went wild.

Undoubtedly, the Germans had used the molds with radioactive material.

He flipped off the switch and stuffed the counter back into his pocket to avoid interest from Conti. He actually felt himself shaking slightly as he stood there.

This room—like the last—and everything in it was radioactively hot! There was no telling how contaminated, but even the air they breathed could be poisonous. He couldn't stay here a second longer than necessary!

Scared, and fighting back an urge to run out, he hurriedly looked around.

The Geiger counter told him only that the molds had once held radioactive material, not what kind. But there was little doubt in his mind: it had to be uranium.

He studied the molds with his flashlight. They had been crafted to create metal cylinders of various diameters and depths. Cavanaugh took quick measurements with a canvas tape measure and made notes on a small notepad. Later, he could calculate whether the general dimensions would be sufficient to produce a supercritical mass of uranium. Assuming two similar pieces were rapidly brought together, of course.

As soon as he stepped outside, he took a deep breath of air, closing his eyes as he did so. Like a child, he wanted it all to go away when he opened them again.

"You okay?" asked Conti.

Cavanaugh nodded. They needed to get out of this whole complex as soon as possible. Ditch their clothes and shower.

192

Conti sensed Cavanaugh's concern. "What's wrong?"

"The lab," said Cavanaugh, "it's contaminated. Dangerous."

"Radioactivity?"

Cavanaugh gave up worrying about security.

"Yeah," he said quietly.

The other small buildings were offices and living quarters for maybe several dozen men. In one room, heavy-metal file cabinets were open and empty. Desk drawers had been pulled out and thrown to the floor. Cavanaugh couldn't tell if the building had been hastily vacated by the Germans, along with anything of importance, or if it had been recently ransacked by the Russians.

Rudi rejoined them as they walked to the largest of the buildings, which appeared to sit at the edge of the complex. Cavanaugh guessed it to be maybe twenty feet high and maybe fifty or sixty feet long.

Beyond it, in the distance, he thought he could make out the faintest line of light on the horizon. Dawn couldn't be more than a half hour away. There wasn't much time.

The building was one large room.

Conti pointed his flashlight at the ceiling. "Look," he said. "A hoist and pulley. Designed to lift and move something very heavy."

Cavanaugh walked over to a pile of crates and poked around. All were empty. Their surfaces, however, indicated that they had been constructed recently and had never been used. The wooden slats still smelled fresh.

Cavanaugh started to walk away when his flashlight caught some lettering on the side of one box. He knelt down and studied it.

The stenciled words were in English. Part of the first line—a proper name—was blurred under a smear of paint, but the rest said "Imports, Ltd." And underneath, in slightly larger letters, were the words "Typhoo Tea." What in the hell did this mean? he wondered. With his flashlight he checked out each of the other boxes; none of them had similar lettering. A few had numbers stenciled on their sides, although neither the numbers nor their sequence seemed to suggest anything more than some kind of identification system.

Cavanaugh stood up and thought for a moment. The boxes were too new to have been salvaged, and it was unlikely that the Russians would have hauled them here from another location. So what were the Germans doing with them? From the other side of the room he heard Conti call his name.

"Over here," said the voice. In the emptiness of the large room the whispered words echoed gently. Cavanaugh headed toward Conti's beam of light.

"What?" he asked.

"I found some papers."

"Where?"

Conti shone his flashlight on a workbench attached to one wall. "There," he said, "stuffed in the rear of that drawer. The Russians must have missed them."

"What are they?" If they were scientific or technical, they might answer a lot of questions.

Conti hesitated for a moment. He flipped through the small stack page by page. "I'm not sure," he mumbled. He handed some sheets to Cavanaugh.

Cavanaugh could tell they weren't scientific. Instead, they looked like bills of lading. He could make out the German words for "railroad" and "delivery schedule," as well as recognize the names of several German cities.

"My guess is they're shipping or delivery orders."

"Probably. But look at this." He handed Cavanaugh a sheet of paper.

The first thing he noticed were the words *Streng Geheim* stamped in large letters at the top. German for "top secret." It was a typewritten letter, with some numerical information in the text; but it was on the stationery of the Krupps Armaments Works in Essen. Another word he recognized was *Geschützrohr*, the German word for "gun barrel." Cavanaugh felt something click inside his head.

"Is this about artillery barrels?" he asked. Somehow, he felt he knew the answer.

Conti scanned it and nodded. "Yeah. About delivery to some experimental group. Part of the SS, I think."

Cavanaugh let out a soft whistle. He remembered the aerial photographs and the trucks that had been identified as having been SS vehicles.

"The language is vague," added Conti, "but it looks like they made, no, they *delivered*, six 'special' 150-mm cannon barrels in February. Or maybe the word is 'modified' artillery barrels."

"Six? Jesus!" Now they had to consider the possibility that the Germans had six atomic bombs! He folded the paper and stuck it in his notepad. "Let's find that pit."

194

As they stepped outside, Cavanaugh noticed that the sky was changing colors at the horizon. The buildings, the trees, everything around them was becoming more distinct. He looked at his watch: it was a quarter after five.

Cavanaugh began to get a better sense of the layout. All the buildings were temporary at best; all were made of wood with tar-paper roofs. As far as he could tell, the buildings seemed fairly close to one another, except for the chemistry lab, which was farther out than most. The buildings were linked by dirt roads and small footpaths. Trees had been left between buildings, perhaps to help camouflage them from the air.

Fifty feet away, barely visible in the pre-dawn light, was a small ridge, maybe a foot high, of shoveled dirt. Jesus! He prayed that this was the goddamn pit he was looking for.

Light was now flooding across the sky from the horizon like water suddenly released from a dam. Cavanaugh remembered a childhood prayer, something he always used to utter when he was at bat or before anything important. Sometimes he repeated it so often that it became a chant: *Jesus, Mary, and Joseph; Jesus, Mary, and Joseph; Jesus!*

The mysterious pit, the rough circle that before now he had seen only in photographs was much deeper and more irregular than he could have guessed. The hole had been scraped out of the earth by a bulldozer and the dirt pushed crudely to the sides to clear the depression itself. It took several seconds for Cavanaugh to realize that the gun barrels weren't there!

"Oh, shit," he said, "where the hell are they?"

Conti just stared.

Cavanaugh felt slightly faint, even a little nauseous. Nothing really mattered but the barrels.

Conti started walking around the pit. "Wait!" he shouted. "They've been moved. Dragged. Look." He pointed toward a series of ruts that ran from the bottom of the pit up one side and over the berm.

Cavanaugh muttered his prayer again: *Jesus, Mary, and Joseph!* Suddenly, there they were: three long black pipes, laid neatly side by side.

"The Russians," mumbled Conti. He bent down and plied loose dirt off one end of the nearest barrel. "See," he said, "it's moist. That means it was moved in the last day or so."

Cavanaugh bent down to study the closest one.

"We don't have much time," reminded Conti. They no longer had the protection of night.

Cavanaugh studied the breech end; with its loading handle and lock it looked to him like a conventional weapon. It wasn't until he walked to the other end that he saw that the muzzle had been covered with a different type of metal, cylindrical in shape, but larger in diameter than the barrel itself. And maybe a foot long. It looked as if it had come from the molds inside the laboratory building.

The device was attached with screw-in bolts but looked as if it could be easily removed. And the barrel itself looked like it had been cut in half and reassembled. For shipment, thought Cavanaugh, that had to be it.

Oh, Holy Mother. Now that he could see it up close, instead of in a photograph, even touch it, the weapon took on more of the characteristic of Little Boy. The oversized cylinder on the end of the barrel had to be a tamper, a thick metal "shield" used to "reflect" neutrons back into the uranium.

"Got a knife?" he asked Conti.

The man nodded and handed him a pocket knife.

Using one of the blades as a screwdriver, Cavanaugh managed to remove the bolts. He pulled the cylinder off the barrel and let it drop to the ground. It had to weigh over a hundred pounds.

The cylindrical piece of metal—it was at least twelve inches in diameter—was hollow and undoubtedly intended to hold another cylinder inside. In Little Boy, the smaller cylinder would be the "target" half of the uranium. And unless Cavanaugh missed his guess, this metal bucket was uranium.

Cavanaugh took a deep breath. This was an atomic bomb. Unsophisticated and basic, but with the essential features of the Los Alamos gun bomb—it was like its cousin.

Cavanaugh couldn't tell from the weight of the metal if it was uranium. It could be lead, or maybe some combination of metals. Maybe it was just a prototype made by the bomb's designers as a device for taking measurements. Surely the Germans wouldn't have left this much uranium behind? If so, its value was incalculable!

With the knife, he made a deep V-shaped scratch—the metal was soft enough for that—and extracted a sliver of material. It had the consistency and tensile qualities of lead. He folded a piece of paper from his notepad around it and stuck it between two pages; it was the

196

most protection against radioactivity that he could manage right now. Later, he could have Los Alamos analyze it. That would tell them not only if it was uranium, but its purity.

Cavanaugh sat back on his haunches, trying to assess what he'd found.

There were a lot of questions. If this was a tamper—and it had all the characteristics of one—where were the uranium target and projectile pieces? And what about a source of neutrons? Polonium, for example? This would make a nuclear explosion more probable, certainly more efficient.

The indentation in the middle of the barrel was apparently where it could be disassembled into two pieces. Again, to make the entire weapon more transportable.

Conti evidently had been watching him. "Something important here? New type of weapon?"

Cavanaugh nodded. "Possibly."

As quickly as he could, he began to take measurements: total length of barrel; diameter of bore; dimensions of outer metal sleeve.

"The camera," he ordered.

Conti took a Leica out of his pocket and handed it to Cavanaugh, who took it and began a series of close-up photographs. He paid particular attention to breech and muzzle ends and the heavy piece of metal on the ground. He also photographed the other two barrels, none of which had a metal attachment.

There was probably other useful evidence in the laboratories or buildings, but no time to go back. There was, however, enough in the pit to tell Groves what the man wanted to know.

Thank God, Cavanaugh thought, the Germans got these weapons too late to use them.

Conti gestured to Rudi to join them. Cavanaugh could hear birds chirping in the nearby trees. Dawn was here.

He had one last thing to do. He wanted to measure each of the remaining barrels just to be sure that they were identical to the first. He bent down with his folding ruler when he heard the two men talking.

"Rudi says we have to leave. It's not safe to stay around here."

"Okay," said Cavanaugh. He made notes in his pad, then saw the shipping order in German from Krupps. Suddenly he remembered the data it contained.

Six artillery barrels! Krupps had delivered *six* barrels, but there were only three here.

He turned to Conti. "There's only three here!"

"What?"

"Only three barrels. The shipping orders said six. There's only three here."

Cavanaugh jumped up and looked around. There was nothing else in sight and the sun was just over the edge of the horizon. He could see clearly for hundreds of yards.

"The Russians have them?"

Conti shrugged. He wasn't sure what Cavanaugh was so worked up about.

"We gotta go," he said. "Now!"

"We've got to find the other barrels. See if they're here."

Rudi said something.

"No. We need to *leave*, goddamn it!" Conti grabbed his arm.

"Okay," he said slowly. He took one last look at the three dark cylinders.

Jesus, Mary, and Joseph.

Chapter Eighteen

avanaugh was no more than six feet behind Conti and the German when the noise reached them. It was faint at first, no more than a rumble, but increasingly it became the sound of a truck motor. Somewhere nearby.

All three men froze for a moment, glancing one way, then the other in order to pinpoint the source. But it was too vague still, and the buildings could be reflecting the sound from a number of directions.

"Hurry!" said Conti. For the first time in two days, his voice had a trace of fear in it. He and Rudi started to run.

Dear God! prayed Cavanaugh. They were so close to safety; the truck was less than a mile away, the border eight or nine. And now they could be caught! No danger, he remembered Conti saying, and yet why was the little son of a bitch running like hell?

The three of them stopped at the chemistry building and flattened themselves against its wall. The German edged his way down to one corner, Conti to the opposite end; the noise from the truck was louder.

Cavanaugh saw Conti cautiously stick his head around and then bring it back; he turned to the others. He didn't speak the word, but his lips said, "Nothing."

But the sound grew louder. Cavanaugh felt himself tighten involuntarily all over; he clenched his hands and pressed his head back against the wood-slat wall. He shot quick glances at both Conti and Rudi: both men were frozen where they stood, stealing a look only by moving quarter-inch by quarter-inch.

Conti motioned him over. Taking a deep breath, Cavanaugh crept down the side of the building until he was inches away from Conti's head.

"It's a goddamn Russian truck," Conti whispered. "It just pulled up."

"Where?"

"Other side. A mile, maybe three-quarters, away. The sonnavabitch is just sitting there with the motor running."

Cavanaugh could see that Conti was sweating heavily. The motor noise shifted, then began to fade.

"The sonnavabitch is leaving," murmured Conti. "He's pulling around."

Cavanaugh felt the pressure in his chest ease a little. Maybe they were going to make it out after all.

Conti took a deep breath and sighed. "That was goddamn close."

Rudi walked over and joined them. "I think he was lost maybe."

Conti nodded. "I only saw two guys in the truck. You see more?"

Rudi shook his head.

"Probably lost," repeated Conti meekly. "We'll give them five minutes and then get the hell outta here."

Cavanaugh looked at his watch: it was almost six o'clock. The sun was already over the horizon. Bit by bit the shadows were receding as the yellow-red globe lifted. He could feel its warmth penetrating through the layers of clothes. His notepad and the Leica were still gripped tightly in his right hand.

Before he did anything else, he rewound the film into its canister and took it out of the camera. He put the film and his notepad into his pocket and gave the camera back to Conti.

Conti nudged him. "Let's get out of here."

Rudi took the lead. Conti followed and Cavanaugh took up the rear. Every few minutes he turned around and looked to see if anyone was following. He saw no one. The complex of wood buildings grew smaller and smaller.

There were just at the edge of the forest when the first shot was fired.

At first, Cavanaugh didn't know what it was. Then he heard a second shot. Then dozens. Somewhere above him, a tree branch shattered and fell to the ground. Bullets began to prick the canopy of foliage, making a sharp whistling sound as they did.

When he turned around, still moving forward, he saw four or five small figures standing near one of the laboratory buildings. They had rifles in their hands. Where in the hell had they come from?

"Holy shit!" he yelled.

Ahead of him, Rudi and Conti had also turned to look; they hesitated only a moment—just long enough to see the shots came from Russian soldiers—and then started running again through the trees.

"Don't stop!" yelled Conti.

Cavanaugh ran as fast as he could; he knew the deeper they penetrated the forest, the less visible they would be. But then what?

Breathing hard, his heart pounding, he saw Rudi and Conti stop and fall behind some dense bushes. When he caught up, they were on their knees staring wide-eyed through breaks in the foliage.

Rudi said something in German. Conti nodded, and before Cavanaugh could say anything the man took off to the right, into the heart of the forest.

"Where's he going?" said Cavanaugh, saying each word between deep breaths.

"He can't afford to be caught. He's taking off on his own. He'll catch up later."

"What about the truck?"

"Useless. Those guys could radio ahead. The road's too dangerous."

"What'll we do?"

"Stay in the forest. Put some distance between us and them."

"Won't they come after us?"

Conti had a wild look in his eyes. He shook his head. "Don't know. They probably think we're Germans. Scavengers."

Cavanaugh felt relieved. At least they wouldn't wonder what Americans were doing poking around. He smiled nervously.

"Don't relax," said Conti sharply. "If they think we're Germans, they'll shoot to kill."

Cavanaugh wanted to cry. It was all too much. He wanted to say something to Conti but couldn't find the words. Shout some obscenity. Why was all this happening?

There wasn't time. Nearby they heard a truck approach: the same grinding sound that all Russian trucks seemed to make.

"Shit!" said Conti. "We're too close to the road."

The truck stopped. Voices drifted through the trees.

Conti put a finger to his lips. Then he pointed straight ahead, presumbably in the direction of the American Zone. He pulled Cavanaugh over by his shoulder and whispered.

"That's where we're going," he said. "We're splitting up. You're on your own."

Cavanaugh broke loose and jerked back. "What?" he hissed.

Conti was already up.

Cavanaugh was so surprised that he just sat there, watching Conti disappear into the trees. Then the voices got louder and the shooting started again. Automatic-weapons fire.

He jumped up, his heart racing again, and looked around. He knew which way to go, but was it safe? The voices grew closer. This was no time to think.

He started running. The earth crunched; small twigs and branches snapped underneath. The firing seemed to be all around him. Shadows seemed to move in the nearby bushes.

He kept running. Oblivious to the sharp pain, he tried to push away the intertwined branches as he ran. They slapped and pricked his hands and arms. The sharp, needlelike end of one caught his sleeve and jerked his hand behind his body. He could feel blood well up where the branch had cut his wrist.

He ran until he could hardly breathe; the sweat was running down his forehead and face. He could feel the layers of clothes turning wet and sticking to his skin.

When he finally stopped, he forced himself to keep walking, but had to hunch over to make breathing easier. His heart seemed ready to explode.

When the breathing eased, he tried to clear his mind. He had no idea where he was or even how close he was to the road. All he remembered was that it was a country road, one that looped north before it turned down again into Mühlhausen. The endless trees gave no sense of direction. He just had to pray that he had run more or less straight, and hadn't, in his panic, made a circle.

202

He thought about it. The only thing he could do was to drift to the left and try to pick up the road again. Stay hidden in the trees along its edge, and hopefully make his way back to the border. Cavanaugh tried to angle his direction: not immediately to the left, but at a slow angle. Enough to put him well ahead of the Russians. Assuming, of course, they were stupid enough to stay in one spot. *Jesus, Mary and Joseph!*

An hour later he found the road. At least, he *hoped* it was the same road. But he had been on it at night and there was nothing distinctive that he could remember about it.

He noticed almost immediately that the road curved and straightened, curved and straightened again. That meant he had to stay well off it, since there was no way he could see in advance a car coming in front of or behind him.

That wasn't always easy. The bushes were sometimes so dense, or the trees so close together, that he had to make frequent detours around them. Then he had to locate the road again. When the forest was relatively clear, he jogged, just enough to pick up his time but not enough to burn every ounce of energy he had left.

Cavanaugh alternated between cursing and praying. Every time a car or truck drove by he stopped and fell into a crouching position where he could watch without being seen. He was hungry and tired. And when he couldn't run anymore, he struggled to plod along, often tripping and falling. His hands were cut and bruised, his clothes soiled and torn.

It was nearly eleven when Cavanaugh reached a series of clearings and small farmhouses. He sidestepped them as best he could, always feeling that someone, behind a window, or hidden in a barn, was watching him. He expected the Russians to appear at any moment.

Actually, he saw them first.

The first time was when he saw four or five Russian soldiers interrogating a fat German woman near a farmhouse. They could be after food, wine, anything, he told himself.

The second time was when he almost walked into a clearing where a dozen tents had been set up. The beat-up trucks with red stars painted on them told him everything he needed to know.

He backtracked fifty yards and wound his way around them.

Twenty minutes later he saw something that almost made him shout.

Three jeeps were parked by the side of the road. Two were Russian, but one was American. Six or seven men were standing around, the majority wearing Soviet uniforms; they were talking and smoking cigarettes.

Cavanaugh hid behind a tree and tried to decide what to do. He didn't want to have to explain what he had been doing in the Soviet Zone, but he wanted to get out of the goddamn forest as soon as he could. He could just walk up. Or he could start a fire or something, shoot his gun, anything to create a diversion, then make a run for it. But he knew he had to decide quickly.

He peeled off his civilian clothing and kicked it into a low bush nearby, then he adjusted his uniform as best he could and tried to smooth his hair. He didn't have the faintest idea how he looked, but he didn't give a damn.

A motor turned over. The Americans were back in their jeep. *They were gonna leave without him!*

This was it. Without thinking, he stepped out from behind the tree and starting running for the group. At first, no one saw him.

Then a Russian turned around and suddenly lifted his rifle.

Cavanaugh shouted. "Hey! I'm an American!" He stopped running and started to walk. One of the Americans stood up in the jeep and stared at him.

They were fifty yards away. Several other Russians lifted their rifles and aimed them at him.

"American!" he shouted. He didn't know what to do next. Then he reached into his jacket and pulled out a pack of cigarettes. Lucky Strikes.

"American!" he shouted again.

He was now close enough to hear one of the GIs say, "What the hell?"

The Russians began to shout at him. Cavanaugh kept on walking, holding the cigarette package in his hand. One of the Russians grabbed his sleeve as he passed by.

Cavanaugh jerked it free and touched the jeep. He knew damn good and well the Russian rifles were still aimed at him.

"I got lost," he said. He could barely speak and he knew he looked like shit.

There was more conversation; everyone was talking at once.

"Who the hell are you?" someone asked in English.

"My name is Cavanaugh." He took a breath. "Captain Cavanaugh. I got lost early this morning." Without asking, he climbed into the jeep. At least now the Russians would have to shoot all of them.

Then he remembered the clothes he had thrown away. In a pocket were his notes and the roll of film.

An hour later, Cavanaugh was in a camp drinking coffee. Someone had produced scrambled eggs. He thought he had never tasted anything so good in his entire life. Someone else brought a sticky lotion to put on his cuts. One hand was wrapped in a bandage.

He was so relieved that he didn't even care that he'd lost the film and his notes. He was alive.

The group commander was on his way, a major to whom Cavanaugh would have to explain. He didn't care. He was so glad to be back that he couldn't stop grinning. Jesus, he kept saying to himself, they must think I'm crazy!

"Cavanaugh?"

He turned around and saw Conti walking toward him. He didn't have a scratch on him.

"Thank God. You made it." The man was grinning. "Tight, huh?"

Cavanaugh just stared. This son of a bitch had abandoned him back there. He gripped his metal cup so tightly that his hand started to hurt.

"Bastard!" he said.

Conti's grin faded; he smirked. "You'll live."

Part Seven

It is possible the Germans will have . . . enough
[fissionable] material accumulated to make a large number
of gadgets which they will release at the same time on
England, Russia and this country.
              —Edward Teller and Hans Bethe
        in a memorandum to Robert Oppenheimer, 1943

Chapter Nineteen

*L*ytton-Harte methodically examined each photograph, holding them delicately by the corners with his fingers. There were six of them. Dense clouds of smoke billowed from his pipe every time he inhaled.

William Canning, his assistant, tried discreetly but unsuccessfully to wave some of the smoke from his face with a small gesture of his hand. He wasn't a smoker himself and disliked the way the smell permeated everything it touched. His wife often said she could smell him coming home at the end of the day before she saw him. Unfortunately, working for the DDG meant almost constant exposure to an acrid blend of Turkish and Virginia tobaccos.

"You see," he said softly, "it was the rather unusual shapes of the canisters that first drew our attention. And then there was the weight."

Lytton-Harte raised one photograph. "These?" he asked. Canning nodded.

The photographs were of two cylindrical objects, one larger than the other. The smaller of the two appeared to be solid; the larger was almost twice as large, but hollow in the center. Clearly, the smaller cylinder was meant to go inside the larger one. A ruler placed in the foreground of each photo told Lytton-Harte that the smaller canister was six by six inches. The larger canister was approximately eight by perhaps seven inches.

"We have precise measurements," said Canning, "and weights." He glanced at his notes and read off the numbers to Lytton-Harte.

"They're not lead or some other conventional material?" the DDG asked.

"No. Their weight prohibits that. The density per unit of weight leaves only one substance."

"Uranium?"

Canning nodded. He was rather proud of the way he had handled this assignment. A week ago they had received a report from Southend about an odd discovery. A few days later they had the cylinders and companion objects in their hands in London and absolutely no idea what they were. His assignment had been to find out *what* they were—discreetly, of course—and report back. And today, less than four days later, he had the answer.

"Extraordinary," mumbled the older man. "Positively extraordinary. They're certain? Your experts?"

"Absolutely." His scientific advisors had been clear on that.

"And they're intended for a weapon of some kind?"

"It's very likely." Unfortunately, his men had been far less certain about the purpose of the cylinders.

Lytton-Harte lifted one heavy eyebrow and stared at Canning.

"You see," added Canning quickly, "the uranium is enriched—that is, not only refined, but with a larger percentage of a specific uranium isotope present." Canning felt his scientific understanding of all this was at its edge. "And the smaller piece fits the larger one exactly."

Lytton-Harte's face seem to cloud over. "What does that mean?" he asked.

"Essentially, that the uranium can be used in a weapon. Of a type we simply aren't aware of. It could well be the sort of thing the Americans are working on."

The Americans! thought Lytton-Harte. Of course. That reminded him of Philip Cavanaugh, whose name had just crossed his desk in a cable from a British agent in Germany.

"And where did they find these?"

"The port at Southend. On a fishing boat of British registry. But one that had been seized by the Germans when they captured Antwerp in 1940. It spent all of the war there. The boat was only released back to its owners in April. They, in turn, engaged a Dutch commercial fisherman to bring it back to England."

"But it had cargo?"

"Yes. There was a bill of lading attached to the cargo, you see, that the captain registered with the Harbormaster at Southend. Supposedly intended for an establishment here in London. The address was fake, and the company doesn't exist. But the Germans had obviously sought an air of authenticity."

"This wasn't planned by the owners?"

"No. They knew nothing of it. Their agreement with the Dutch captain indicates that the boat was to be returned to England as soon as possible. Nothing else."

"And you believe them?"

"There appears to be no reason to doubt them. It's an old and established company. It was apparently something the captain arranged on his own."

"And this was the entire cargo?" Lytton-Harte made a rasping sound as he inhaled his pipe; the last of his tobacco had burned down.

"No. There were a number of crates of Indian tea."

"Tea? Curious. What address did they give?"

"The address is a series of bombed-out buildings. Hit in '43. The street was, ah—" Canning checked his notes. "Carlisle Lane. A stone's throw from Lambeth Palace."

Lytton-Harte looked up from the photographs with a jerk. "Charlie's house? Extraordinary!"

The Deputy Director General, was referring to his old friend and schoolmate, the present Archbishop of Canterbury. He was the only person that Canning had ever heard the DDG refer to by his Christian name.

Lytton-Harte selected a fresh pipe from the small rack that sat on his desk. The coincidence of the false address was probably no more than that, he thought. But the proximity to his old chum was odd, even amusing, in a dark way. He had to remember to tell His Grace when next they met.

Then he remembered Philip Cavanaugh. This business had given him an idea. There was another piece of intelligence they had, something largely discountable, but it could prove helpful here.

The DDG reached over and rang his secretary on the intercom. "Get

Brooke in here, will you?" Then he looked back at Canning, who was studying his notes.

"And these experts of yours, they can be trusted? He used one brown-stained thumb to press the tobacco down in his pipe.

"I believe so. They weren't told that the uranium was German. No doubt they think it's ours."

"Good," said the DDG. Canning was a sharp one.

He lit his pipe and thought about the Americans again. "I don't believe the Americans would be forthcoming with information on their new weapon if we ask directly, do you, Canning?"

The man with the large brown eyes shook his head. As far as he was concerned, the last few months had revealed the Americans to be a thoroughly untrustworthy lot. In that, he shared the DDG's opinion fully.

"Well then, with a little luck we might trick it out of them."

He carefully placed the photographs in a file and closed it. "And you've seen the intelligence report on the Leningrad explosion?"

He referred to a new report from a source within the Soviet Union that described a large explosion a few weeks ago somewhere outside of Leningrad. Details were sketchy; some Russian sources said it was only an ammunition storage dump that accidentally caught fire and exploded. Many people had been killed; other reports said that many more were ill, as if the symptoms had been brought about by poison gases. There was the possibility that because of its size, it could be nuclear in origin.

"Yes."

"Could it be, ah, atomic?"

"Impossible to say, really. We have so little information. It may have been a large supply of mustard gas. We have had reports for years of Russian efforts in that direction."

Lytton-Harte stared at the ceiling for a moment. "Brooke might be able to help us," he said slowly.

A look of surprise crossed Canning's face. He didn't much care for Brooke. Too young, too unorthodox for his taste. Certainly not a career man.

"Ah," said Lytton-Harte, "don't despair. Our younger colleagues have their value. But you must know what it is and how to exploit it." He leaned slightly forward, as if to share a great confidence. "No word of our discovery to others, mind you."

There was a knock on the door.

"That's Brooke," said Lytton-Harte. "I'll see him alone."

Canning nodded and got up. The door opened and Christopher Brooke walked in. Both men nodded perfunctorily to each other but said nothing.

"Brooke. Good. Do sit down."

Brooke took a seat and noticed immediately that it was warm. Canning had been sitting there.

Lytton-Harte waved a cablegram at him. "You know that the American, Cavanaugh, is returning to London?"

Brooke nodded. He had seen the telegram that morning. It had come from one of their agents in Germany. As much as possible, Cavanaugh's entire journey had been tracked.

"You have any idea what the man's been up to there?"

"Not really," said Brooke. "I assume he's been with the SHAEF people."

"He told you nothing when you met? Nothing about his purpose there?"

"No." Brooke had reported all this. The DDG was up to something.

The bushy eyebrows trembled as Lytton-Harte lit his pipe again; he inhaled deeply several times to get the tobacco burning uniformly.

"Did you know that before he left London, ah, the last time, he had several suspicious telephone calls? Very oblique language, setting up meetings in parks, that sort of thing."

Brooke looked surprised.

"Yes, indeed. We 'dropped in' on his calls, you see. Rather interesting. This chap he met in the park. An American. With their Office of Strategic Services."

Brooke didn't respond. He did remember, however, that the Americans had an intelligence operation known as ALSOS. Perhaps Cavanaugh was associated with that.

"He also dropped out of sight for several days in Germany. Did you know *that?*"

Brooke vaguely remembered another cable from one of their intelligence sources. It noted that Cavanaugh had broken away from the special SHAEF scientific team. At the time, Brooke hadn't made much of it.

"Well," said Lytton-Harte testily, "he did. Several days. And we have no idea where he was."

Brooke just sat there. The DDG rarely asked a question because he wanted an answer.

Lytton-Harte, however, chose not to pursue Cavanaugh's mysterious trip. Instead he changed the subject.

"You've seen the report from Southend? The one on the uranium canisters?"

Brooke hadn't actually read the report, just glanced at it in transit from Canning to Lytton-Harte. It was a common trick he used to stay abreast of inter-office traffic, although he could hardly afford to acknowledge it.

"No," he said.

Lytton-Harte stared at him for a moment. "Ah, quite a remarkable discovery." He explained.

Brooke was surprised. He knew about the uranium discovery, but not that it could be part of a weapon. *That* was news.

"You see, Brooke, we now have something your American friend can help us with. What do you think his schedule will be when he arrives here?"

Brooke repeated what the DDG no doubt already knew. "As I understand it," he said, "Cavanaugh is returning to London today. Probably to catch a flight back to the States."

"Yes," said Lytton-Harte, "I think that's likely." Smoke billowed up to the ceiling. Brooke noticed that the bowl of the pipe was shaped like a lion's head.

"But he may not get out," said Brooke. I understand we're in for a bit of foul weather."

The Deputy Director took several large puffs on his intricately carved pipe and turned to stare out of his window. Finally he mumbled, "Is he approachable?"

Brooke was confused. "For what, sir?"

Lytton-Harte continued to stare silently at the lighted window. The morning sun now illuminated his profile as well as the dense mass of wiry white hair above his forehead. In that light, Brooke thought the head looked like the bust of a Roman emperor.

"I mean," Lytton-Harte rumbled, as his voice slowly picked up volume, "can we persuade him to talk to us about, ah, sensitive matters?"

Brooke thought for a moment. The "we" probably meant himself. "I don't know, really. He seems perfectly straightforward. Very American in that respect."

Being straightforward was something Brooke had come to associate with most of the Americans he had met at Harvard and during the war. They had a lively, almost naive quality that let them say what they meant. At least, most of the time. It was frequently disarming, sometimes off-putting, at least until one learned that it wasn't intended as an offense. It was mostly a matter of style: informal. And rather different from the circumspection so artfully practiced by his countrymen.

"Yes," said Lytton-Harte, "American. Indeed." He opened his file again and reread the brief intelligence report.

"Can we trust him to keep, ah, information to himself? Information we might give him? I mean about the Southend discovery."

So that was it. The fog lifted briefly on Lytton-Harte's machinations. He wanted Cavanaugh to confirm that the uranium cylinders were the components of a bomb. An atomic bomb. Clever, but not likely, thought Brooke, who said so.

"No. And once he leaves Britain, he's out of our reach. But I'm not sure he'd tell us anything anyway. Secrecy and all." Cavanaugh had been scrupulous the night the two of them had drinks together.

The Deputy General pondered this a moment. "Then it's a gamble. Is it possible to intercept him? At the American air base, I mean."

"Only if he stays over. Even then, it would be difficult to talk with him at an American air base." Brooke paused. "If, indeed, we want to talk to him at all."

More smoke rose from the lion's head. "Oh yes, I think we shall want to talk with him." He motioned generously but slowly with his hand. Brooke had never known Lytton-Harte to move quickly. "He might just help us with our little discovery."

Brooke wondered how likely that was. After all, he would be asked to reveal—directly or indirectly—some aspects of his work in Los Alamos. That would be asking too much.

"Well then," said Lytton-Harte, "we need to lure him away from his colleagues. And we need luck."

"Luck, sir?"

"Yes. A delay perhaps, bad weather, something that keeps the good Dr. Cavanaugh in London for a day or two." He took several long puffs on his lion's-head pipe. "See what you can do. We'll talk again."

Lytton-Harte watched Brooke leave. The heavy door shut and once again he was alone in his great office.

Could Brooke be talked into staying with the Service after the war? he wondered. So many men were leaving, or talking about it; the air was positively thick with chatter about a return to normalcy. Only the

Japs to give the final thrash to and all that. Ah well, how many of them, Brooke included, knew—really knew—what was ahead? Not many, he ventured, but then, that was typical of the young: naive and idealistic. Once, a long time ago, he might have felt the same way.

His reverie was broken by a single sharp ring of his telephone.

"Yes?" he said gruffly. It was his secretary, Mrs. Morley.

"You said to remind you about your appointment this afternoon with Major Kaluzny."

"Who?"

"The military attaché with the Soviet Embassy."

"Yes. Good. When?"

"Thirty minutes. Shall I have tea brought in?"

Lytton-Harte thought a minute. "No," he said, "best not to encourage him to stay."

"Right."

He started to hang up when suddenly he thought of something else.

"Mrs. Morley?" he shouted, hoping to catch her.

"You needn't shout," she said calmly, her voice crackling over the antiquated telephone. Little bothered her these days; she had lost both her husband and her home during the blitz in 1940.

"Ah, yes, well, see that I'm not disturbed for a bit, will you?"

He hung up and reached over to unlock his desk file. Then he unlocked a second lid, a metal one, and withdrew a small folder. Inside were a collection of Ultra intercepts he'd gathered during the last few months of the war.

Each page—there were several dozen—was stamped "Most Secret," and had come from the Ultra cryptographers at Bletchley Park outside of London. Each sheet contained decoded German military or diplomatic transmissions.

Each one vaguely resembled a telegram, with several lines of data identifying where at Bletchley the decrypt had been made, to whom it was sent, the date and time, and the intelligence priority ranking, which indicated its urgency.

Lytton-Harte had assembled this small collection during the spring. Within MI5, only he and the Director General were authorized to see the Ultra material, undoubtedly the most valuable source of intelligence they had.

This particular file contained all the Ultra references to German sabotage or reprisal activities in Britain, real or threatened, that had been generated during the final months of the European war. Much of it was vague or veiled, and most of it had been empty posturing by the increasingly desperate Nazis.

There were, however, two exceptions, two Ultra decrypts from late April, just weeks before the final capitulation of Germany, that still interested Lytton-Harte.

He thumbed through the file, pulling the two decrypts he had in mind. The first, the most provocative, was on top:

REF CX/MSS/T367/T45   KV 9177

ZZ

SIGNALS SENT FIFTEENTH APRIL 0530 HOURS FROM FÜHRERBUNKER
BERLIN TO (1) CAPTAIN VESSEL U180 AND (2) SS SPECIAL DETACHMENT
STAGHORN ORDERING ACTIVATION OF OPERATION LAST SHOT—DETAILS
UNSPECIFIED EXCEPT TO PROCEED TO TARGETS IN UK AND US—U180
BELIEVED PRESENTLY OFF SPANISH COAST—SS DETACHMENT STAG-
HORN BELIEVED OPERATING SOUTH COAST IRELAND IN ACCORDANCE
WITH INTELLIGENCE SIXTH APRIL—FIRST MENTION OF OPERATION
LAST SHOT—NO FURTHER INFORMATION. 151522z/4/45

"Last Shot." This mysterious Nazi operation still intrigued him, although, two months after its discovery, he still had learned nothing more about it.

He had first read this decrypt on the afternoon of April 15, barely two weeks before Hitler's suicide and three weeks before the German capitulation. Whoever translated it had assigned it a low priority at the time: two z's only. If it had been thought urgent, it would have gotten four, maybe five, z's. But there was no telling why the experts at Bletchley gave it the priority they did.

Of course, he'd immediately ordered a review of the records for any previous mention of anything called Last Shot, especially among their files on Irish-Nazi collaborators. There was nothing. Through the DG, he'd had MI6 queried, again with no results. Even the captured files of the Abwehr, the military-intelligence division of the German General Staff, had been perused in May, with no luck.

The end of the war relegated the decrypt to the inactive file. Along with the second one, dated April 17, also originating from the Führer-bunker. This one mentioned the same SS Staghorn Detachment, although it had been sent to a German unit supposedly operating in Poland at the time.

Lytton-Harte stared at the two intelligence reports. Certainly, with the end of hostilities, there was no one else interested in Last Shot.

And he had been just about to agree, except for two events, both within the last few days. One was the surprise discovery of uranium—German uranium—in England; the second was a tantalizing tidbit that had stumbled out of the interrogation of a former Nazi, now talking his head off in the hopes of avoiding imprisonment.

His telephone rang again.

"The Soviet attaché," said Mrs. Morley.

"Right. Give me another moment, Mrs. Morley, then send him in."

Lytton-Harte gathered the file together and returned it to his desk safe. A moment later he heard a knock and the door opened.

Major Kaluzny stepped stiffly in, a tall man whose half-bald head accentuated his large forehead.

"Ah," he bellowed, in thickly accented English, "I am pleased to meet the Deputy Director General." He cleared his throat briefly and added, "today."

"Yes, indeed," mumbled Lytton-Harte, who deliberately slowed his rise from his leather chair. "Good morning, Major." He shook a moist Russian hand and offered the chair opposite his desk.

"I send you the greeting of my Ambassador," Kaluzny said.

Lytton-Harte nodded and noticed that the man was sweating profusely, especially on his expansive forehead, where large beads had formed.

"Thank you. I trust that you'll give the Ambassador my good wishes?"

"Oh, yes, yes, of course." The man produced a handkerchief from his pocket and wiped his forehead. He smiled and revealed nicotine-stained teeth. "London is very warm, yes?"

"Quite. Summer, you know."

For a moment neither man said anything. Lytton-Harte was feeling uncomfortable. And put out. These Russians were always slow to the point.

"Ah, yes, the Embassy said you had something important to discuss? Something of an intelligence nature?"

"Yes, yes, of course. Very interesting. I think you will agree."

Lytton-Harte raised an eyebrow and waited.

"Yes, very interesting to us," he repeated. For a moment, Kaluzny studied the room. "Very nice," he said. "I have seen many English offices. They are very nice."

Lytton-Harte nodded again. Very slowly he pushed a small silver box toward Kaluzny. It contained only Player cigarettes, nothing that he himself would smoke.

"Cigarette?"

"Oh, yes, thank you."

Lytton-Harte refilled his lion's head pipe and lit it. Then he settled back and waited for the Russian to talk.

"We understand you are holding a German prisoner here in London," the man said between drags on his cigarette.

"Oh yes? I dare say we have many."

"This man is special. A very important Nazi." Kaluzny officiously opened a small valise and withdrew a single sheet of paper and handed it across the desk.

Lytton-Harte noticed immediately that it had been impeccably typed on an English-language typewriter. The syntax, however, revealed that it was a translation from the Russian.

"He was very important," the major said. "Very close to Himmler, we are thinking."

The DDG glanced again at the paper, the name on the abbreviated dossier was well known to him. Damn right they had the man. And safely stashed away outside of London.

"There are many former Nazis around, Major. Why are you interested in this man?"

Another nicotine smile. "As I tell you, he was very important. We believe he had much to do with a special anti-Soviet campaign at the end of the war."

This was interesting. Lytton-Harte leaned forward slightly. "A special campaign, you say?"

"Yes. One directed at destroying special targets behind our military lines. Industries. Government offices. You would say to get even, I think."

"Well, that's all over now, I trust."

"Yes. Maybe. But we have information that some of these, ah, activities were planned to occur many months later."

"How so?"

"We are not so certain about that. Perhaps to use Nazi partisans who have not yet been found."

"I see. And your sources of information?"

"That I cannot say. But if we could have this man . . . interrogate him. Yes?"

219

Lytton-Harte carefully picked up the Russian's dossier. "His name is Brunig?"

"Yes."

"I will see if we are holding the man. It may take a while."

The Russian smiled again. "Oh yes, you are holding him. We are sure of that."

"Yes, well, I shall certainly try to confirm that for you."

Kaluzny sat in his chair for a moment, until he finished his cigarette and then squashed it firmly in the ashtray near the edge of the desk.

"Yes," he said, rising from his chair, "your cigarettes are good, but I think the American ones are better. Don't you think this is so?"

Lytton-Harte smiled faintly, but not out of humor.

"Quite a matter of taste, don't you think?"

Chapter Twenty

Cavanaugh's head throbbed. The noise in the vast terminal echoed again and again, exacerbating a headache he'd developed somewhere over the Channel. The NCO on the other side of the wooden counter was telling him there was no way to get back to the States until tomorrow.

"No planes. Full. Got it?"

Cavanaugh shook his head. Did the whole goddamn Army work like this? Very slowly, he said, his voice carrying more than a trace of exhaustion, "It's important, okay?"

The NCO with the mustache rolled his eyes. Nearby, a group of young GIs, still a little drunk from the night before, were singing—or trying to sing—a few lines of "How Dry I Am."

Cavanaugh was now several days behind schedule. The collection of military papers he had with him didn't account for that. And right now, there was no one in England that he could turn to. Not with the restrictions Groves had placed on him.

He leaned closer to be sure that the man could hear him. The voices around him seemed to be swelling in volume. It was midafternoon, or at least he thought it was. He had been on a couple of flights from Germany that seemed to stop every thirty minutes along the way.

Running through his head, like the flickering images of a silent movie, were the events he had just left: Mühlhausen, the radioactive-enrichment building, the ominous gun barrels, the old dead man in the road. The chase through the forest. The lost notes.

"Look," he implored, "I know everyone wants to go home, but . . ." He fumbled for words. How could he tell this man what he knew? "I *gotta* get back to D.C. It's important," he repeated.

The three-striper gave him one of those looks that said he'd heard it all before.

"You look," he finally said to Cavanaugh, pointing around the room with his hand. "What do you see?"

Cavanaugh didn't bother to turn around.

"Generals. Colonels. You get it? They wanna go home too, and they goddamn outrank you."

Cavanaugh shrugged. If only he didn't feel so bad. If only he could tell this jackass what he knew. If only he could call Gilbert; the man would arrange something. Instead, he said, "Okay, when?"

"Tomorrow. Earliest. I mean it."

Cavanaugh nodded and grabbed the stack of military orders from the counter. There was nothing he could do but send a message that he'd be delayed. Then he remembered something else and whirled back around. The NCO was ten feet away.

"What about a hotel?" Cavanaugh shouted. Where in the hell was he going to stay tonight?

The other man didn't bother to stop walking. "Check with billeting," he shouted back and then mumbled a one-word obscenity. Cavanaugh started to give the guy the finger but changed his mind. Right now, the little son of a bitch controlled what he needed most: an airplane back to the States.

Tired and exasperated, he found the communications desk and sent a telegram to Headquarters, Army Corps of Engineers in Washington, informing them that he would be at least twenty-four hours late. Just that. No mention of General Groves or anyone at the Manhattan Project offices. He had been told to do that, nothing else.

Then he found the billeting office, which was easily identifiable by the crowd of men hanging around. His luck was no better there than at the flight-operations desk. No rooms in London anywhere. Maybe space in the base's officers' billet, but just in case, there was always a couch here in Base Ops.

Cavanaugh walked away with his name on a list and a number—127—just in case a hotel room opened up. Unlikely, said the lieutenant in charge. But hell, he said cheerily, you never knew, and Cavanaugh could always call back later and check; he sounded exactly like a man with his own room.

He stumbled back into the waiting room and found his duffel bag—what there was of it—and flopped down in one of the metal chairs that seemed common to every government installation in the world. All he could do was wait to see if a room became available. Or drink in the Officer's Club. With his hand he massaged his forehead and then pressed lightly on his eyes.

Oh, God, how much he wanted to go home, back to his bed in Barracks A at Los Alamos. Right now, he couldn't even remember how long he'd been gone, nor could he imagine what had happened since he'd left.

At least he could tell Groves what he wanted to know.

Mentally, he tried to put himself back in Los Alamos, and the schedule of work as he remembered it. As of the day he left. Or rather, the night. He didn't think he had missed the Trinity Test yet, but there was no way of knowing for sure.

By now, his team would have disbanded, men shifted to preparations for the Test, or already sent overseas to Tinian Island in the Pacific to assemble the bombs for Japan. No, that wasn't right, he realized: those guys had shipped out a month ago. Or—hell, he wasn't sure about any date anymore. He rubbed his eyes again and stared into the milling passengers.

Someone was standing a dozen feet away staring at him.

"Cavanaugh?"

Cavanaugh lifted his head and saw a man in a British Army officer's uniform.

Brooke suddenly remembered the American penchant for first names. "Phil? It's Christopher Brooke. Remember?"

Cavanaugh smiled and struggled to get up. Brooke was the first friendly face he had seen in what seemed like ages.

"Yeah," he said. He shook hands. "What the hell you doing here?"

Brooke smiled his hail-fellow smile. "Had some business out here with some of your chaps. And you? On your way back to the States?"

Cavanaugh managed a weak smile. "Eventually, I hope." He shook his head. "Maybe tomorrow."

Brooke forced himself to look sympathetic. Inside, he almost laughed. The DDG would be pleased. Luck seemed to be on their side after all.

Solicitously, he asked, "Weather?"

"No," said Cavanaugh, "no space." He looked around. "Outranked."

"Need a ride into London?"

"Nope. No room there, either." He pulled a cigarette from his pack and offered one to Brooke. "This just isn't my day."

Brooke was thinking fast. He needed Cavanaugh somewhere where they could talk. Somewhere where he could be approached, under the right circumstances. And it sure as hell wasn't likely on an American air base.

"I can get you a hotel room." He hoped he sounded genuine.

Cavanaugh just stared at him.

Brooke laughed. "Connections, you see. My unit. Not fancy, but good for a lie-down. Hardly the Dorchester."

"With a bath?"

"A private bath? Well, maybe." Hell, he thought, surely MI5 could arrange that. "Let me call."

The idea of a long, hot bath grew in Cavanaugh's mind until he could almost feel the hot water lapping all over him. Then he remembered what he was doing here. He couldn't afford to miss another plane. *That* was more important.

"Nah," he began, "I don't think I can, really. My plane, and everything."

"I thought you were leaving tomorrow?" Brooke's excitement suddenly evaporated.

"That's true, but I don't know exactly when. Maybe early tomorrow, maybe late. But I've got to stay around here and catch the first one I can." He tried to force a smile. "Thanks just the same."

Brooke nodded. Now what the hell did he do now? Then he had an idea.

"What about dinner? In the city? I can have you back in a couple of hours." This was it: either the American would go for it or he wouldn't. There wasn't anything Brooke could do if Cavanaugh said no. He thought of the Deputy Director, his large round head staring at him from behind the oak desk.

Suddenly Cavanaugh broke into a big smile. "That sounds great. My treat."

"Right," said Brooke. "Let's stow your kit."

Brooke looked in the mirror and combed his hair. The marbled bathroom was large and the sound of running water echoed throughout.

He wasn't looking forward to the next few hours. Poor, simple Cavanaugh. No, he knew, not simple. Informal. And unsuspecting.

Right now the poor man was sitting at a table outside waiting for him to return. Then they would eat.

In the DDG's Machiavellian plot, Brooke was to be the first course; Lytton-Harte the second. And somehow, at the end of it, according to the DDG's plan, Cavanaugh would break his oath of secrecy and tell British Intelligence what they wanted to know. Even a little bit would be a lot, though, considering how little they knew about atomic weapons.

It was certain, as the Old Man pointed out, that Cavanaugh and the Americans were undoubtedly up to something. The man had inexplicably disappeared in Germany. And despite their best efforts, British agents had not been able to track him down for four days. Even amid the chaos in Germany that was unusual.

Brooke straightened his tie. He could be with Augusta right now. He hadn't seen her for days, it seemed, and one couldn't let a woman like that be alone for too long. That could be costly.

But right now he had to do what he was ordered: ply Cavanaugh with liquor, charm him, and apprise him of England's post-war plight. After all, he'd set the stage with the American over drinks a week ago.

Then and only then, when the hapless man was warm and toasty, was Brooke to turn him over to Lytton-Harte.

They were on the second floor of a large restaurant called Simpson's, which Brooke described as famous for its beef, a dish he confessed he thought Cavanaugh would prefer. The room was vast, almost two stories high, with tall windows that overlooked a hotel. Waiters were carving slabs of beef on steaming metal trolleys that were pushed from table to table.

The two of them sat on a corner banquette, conveniently isolated so that it wasn't difficult to talk. Like the Dorchester, the restaurant had an elegance that seemed to Cavanaugh to come more from the atmosphere than from any particular item within it: the tablecloth was frayed and the china chipped here and there along the edge of a plate or bowl.

The liquor was taking effect. First the drinks—American bourbon—and then the wine, some sort of claret. Now he felt better. Still tired, but the images from Germany seemed to be ebbing. The flight home became more certain, yet less urgent.

Brooke was talking, being wonderfully amusing about life in England both before the war and during it. He deftly balanced the difficult times with small, warm human moments so that Cavanaugh found himself slightly envious that he had missed it all.

He had stories about Los Alamos, of course, but he didn't know if he could tell them. All of them at the lab had been warned, repeatedly, about talking, especially about their work and the people they worked with. And there were the war posters: "Loose Lips Sink Ships, Tall Tales Tell the Enemy, He's [the enemy] Listening"; that sort of thing.

Something Brooke said reminded him of a story about Enrico Fermi eating Mexican food for the first time in New Mexico. It was really funny, and for a moment Cavanaugh considered telling it; after all, he could change Fermi's name. Then he realized that it wouldn't be as funny unless you knew the man was Fermi; there was something about an Italian physicist who spoke little English ordering tacos in Santa Fe. And there was Niels Bohr, one of the Immortals, listening to a WAC explain in a Texas accent the lab's eccentric system for classifying papers.

"And after the war?" asked Brooke. He had just talked about his plans for the future.

"Don't know," replied Cavanaugh. A lot rested on the success of Trinity, he figured. No one would be particularly interested in a physicist whose project had failed after three years and God knows how much money. But he couldn't say that either.

"Maybe back to a university somewhere. I'm interested in astrophysics."

Brooke nodded. "I'm not sure what England will be like when the war ends. Really ends, that is. And everyone comes home." He thought about his father and brother. Would the family income support all of them if the economy failed to pick up? "I suppose we'll make the best of it. We don't really have a choice."

226

Cavanaugh nodded.

"And your present work," asked Brooke, "it's going well?"

Cavanaugh felt the tiniest alarm ring inside him. "I think so," he said. "We'll know more soon." Was that saying too much? he wondered. Probably not. After all, Brooke and a dozen others knew he was from Los Alamos. And everyone associated with ALSOS knew that Los Alamos was working on a bomb of some kind.

"I envy you," said Brooke suddenly. He was holding his wineglass in his hand, staring into the ruby-colored liquid.

Cavanaugh gave a short laugh. "Why?"

"Oh, your country, I suppose. It's rich, powerful. Informal." He smiled. There was that word again. "And your work. I envy that."

He gently rested the glass on the table and looked around the room. The occupants were a mixture of uniforms and civilian clothing. He leaned forward slightly.

"We don't know much about Los Alamos, of course. Maybe we shouldn't know anything. But we have some chaps there, you know. They're naturally incommunicado during the war, so there are only hints about the work."

Cavanaugh said nothing. Was Brooke pumping him for information? An image of General Groves flashed across his mind. The tiny alarm inside him rang again.

Brooke smiled. "Don't be surprised, old boy. It's not hard to put things together. After all, we plodded along the atomic road quite a bit before the war. Gave it up to concentrate on radar."

Cavanaugh decided to try and change the subject. "So America's rich?" It was a poor attempt. Any jerk stepping outside could take one look at a city bombed on and off for five years and guess that America had to be better off.

"And powerful," added Brooke. "Yes, I'd say you people are going to come out rather on top. Wouldn't you?" As hard as he tried, he knew he'd revealed a trace of bitterness. He had to control that. It wouldn't do to offend this man, or make him uncomfortable. Not tonight. Not when he had to wheedle cooperation out of this American.

Cavanaugh shrugged. There was a lot of talk about who was on top these days, but he hadn't thought much about it. The business with the Russians had scared him, however; he certainly didn't want *them* on top.

Brooke moved to soften the conversation. "Well," he said, "we'll all be winners of a sort when the war ends. Especially those of us in the West." He turned and looked straight at Cavanaugh. "Especially if what you're working on proves successful."

"Yes," said Cavanaugh quietly. It was strange, but until this moment he had always assumed that the bomb was something uniquely American. It had never crossed his mind that it would be shared with anyone else: allies, fellow victors, co-conquerors aside. Even with Brits working at Los Alamos. That was probably stupid, he knew, but most of his time on the mesa was spent working on the bomb, not thinking about who would control it after the war.

The room was suddenly very small. And very quiet. Brooke reached for the Haut Brion and poured the last of it into both their glasses. The transparent red liquid glistened.

"I know you can't talk about your work," said Brooke, "but I think you'd agree that the work of Los Alamos will substantially shape the post-war world. Especially politically."

"Uh, probably," said Cavanaugh. He didn't even like to hear the name Los Alamos mentioned in public.

The uncomfortable feeling inside him was rising, although he knew it was only partially related to atomic secrets. It was also that someone—in this case, Brooke—was suddenly raising issues that Cavanaugh had never thought about.

"I don't know, really; I mean, I haven't thought about it much. I haven't had time." In fact, he didn't know anyone at Los Alamos who was talking like this.

Brooke sensed Cavanaugh's discomfort. This was it, he thought. He had to press now or not at all.

"I'm thinking of the Soviets, of course," he said, choosing his words carefully. He didn't want to appear glib. He sensed that Americans rarely felt comfortable with that trait in the British, and Cavanaugh, poor Cavanaugh, probably not at all.

For a brief moment he thought about all the conversations he had had with friends and colleagues about the Americans. The attitudes always varied between gratitude and constrained resentment. "Overpaid, oversexed, overhere" went the popular saying. Most of this missed the point, Brooke felt; the Americans were unsophisticated, perhaps, but always genuine. And Cavanaugh seemed to exemplify what Brooke believed.

"I think we have much to fear from them. Especially now that they occupy so much of eastern Europe."

228

Cavanaugh nodded. It was as if Brooke and Groves had shared views with one another. He also thought about running for his life in the forest outside of Mühlhausen.

"I don't think we want your *work* falling into their hands." Brooke ever so gently emphasized the word.

Cavanaugh wanted to say something to the effect that it was out of his hands. Or maybe that they didn't even know if the damn things worked yet. Or, like his mother would say: Don't count your chickens before they hatch.

He saw Little Boy wrapped in its metal suit on a hoist back in S Site; the rounded nose turned to stare at him like a giant black eye.

"Can you imagine if the Germans had succeeded?" Brooke asked. That's it, he thought; Cavanaugh would either bite or he wouldn't.

"No," said Cavanaugh. The alarm inside him was ringing louder now. It was time to go. "But fortunately, they didn't succeed."

That wasn't exactly a lie, he reasoned. The gun barrels at Mühlhausen represented an *attempt* at an atomic bomb. They had never been used; there was no proof that they would even work. Suddenly, Cavanaugh wondered if the British knew about Mühlhausen and Brooke was just playing with him.

"It's late. I've really got to get back and catch some sleep before tomorrow." He looked around for the waiter. "Can we get the check?"

Brooke just sat there. Finally, he said, "Of course." He leaned forward again, speaking softly. He was preparing another jab. An older couple was staring in the direction of their table; the man wore pince-nez glasses.

"I don't mean to make you uncomfortable, but—"

"Oh, you haven't," interjected Cavanaugh. "Really. It's just that I'm tired. It's been a long trip. Tiring."

A tiny grimace crossed Brooke's boyish face. He ignored Cavanaugh's plea to go. "You see," he began, "it's just that *if* they had succeeded in making a new weapon, there is every reason to believe they would have used it *against us.*"

Cavanaugh noticed that Brooke's voice had changed. He was speaking in low tones, but the voice had a sharp edge to it.

"I can't quite put out of my mind that I live in England, that my family lives in England. And that living here means we could have been victims of such a weapon." Brooke hesitated. "Or that we still could be."

Cavanaugh tried to laugh but couldn't. The conversation had turned

229

very serious. Brooke's easy wit and charm had disappeared, leaving Cavanaugh feeling very uncomfortable.

"But the Germans didn't succeed," Cavanaugh meekly repeated. "I mean, it would have been terrible if they had. More terrible than most people can imagine. But it didn't happen. Not here." What was it that Brooke had said? That last sentence? Something like ". . . we still could be"? That was a curious thing to say.

Brooke pulled a big five-pound note from a black wallet and threw it down on the table.

"Oh, no," Cavanaugh said. "This is on me." He fumbled around in his back pocket for his own wallet.

Brooke reached over and put his hand on Cavanaugh's sleeve. "Oh, no," he said, "you're our guest."

" 'Our' guest?" asked Cavanaugh.

Brooke smiled. "Just a figure of speech, old boy. You're England's guest tonight."

They started out the door, Cavanaugh still arguing about the check. Brooke suddenly stopped.

"Need to use the WC, old boy? I've got to make a call."

Brooke was uncharacteristically silent during the ride out of London.

Cavanaugh sensed that he had somehow offended Brooke, or at least put him off in some private way. Brooke wasn't exactly pouting, but he did seem unusually quiet. Perhaps it was their conversation at dinner, which just at the end had seemed to turn sour. Had he perhaps appeared insensitive to the dangers England had faced in the war? Surely Brooke didn't expect him to talk about his work at Los Alamos. . . ?

He unconsciously gripped the door as they made a turn off the well-lit street; he still wasn't accustomed to driving on the left side of the road.

"I'm going to take you back a different way," said Brooke suddenly. "Less traffic, I think." He made another turn down a darker street.

Cavanaugh said nothing. He sort of liked the wind from the open window in his face, and although the effect of the alcohol was ebbing, he still felt mildly comfortable. Or mildly incandescent, as one of his college roommates had been fond of saying.

Block by block, the city dissolved behind them. They seemed to be entering a patchwork of suburban countryside that was a mix of houses and small farms.

230

"I don't remember any of this," he said.

"It's a different part of London," replied Brooke. "Near Surrey."

"You sure this'll get us to the air base?" Cavanaugh said it jokingly.

Brooke kept his eyes on the road. "Eventually."

They drove through a small village called Ham Common, where some of the houses had tall thatched roofs. Warm, soft lights glowed through the windows from the interiors.

Brooke began to slow down and appeared to study the left side of the road.

Cavanaugh thought that curious. "Looking for something?" he asked.

"I've got to make a quick stop. It's right around here."

"What about the air base?" asked Cavanaugh. He thought about his bed. "I don't want to get there too late."

"This won't take long," said Brooke cryptically. A stone fence came into view.

"Ah," he said, and began to make a turn.

Out of the corner of his eye, Cavanaugh caught a fading wooden sign partially covered by greenery. It read "Latchmere House."

"Someone lives here?" Cavanaugh turned and tried to read Brooke's face.

"Sort of."

Something about all of this seemed out of place to Cavanaugh. Brooke had said nothing earlier about stopping at someone's home. In fact, the man had said damn little the last thirty minutes. At the end of the driveway was an ugly Victorian house.

"What sort of place is this?" he asked.

Brooke didn't reply.

Cavanaugh unconsciously gripped the door handle, although the car was slowing down. "What's going on?" he asked.

Brooke pulled up to the front of the house and stopped. Lights were on and the front door opened. Slowly he turned to face Cavanaugh.

"Remember when I told you at dinner how vulnerable England was to German attack? Especially if they had a new and powerful weapon?"

"Yes, but—"

Brooke cut him off. "Well, we have some information, some intelligence, that is rather frightening." He paused, as if he wanted the effect of his words to sink in.

Cavanaugh was confused. And uncomfortable. What the hell was Brooke talking about?

"What does this have to do with me?"

Brooke looked at Cavanaugh and then up at the door of the house, where a man stood. Right now, he was only a dark shadow highlighted by the inner light of the house.

"You may be able to help us. To confirm something."

"What?"

Brooke didn't answer. The dark figure continued to stand motionless in the doorway. Then it spoke.

"Captain Brooke?"

Brooke popped his door open and started to get out. Cavanaugh reached over and grabbed his arm. Hard.

"What the *hell* is going on?" He didn't like any of this.

Brooke seemed to hesitate a moment before he pulled himself free. "I told you," he said firmly, "you might be able to help us." He looked again at the figure in the doorway. "It won't hurt you to listen."

"Oh, Christ," mumbled Cavanaugh. His mind was racing. He could get out of the car and run for it. But where? He could go in and talk with whomever was standing on the porch. He could reach for his duffel bag and pull out his gun. But for what? These sons of bitches were his goddamn allies, for Christ's sake!

"I really must ask you to come in, Cavanaugh," said Brooke softly. Then he remembered something about Americans. "Please, Phil. You can't imagine how important this could be."

Cavanaugh sat in his seat a moment longer, fingering the leather upholstery with one hand, still gripping the door handle with the other. Then he let go and slowly got out of the car.

Chapter Twenty-one

Canning knocked on the door and stuck his head in. "They've arrived, sir."

"Good," said Lytton-Harte. He stood by the large fireplace warming himself. In a moment he would get a drink. He would probably need another by the time this evening was over.

Brooke apparently had succeeded. Good man. He and the American were outside. No doubt the American was mad. Or confused. Or both.

It was going to take everything he had in him to pull this off, he thought. And as much as he disliked Americans, he had no wish to be rude. After all, he wanted information. And what he wanted was obtainable by no other means he could think of. With luck and skill— certainly with skill, since he believed more in that than in luck—he would have just enough information at the end of this little session to tell him that the German uranium canisters were indeed part of an atomic bomb. And, more important, how they could be made to work. That information would be terribly helpful.

The experts had guessed that the uranium belonged to a bomb of some kind. They just didn't know what the bomb looked like, and no one knew if one was somewhere in England. If they had any hopes of finding it—or anything like it—they needed more information. They needed what this American undoubtedly knew.

What he was going to trade was another piece of intelligence. Something they had picked up under interrogation in the last two weeks. Nothing too valuable, of course, but enough to give this session its patina of reciprocity. That was the gentlemanly thing to do.

He turned to Canning. "Is our other guest ready?" he asked.

"Waiting," replied Canning.

Lytton-Harte nodded. Now he would show the Americans who *really* won the war.

It was cold inside the house. And dark. The foyer existed in a dim half-light from some softly glowing electrical sconces on the wall. A hallway directly ahead seemed to disappear straight into darkness.

Cavanaugh walked silently behind Brooke down the dark hallway, only half noticing the heavy brocade wallpaper with its hint of former elegance. A door clicked behind him and the mysterious doorman disappeared along with their coats. To make a break for it now would mean running outside in the cold.

Brooke stopped at a door and knocked softly. It was clear to Cavanaugh that the man had been here before. Slowly his discomfort, his uneasiness were replaced by a new emotion: he was mad at this damn little game the Brits were playing. The dinner, the solicitous conversation had been to set him up!

The room they entered was spacious without being large; it must have been a library once, with its high ceilings and wood-paneled walls. But there was little furniture and the bookshelves were empty except for a few scattered volumes.

At the opposite end was a fireplace and before it an arrangement of sofa and chairs. Reflected light danced off the arm of the leather chair nearest the fire. Two men sat talking quietly until one looked up and saw Brooke and Cavanaugh; suddenly they were both silent. Slowly the older of the two men rose, then the younger. For a moment, no one spoke, and both pairs of men simply stared at one another.

Finally, the older man cleared his throat. "Ah, Dr. Cavanaugh."

"Doctor" instead of Captain. And it wasn't so much a question as it was a declaration.

Cavanaugh only stared. The old man was on the short side, stocky, with a round, fleshy face and wiry hair. The younger man was of medium height, thin, with a schoolboy's round, lineless face. His eyes, which were large and dark, gave him an inquiring but nocturnal look.

"Do please sit down." The older man motioned toward a chair by the fire. "Warm up. I suspect it's rather damp outside."

Cavanaugh was about to object when the man spoke up again.

"I apologize for the manner in which you've been brought here. A bit dramatic, I know, but I think you share our concern for secrecy. A drink?"

Cavanaugh shook his head and slowly walked toward the edge of the couch. The thin man disappeared into the shadows. Out of the corner of his eye, he saw Brooke at a small table pouring something into a glass from a decanter.

"Was it necessary to kidnap me?"

A very thin smile broke out on the older man's face. He had returned to his chair by the fire and looked directly at Cavanaugh.

"Now, I would say that's dramatic as well," the older man said. "But there is a great need for discretion at the moment. *Please* sit down."

Reluctantly Cavanaugh took a chair diagonally opposite the old man. These men were schoolboys playing spies. "Who the hell are you" he asked.

"My name is Lytton-Harte. I'm associated with the War Office." Not quite a lie, but certainly an exaggeration. Or at least a distortion. But then, how would this American understand the nature and purpose of MI5?

"What do you want?" It was as direct as he could make it.

The older man turned and looked briefly at Brooke, then at the fire. He wouldn't be hurried.

"These are difficult times, Dr. Cavanaugh, very difficult." He turned slowly back to look at his captive. "The war in Europe is over, sir, but now we must live with its legacy."

High-minded, thought Cavanaugh, and obscure. What was the point, the *real* point of all of this?

"What do you want from me?" he repeated.

"It is, ah-h, what you know that could be useful," said the man slowly. His assistant, the thin man with the youthful face, quietly reappeared and whispered something in the older man's ear. "Ah-h yes," the old man mumbled.

Cavanaugh noticed that the man distorted his words, almost slurred

235

them, as if he had been drinking. Something like a drunk Winston Churchill.

Brooke took a sip of his brandy and smiled to himself. The DDG always had the good stuff. But poor Cavanaugh; the man must think we're off our bloody rockers. Or worse, that we intend to do something awful to him. Thank God, his own part was over; the DDG had it now. It was unfortunate, though, because under other circumstances, he and Cavanaugh might have been friends.

"What do I know?" asked Cavanaugh.

"It's your work, Dr. Cavanaugh. You see, we know something about what you do."

Cavanaugh wasn't surprised. "I can't talk about my work. You certainly know that." Oh, God, how he wanted to be back at the air base. He thought about tomorrow; at least he would leave all this shit behind him.

From the couch, Brooke quietly interjected. "This is difficult for us—"

"Difficult for *you*?" shot back Cavanaugh. "You bring me here in the middle of the night to ask me to talk about my work? What makes you think I'd do that? What in the *hell* makes you think I'd talk about *anything* with you?"

"It's important. And we're all on the same side."

Cavanaugh felt his face flush. "If it's so goddamn important, why can't we talk in the daytime, in an office somewhere? Officially?"

The old man rumbled something from his seat. The worn leather creaked as he shifted his portly body. "Officially, our conversation can't take place."

"Why?" Cavanaugh jerkily stood up. He had had enough.

"Please sit down."

Cavanaugh shook his head. "Not until I know what all this is about. What the *hell* do you want?"

"We want you to look at something." Brooke's face seemed almost pleading.

"*What*?" Cavanaugh released his grip on the edge of the chair. He could still make a run for it. He could be out of the house in less than sixty seconds. And then . . . and then what would he do?

"Yes. Just look at something; that's all. You see, we found something here in London, just a few days ago."

"Why would I know anything about it?"

"You can tell us if it's part of a bomb," said Lytton-Harte. "An ahh-tomic bomb."

Cavanaugh tensed from one end of his body to the other. This was exactly what he didn't want to hear. "Oh, shit," he said.

Lytton-Harte winced slightly. He never approved of vulgarity, but then, this man was an American. He cleared his throat and leaned forward in his chair.

"You are not being asked to reveal secrets, Dr. Cavanaugh. We respect you, and our American allies, too much to do that. But you might, ah-h, indicate if this material *could* be part of such a weapon."

Cavanaugh couldn't believe what he was hearing: a neat but still devious request. Even to *identify* something was to reveal part of what he knew. "I can't do that," he said.

Lytton-Harte would not be put off so easily.

"You could *look* at what we have, sir. That would involve no compromise. And what you learn will be of considerable interest to your government. I can assure you of that."

"What good would it do? I still couldn't tell you anything."

The old man stood up, grasping the edge of the green leather chair as an aid. "*That's* a decision you can make when you see what we have. To *look* will compromise nothing."

He motioned to the young man next to him. "Canning? Is the, ah-h, material ready?"

The dark-eyed man nodded; his hands were clasped together.

Cavanaugh made a quick decision. He would look at what they had; he could always stall or say nothing. Or lie. Maybe he *could* learn something. Groves would appreciate that. And besides, what else could he do?

They walked down the hall together, the four of them; as they neared a door the thin man named Canning scurried ahead of them to open the door, then stood submissively aside to let them pass.

This time, a flood of light spilled out from the room on the other side. Before he stepped in, Cavanaugh caught sight of another man— someone in uniform—receding into the darkness of the hallway. He only had a second, but he thought he saw a gun holster on the man's hip.

This room was small; it looked as if it had formerly been a kitchen: the walls were painted flat white, and the floor was covered in small black and white hexagonal tiles. A bank of naked light bulbs on the

237

ceiling was the source of the harsh illumination. In front of them was a table with several objects, including two dark metal boxes.

At first glance, none of the objects seemed particularly unusual; none seemed to leap out and shout that it belonged to a weapon. To an atomic bomb.

"Take a closer look," said the old man. Canning had already moved to one end of the table, Brooke to the other. Cavanaugh took a cautious step, then another.

He could tell that the two metal boxes, maybe two feet square, had been pried open. The smaller objects included two small plugs, almost certainly fuses, with wires extruding from one end. There was also a smaller anodized metal box that was devoid of nomenclature and detail except for several electrical plugs at the base. That was interesting. A brown gunnysack sat next to the black box.

"What's in the small box?"

"Take a look," said the old man.

Cavanaugh hesitated for a moment. The top of the black box was hinged along one edge and clasped on the other. He flipped the clasp and lifted the cover. Inside were wiring and several German-made electrical components. There was also a place for batteries.

"A condenser?" he asked.

"Yes," said the man named Canning. "We're told that it stores an electrical charge."

Cavanaugh nodded. The unsettling feeling in his gut grew. His anger was rapidly being displaced by an uncomfortable realization that parts of a weapon might well be on the table. There wasn't a weapon here, not a conventional one, anyway, but there were *parts* of one. Or, at least, there were parts for something out of the ordinary.

"And the sack?" He hesitated to touch it.

"Black powder. Packaged in small bags. The sort of thing commonly used by the Germans to propel their artillery shells."

Cavanaugh's heart skipped a beat. Explosives. Fuses. Electrical systems. It was beginning to look more and more ominous.

He continued around the table, studying each object, oblivious to the fact that the others were studying his reactions with equal intensity. At last he came to the two large metal boxes with the broken latches. As he tried to pull the first one toward him to examine it, he found it wouldn't budge.

"Try again," said Canning. Cavanaugh didn't bother to look at the man's face, which had a thin smile on it.

238

He grabbed the box with both hands and struggled to move it; it slid only a few inches. The thing was damn heavy!

"Jesus, it must weigh over a hundred pounds."

"More like a hundred and fifty, actually," said Canning. "Around seventy kilograms."

Cavanaugh leaned forward and lifted the top half of the box. Somewhere, in the back of his mind, he knew that it wasn't booby-trapped. These guys had already looked at it. They knew what was inside.

Lying on a wooden cradle was a metal cylinder, one of two Lytton-Harte knew had been found in Southend.

Cavanaugh gasped. He could be wrong—he hoped like hell he was wrong—but it looked as if it had come from the mold at Mühlhausen; if it was, it would be the projectile piece for a gun bomb! It was the right shape and size, more or less.

He extended his fingers and made a quick estimate of its dimensions: it was six inches in diameter and the same height.

Oh, Jesus! The physics worked out at Los Alamos suggested that a projectile needed to be the same height as width for maximum effect in a bomb. The target needed to contain a larger amount of uranium, but could vary in size to fit the projectile.

Dammit! he wished he still had his notebook with its measurements. Then he would know for sure if this came from Mühlhausen.

He lifted the object up, struggling to do so.

"Approximately fifty kilos," said Canning mechanically.

Cavanaugh wondered if these people knew what they had on their goddamn table. Carefully, he let the large slug fall back into place. Its weight alone suggested that it was uranium. Very possibly enriched uranium containing just enough U235 to make an explosive chain reaction feasible.

The contents of the second box were therefore no surprise to Cavanaugh: a large cylinder of metal, whose center was obviously designed to accept the smaller slug. He didn't even bother to pick the bucket-looking object up. It was the target half of a bomb.

"Sixty-five kilos," intoned Canning.

Cavanaugh started to close the box when something in the center of the large cylinder caught his attention. He reached in and lifted out a metal pellet the size of a tube of lipstick. He pointed to it.

"Yes," said Canning, "we've examined that."

"And?"

"It's radium, coated in beryllium."

The source of neutrons! Critical to the chain reaction needed for an explosion. Cavanaugh had wondered about this in Mühlhausen; but clearly the Germans had figured out the need for extra neutrons. And radium was a perfectly acceptable source.

Cavanaugh stared at the table. A dozen thoughts were rushing through his mind at once: the problem of telling the Brits what they had; the realization that the Germans had succeeded. But most of all was the special knowledge that only he possessed: that there were six gun barrels produced by Krupps, only three of which could be accounted for. This table contained the nuclear elements for one of those six.

It slowly dawned on him that there was another question, perhaps even more immediate than the others: Were these objects from the secret laboratory in Mühlhausen?

The old man emitted a rumbling sound, then spoke. "We've been told this is highly enriched uranium, Dr. Cavanaugh."

All he could do was nod. The old man's line about these being "difficult times" came hauntingly back to him. Never had he felt less secure, less certain about what to do, than right now.

"Where did you find these?" he asked. Had the British, through some extraordinary turn of events, been to Mühlhausen?

"That is the problem, sir."

"What do you mean?"

"As I told you, these objects were found near London. Less than a week ago." Lytton-Harte's normal face usually revealed no emotion; this time, however, he looked genuinely concerned.

Cavanaugh blanched. He literally felt the blood rush out of his face. For a moment, he felt as if he might faint, or be nauseous. Instead, he gripped the table with both hands and leaned on it.

Cavanaugh's face told Lytton-Harte a great deal of what he wanted to know.

"How did they get here?"

"We presume by boat. We don't know by whom, and that's rather a worry to us."

"Yes," mumbled Cavanaugh.

Lytton-Harte was looking intently at him; the expression on his face was grave. "That's why we must know what these objects are. And if they fit together to make one of your, ah, secret bombs."

Of course they'd want to know, Cavanaugh thought. But Groves had said—Oppy and everyone else had always said—the work at Los Ala-

240

mos was the greatest secret of the war. In the history of the nation, probably.

He shook his head. "I don't have enough information to know precisely what kind of weapon these are part of," he said quietly. He pointed at the cylinders. "But obviously, uranium can be used in a bomb." Perhaps they would let the matter go at that.

On the opposite side of the table, Lytton-Harte looked at Brooke, then at Canning. He would press the point.

"Have you seen anything like this before?"

Images formed in Cavanaugh's mind. There was Little Boy in Los Alamos, naked on its hoist, with its uranium target and receptacle not unlike these cylinders in London, half a world away. And the discoveries in Mühlhausen. Yes, he knew what these things were.

"You must help us," Lytton-Harte pleaded, managing to ask and retain his dignity at the same time.

"I can't," said Cavanaugh. "I really can't say more."

Can't or won't? wondered Brooke. And what now? What else could the American be expected to say? For all practical purposes, they had their answer: Cavanaugh had revealed it by the expression on his face. These were the components of a *bomb*, by God! They had suspected it days ago, when the chemists from Cambridge had confirmed that the metal cylinders were uranium. There could be only one purpose for so much refined uranium: to make a weapon of some kind.

But there was still the question of what Cavanaugh was doing in Germany. Where had he been? Brooke wondered. What had he seen? Did it have anything to do with these uranium cylinders?

Lytton-Harte turned to Brooke and Canning. "I'd like to speak to Dr. Cavanaugh alone, please."

Both men nodded and quietly walked out. For a moment there was only silence as both Lytton-Harte and Cavanaugh stood without talking under the harsh glare of the electric lights.

"This isn't all we have, you see," said Lytton-Harte.

Cavanaugh looked up from the table. "What?"

"There's more. Information that's rather frightening."

Cavanaugh wondered what else he could possibly be hit with tonight.

"I want you to see someone, and hear what he has to say. Then you can go if you like."

"Who?"

A dark, pensive look crossed the old man's face. "A prisoner. A German prisoner."

Chapter Twenty-two

*I*t seemed to him as if the whole night had been spent in a succession of small rooms: first the dining room of the hotel; then the library and the room with white walls in the old Victorian house. And now this tiny room, no more than a closet, with the one-way mirror.

Cavanaugh stood in the dark next to the old man. The man was a good foot shorter than he. The two of them, and a third man, someone he had never seen before, were staring through a small window into another room.

On the other side were two men at a table. One, with glasses and a tweed suit, sat with a small pile of papers in front of him, questioning the other in German. The second man wore a suit but not a tie; he was heavily built and hadn't shaved for a while. With each question he rolled his eyes, swung uncomfortably back and forth in his chair, and clasped his hands together. His voice, which Cavanaugh could hear over a tinny-sounding loudspeaker above his head, was tired and irritated. The man seemed resentful of the questions. From time to time, he suddenly stopped in mid-sentence and struck a pose: he would angle his head back and peer arrogantly at his questioner, much like a bird would eye a worm before eating it.

"Who is he?" whispered Cavanaugh.

Lytton-Harte hesitated for a few moments, then spoke quietly. "He was a member of the Schutzstaffel, the SS, close to Himmler but attached to Hitler's immediate entourage. He claims he had access to Hitler, even in the bunker. His name is Brunig."

"Why's he here?" There had to be thousands of ex-Nazis around, so why was this particular man in London?

"We brought him here for questioning. He was captured in Italy aboard a ship sailing for South America." A lie. He had been captured in Vienna and brought to London a few weeks ago.

On the other side of the mirror the interrogation was heating up. Cavanaugh could only understand bits and pieces of the conversation in German. He could tell, however, that the captive was objecting to answering the same questions over and over.

Lytton-Harte bent over and whispered something to the quiet man on his right. The man nodded and stepped out of the tiny room. Moments later, he appeared on the other side of the mirror with two mugs of tea. He quietly set them down on the table and left again.

"That's the signal to begin some, ah-h, special questioning," whispered Lytton-Harte. Even whispering, his voice tended to resonate within the small chamber.

Cavanaugh was interested but confused. What "special" questioning was the old man referring to? In fact, what was the connection between this German and the cylinders of uranium he had seen less than half an hour ago?

There was a lull in the conversation in the other room. Both men were sipping from their mugs and staring at each other. Suddenly, in English, the German asked for a biscuit. In English, the interviewer said they would eat later. That, thought Cavanaugh, was the bait: talk and then food. Such a simple equation; hell, they had tried it on him earlier this evening.

Behind him, the door opened and the quiet third member of their party re-entered. The interrogation started again, and, in a low voice, the third man began to translate.

"The interrogator is saying that he wants to talk about the vengeance plot again." His voice was curiously monotone, and contrasted with the tinny sound from the speaker. His translation of the German coincided with a word that Cavanaugh instantly recognized: *Rache*, the word for "revenge."

The questioning took on an eerie quality, magnified somehow by the tiny dark room the three of them inhabited. Cavanaugh could smell the old man's pipe tobacco, as well as his own musty, day-old sweat. On the other side of the glass window, the German and his interrogator spoke, moved their lips and gesticulated, their voices mechanically altered by the antiquated speaker above Cavanaugh's head. And the thin, reedlike quality of that reproduction was laid over, like blankets on a bed, by the dull droning of the translator.

" 'I'm only telling you what I heard,' " repeated the translator. The questioner nodded, then pressed on.

Cavanaugh found himself leaning closer to the glass in front of him to watch the German's face as the man spoke. There was something about the way he rocked back and forth in his chair, and twitched his mouth and eyebrows, that Cavanaugh found fascinating. Except for this expression of nervousness, it was a disingenuous face: there was neither truth nor deception on it. Either the man was very practiced at deception, or he thought too little of his interrogator to tell a lie.

Cavanaugh found a hand gently placed on his arm, pulling him back; he turned and saw the old man nodding with his head to move away from the false window.

" 'Tell me simply,' " repeated the translator, " 'about these special weapons.' "

Cavanaugh instinctively leaned forward again.

" 'Yes, yes, I told you. They were, how do you say, very special. Very secret.' "

" 'But what were they?' "

" 'I don't know much, just that they were very scientific. Powerful.' "

" 'Scientific?' "

" 'Yes, you know, scientists designed them. We were very advanced. Germany had many such efforts.' " The translator clasped both hands together in front of him and rocked back and forth as he talked.

" 'Efforts like this special weapon?' "

" 'Yes. Our rockets were a good example.' "

" 'But this weapon was different?' "

The German hesitated. Cavanaugh focused all of his attention on the man's face. Surely there would be some clue to the German's truthfulness on his face.

244

" 'Yes, different. Using some new technology. Some break-through.' "

Cavanaugh stared. The face appeared sincere.

" 'But you don't know what kind of, ah, development it was? That is, what kind of breakthrough had been made?' "

" 'No. We, the SS, were brought in only at the end. That is, I only learned about it at the end. In March, or April, maybe. But I think for a long time the work on this weapon was underway."

Cavanaugh shifted from one foot to the other, and then back again. The conversation seemed like an inconclusive Ping-Pong game. Back and forth. Question and answer. Question and clarification.

"Where is this going?" he whispered.

Lytton-Harte shook his head. "These sessions can go on a long time. Our man is good, though. He'll try to bring the German around straightaway."

Cavanaugh wondered how long he would have to stand there. In the darkness he couldn't read his watch; he had no idea of the time, although his fatigue was rapidly returning. Then a sentence from the translator suddenly galvanized him.

" '. . . from Norway?' "

Norway! The name clicked. Norway could mean heavy water, and heavy water was an excellent medium for nuclear reactors.

" 'Yes. I remember being told that Norway supplied some of the raw materials for the new weapon. But when Norway fell, we were able to find other sources in Czechoslovakia.' "

That also clicked in Cavanaugh's head. There were reportedly large deposits of uranium in Czechoslovakia.

" 'And do you understand, do you know, what these materials were?' "

The German shook his head. *"Nein."*

There was more conversation and Cavanaugh slowly discerned the questioner's line of interrogation. He had artfully asked and reasked several questions in order to check the answers; satisfied, he now seemed to be setting the groundwork for a different direction of interrogation.

The translator never let his eyes wander from the men on the other side of the mirror. Only once or twice did he falter, searching for some English equivalent to a German word or expression. Several times he cleared his throat.

" 'And what were these weapons, uh, intended for? That is, what was their purpose?' "

The prisoner snickered. " 'To win the war, of course. But they came too late. Like the—" The translator paused at the word but Cavanaugh knew it: *Vergeltungswaffe* referred to the V-1 and V-2 weapons. The German seemed almost to spit. " 'They came too late as well.' "

" 'So what did Hitler decide to do then? I mean, when it was too late to use them in the war, what did he want these special weapons for then?' "

" 'That is what I told you. Hitler wanted to use them against the Allies, the major Allies, as a, what do you say—' " He searched for the words. " 'A parting shot.' "

Cavanaugh thought of the gun barrels in Mühlhausen. And the uranium cylinders several buildings away. The German seemed almost flippant as he said this. Did he even know what an atomic bomb was? What it could do?

" 'What do you mean by that?' "

The German waved one hand in the air. " 'You know, he wanted one last strike at his enemies. I think maybe Hitler didn't care if they arrived after the fall of Germany. What mattered to him was that he could strike back from his grave.' "

" 'Who did he want to strike back at?' "

The German smiled wickedly. " 'The Russians, of course. The Americans. And you.' "

" 'Not the French?' "

There was laughter. " 'They are—what do you say?—*ausschweifend.*' "

The translator paused a moment. "I think he means 'dissolute,' " he said quietly.

" 'Hitler thought the French would collapse of their own decadence.' " The German shifted in his chair and wiped his brow with a dirty handkerchief. He said something in a low voice that Cavanaugh couldn't hear.

The translator leaned toward the speaker. "I think he said he's tired. That he's said all this before. Yes. Now he wants to know why the interrogator is going over all this again."

The German raised his voice. " 'This is all academic. There was a plan, yes. But no one to carry it out.' "

The questioner, however, persisted. " 'But if there had been a way, if there had been men, what would they have done?' "

246

The German shrugged. " 'I told you. A small team of very special SS, very experienced, would take these weapons to the cities Hitler had chosen.' "

" 'And what would they do with them?' "

The man's face froze for an instant, then relaxed. The sour look returned to his face. " 'Use them, of course.' "

The words chilled Cavanaugh. Suddenly Mühlhausen and London were connected in an immediate and terrible way.

The gun barrels in Mühlhausen were prototypical atomic bombs. Somehow, secret Nazi scientists had succeeded in understanding that uranium could be made to explode. And somehow, they had found enough uranium to enrich through thermal diffusion to form into the fissionable male and female halves of a weapon. One set had been brought to England. Perhaps with a gun barrel; perhaps as the first of several secret shipments. Other bombs could be on their way to America and the Soviet Union.

But what frightened Cavanaugh most was the fact that only he knew about the gun barrels. He had the missing piece. And now he knew about a final vengeance plan that included his own country!

Cavanaugh leaned clumsily back against the wall. The last of his energy drained from him. For over a week he had lived with the uncertainty of his mission, in a foreign land, surrounded by people who wanted him for their own purposes. And for several days he had lived—alone—with the awful discoveries in Germany. And now this.

Lytton-Harte sensed Cavanaugh's shock. He hesitated for a long moment, weighing how to push Cavanaugh into telling him the last of what he wanted to know. His instincts said there would be no better moment than this.

"You see our dilemma," he began softly. He motioned to the translator to leave.

"Perhaps you'll take that drink now?"

Cavanaugh nodded and let himself be led down the hall to an unused office. It was just the two of them. The only light in the room came from a desk lamp. Part of the time, as Lytton-Harte spoke, the old man's face drifted in and out of the path of light. Cavanaugh sat on the couch, clutching his drink—he had no idea what it was—and just stared into the room.

Lytton-Harte carefully weighed what he would say. There was a delicate line here, one too easy to cross and therefore to give away more than one would gain. That wouldn't do. Not if what their German captive had said was true. There was so much at stake here, including the undeniable fact that the Americans had a weapon, or would have shortly, a weapon they might, after all was said and done, not share with the British. Damn it all!

He took a deep breath and tried to muster his most soothing voice. He had used it often enough on his colleagues in M15.

"I speak to you," he began, "in complete honesty." Lytton-Harte paused briefly to collect his thoughts. This was the crucial point. What he wanted now—what he was willing to risk in the already tentative relationship with American Intelligence—was to convince this young man on the couch of his sincerity. With that would come information.

"If what Brunig says is true, or substantially true, the Germans dispatched these special weapons to their enemies. We have to assume that they would send them to the capitals of our nations, of course. There, they could do the most damage. And with the war over, military targets would have lost their—how shall we say—their appeal."

He took a sip of his own drink. It was brandy, hardly of the quality he preferred, but right now it would do. Unfortunately, the American wasn't drinking his.

"We also have to assume that the, ah-h, uranium cylinders are part of a such a weapon." He fell silent and let his large head drop forward as if exhausted. "Consequently, we have to assume that this improbable plot is indeed fact and not fiction."

Cavanaugh stared at the old man. In the half-light, he had an avuncular quality.

"What I need to know, Dr. Cavanaugh, is whether you think that uranium was intended for an atomic weapon of some kind?"

Cavanaugh sighed. "Yes." He barely said it.

Lytton-Harte leaned against the edge of the desk. He deliberately chose not to sit down. It was uncomfortable for him, but he wanted to maintain a position of height; it was his theory that under circumstances like these, it could be intimidating. And any edge would be welcome in this dangerous game.

For a moment he looked out the blackened window. The wartime blackout curtains were still in place. There was nothing to see but a rectangular patch of darkness. Cavanaugh would report the events of tonight, of course. That was inevitable. And he would report this interrogation. That was inevitable, too. The Americans would object, possibly vociferously. They would be angry that an officer of theirs had been subjected to a kidnapping and drilling.

Lytton-Harte smiled to himself. This evening wouldn't help Anglo-American relations, but then, MI5 was on to something. *He* was on to something. A way of getting what the Americans had without having to rely on them. *That* was worth risking their wrath.

"You understand, Dr. Cavanaugh, we must think of this Nazi weapon, and this so-called vengeance plot, as still possible, still dangerous. Therefore, we must know more about the weapon itself. Clearly, what we found was only part of a weapon." He made it a declaration, rather than a question. It would be easier for Cavanaugh to respond to that.

Cavanaugh sighed. "Yes. Only part." His voice was still a whisper.

"I understand the confidence you must protect, your oath of secrecy, as it were. But also understand that we are under great pressure to find the rest of this bloody bomb. There are many lives at stake, and there could be others out there." Lytton-Harte's voice grew hard. "And we don't know what to look for."

Cavanaugh thought of the gun barrels. The missing ones. He felt the nausea rise inside him. He knew what the man was asking for, what he should say to help them out. But yet—

"Dr. Cavanaugh? This uranium was found in London. Parliament is in London. Buckingham Palace is in London. Indeed, several million people live in this city. Think of that!" Lytton-Harte found his voice rising. After all these years, his methods were almost instinctive now. He eased naturally back into his normal voice.

"We must have some clue, some idea, of what to search for. *Lives* are at stake."

Something turned inside Cavanaugh. What the hell! he told himself. Little from his past made sense after the last week. Los Alamos was far away.

He began slowly. "The cylinders, the uranium pieces have to be brought together very quickly. Simply pushing them together won't do."

"You mean explosively?" asked Lytton-Harte. He hoped the hidden microphone in the room was working and Canning was taking notes. Good notes.

"Yes. Explosively. They could be fired into one another."

"How do you do that?"

"With a cannon. In a pipe even. But one half would need to be fired at great speed into the other half." With those few sentences, he realized that he had given away the greatest American secret he knew. What the hell was his oath of secrecy worth now?

"How big would the cannon have to be?"

Cavanaugh shook his head. "Six feet. Eight. Enough for the first half to avoid something we call predetonation. A fizzle. I really can't say more." He hoped like hell the old man wouldn't press the point.

He didn't. Instead the man asked something else. His question came out in the form of a rumble.

"You saw the uranium. If it was to be used in a bomb of some kind, a weapon, how powerful would it be?"

"I don't really know." And Cavanaugh didn't. There were so many variables. How much of the uranium was U235. Total mass. Manner of assembly. The force of the propellant. Nuclear cross sections.

"There are many factors," he said slowly. "If the weapon worked— and that's a big 'if'—the explosion could vary."

"By how much?"

Cavanaugh shrugged. "From several hundred pounds to several thousand tons of TNT equivalent. Maybe more."

"And what would that mean in terms of destruction? Loss of life?"

"At the low end, the same as a conventional air-dropped bomb. Plus some radioactivity. And at the high end . . ." He hesitated.

"And at the worst?"

"Dozens, maybe hundreds, of square blocks. Maybe hundreds of thousands of lives." He didn't say it again, but there was also the radioactivity. No one knew for sure how much would be produced in an atomic explosion, and how it would affect human life in the fallout area.

For the first time in his long, cynical career, Lytton-Harte was stunned. He had heard figures like these before, in the early 1940s, when Britain still had its Tube Alloys Project. But in those days, the numbers were mostly speculation. Mathematics. The sort of thing scientists dealt with.

He pushed himself off the edge of the table and stood there, unable to think of anything else to ask.

"I think we need to alert the Russians," said Cavanaugh softly. He was thinking of Mühlhausen.

Lytton-Harte nodded. "Of course."

"And my government."

"Certainly."

There was a knock on the door. Cavanaugh barely heard it. He stared into the room, confused and angry with himself, and still slightly dizzy. He had said more than he should have; he had learned more than he'd ever wanted to know. And right now, he didn't know whom to trust. Then he looked up and saw Brooke standing next to the old man.

"I can take you back to the aerodrome now," Brooke said. His voice sounded almost apologetic.

Cavanaugh just stared at him.

Brooke flinched. "Or we can have a driver take you?"

Cavanaugh nodded slightly. Goddamn sons of bitches. "Yeah. A driver."

Part Eight

AUGUST 1991

LONDON, ENGLAND

It is certainly a good thing for the world that Hitler's
crowd or Stalin's did not discover this atomic bomb.
   It seems to be the most terrible thing ever
discovered, but it can be made the most useful.
                              —Harry Truman, 1945

Chapter Twenty-three

*I*t was a brief ride to the Archbishop of Canterbury's residence: from Whitehall straight down St. Margaret and Abingdon streets, then over the Thames across Lambeth Bridge. The ancient stone palace sat at the junction of Lambeth and Lambeth Palace roads.

Ramsden and Solomon sat in the backseat of a Ministry car. Their meeting with the Archbishop was in just fifteen minutes.

"We might be late," said Solomon, looking at his watch nervously.

Ramsden said nothing.

"I'm told His Grace is a very punctual man."

"Indeed," mumbled Ramsden, "a man of God should be."

Two days of polite, even ceremonious, negotiations had produced a meeting between the Archbishop and Ramsden. The purpose was, of course, extremely sensitive, given the nature of what Ramsden hoped to discuss. But as Sir George argued, if you couldn't trust the Primate of All England, just whom could you trust?

The car turned into the private entrance of the palace, which was actually a complex of buildings, many of which he had visited during public days; he remembered the Gatehouse, the Great Hall, the Post Room, and the Chapel.

Let's see, he mused, the Gatehouse, the imperious four-story castle, is the earliest building; from the 1400s, he remembered. That contained the library and archives. Were the missing files of MI5 hidden there?

That was Ramsden's guess. It was also his hope. The only one he could think of that made sense, given the mélange of facts and half-facts he had collected.

The events of July 1945 had been code-named "Archbishop" ostensibly because a German agent had been captured near the palace. But that didn't tell them where the missing files were. Lytton-Harte, a man Ramsden had been forced to learn about, had not been a simple man. No, more was at play. And Ramsden had one piece of incidental information that worked into all of this: both Lytton-Harte and the Archbishop of Canterbury had been schoolmates—Harrow, Eton, Christ College.

He smiled to himself. It was a hunch, no more than that, but by God! it was great fun.

He and Solomon were ushered into a waiting room by a rather frumpy older man in a clerical collar who extended his hand and bowed his head politely as he was introduced, first to Ramsden, then Solomon. Ramsden had the distinct impression that Solomon was also enjoying himself immensely. That was curious, he thought, since Solomon had converted to the Church from Judaism only after marrying an Anglican. It seemed a matrimonial convenience at best. And in Ramsden's experience, a visit to a prelate—any prelate—was hardly a religious experience.

Ramsden studied the room. The dark, rich paneling was from the last century, as was most of the heavy furniture. There were somber portraits in oil of the Archbishop's predecessors on the wall, all suitably stiff and glum-looking. Such was immortality. The air was a mixture of age and mustiness, a hint of decay mixed with the telltale smell of tobacco.

A moment later, one of the double doors under a heavy curved arch opened and the frumpy man nodded kindly and said, "His Grace will see you now."

Ramsden changed his mind when he entered the Archbishop's study. Momentarily, at least. The initial effect was almost religious, though no doubt intentionally staged. The room was rectangular, with mar-

256

velously high ceilings that curved toward one another. The wood paneling appeared even older and more lustrous than that of the anteroom. Ramsden had to admit that he was impressed.

The Archbishop himself sat behind a large desk strategically placed in front of a series of tall, thin windows that ran the length of the rear wall. Sunlight fell through hundreds of tiny panes of glass, each one thick and slightly dim with age, which seemed to slow the light as it passed. To Ramsden, the primate looked enveloped in celestial light.

"Good afternoon, Your Grace," he said, wondering if his voice carried to the opposite end of the room.

The man rose and walked to meet them halfway. "Ah, Mr. Ramsden."

The Archbishop was comparatively youthful, perhaps in his middle fifties. He appeared well cared for, trim and slightly bald. His face was aesthetic rather than handsome. To Ramsden, he appeared more of a professor than a prelate. He also wore a heavy dose of cologne, of a variety that Ramsden thought far too cloying for a man of his position. The prelate led them to a couch and several chairs in front of a massive stone fireplace.

"Quite lovely," said Ramsden. He ran his hand over one of the gargoyles on each side that gave the illusion of supporting the mantel. The Archbishop took a seat in one of the chairs while Ramsden took a position on the couch opposite him.

"You have an interest in these things?" the Archbishop asked.

Ramsden wasn't sure if the Archbishop meant the gargoyles or architecture in general. "Yes," he replied ambiguously; "architecture is an interest of mine."

Solomon simply smiled and took a seat next to Ramsden.

"Your request leaves me curious," said His Grace suddenly.

"Indeed, it's a curious business." Ramsden leaned forward slightly on the couch; the leather creaked and groaned as he shifted. It was an old practice of his, to lean forward when speaking of confidential matters. Here, he realized, it was only for effect.

"We have reason to believe that certain papers, files from the last war, were given to one of your predecessors." Ramsden explained about the visit to Canning and those facts he felt he could share regarding the remarkable tale of the Archbishop File.

The present Primate of All England barely lifted an eyebrow. "I still find it curious," he said, "but I nonetheless had our historian search the archives. Especially those related to the late Archbishop. You see,

I really don't understand why such papers would be given to the Church for safekeeping. Especially when they concern, ah, intelligence matters."

Ramsden nodded apologetically. "There is no explanation, Your Grace. We surmise they were given to your predecessor because of his friendship with the late Deputy Director General of MI5."

"Extraordinary. But why?"

Ramsden shrugged. He suspected the answer but it wouldn't do to offer his speculation to this man. "Perhaps it was done for safekeeping. At a time when the conventional procedures were, oh, inconvenient? In any case, I rather think the Deputy Director intended to reclaim them. But as I said on the telephone, the man died not too long after the war."

"Yes. Curious. Well, I'm sorry to say that our historian found nothing like you describe. And I assure you, he is a very thorough man."

Ramsden's heart fell. He had truly been hoping this would be the end of the search, that, with the missing files, the dozen odd, dangling questions would be answered, and the puzzle would be assembled.

"That is unfortunate indeed."

The Archbishop sensed Ramsden's disappointment. "I am sorry," he said. "Of course, if you have any other information, any lead, we should be glad to make the search again." He cleared his throat. "I am interested, however, in one point."

Ramsden looked up at the man with the aesthetic face.

"What could be so important about these files? After all, the war has been over for nearly half a century now."

Ramsden knew he couldn't mention the atomic bomb. Instead, he said, "There were events, at the end of the war, which would be greatly clarified with the information in those files. If we should find them, that is."

The Archbishop looked perplexed but pressed no further. Ramsden sensed that the man was discreet enough to realize that some arcane political matter was at stake. But then the Archbishop straightened and looked at Ramsden with renewed interest.

"Have you checked with the late Archbishop's assistant? Perhaps he has some idea of the final resting place of these papers."

"An assistant? Still alive?" Ramsden sat up himself. Perhaps not all was lost.

"Yes. I believe he's still alive. That is, he was last year. I can get the name for you."

258

"That would be very helpful. Perhaps our last hope, in fact."

The Archbishop pursed his lips. "We cannot let you lose hope, Mr. Ramsden. That would be unforgivable of us."

Yes, mused Ramsden. Now he had hope, but did he have faith?

The assistant was indeed alive. The ever-enterprising Solomon found him with the help of the Archbishop's secretary. The man, the right Reverend Sebastian Tweed, was in retirement at a home for elderly Anglican prelates in Chiswick, a suburb of outer London.

Ramsden immediately dispatched Solomon to interview him.

Tweed was alive, but barely, reported Solomon late that afternoon. The man was emphysemic and struggling with collapsing kidneys. Solomon dryly reported the man's condition with unintentional humor: "The administrator of the home says Tweed could take his last breath any day."

Fortunately, he lived long enough to remember that His Grace and Lytton-Harte frequently exchanged gifts. The one object that had struck the Right Reverend Sebastian Tweed as particularly remarkable was the gift of an old, worn leather valise that Lytton-Harte had given to the Archbishop.

Tweed had assumed that it had some special meaning to the two of them and remembered it only because the valise had arrived in the summer of the last year of the war. Not at Christmastime, as usual. It had, recalled Tweed, smelled of summer heat.

Unfortunately, the old prelate didn't remember what had happened to the gift.

Ramsden immediately placed a call to the palace asking if, by any chance, any of the late Archbishop's possessions were still at Lambeth Palace.

The palace historian called back two days later and said yes, there were several boxes of old things in storage. No, he said, they could not be examined without the express permission of the Archbishop.

Ramsden drew upon his newly found reservoir of hope and called the primate directly. His hope was justified: if it was important, the contents could be looked at. And if there were state papers, they could be taken for study.

The storage room was in the basement of the Great Hall at Lambeth Palace, terribly dank and moldy. Ramsden worried that anything stored there, but especially paper, might not have survived forty-five years. Fortunately, he was wrong.

The old wooden boxes were pried open and carefully emptied by the historian. The man's face matched his work, it was heavily lined, with the look of years spent in ancient surroundings. The valise came out with a coating of dust and mold but the initials were unmistakable: it had belonged to Lytton-Harte.

The clasp came off its mount at the historian's first touch. The black leather was in better shape, but barely. The old man with the lined face laid it flat on a table and carefully lifted its flap, then lifted the upper half of the valise itself. Even from the edge of the table Ramsden could see an inch or so of brown paper inside.

Somehow, he knew this was it!

Very gently, with obvious practice, the historian extracted a package wrapped in simple brown paper and tied with thin string. From Ramsden's position, it looked like a package you might be given at a book or stationery shop. The pace of the historian was maddening to Ramsden, but he said nothing. The old man untied the strip and gently pried open the wrapping paper.

The very first sheet was a small piece of personal stationery, maybe five by six inches, with something written in hand. The second sheet, more common in size for government work, was typed but contained two large words at the top that had been rubber-stamped years before.

They said simply, "Most Secret."

Chapter Twenty-four

*I*t was the sound of the clock that made him look up. The old grandfather clock that a previous Deputy had generously donated to the Ministry. Or left behind after retirement or death. It was in the hall outside his office.

It struck a number of times, and Ramsden was as taken with the graceful, mellow sound of each stroke as he was with the fact that he'd heard them. Usually, during the day, the outer office was too busy, too loud with telephones and conversation; the chimes were ordinarily lost in the technological and human melee.

He took off his glasses and laid them on the desk; gingerly, he rubbed the bridge of his nose and then pressed fingers to his eyes. He had been reading since late that afternoon.

The clock on his desk—an old gift from Edith, his late wife—read ten o'clock. Could he have been sitting here all these hours? Obviously so, because for the first time all day he felt the weariness that ran

261

from his head to his feet. Solomon had left hours ago, sometime around seven or seven-thirty, he remembered. They planned to meet first thing tomorrow morning to prepare a report.

But right now Ramsden was musing on history. Or rather its nature. One moment it seemed fixed, its characters cast and facts printed in black and white. And yet the next moment, just when one was feeling comfortable with the lay of it, history suddenly changed. A new fact, or character, or sheet of paper changed it all.

Or did it? Well, others could read the Archbishop files and decide for themselves. But God! what a discovery.

He glanced at his desk. The files were neatly arranged in one pile; last week's scientific report on the German gun barrel was off to one side. The information in that report—the precise measurements executed by the weapons people—left no doubt. The canisters of purified uranium found in 1945 would almost certainly fit the recently discovered gun. Together, the two would form the crucial elements of an atomic bomb. Ironically, information from two different generations made this definitive assessment possible.

A lot of what was in the files surprised him. Certainly the complex maneuvering by Lytton-Harte to get information out of the American named Cavanaugh. Really quite devious. And fairly successful, all things considered.

The small collection of intelligence reports from that murky period was equally fascinating. There were three of particular interest.

The first report was either startling or meaningless, and after nearly fifty years there was no way to be certain which it was.

Ramsden reached over and picked it up. Dated July 30, 1945, it was typed on M15 stationery, the paper yellowed like the rest of the stack, and prepared by Lytton-Harte from several sources within the Soviet Union. It reported a mysterious explosion somewhere outside of Leningrad. There was no official statement from the Soviets, but M15's source in Moscow reported several rumors: an Army munitions dump; sabotage; an accident at an electric generating plant. No firm explanation; just these rumors. Reportedly, however, the government was as perplexed as anyone about the event. And there were apparently many deaths from the explosion.

Why was this odd piece of unsubstantiated intelligence in the Archbishop files? Ramsden could only guess that Lytton-Harte believed that the explosion might have been nuclear in origin. That meant the existence of at least two Nazi bombs.

Ramsden shuddered at the thought. There was no way to be sure about the explosion or its cause. Too much time had passed for that.

The second intelligence report was briefer. Once again, a source within the Soviet government reported the execution of several Nazi "saboteurs"—four men captured in Leningrad and identified as SS officers. This memo was dated August 7.

By itself, the report would have meant little, certainly originating as it did from within the Soviet Union, where the military were executing hundreds of former Nazis in 1945, wherever they found them. But in the context of the events in 1945, and the rumors of a large and inexplicable explosion, it seemed to lend even further weight to the Nazi plot. Lytton-Harte obviously thought so because he had included this memo in his secret Archbishop file.

The third report, untitled and undated, contained Lytton-Harte's discussions with several Russian officials stationed in London immediately after the war. Ramsden couldn't be sure—the notes were frustratingly vague—but he sensed that even then the Russians knew something of a new, powerful German weapon. Perhaps they even knew it had been destined for use against them.

Earlier in the day, Ramsden had had only the briefest conversation with the Home Secretary. Enough to tell him of the find and to suggest that after a casual glance of the valise's contents he was sure his earlier suspicions had been correct. Intelligence *had* known of the German atomic bomb in July 1945. But there was even more shocking information. He had promised a thorough report by mid-morning of the next day.

Outside, London traffic had thinned to evening levels. Ramsden could pick out the telltale roar of a double-decker as it passed nearby and the occasional honking of private cars and taxicabs as they jostled for territory on London streets. His own office was very quiet; therefore the chimes of the grandfather clock had seemed like small explosions. He was virtually alone on his corner of the floor.

The night always contained an eerie quality for him, but tonight he seemed especially affected. His lamp illuminated the top of his desk and the papers with their faded "Most Secret" stamps; the table lamp against the wall assured him that there was more to his office than his desk. But the files—the much-sought Archbishop files—were like a window to the past. And through that window the turbulence of a summer almost fifty years before had suddenly re-emerged in a vivid and troubling way.

For Ramsden, the most intriguing revelation of all was Lytton-Harte's secret dealings with the American.

Ramsden had just leaned back in his creaky leather chair to reconsider all this when the telephone rang. The sudden harsh sound startled and frightened him. He clumsily grappled with the receiver.

"Hello?" he said, his voice searching for steadiness.

"Ramsden?" The voice was unmistakable. It was the Prime Minister! "Good. I caught you."

"Yes, Prime Minister."

"I was told you were still working."

Who could have told the PM? He'd been alone for hours. Was someone watching him?

"I understand you have something. Something about the South Bank discovery."

So the PM already knew! But how? From whom? The Home Secretary had expressed little surprise or interest. But then, he wasn't running for re-election. "Yes, it's true. Just this afternoon. You've already heard?"

"Yes, yes. You've had a chance to see it?"

What else would he have done but read the material? "Yes, Prime Minister. It's rather provocative."

"Provocative, Ramsden, or shocking?"

Ramsden thought a moment. "Yes, 'shocking' would be the word."

There was a pause on the other end and then a voice filled with resignation. "I rather feared that. That presents a problem."

"A problem?"

The Prime Minister seemed to sigh. "The times, Ramsden. This is a time of great political change. The dissolution of the Soviet empire. Most fortuitous for us." He hesitated. "I say, Ramsden. Who else knows about these files?"

"Only Solomon, my assistant, and the Home Minister. And the Archbishop, of course, and one of his assistants."

"They've read the material?"

Ramsden made a quick decision. "No, only myself."

"Good. We must keep it that way. I shall want to see them for myself, tomorrow, as soon as possible."

"I'm preparing a report."

"Yes, a report. Good. But I want to see the files themselves. You'll send them over?"

Ramsden felt the anxiety rise in the Prime Minister's voice. But then, this sort of discovery, if it was made public, could quite possibly create an uproar. "Yes," he said. "In the morning."

"First-rate. And, Ramsden?"

"Yes, sir?"

"Lock them up tonight. I don't want anything to happen. Is that clear?"

"Of course, Prime Minister." Ramsden said good night and hung up. That was the first telephone call he'd ever had from the PM.

Ramsden was greeted at his office the next morning by a strangely nervous Mrs. Pratt, his secretary.

Instinctively, he scanned the room and saw two odd-looking men sitting on the low couch against one wall of Mrs. Pratt's office.

"Who are those dour-looking men?" he asked.

"From Number Ten," mumbled Mrs. Pratt. "The PM sent them over."

"Hmm," said Ramsden. "They're waiting for me?"

"Yes. They're really quite dreadful. Gangster types with security cards."

"Ah." Ramsden could guess what they wanted. He opened the door to his office and stepped in, followed quickly by Mrs. Pratt.

"No need to worry, Mrs. Pratt. They don't appear to be terrorists."

The older woman dropped her voice. "It's not them. It's something else."

Ramsden turned slowly around to look at his long-time secretary. They had worked together for almost fifteen years, and this was the first time he'd known her to sound so odd. As if she were frightened.

"What is it?"

"Your office. Someone was in it. Digging around. Mine too. I guess last night."

Ramsden smiled. "No, Mrs. Pratt. Not someone. Me." He laughed. "I worked late last night. Till perhaps half past ten."

Now it was her turn to study him. "And you left your desk file unlocked? And opened mine as well?"

"I beg your pardon?"

"Yes. My desk file was unlocked this morning. And I distinctly remember locking it last night as I left. Always do. And I checked your desk. Also unlocked."

Ramsden glanced around the room. Nothing seemed particularly out of order as far as he could see. He walked over to his desk and examined the file drawer. There were tiny scratches around the keyhole, but he could have made those on any number of occasions over the years. He pulled on the drawer and it slid easily open. Could he have left it unlocked?

He quickly thumbed through the small collection of folders and then felt around for a small envelope he kept at the rear of the drawer. He found it. Inside were fifteen 10-pound notes; whoever opened his drawer hadn't been looking for cash. He closed the drawer.

Had he somehow left the drawer unlocked? Was Mrs. Pratt wrong about her own desk? Someone *could* have come to their offices after he'd left last night. But who? He looked over at Mrs. Pratt, who was clearly upset.

"What do those lugubrious men want?" he asked in a comforting tone.

"Some files you promised to the Prime Minister." Mrs. Pratt shook her head; her short gray hair stayed plastered by some invisible force to her skull.

Ramsden peeked through the open door to the outer room. The two men sat quietly on the couch, both dressed in rumpled pin-stripped suits. He waved them in.

"Thank you, Mrs. Pratt. I'll speak with them now."

He walked over to his desk and opened his briefcase and extracted the Archbishop files. For some reason, he had decided to take them home with him last night. At the time, it had seemed the safe thing to do. And by taking them home he had almost certainly kept them from falling into the hands of whoever had been there last night. *After* he'd left at ten-thirty.

There was a polite knock on the door. One of the men, who spoke with an East London accent, introduced himself and his partner and said that they had come for "certain files," as promised to the Prime Minister.

Ramsden was tempted to dodge the request by asking for clarification. Instead, he indicated he wished to verify the Prime Minister's request by telephone. He assured them it was because of the importance of the documents.

The Security men were nonplussed. Apparently, the move struck them as prudent. Or perhaps procedural. They agreed to wait while Ramsden made a call. But he couldn't reach the PM himself; the great man was unavailable. And then he couldn't locate anyone at the PM's office who might know.

He was explaining this to the dense-looking men from Security when the telephone rang in the outer office. A moment later his own phone rang. Mrs. Pratt told him it was William Ackersly from the PM's office at Downing Street.

Ramsden knew Ackersly well enough to dislike him. The man was an assistant to the Prime Minister, young, terribly conscious of public relations, and too arrogant for either his age or his talents. But he was powerful and was said to speak for the PM.

"Ramsden?"

"Ackersly." Ramsden's voice was neither warm nor distant. Just the sort of tone crafted over a lifetime of bureaucratic survival in which PMs and their assistants came and left.

"Our men are there?"

"Do you mean the gentlemen from Security?"

"Yes, of course. Who else?" He made no attempt to conceal his irritation. That got him a poor mark, thought Ramsden. Never reveal irritation or disappointment.

"Yes, they're here and asking for the, ah, files we discovered yesterday at Lambeth Palace." He rather imagined Ackersly shaking his head at this point.

"Good. Give them over, will you?"

"Well, I haven't quite finished writing a report for the Prime Minister yet."

"Ah, don't bother. I think the PM would prefer a briefing in person."

So, thought Ramsden, nothing on paper. Already preparations to eliminate a paper trail.

"I've promised a report to the Home Secretary as well."

Ackersly emitted a sharp sound; he was more agitated now. "Well, take that up with him personally, of course. But the Prime Minister is most anxious to see what you've found. As soon as possible."

"Of course. I'll send them right along."

Ackersly issued a terse "good," and then hung up.

Ramsden stuffed the Archbishop files into a "Classified" envelope used for mail between Ministries. Then he had Mrs. Pratt prepare a receipt for the material and took pains to be specific about the contents of the envelope. There would be no doubt that he had turned the papers over.

The Security men didn't flinch. Nor did they ask why Ramsden kept material of such obvious importance unprotected on the top of his desk. Instead, the man with the East London accent signed eagerly and put the envelope into an attaché case with a small chain connected to his wrist. They said good-bye politely and left.

Moments later, Solomon knocked on Ramsden's door.

"Well," said Ramsden sarcastically, "you saw the PM's representatives?"

Solomon nodded. "What did they want?"

"The Archbishop files. They're on their way to Downing Street as we speak."

"What about our report?"

"We'll do it anyway. From memory. The specific contents aren't important, just the implications." He paused. "And the consequences."

Their conversation was interrupted by Mrs. Pratt ringing on the telephone. "The Home Secretary wants to know if you can meet with him?"

"Of course. When?"

"Right now. Just you."

"Certainly. Tell him I'm on my way." He hung up the phone, slowly resting the receiver on the cradle. So now it was his own Secretary calling. The PM must have talked with him just minutes ago. Or perhaps last night.

He was almost out the door when he caught himself. "Oh, say, Walter?" It was the first time he remembered using Solomon's first name. He stepped back into his office and closed the door.

Solomon looked up, puzzled by the informality.

"On second thought, I'll do the report myself. You haven't read these files. You know they exist, but you haven't read them. Do you understand?" Ramsden could at least protect his assistant.

Solomon blinked several times before he replied. Ramsden had known the man too long not to know that he understood.

"Yes, I do," Solomon said. "Yes."

Part Nine

JULY 1945

WASHINGTON, D.C., AND ALAMOGORDO, NEW MEXICO

When the hurlyburly's done,
When the battle's lost or won . . .
—William Shakespeare, *Macbeth*,
Act I, Scene 1

Chapter Twenty-five

*W*ashington: pristine and untouched by war. And green and bathed in summer sunlight. Cavanaugh was so glad to be back that he almost cheered when the plane touched down. Home. Almost home.

He didn't even wait for an Army car, but grabbed a cab directly to the War Department.

He had a long list prepared of things to do. It was in his head, at least a dozen items, although the first two seemed more important than anything else.

Making the list had occupied most of the agonizingly long flight between London and Washington. He had slept twice, dozed, really, out of sheer exhaustion. Most of the time, his mind had reeled with memories: incidents, conversations, impressions—they ran together in a mental soup that he struggled to keep clear, defined.

First he had to talk to Groves. Tell him everything he could remember: Germany. England. Put it all down on paper if that's what the General wanted. Even about the old man outside Mühlhausen: his death would never be right, but it might be easier to bear if Cavanaugh could at least get it off his chest.

God! he had no idea how Groves would react. Especially to what had happened his last night in London. There was no way he could withhold what he had done and heard. He would tell the truth about everything, no matter the cost.

But as soon as he could—and Jesus, he hoped she was still there!—he wanted to see Christine. On the plane he had pulled her handkerchief out of his pocket and smelled it; there was only the faintest hint of her left. Maybe it was all in his head, but there was still a trace, enough to make her face, her smile vivid in his mind.

Then he wanted to get home. Back to New Mexico and his work and the Test. He didn't want to miss that. He just hoped that Groves would let him go back.

And somewhere on his list, either fifth or sixth, he couldn't quite remember, he wanted a shower. A hot, American shower. Fifteen minutes at least; maybe thirty if the water held out.

He'd sent a cable from the U.S. air base in England saying he was on his way back and when to expect him. But nothing of his mission nor his findings. He had been warned about that. He couldn't even say that he had something to say.

Now Cavanaugh waited impatiently at the security desk in the lobby of the War Department Building. There was no pass for him waiting, not even his name on a list. Had they even gotten his goddamn cable? He wondered. Next to him, in a lump, was his duffel bag.

"What's the holdup?" he asked.

The young MP behind the desk shrugged. "We called. They gotta send someone down."

Cavanaugh nodded. He had taken only a few minutes at the airport to use the bathroom and check his uniform. The insignia seemed right, but how in the hell did he know? They wore different stuff in Europe, or nothing at all except rank and a badge on the arm identifying the infantry group, or whatever, and in his case, the Army Corps of Engineers.

Goddamn it! What was the holdup?

The telephone rang on the desk. The GI answered it, said something and then looked at Cavanaugh.

"Some guy's on his way."

He shifted his weight from one foot to the other and lit a cigarette. None of the faces in the lobby were familiar, but everyone looked the

272

same; as far as he could tell, it was the same sophisticated crowd that had come and gone the last time he stood there.

Behind him, over the din, he heard a voice calling his name. He turned around and saw Christine walking toward him. At first he was so surprised to see her, so delighted, that he failed to notice the somber look on her face. He dropped his cigarette and rushed toward her, just managing to touch her arm with his hand to hug her when she hesitated and then pushed him back. Or moved herself back.

"Good to see you again," she said evenly. There was no emotion in her voice.

Cavanaugh was confused. No, he was stunned. Her greeting was nothing like what he'd expected, certainly nothing like what he'd wanted. Had she forgotten the night they'd spent together or put it out of her mind the way you do with things you later regret?

She looked around him to the GI. "Thanks, Corporal," she said. "I'll take him from here." Her face broke into a small smile. The GI winked and touched his forehead with a single finger in a fake salute.

"Good trip?" she asked. "This way."

Was that all? "Yeah." Cavanaugh was still too shocked to feel anything. But then he began to feel his insides churn.

"Hey Captain!" the corporal shouted. "Sir!"

Cavanaugh didn't hear him; he would have kept on walking if Christine hadn't stopped and turned around.

"What about your bag, Captain?" The GI pointed to Cavanaugh's duffel bag which still lay near the desk.

"Oh yeah," he said. He walked back, picked it up, and started after Christine.

They walked down a hall until she pointed to a door on their right.

"This'll be quicker," she said, and pushed the door partially open for him. He stepped in, ignoring the plaque next to the door that probably identified the room or stairwell. Then he stopped.

They were in a closet of some kind, with washtubs on rollers and mops hanging on the walls. Before he knew it, Christine came in behind him and closed the door. When he turned around and started to say, "What the hell?" she suddenly rushed forward and hugged him. Hard.

Then she kissed him, again and again. "Thank God, you're safe," she murmured.

Cavanaugh didn't try to figure it out. Instead he held her so tightly he suddenly feared he might crush her; he relaxed and melted his mouth into hers. "Oh, God," she said again, pressing her face close to his.

Then she stepped back a bit, still keeping both her hands on his torso, and looked at him. Her face was flushed, even more lovely than he remembered, and seemed to take his face in, looking at everything at once. Suddenly she caught his expression and broke into a laugh that she quickly stifled with her hand.

"Oh, that," she said, nodding her head backward. "I couldn't say hello properly out there. Not in public. Too many people gossip."

He smiled, feeling at once relief and joy. He momentarily forgot everything he so urgently planned to tell Groves.

She dropped her hand, revealing again her lovely smile. "We'll say hello again, okay? Later?"

Cavanaugh didn't reply. Instead he gently pulled her close, never losing sight of her face until he bent down to kiss her.

Cavanaugh's good feelings, his momentary respite from all that he had been through, lasted until he was upstairs, in the conference room of the Manhattan Project offices. Sitting at the table across from Gilbert, his sense of urgency, his anxiety returned in full force.

"Well, where is he?" Cavanaugh couldn't believe that Groves had left town. Hadn't the man gotten his goddamn cablegram from England?

"He's on the road. He left yesterday afternoon." Gilbert's voice revealed no reaction to Cavanaugh's surprise. Instead, he had a calm, patient look, one he had cultivated and used when briefing important, but technically uninformed, Army brass.

Cavanaugh did some simple arithmetic. The cablegram had almost certainly gone out yesterday morning and, given the time difference, would have arrived in America in time to be read during the day. Groves would certainly want to hear all that he knew!

"But he wanted to talk to me as soon as I got back."

He frowned. "But he wanted to talk to me as soon as I got back."

"He did. But you're at least two days late. You were expected Wednesday. It's Friday."

"What about Franklyn? Where the hell is he?"

"On the road too. Left two days ago for an inspection tour of Oak Ridge."

"Jesus Christ," murmured Cavanaugh. What the hell was he supposed to do now? "When will Groves be back?"

Gilbert shook his head. "Don't know. Couple days, I think. This trip's been planned for a while."

Cavanaugh's mind raced. What could he tell Gilbert? How much of what was brimming inside his head could he possibly share without violating his promise to Groves: to brief the General, and only the General, in person. He sighed. Probably nothing.

"Didn't he get my cable?"

"I'm sure."

"Well?" Cavanaugh took a deep drag on his cigarette and drummed the edge of the table with his other hand.

"Well what? He's gone. I've sent a cable to the next point where he can be reached asking for instructions." Gilbert leaned forward solicitously. "You just gotta wait."

Cavanaugh sighed and rolled his eyes wearily. He had no idea what his information was worth. Or how reliable it was. But someone else needed to make that assessment, not he. And Jesus, it had to be done soon! If there was a chance, no matter how small, that Hitler's final vengeance plot was true, then . . . then someone needed to do something.

"How long until you reach Groves?"

"Sometime today. Soon maybe. But he may not respond immediately."

"Why not?" Surely Groves would react in some way. He was known for details like that.

"I really can't say. I mean, there's a lot going on."

Then Cavanaugh remembered Trinity. "It's the Test," he said loudly. They've set the test date!"

"Shh," ordered Gilbert. "Not so loud."

"Well?"

"We're not supposed to talk about it in the office."

"Gilbert, for God's sake, I helped make the goddamn thing!"

Gilbert lowered his voice even more. "It's set for next week." The Test was set for Sunday, maybe Monday, depending on how soon Los Alamos would have the bomb ready.

"Oh, God," moaned Cavanaugh. "What day? I've gotta know. I've gotta be there!" Next week? That left only a few days to catch a train, or hopefully a plane, back to New Mexico. Jesus Christ! The Test was what he had worked so hard for for a year and a half.

Gilbert stalled "I don't know exactly when. Depends on when you people get your act together."

"Why can't I get a plane today?" Cavanaugh pleaded.

Gilbert slowly shook his head. "I can't do anything, I can't arrange anything until I hear from Groves. You understand, don't you?"

"No. I just want to go home. Now. I want to make the Test." He thought of all the experiments he had designed to measure aspects of the explosion: detonation simultaneity, blast intensity, things like that. And his friends and co-workers. They were probably already at Trinity, setting everything up, waiting, sweating in the New Mexico sun, shooting the shit. It was the big moment, and Jesus! he didn't want to miss it.

"Gilbert, *please*, get to Groves. I've got to talk with him right away, and he promised I'd be back in time for Trinity."

"I'll do my best, Phil, but I can't promise. You know that."

"Yeah." Cavanaugh looked out the window, at the wall that partially blocked the view.

"Why don't you get some rest?" Gilbert suggested. "We'll find you a room somewhere. You can shower, get some sleep. I'll get back to you as soon as I can. I promise."

Gilbert looked straight across the table at the other man. He knew damn well that Cavanaugh was going straight to Christine's apartment, the lucky son of a bitch. At least he had that going for him.

He watched Cavanaugh walk down the hall. Probably back to Christine's. Everyone knew Cavanaugh had spent the night with her two weeks ago. Even the General. But at least the lieutenant was family. She knew enough not to ask questions, and not to let Cavanaugh talk.

And if he did accidentally let something slip, well, it wouldn't be catastrophic. Besides, she would report whatever had been said back to Gilbert. She had been instructed to do that. That had been Groves's idea, but Gilbert had been told to implement the order. And if she wanted a career after the war, and a clean record, she would comply. She was an ambitious girl. And a beautiful one.

Gilbert thought about Cavanaugh and shook his head. Lucky son of a bitch.

The evening wasn't what either would have wanted. Christine cooked a wonderful dinner, served with wine and candlelight. God only knew how many coupons she had used to make it. There was even soft music from the radio in the background.

But somehow, despite the dinner and, above all, her presence, Cavanaugh couldn't quite get his disappointment out of his mind. The

276

prospect of missing the Trinity Test lingered in the back of his head throughout the evening. It was part of every conversation and every look between them.

The food was wonderful, but he couldn't find his appetite. She was charming, but he was slow to respond; they were like a theatrical team whose performance is spoiled when the timing of one partner is off by even a few seconds.

She noticed it, of course, and did everything she could to compensate. But she knew something was on his mind. And he knew that she was working too hard.

"I'm sorry," he said for the tenth time during the evening.

"Don't worry," she said—again. "You're tired, you've been through a lot, I know."

He believed her. And what made him love her even more, and therefore feel even more guilty, was the fact that she *did* understand.

She sat across the tiny table from him, within touching distance, and now she placed her hand quietly on his, like a gentle caress. He turned his hand palm-up and took her hand and curled it within his own.

"I can't tell you how much this means to me, to be back here with you. I thought about it so often over there." He smiled, then shook his head. "But I'm not much of a date tonight."

"You've got a lot on your mind. Don't worry. Just relax." She reached over and poured a little more wine into his glass. "Why don't we just sit for a while?"

He nodded. Holding her on the couch, both of his arms wrapped around her, he closed his eyes and tried to clear his mind. Christine felt so good, so soft and warm; her perfume, which he recognized instantly, drifted up to him.

"I saw a man killed," he said suddenly. It came out of him unexpectedly.

Christine turned slightly to look into his face.

"I was in a truck, at night. We ran into him."

"My God," she said softly. Very gently she took his hand and squeezed it.

"He wasn't killed right away. Someone—" He hesitated. "Someone broke his neck. Killed him. To keep him from talking."

"A German?" she asked.

"Yes. I mean, I guess so. It was in the Soviet Zone—" It didn't even occur to him that he shouldn't have mentioned the Soviet Zone.

Christine turned suddenly and put her finger on his lips. With only the light from the candles, he looked into her face and saw her frown. Or turn serious.

"It's not your fault," she said. "You can't blame yourself."

"But—"

"Shh. Bad things happen. And if you didn't intend to harm him . . ." She didn't finish. Instead she lowered herself on him and put her face next to his.

"So many bad things happen," she whispered.

He sighed. "There were other things," he began, "things I learned about."

She put her hand back on his mouth. "Not now," she said.

The man with the blond hair watched the sunset from the window. It wasn't as impressive as some he'd seen, especially back home, but it was pretty.

He stood at the window on the third floor. Just high enough to see over the rooftop of the building across the street. Washington's taller buildings popped up irregularly in the distance. Beyond them was countryside.

As far as he was concerned, the city wasn't especially beautiful. The buildings were too low, too plain to be of any real interest to him. Not like his own city had been. And it was hot here, even humid, and that made walking and being outside uncomfortable. In this, he differed from his colleagues. They seemed to like the place.

But they all agreed this country was rich, however: the cars, the clothes, the staggering availability of food and goods. None of them had ever seen so much at one time. Every day. And most of it could be had for money. No coupons needed. No black-market contacts. Just American dollars.

The one thing he did like was the cigarettes. All the American brands. He could buy his favorite anywhere: Pall Malls. And as many as he wanted and for almost nothing.

He couldn't imagine what life in Germany was like now. He had been gone for so long, and all he and the others had was the news from foreign newspapers. The war was over, or so the papers said, but there was no word of friends or colleagues. It had been three months since he had last worn his major's uniform.

The pain in his head came back. It always started as a pinprick in his neck and worked its way through his head. It happened every time

278

he thought about the Americans and their wealth. A nation made rich by the same war that had devastated his own. And all artificially contrived, of course. Phony, made possible by a nation and a people concerned only with their own pleasure. That sickened him. There were no restraints here.

He also resented the fact that there was no destruction in the city. No rubble, no neighborhoods totally flattened by aerial bombing. During the day, families picnicked in the parks; at night, the streetlights came on and people walked around. There was not a single window boarded up; not an air-raid shelter in sight. No hint of war.

Scheisse! He hated these Americans.

Behind him, a voice spoke.

"Werner?"

He whirled around. "No! I told you. Simon. Always use the English." The man nodded. "What time tonight?"

The blond man looked at his watch. A new American one. "Nine," he said. "After dark."

Chapter Twenty-six

$\mathcal{G}$ilbert looked at the Army telegram one more time and then let it gently slide from his hand so that it wafted down in an arc to the ink-stained surface of his desk blotter. All he could see now was a single line of typed copy: the transmission code that indicated the telegram had originated in California Friday night.

Cavanaugh wasn't going to be happy. Reached on the West Coast, Groves had finally responded to Gilbert's inquiry. It was direct: Keep Cavanaugh in Washington until the General returned but offer no explanation. And maintain surveillance and inform Groves of any unusual events. The estimated return date was Tuesday, July 17, possibly the day after if there was a snag in the work in New Mexico. Groves was in California, ostensibly checking out a Manhattan Project laboratory. In reality, he was making a long, circular trip to Albuquerque as the last stop before heading for Trinity. For some reason, the Old Man wanted to disguise his real travel plans.

Gilbert pulled a map of the United States out of his desk drawer and unfolded it. Groves was in Los Angeles, but was planning to fly to New Mexico today. Gilbert ran his finger across Arizona to New Mexico. Then he slowly ran it down several inches to an unmarked spot on the map. The closest towns were Alamogordo, slightly to the north, and Las Cruces, slightly to the south. El Paso was even farther south. The invisible point was Trinity, where the Manhattan Project's experimental atomic bomb awaited detonation.

As a last resort, Groves could probably be reached in Albuquerque later in the day. Once he left by car for the desert, however, he would be effectively out of touch; a combination of security precautions and crude communication lines. If Cavanaugh had any hopes of appealing Groves's decision, he needed to do it today.

Gilbert folded the map up and sat back in his chair, thinking about it all. Even if he helped Cavanaugh draft an appeal, it was highly unlikely that Groves would change his mind. When it came to security, the Old Man was a maniac. And besides, it wouldn't help Gilbert to be involved in anything that looked as if he were challenging the General's decision. No, he would just have to give Cavanaugh the bad news straight on. Or soften it somehow.

He reached over and grabbed a file folder from his desk and skimmed through it one more time. The file contained everything the Office had on Philip Cavanaugh. Groves had ordered it prepared before he selected him for his mysterious overseas assignment.

The file didn't have anything particularly interesting in it, at least as far as Gilbert was concerned. Some of the background data he already knew, since the two of them had been in college together. There was a copy of his employment application at Los Alamos, although the name "Los Alamos" was never mentioned. A copy of his résumé, basically a list of his college courses and the part-time jobs he had held as a student. Some background on his parents. Several photographs. A security review, which ruled the man "loyal." Paperwork related to his trip to Europe. And some recent memoranda from Major Franklyn about Cavanaugh's "suitability." Gilbert pulled one memo out.

A line popped right out at him: ". . . bright but inattentive to detail . . ." Oh, boy! That was Franklyn's way of saying that Cavanaugh took Franklyn less than seriously. Gilbert smiled. He caught another line: ". . . obviously accustomed to an unstructured setting . . ." That was a cheap shot at Los Alamos that Groves no doubt shared. And still another Franklynism: ". . . somewhat immature, as evidenced by his unreasonable resistance to authority . . ." Gilbert laughed. Cavanaugh must have insisted on smoking in the major's goddamn office!

Gilbert thought about the file. What was interesting about Cavanaugh wasn't on paper. It had to do with his trip to Europe and what happened there.

Something had gone on, something out of the ordinary. He could tell it by the look on Cavanaugh's face yesterday, and the way he'd acted. He had been anxious, really nervous, about talking with the General. And there were the other things.

One was the cablegram from G-2 in London. Manhattan Project Security had received a report about a long dinner Cavanaugh had with an English officer named Brooke. And Brooke, as G-2 knew from its own files, was part of British Intelligence. This report had come as a routine follow-up on Cavanaugh's activities in England. The follow-up had been ordered by Groves himself.

And then, there was the trip itself: Cavanaugh's secrecy-shrouded trip to Germany. Why had he been sent there? The intelligence report from SHAEF—from the very team that Cavanaugh had been part of—reported nothing new from a second sweep of southern Germany, although it did confirm the French were now actively involved in the scramble for Nazi technology. In fact, Gilbert knew from other sources that a formal protest had been filed by the French Army Command with General Eisenhower about "unauthorized" American Intelligence activity in the newly created French Zone of Occupation in Germany.

They didn't know half of what was going on. But what Gilbert found most intriguing were the days unaccounted for between the so-called sweep of Nazi atomic laboratories in southern Germany and Cavanaugh's reappearance in London. That made three or four days when there was no mention of where Cavanaugh had been, nor what he had been doing. What the hell had happened?

Gilbert knew that it had something to do with General Groves and one of the Old Man's pet projects. Something special and secret. And probably technical. Why else would Groves send a scientist from Los Alamos when someone from headquarters would easily do?

Clearly, it had something to do with the race for German wartime scientific achievements. But what? All of Gilbert's subtle probings the last few weeks hadn't revealed a goddamn thing. Franklyn probably knew some of it, but he wasn't talking. And Gilbert's friends at the Pentagon were all ears for any news of the Manhattan Project.

Gilbert thought about the last year or so. Several times, very judiciously, he had let small pieces of information drop to his friends there. No technical secrets, of course, not that he knew any, but just updates on the Project efforts. The sort of thing that was only officially shared with maybe a dozen top people, including the President, and never with the next level down.

The news Gilbert shared was always something basic, for instance, that Hanford was finally delivering plutonium, or that Los Alamos had finally settled on two distinct bomb designs. Never any more than that.

It was all friendly stuff, among *family*, as it were.

He had a reason, of course. The Manhattan Project wouldn't continue much longer once the war in the Pacific ended. Men would come home and there would be a scramble for jobs. If he could stay in the Army, he would at least have something to do, and given the nature of the atomic bomb, it could be a pretty damn interesting job. But to survive, to advance in the military, he needed friends outside of the small, closed world of the Manhattan Project.

That was why he cultivated the friends he did, with small pieces of information, about a project that more and more people were growing very interested and excited about. Groves would exile him to Alaska if he knew what Gilbert was doing, of course, but it was worth the risk. And besides, the war had to end soon. The Manhattan Project would end with it.

Gilbert leaned forward and rested his arms on the desk. One of his friends at the Pentagon had noticed that Cavanaugh had become a captain in the Corps of Engineers. And he had wondered about the sudden, high-level trip to Europe. Casually, the man, a colonel, had inquired about Cavanaugh, although at the time Gilbert had been as surprised as anyone to see Cavanaugh go on that mission.

So what had the man done in Europe? That was what Gilbert and his friends in the Pentagon wanted to know. But Gilbert needed more information. And that meant getting it out of Cavanaugh before the man returned to New Mexico.

Cavanaugh put the receiver back on its hook. He didn't know what to feel. Gilbert had put it as good news and bad news: good news that he had reached Groves, bad news that Groves wanted him to stay in Washington. No explanation.

Gilbert had been honest, at least. And there was still a chance that

Groves could be persuaded to let Cavanaugh make Trinity—the date, according to Gilbert, was still uncertain, but set for next week. There was still a chance.

Cavanaugh flopped back down on the couch, gloomy and disheartened. Somehow, he had to force himself to put the Test out of his mind and remain optimistic—there was a chance! At least he wasn't as tired as yesterday; sleeping until ten that morning had helped a lot.

Christine had left early for work—he had no idea when. Washington, like Los Alamos, was still working a seven-day week. She had left him coffee and a note telling him where to find the eggs and bacon. There was even a bowl of fresh fruit sitting on the dining-room table—miraculously cleared from last night's dinner—along with fresh flowers and the Saturday morning newspaper. God, what a girl!

And last night . . . He had been so tired, so depressed, that he had surely ruined their dinner. No matter what she said. And in bed, he'd been way off, terribly anxious to make love on the one hand, somehow unable to put all of himself into it on the other. And despite all that, she'd left him breakfast and this small message at the end of her note:

X X X X
(lots of love)
C.

Wearing only his underwear, he picked up the newspaper and set it on his lap. The headlines were mainly about the war in the Pacific and a Congressional hearing about war profiteering. He knew it was silly, but he half-expected to see an article about a German civilian killed in a hit-and-run accident and abandoned in the Soviet Zone. And that this victim would also have a broken neck.

Cavanaugh didn't bother to read the text. Instead, he scanned the headlines, looking for something that interested him. It was strange, but for the first few days in England, after he first arrived, he'd felt out of touch, desperate for news about America. The English newspapers covered the war all right, but mostly the events that affected their own country. America was an ally, a partner in the post-war world, but Los Alamos didn't even exist. His interest had faded to concern over survival. Now he had a real American newspaper and he was having trouble reading it.

What he needed to do was to dress and get back down to the War Department and keep the pressure on Gilbert to stay in contact with

284

Groves. He started to fold the newspaper when his eye caught a small headline at the bottom of the page; it said simply, "Nazi Sailor Hospitalized." The article itself wasn't long—just a couple of inches—but reported that a man in civilian clothes but with German Navy papers had been found on a place called Tangier Island, somewhere south of D.C. in the Chesapeake Bay. The man had been discovered by local fishermen and turned over to the Coast Guard, which kept a small installation on the island. The sailor had been shot three times at close range but somehow miraculously survived. He was now in critical condition at a naval hospital in D.C.

Something about the event struck Cavanaugh as odd. What in the hell would a German sailor be doing, heavily wounded, on a small island in the Chesapeake Bay?

The telephone rang. He jumped slightly, then scrambled up to reach the phone in the small hallway. It was Christine.

"Good morning," she said cheerily.

"Yeah, good morning to you too." Just hearing her voice made him think about last night.

"I knew you weren't asleep."

"Oh yeah?"

"I just saw Gilbert. He told me the news. Sorry."

Trinity seemed as far away now as Germany. "There's still a chance."

Christine hesitated. "Sure."

All of a sudden, he didn't know what to say. Neither did she. They both clung to their phones in a long, uncomfortable silence.

Then Cavanaugh remembered the item in the newspaper. "Listen," he began, "I saw something in the newspaper. Something curious."

"What?"

"An item about a German sailor. Front page on the bottom."

"I saw that. He's in a hospital or something."

"Right." His mind was now clicking and telling him contradictory things: find out more; leave it alone, it's not your goddamn business.

"Listen, can you do something? I mean, find out something?"

"Maybe. Find out what?"

"The sailor. Can you find out more about the guy?"

There was a pause. "Well, I can try. But why?"

Cavanaugh hesitated. He didn't know how to explain, even to himself, why he was suddenly so interested. And even if he did, he wasn't sure how much he could say that wouldn't require telling someone, maybe Christine, about London.

"I know it sounds silly, but if you could find out anything, I'd appreciate it. I'm just interested. Really."

She gave a small laugh. "I'll try. Strictly unclassified stuff, of course."

"Of course," he replied. "Anyway, I'm dressing and coming down to your office."

"When?"

"In a few minutes. As soon as I clean up. And, listen."

"What?"

He lowered his voice. "About last night?"

Her own voice grew very soft, almost inaudible over the telephone line. "Yes?"

"I'm sorry. But maybe we could give it another shot?"

Chapter Twenty-seven

*C*avanaugh was a block away from the new War Department Building when he spotted a bookstore.

"Pull over here!" he suddenly shouted.

Startled, the taxi driver jerked upright in his seat. "Jesus," he said under his breath.

"Yeah, here, that's fine." Cavanaugh fumbled through his pockets for his money. A crumpled wad of bills appeared and he started to pull a single until he realized he had military scrip from Europe. He rooted around in his pockets again and came up with a dollar bill that he threw into the front seat. "Thanks."

Minutes later he was walking quickly down the sidewalk toward the War Department with a sailor's map of Chesapeake Bay rolled in a tube under his arm. He nervously tapped in on the floor as he waited at the security desk for an escort to the Manhattan Project offices. It was Christine who greeted him. She could tell by his face that he was agitated.

She smiled. "What's all this about? You're supposed to be resting, remember?"

He smiled nervously. "Yeah, I know," he said, as he tapped the rolled map against his leg.

"Here," she said, clipping a security pass to his breast pocket. It was similar to the one he wore in Los Alamos. "This is good for the next few days. Now you don't need me to come and get you."

"Let's go," he said, taking her arm. He didn't care who saw them together now.

He had thought about what to tell her in the taxicab: to find an explanation somehow for why he was interested in the German sailor. But he couldn't find anything that made clear-cut sense, not without violating his promise to Groves.

The rational part of him said that it was nothing, coincidence at best, that a German sailor had been washed up on an American island. But some other part of him said to be wary, that such a seemingly coincidental event might actually be part of something larger, something more dangerous. At some level, he had to take seriously the possibility that if the Germans got an atomic bomb to London, and possibly to the Soviet Union, they could have one here as well.

For the moment, though, he would just say he found it interesting and try to leave it at that.

Cavanaugh sat down in Christine's office and lit a cigarette. Then he remembered she didn't smoke. "Oh," he said, "can I?"

She nodded.

He looked around the tiny office and at the empty desk next to Christine's. "You got a roommate?"

"Uh-huh, but he's not here right now. We can talk." She looked at the rolled-up map next to his chair. "What's that?"

"A map. Of the Chesapeake."

She slowly shook her head. "You're really taking this seriously, aren't you?"

He made a half-grin, knowing that what he was going to say was probably something she had heard many times. "Trust me."

Christine rolled her eyes. "Okay, this is what I found out. Your sailor *is* German. They found papers on him. But . . ."

Cavanaugh lifted an eyebrow.

"But he may also have been SS."

Oh, shit! thought Cavanaugh. That was one more tiny weight in favor of being concerned. "Why do you think that?"

"They. Naval Intelligence, actually. Because he has a recent scar under one arm, near the armpit, where members of the SS often had their serial number tattooed. No one is sure, but the scar tissue is very new."

"Jesus."

"His papers, or what was left of them after being in the water for a while, identify him as a German merchant sailor."

"How did he get here, do they know?"

Christine shrugged. "No one knows. There was a commercial cargo ship that docked last week in Baltimore. Spanish registry, I think, that came from South America. He could have come on that and jumped ship."

"Baltimore?" Cavanaugh hadn't had time to look at the map, and for the life of him he couldn't remember the geography of this area.

"It's farther up the Chesapeake. Look at your map."

Cavanaugh unrolled the map and began to spread it out on her desk. "What do they know about him? Anything?"

She shook her head. "Not much. He was shot several times and probably left for dead. No one knows who did it or why."

"What hospital is he in?"

"The Naval Hospital. Down by the river." She looked at him curiously. "You've got to tell me what this is all about. I can't go on making inquiries without getting the Navy guys real interested in why I want to know. In fact, I don't think that Groves would approve of this. It's drawing too much attention. *Someone*"—she emphasized the word—"is going to get interested in us."

Cavanaugh knew that being cautious wasn't going to get him anywhere. Too much was going on for him to worry about getting caught in bureaucratic games. "But the guy is still alive?"

"Yes. Barely. Apparently, he's in and out of consciousness. Naval Intelligence hasn't been able to ask him a lot of questions." Impatiently, she grabbed one end of the map to keep it in place. "Here," she said, pointing, "is Baltimore. And here is Washington."

Cavanaugh stood up and looked down at the map. With his eyes, he followed the Chesapeake down to the point where it was joined by the Potomac, and then wound its way down to the Atlantic. The merging of the Potomac into the wider Chesapeake formed a crude Y.

The tiny, irregular form of Tangier Island was just where the two estuaries met.

"My God," he murmured. Tangier Island was conveniently located

289

where the Potomac enters the Chesapeake Bay. If—and this was a big "if"—someone wanted to bring an atomic bomb to Washington, they could stop at Tangier Island, unload it from a larger ship, and reload it onto a smaller craft for the journey up the Potomac.

Christine caught the strange look on his face. "What are you looking at?"

He sat back in his chair. Was he making all this up? Was he over-reacting, simply because he had a half dozen odd pieces of intelligence? Jesus, he was on the edge!

Just to be sure, he looked at the map once more. The entrance to the Potomac was northwest of Tangier Island. From there, one could travel upriver past dozens of small riverside communities: Colonial Beach, Morgantown, Widewater, Indian Head, Mount Vernon, and then pass by Alexandria on the left into the District of Columbia.

Cavanaugh couldn't be sure, but it looked like a distance of 100, maybe 125 miles. It wasn't a quick trip, but it appeared that it could be made in a small boat in a couple of days. Or nights, traveling to avoid attention.

South of Tangier Island, at the mouth of the Chesapeake, were Cape Henry, Newport News, and Norfolk, where the Navy had giant bases.

His head started pounding. There were all kinds of questions. "How could a Spanish ship get past the Navy at the Cape? I mean, wouldn't the Chesapeake be closed and guarded because of the war?"

Christine shook her head. "Not to all neutral commercial ships. And I think things have loosened up since V-E Day. More open, you know."

But still, he wondered how a big ship like a freighter could stop in the middle of the Chesapeake and unload men and cargo without drawing a lot of attention. At night, maybe?

"They found this guy on this island, right?" he asked. He tapped the small irregular oval that was Tangier Island.

"Some local fishermen found him and called the Coast Guard."

"Was there anyone else? Did they find anything besides the sailor?"

Christine laughed. "I don't know. I didn't ask all that." Then her face turned serious; suddenly she understood that it wasn't a game for him. His face was far too intense, too hard, to mean anything less. "What's so *damn* important about this?"

There was a knock on the door. A young woman in a WAC uniform peeked in. "Lieutenant?"

Christine waved her away. "I'll be right there." She got up from her desk and grabbed a pile of papers. "Look," she said softly, "I've got to take these down the hall. It's going to take a while. We'll talk about this at lunch, okay? It's just thirty minutes or so."

Cavanaugh nodded. He needed a few minutes to think this through.

Christine laid a hand on his shoulder. "I'll meet you downstairs. In the lobby. You've got your pass, so you can come and go now."

Cavanaugh walked downstairs, but took the wrong stairwell and ended up on a different side of the War Department Building. It was warm and beautiful outside: the sky was a clear blue with puffy white clouds that reminded him of the great atmospheric displays that formed over the Jemez Mountains in New Mexico. On any other day he would be glad to be here, certainly glad to have an evening with Christine to look forward to. But the German atomic bomb just wouldn't go away.

Someone shot that sailor, he reasoned, that much was clear. Cavanaugh tried to think through the possibilities. The sailor might have surprised a local resident, who shot him in fear, and then left him to be discovered. Or he could have been shot by other Germans, other SS men, and left for dead. But why? Had he refused to do something, or had he suddenly become extra baggage? That seemed more likely.

Across the street Cavanaugh saw a truck unloading. Jesus! the goddamn bomb would almost certainly have come over from Germany in boxes. Otherwise, everyone would know what was being shipped.

He quickly looked around. There was a public telephone booth down the street.

He ran for it and dialed the operator. "I need Tangier Island, Virginia," he said, puffing heavily. "It's in the Chesapeake Bay."

There was a pause on the other end.

"How do you spell it?" the woman asked. She spoke in a thick Southern accent.

Cavanaugh spelled it. He tapped the side of the glass booth with his fingers.

"Yes?" the woman said.

"Yes what?"

"What number do you need?"

"Uh, the Coast Guard Office." He could hear pages being turned on the other end of the line.

"That's a long-distance call," the operator said. "Seventy-five cents, please."

One by one, he dropped in three quarters, which hit an internal box with a dull clink. Something clicked and there was static on the line. The call sounded like calls in Los Alamos did.

For a long time, there was nothing but static, then he heard the faint sound of a phone ringing. Then another click.

"Yeah?" It was a man's voice.

Cavanaugh hesitated briefly. "Uh, is this the Coast Guard?"

"Yeah," the man repeated.

"On Tangier Island?" He pressed the receiver hard against his ear to filter out the street noise.

"Yeah. Whattaya want?"

"Listen, I'm calling from Washington. Was it you guys that found the German sailor? The one who was shot?"

The person on the other end hesitated. "Yeah. Who wants to know?"

"This is Major Franklyn. Army Intelligence. We're interested in this sort of thing."

"Whattaya need?" The static began to warble, as if someone were deliberately jiggling the telephone lines between the two phones.

"Just some information." Cavanaugh desperately tried to sort out all the questions he had. "Were there any others? Germans, I mean?"

"We didn't find any. But there might have been."

"What do you mean?"

"We found an extra shoe about thirty feet away. Floating in the water. It was a different size."

"Was it German?"

The voice laughed. "Hell, I don't know."

"What about—" There was clicking on the line. "Hello?" he said.

The operator came back on. "That'll be another seventy-five cents," she intoned.

"Where you calling from, buddy?" asked the Coast Guard man.

Cavanaugh quickly fished around for another seventy-five cents. "Uh, we're using commercial lines," he said. God, he hoped the man fell for that.

"What about equipment? Boxes? Anything like that? Did you find anything?"

There was a long pause and Cavanaugh heard the man talk to someone nearby. "Only some broken crates."

Cavanaugh's heart leapt. "What kind? How big?"

"Hell, I don't remember. Pretty big. But they'd been broken up, see. We found them in pieces. And some had been burned, like someone

292

tried to light a fire but it went out. But they was probably big. Like maybe you'd put car parts in."

The gun barrels? Cavanaugh guessed. "You see any kind of markings? Foreign lettering?" Typhoo tea. *Say Typhoo tea!*

The man talked to the other man again. "Nah. There might have been some, but no one here remembers for sure. Whattaya want to know all this for, anyway? The Navy's got the guy in a hospital somewhere. Why don't you ask them?"

Just maybe I'll do that, thought Cavanaugh. "Well, the Army and Navy don't always talk," he said with as much humor as he could muster.

The man laughed. The static worsened, and the low, warbling sound began to drown out the man's voice.

"Anything else?" he shouted.

Lots, thought Cavanaugh, but he didn't have time. Nor another seventy-five cents. "No, thanks."

"Sure. And who'd you say this was?" The static worsened.

"Yeah, good-bye," Cavanaugh shouted, and hung up the phone.

Gilbert studied her face from across the desk. She was staring at the floor, obviously uncomfortable. She was quite a prize for Cavanaugh. Not quite Gilbert's style, though; he really liked the voluptuous type more. More curvy, brassier, or more outgoing, maybe, that sort of thing.

He had waylaid her on her way to lunch, probably with Cavanaugh. She had protested, but he had insisted. Just a few minutes.

It was immediately clear that something was on her mind, and no doubt it had to do with the man from Los Alamos. The problem was her reluctance to talk about it. He sensed that it didn't have anything to do with their relationship; in fact, he wondered what kind of relationship they could have after only a couple of meetings. Sex was great, but . . .

"Look," he said calmly, "he seems worried about something. I could sense that yesterday. And today, today I'm told he rushed in here all in a fuss."

She continued to stare at the floor. "I'm not comfortable with this," she said softly.

Gilbert nodded, even though she wasn't looking at him. "I know." He didn't, really. But then, he had never had a personal relationship that mattered all that much.

293

"I didn't mean for us to get involved. But we are, sort of. And I don't like the feeling that I'm supposed to spy on him."

"It's not spying. You know as well as I do that Groves wants to keep an eye on him. He was on a very special assignment. Very important."

Slowly she lifted her head and looked out the window. She had been asked point-blank what Cavanaugh was up to. But the hell of it was, she didn't know. Not really.

"He saw something in the newspaper, that's all." There was no need to mention that he had let slip the fact that he had been in the Soviet Zone in Germany.

"What?"

"An item about a German sailor. The one that was found by the Coast Guard."

That struck a note somewhere in Gilbert's memory. "The story in today's newspaper?"

"That's the one."

"What the hell is he interested in that for?" This was interesting.

Christine shrugged. "I don't know; he just seems, well, *upset* about it." She prayed that Gilbert wouldn't ask too much.

"What does he want to know?"

"Just who he is. How he got here."

Now Gilbert remembered the story. A German sailor, shot or something. Someone in the office would probably still have the paper and he could reread the article. But why was Cavanaugh interested?

"Look, I'm not asking you to spy or anything. I like Phil. We're old college friends. But we can't have someone running around asking a bunch of questions. You know this town. Soon we'll have G-2 calling us. Then someone else. And Groves won't like that."

"I know."

"Who'd you call?"

"A friend at Naval Intelligence. I asked about the sailor. That's it."

"You told him what you found out?"

She nodded.

Interesting, he thought. It must relate to Germany. He had an idea.

"Hey. Talk with him. Suggest *we* talk. Maybe I can help. Anyway, I'm a hell of lot better than Franklyn, and that's who he's gonna end up with on something like this."

Christine shook her head. "I don't know."

Gilbert tapped one finger on his desk. "I'm probably in hot water

294

myself. He ought to be in a barracks somewhere instead of running around town. Groves wanted him exposed to minimal contact. At least until he got back from the Test Monday or Tuesday. I don't wanna lock him up somewhere, but I'll have to do something if he keeps this business up. Franklyn's due back today, maybe tomorrow, and he'll have a shit fit. So will Groves."

Actually, Gilbert wasn't sure when Franklyn would be back, although he vaguely remembered that it was supposed to be next week.

Wearily, she nodded her head. "I'll talk with him. At lunch."

Gilbert watched her go out the door. He leaned back in his chair, heard it squeak, and stretched his arms.

A dilemma was emerging that made him uncomfortable.

Cavanaugh was on to something, something almost certainly related to whatever happened to him in Germany. Or maybe England. He was asking questions about an obscure German sailor. Why? It was also clear that the man was operating under very special instructions from Groves. Had to be. Franklyn knew Cavanaugh was returning and still had left town to inspect Oak Ridge; he wouldn't have done that if he were in on the game plan. And Cavanaugh was nervous, really anxious to talk with Groves.

Gilbert had lied about trying to get Cavanaugh to New Mexico. He'd done no more than cable Groves that Cavanaugh was in D.C. And he'd lied about the date of the Trinity Test. Cavanaugh wouldn't appreciate that. But the question now was: Should he cable Groves again that Cavanaugh had something urgent to report? But if he did that, he would lose any chance of finding out from Cavanaugh what the big news was.

So far, Gilbert had done only what he'd been told to do: cable Groves the moment Cavanaugh returned and wait for further instructions. He'd done that.

But the dilemma was that Gilbert himself was under secret orders from Groves to stay close to Cavanaugh and report anything unusual. Any strange contact by someone else, for example. That, and to keep him away from circumstances or events that might make him likely to reveal what he shouldn't. "Stick like a leech" was the way Groves had put it. Dammit! he should've quartered Cavanaugh on an Army base instead of letting him stay with Christine.

Whatever was going on was big. Gilbert *smelled* it. There was no way in hell Groves, or Franklyn, for that matter, would ever let him in on it. It sounded like the kind of thing that would be very helpful to know and to be able to share with his friends in the Pentagon. Just another play in the Washington information game.

He looked at his watch. It was half past noon, still early in Los Angeles; there was time to reach Groves there. Or he could probably get a cable to him in New Mexico. At Kirkland. But after that, the General would be incommunicado until tomorrow.

Okay, he'd do it. He quickly drafted a cable to Groves indicating that Cavanaugh seemed to be experiencing unusual anxiety, perhaps due to his experiences in Europe. Gilbert noted that Cavanaugh seemed particularly anxious to be debriefed by Groves, and only by Groves, regarding his activities.

Gilbert smiled to himself. That ought to cover him, just in case.

Then he drafted a second cable, this one to ALSOS, London. His query was simple: Did Captain Cavanaugh file a report on any activities?

He rang for a runner to take the messages to the Communications Center.

The runner, a young corporal with reddish-blond hair, said, "You got one to London and one to Los Angeles?"

Gilbert nodded, then suddenly thought of something.

"Hey," he shouted, "just a minute."

He grabbed the cable to Groves and scratched out the Los Angeles address. Then he wrote in the Manhattan Project contact address at Kirkland Field in Albuquerque.

That would buy him another six or seven hours.

The newspaper article had scared the hell out of them.

It was part of their special training to read the local newspaper every day to be aware of events. To get a feel for a foreign city and its people, even to know what movies and concerts were playing.

The article had been on the front page of the newspaper.

The discovery of a German sailor on Tangier Island could only mean their own man. And this was unbelievably bad news!

It also meant that Graber, the one they now called Herman, had failed to do his job. His mistake was inexcusable and now all of them were having to pay the price. And they were so close to completing their work in Washington.

Herman was morosely sitting in the next room; at least, he was aware of what he had done. He had been careless and not bothered to

296

check to see if the sailor was really dead. Simon would deal with him later; right now, he needed both of his men to finish the job.

Simon tried to relax the muscles in his neck by rolling his head from side to side. They were so close and they had come through so much only to be threatened at the very last moment. *Verflucht!*

He thought about the last six months. He had been transferred from active duty in February and sent to a special school where he'd practiced his English all the time and studied American culture. There were only a dozen students. They had been given new names and identities, and had memorized entirely new histories for themselves. Their uniforms had been taken away and they had received ordinary clothes instead.

For weeks they drilled and studied. Then some civilians had come and taught them about a new bomb, one that had never been used before. They had looked at diagrams and practiced assembling wooden dummies. Assembling, disassembling. Over and over. But never any word about what they would do with the real bomb, or when.

He remembered asking, "But Herr Professor, when will we get the real bomb? And when will we use it?" And the only reply he received was, "You will be told when the time is right."

The moment came in April, with a summons from Borman himself to attend a meeting in the Führerbunker. He and two others had made the perilous journey from the Harz Mountains into beleaguered Berlin. They had been briefed and given their orders, but only he had been pulled aside to meet the Führer personally!

He still remembered vividly being told that he had been personally chosen for the most dangerous assignment of all: a secret journey to America with the new bomb. There would be many obstacles to overcome, said the Führer, and the trip might take months. But it didn't matter, because this was the Reich's final blow at the Americans, who, Hitler had said, in a voice so low and tremulous that it was hard to understand, bore more responsibility than anyone for Germany's plight: they had failed to grasp the real threat from the Russians in the east!

Simon sadly thought about Germany. A nation of rubble. And its defeat was not alone due to the Allies but as well to the Germans themselves: those that had failed to give their best, to offer their lives for the greatest race of human beings in history. Now that nation was on its knees, its leader dead in the battle for Berlin. And the blow

Simon was about to strike for the Third Reich was likely to be the last, but it would be memorable.

Berlin! His home. There was nothing left there. His father killed in '41, his mother killed in an air raid last January. His sisters were missing. He was the last of his family.

Perhaps that was why he had been chosen over so many other senior SS men. He'd lost everything but his will. He was young, just thirty, and the men with him weren't much older. And now his work was imperiled by that swine Josef, the man they had left for dead on Tangier Island.

The pain in his neck wouldn't go away. It often stayed with him for hours; sometimes not even sleep would ease it.

They had so little time left. Less than two days to finish their special assignment here in Washington and rejoin the crew on the Spanish freighter. Hopefully, they would still be able to complete the journey back to Buenos Aires. There were friends there, former SS colleagues and sympathizers who would help them disappear and make a life until they could return to Germany for its rebirth. That might be years, even decades, but Simon had no doubt that the time would come.

A frown crossed Simon's face as he thought about the Spanish ship. The captain was an ardent sympathizer only as long as he got his gold. It had taken a second, unexpected payment of one hundred ounces the last minute to get the man to keep his promise: to fake engine trouble just long enough for Simon and his men to unload their small boat and their "package" near the tiny dot called Tangier Island. One day the captain would pay dearly for his treachery.

He turned to his companion. "Ready, Ernest?"

The man nodded. The two of them could be brothers, one slightly taller and thicker, but both blond with similar facial features. Ernest was the man he trusted most. He had to; he couldn't do what needed to be done without someone's help. Just loading and unloading the weapon took two strong men and every ounce of energy they had.

Ernest was tying his tie.

"No. A Windsor. Like this," said Simon. He showed him how to make the knot. "We must look American."

That had been part of their training. All of them spoke English, he and Ernest best of all, Josef the least. They had memorized expressions, intonations, currency, politicians, dates, and events. A schoolboy's life crammed into a week, and all intended to make them appear as if they had lived extensively in the United States.

298

For the last week, they had posed as Swiss diplomats, assigned to the International Red Cross, complete with European suits and the necessary passports and papers. That made it possible to operate in a city like Washington; they could rent cars, buy equipment, and not seem out of place. After all, almost every American male their age was in uniform.

As Swiss citizens, they were foreigners but neutrals. And no one would find their presence in Washington unusual in July 1945. Not with the war over and the fate of the Reich in the hands of the Allies.

But Josef, what a *Trottel!* A last-minute replacement for a much better man who had been killed in an air raid. Josef was clumsy, always making mistakes; he frequently broke into German, or absentmindedly hummed German songs, or used their real names. That was why Simon had ordered him killed once they had succeeded in reaching Tangier Island and unloading the weapon. Simon's mistake, however, had been in giving the assignment to Herman, who had shot Josef but had never bothered to be sure he was dead. Instead, he had made an assumption—a stupid act when the stakes were so high—and sworn on his country that Josef was dead. And now . . . ? Well, they would have to make the best of it.

Simon had a plan. It was risky, but perhaps no riskier than some of the things they had done during the last few weeks. He smiled faintly. Things like renting a boat as diplomats planning a "victory" weekend. Taking different rooms every other night. Buying supplies. Lifting the crates from the small rubber boat to the larger one. Any single act could have tripped them up, revealed their true identity and their purpose. All of them seemingly impossible, but against all odds they had succeeded.

"Let's go," he said to Ernest. He called for Herman.

"You stay here. Be sure the electrical system is working, yes?"

Herman nodded. He was glad to be on his own. He had spent the last few hours in utter disgrace and was looking forward to getting this business over with. Then, at least, there would be no reason to focus on his failure. Three shots, he thought. *Gott!* You would think three shots would kill an elephant! And the *Schwein* looked dead!

Simon put on his coat and stared in the mirror. The overall effect was a cross between European and American styles. The clothes were first-rate, of the highest quality, precisely the sort of things a Swiss would wear. At least, they weren't different from many other for-eigners here in Washington.

They would go to the hospital where Josef was being kept. A telephone call as Swiss Red Cross officials had already told them which one it was.

They needed to know if Josef was alive or dead. And, if he was still alive, how to kill him.

Chapter Twenty-eight

Christine sat stiffly behind the steering wheel of her car. Cavanaugh could tell she was uncomfortable doing this, and knew she was complying only because he'd insisted.

"I don't like this," she said at least for the second time. Her voice betrayed an edge of anger.

"Please," he said.

She shook her head and started the car. "I don't know what's going on."

"I'll explain it. But later." With any luck—if that was the word, he wondered—there would be a logical explanation for everything. For the sailor. For the boxes on Tangier Island. And then he could laugh at how he let his imagination run wild. "How far is the hospital?"

"Not far. Less than ten minutes."

Christine had her doubts about the whole business. *Strong* reservations. She didn't like being asked to spy on Cavanaugh; and she felt damn uncomfortable driving him to the Naval Hospital in an effort to try and talk with a captured German. What had seemed at first like no more than a one-night fling with someone she liked—the sort of affair she knew happened every day in Washington during the war—had turned into something much more. She liked Cavanaugh, maybe even loved him, but the two of them had been swept up in events she neither understood nor cared for.

Phil was acting crazy. She wanted to believe that he had a *reason*—he said that he did—but he was asking things, doing things, that were risky. Out of character. Her career was on the line. Gilbert had made that plain enough.

Cavanaugh saw that the tightness hadn't left her face. What could he do to make her more comfortable? He tried asking about Washington. What was that? he asked, pointing to a building. And that? Her answers were terse.

When at last they pulled into the parking lot of the hospital, she slowed down.

"Okay," she said, "I'll wait for you." She sat back in her seat, still gripping the steering wheel with both hands.

"No," he pleaded. "You've *got* to come. You speak German."

"Phil, really . . ."

"*Please.*"

It surprised her that she went along. She had definitely meant to stay in the car. Even walking up the steps into the main entrance she kept asking herself: am I really doing this? I should turn around . . .

And Phil? She had never seen him like this. His boyishness, his hesitancy had disappeared. He was so determined. He walked right up to the information desk and asked where the captured German was being kept. Christine held back a half dozen yards or so, leaning against one wall. The nurse at the desk didn't flinch. She pointed toward the elevator and smiled as she told him.

"Third floor," he said, grabbing Christine's arm.

The elevator was a slow, wheezing affair that creaked its way from floor to floor.

"What are you going to ask him?" Christine asked. "Assuming they *let* you talk to him."

"Who he came with. What they brought with them."

"What they brought?"

He nodded. The elevator stopped with a small jolt. Cavanaugh stepped out before the doors had opened all the way.

The German's room was obvious. A shore patrol man was sitting in a chair next to the door reading a magazine. Cavanaugh hesitated only a moment.

"Afternoon," he said cheerfully.

At first the guard was taken aback. Then he stood up and started to salute. Cavanaugh waved him back down.

"Just going in for a minute."

He started to protest. "But, sir . . ."

Cavanaugh was halfway through the door. "Army Intelligence," he added. Christine couldn't suppress a smile; she followed Cavanaugh in.

The small room was dominated by a single bed against the opposite wall. In it, asleep or unconscious, was a youngish man, very pale, with a round, pleasant face. He didn't look like a member of Hitler's feared SS; instead, to Cavanaugh, he looked like a farmer or a grocery-store clerk. Next to him was a nurse with a surprised look on her face.

Cavanaugh raised his hand and lowered his voice. "Is he asleep?"

"Who are you?" asked the nurse.

Cavanaugh ignored her question and walked to the side of the bed. The man was breathing regularly but looked as if he had been through the wringer. Tubes emerged from underneath the sheets and drew up in arcs to hanging bottles of clear liquids.

Christine slowly joined Cavanaugh at his side.

"Can he talk?" he asked.

The nurse just stared for a moment. "Does he look like it?"

Christine moved toward the nurse. "We were hoping to talk with him. Just a few questions."

The nurse shook her head. Cavanaugh noticed that her lipstick was larger than her lips and generously applied. "He comes and goes," she said. "The doctor ain't gonna allow no one to talk to him until later."

"Tonight?"

"I doubt it. Tomorrow, possibly. That's what he told those other guys."

"What other guys?"

"The foreign guys. The ones from the Red Cross. They was just here too."

Cavanaugh looked questioningly at Christine.

"It's common," she said quietly. "The International Red Cross would assist any foreigner stranded outside his country."

"You gotta go," said the nurse.

Cavanaugh nodded. He took one last look at the man in the bed,

303

then turned around and walked slowly outside. At least the German wasn't going anywhere soon.

The Navy guard was back in his chair, absorbed in his magazine. A dozen paces down the hall was a man in a white jacket talking with two tall men in business suits. By the stethoscope drooping from one pocket, Cavanaugh judged the man in white to be a doctor. One of the two civilians, the taller one, turned and looked in Cavanaugh's direction. Briefly they locked eyes.

The man had a curious look, not icy exactly, but distant and cool. Also curious. Cavanaugh found himself being examined. His companion's voice was indistinct against the louder noise of the hospital. The doctor appeared to shrug his shoulders.

"Let's go," said Christine quietly.

"I need to talk to the doctor." The conversation between the three men was breaking up; the doctor turned and came toward Cavanaugh.

"Are you treating this man?" Cavanaugh asked. The doctor was easily in his fifties. He had the tired, drawn look of a man who had been on the job several hours past his shift.

"Don't tell me," he said, "you want to talk with the German, right?"

Cavanaugh nodded.

The doctor looked at his watch and frowned. "I'll tell you the same thing I told them," he said, pointing behind his back with his thumb. "The sailor is still in critical condition and won't be up to anything for a few days."

Cavanaugh could see the two men conferring quietly. At one point, both of them stared at Cavanaugh.

"Those are the guys from the Red Cross?" he asked.

"Yeah. Swiss, I think. Who the hell are you?"

"Army Intelligence. We just want to talk with the sailor for a minute."

"Well, not today. And anyway, what the hell does the Army want with this guy? I thought he was Navy property?"

Next to him, Christine spoke up. "Lot of German nationals are trying to get into the U.S., Doctor," she said. "Some are former Nazis."

The doctor shook his head. "I don't think your guy is going to tell you much. At least for a while."

"Why?" asked Cavanaugh.

"Shot a couple times. Dumped in the water. He's lucky he's still alive. And when he talks, it's garbage. The Navy guys have already been here, you know."

"Naval Intelligence?"

"I guess. They talked with him for a few minutes."

"Did he say much?"

"Kept saying 'no, no,' that sort of thing. In German, of course. And something about the 'others.' He talks sometimes in his sleep."

Cavanaugh felt the excitement rise in him. "Did he say who the 'others' were?"

The doctor shook his head. "Hell, I don't know. He talks mostly in German. Check with us tomorrow."

Cavanaugh felt that he had run up against a brick wall. There seemed to be no choice but to come back later. Or give this damn business up.

"You all right?" It was Christine.

"Yeah." He took a last drag on his cigarette and crushed it in the aluminum ashtray. When he turned around and looked, the two tall men from the Red Cross were gone.

"Did you see those guys from the Red Cross?" he asked.

Christine nodded. "Why?"

"Didn't they look young to you?" Something about them disturbed Cavanaugh, but he couldn't put his finger on it.

"I suppose. So what?"

"I don't know. Why would they be here?"

Christine laughed. "I told you. They do this kind of work. The Red Cross helps repatriate anyone separated because of the war. Look what they're doing with displaced persons in Europe."

Cavanaugh was trying to decide what to do next when he and Christine walked outside and headed for the parking lot. They were approaching Christine's car when he noticed a dark two-door sedan moving slowly through the lot in their direction. He hesitated; the occupants of the car looked like the two men from the Red Cross. He couldn't be sure, since the reflection of the sun off the windshield obscured a clear view.

"Phil?" It was Christine. "What's the matter?"

Cavanaugh bent down but kept his eyes on the other car. "Just a minute."

The sedan hesitated, then suddenly picked up speed. It wasn't racing, exactly, but it had to be going fifteen, maybe twenty miles an hour, far faster than it should be going in a parking lot. As it sped by he got a good look at the driver; it was one of the Red Cross men!

Before Cavanaugh realized it, the car was at the exit of the parking lot heading into the street.

"Jesus!" he shouted. Throwing his hat through the open window of Christine's car, he ran down the parking lot toward the street. If he could, he wanted to get the license-plate number. But just as he arrived at the street, another car pulled out of the parking lot from another exit and fell in behind the dark sedan. He had had only a glimpse of the license before it disappeared.

Christine came running up, out of breath. "What is it?"

Cavanaugh just stared. The sedan was already a block away. "Too late," he mumbled.

"I want to know what's going on. *Now.*"

From the look on her face, Cavanaugh could tell she was serious. If he was going to keep on, he'd need her help, and he had to tell her something. He owed her that much.

"Okay. But not here."

Gilbert sauntered by the new WAC and smiled at her. Any other time he'd stop and introduce himself, maybe see what he could get going. She was pretty, though a little plump, but from what he could see he liked her legs.

Right now he didn't have time to pursue anything. A cable had just come from ALSOS in London and he had it in his hot hands from the decoding clerk. There had been only a moment to scan it and already he knew it didn't tell him what he wanted to know. He took the West stairwell, two steps at a time, and hurried into his office and shut the door. He sat down at his desk, unfolded the cable and read it again slowly.

> 15 JULY 1945 SHAEF LONDON
> 1269 ENGINEER COMBAT BATTALION MANHATTAN
> DISTRICT HDQRS WASHINGTON NO INFORMATION ON SUBJECT DURING
> PERIOD IDENTIFIED. STOP. ASSUMED UNDER ORDERS AS PER ASSIGN-
> MENT MDHDQR. STOP. NO REPORT FILED. ADVISE IF FURTHER ACTION
> NEEDED. END.

Goddamn it! Their people in Europe didn't know any more than Gilbert did about Cavanaugh. And Gilbert couldn't afford to make another inquiry, not without attracting attention from the staff here. That sort of news would go instantly to Groves, who'd want an explanation.

And he hadn't learned anything in Washington. His own sources at Navy knew little more than the newspaper about the German sailor.

The Kraut was suspected of being an SS officer, but there wasn't anything conclusive to hang a hat on.

So why was Cavanaugh interested? And where was Leiter? She had left after lunch to pick up something, or so her office said. Gilbert looked at his watch. It was nearly 5 P.M. Leiter wasn't back and wasn't likely to return until Monday. That meant he would have to contact her at home, with Cavanaugh hanging around.

By now his cable to Groves was waiting for the General in Albuquerque. There was no telling how the Old Man would react. But at least he'd covered his ass.

Gilbert sighed and leaned back in his chair. He tried to work his way through what he knew and what options were left.

As of right now, he'd exhausted every source of information in Washington except one. And that was Cavanaugh himself. If there was any chance of learning something—if there was anything to learn—it had to happen before Groves returned. That meant finding a way of talking with Cavanaugh and putting a little pressure on him.

He pulled out his personal directory of Manhattan District staff and made a note of Christine's home telephone number. Very carefully he folded the paper and put it in his pocket. For later.

Outside it was darkening, melting into twilight.

Cavanaugh watched the lighter shadows fade into darker ones. The pale-yellow walls of Christine's bedroom turned shades of ocher, then umber. She lay next to him, her perfume mingled with the scent of sex and sweat. The ceiling fan above them beat a slow and rhythmic pattern, barely moving the air in the small room.

He turned slightly to look at Christine. Her face glistened with a light coating of sweat, as did the one shoulder he could see. Somehow, she had ended up with the sheet, which was coiled around her like a pale sarong, leaving one breast revealed but half hidden by an arm. It was such a sweet sight for him that he felt a rush of affection run through him. It made it all the more difficult for him to do what he had decided to do a few minutes ago.

He started to touch her shoulder, to wake her if she was still asleep, then he drew back. Just a minute more, he thought.

Last night, after the visit to the hospital, he and Christine had stopped at a small diner for a cup of coffee. There, amid the clatter of dishes and Benny Goodman on the radio, he'd told her about the Nazi vengeance plot. He didn't mention Mühlhausen; but why he drew the line at this he didn't know. He *did* know that he had to compromise his promise to Groves and at least tell Christine about the plot.

He remembered that the expression on her face hadn't changed. She didn't even lift an eyebrow. At first, he'd thought she didn't believe him and he felt foolish. Maybe there was lots of talk about all kinds of Nazi plots. But then she'd asked him a few questions: Where had he heard this? What was the source? Any details? Finally she'd said he needed to tell Groves as soon as possible.

She knew there was more to the story, but didn't press him. Instead, she'd dropped her own bombshell: Groves was already in New Mexico for the Trinity Test! His reaction had been immediate and visible.

She had looked surprised and then apologized. "You didn't know it was set for the sixteenth? The information came today," she had said. "Gilbert didn't tell you?"

"No," he had whispered. "He said that, well, he thought it was set for the middle of next week."

That son of a bitch Gilbert had lied to him. There had never been a possibility of his making the Test. No appeal to Groves. But why? Why the subterfuge?

Cavanaugh lay back in bed with his left arm behind his head. The ceiling fan only barely stirred the air; he felt only the slightest breeze on his naked body.

They had returned to Christine's apartment last night, as much to recuperate as anything. He was beat, empty. It was as if everything he'd worked for had been pulled out from beneath him; Groves, Gilbert, the lot of them, they had used him and disposed of him.

Christine suggested he lie down for a while; he did and woke up with her hand on his forehead, straightening his hair. When she kissed him, everything came out at once: his anger, his disappointment, his fear, his desire. Saturday night dissolved into Sunday amid frantic, then lanquid sex, followed by hours of lying around talking, or listening to music. For a while, he was able to push Europe and New Mexico out of his mind.

But now it was Sunday evening, and he was wide awake and left with the realization that he had to return to the hospital and force a conversation with the German sailor.

Part of him wanted to do nothing but remain where he was. Damn Trinity! Damn Groves and the rest of them! But the other part wouldn't let go of the sailor and all the other frightening possibilities he had learned about in Europe.

He reached over and gently touched her shoulder. "Christine?"

Her eyes fluttered for a moment, then stayed open.

"I've got to do something," he said. "And I need your help."

She didn't say a word. Instead, she sat up in bed and pulled the tousled sheet around her.

In the dark, he couldn't make out the color of her eyes, only that they looked sympathetically at him.

An hour later they were back at the hospital.

Groves stood at the back of the room, watching the dozen or so men around him, knowing there was nothing he could do if they made a mistake.

He was in a small windowless room, reinforced on three sides by tons of concrete and dirt. Ten thousand yards away Fat Man sat on its steel tower, just minutes away from detonation. Everything he'd worked for, all the government's money he'd spent, virtually the rest of his career—everything was riding on that curious dark sphere several miles away. The atomic bomb would either work, or it wouldn't. To him, it was as simple as that.

He looked around the room. Oppenheimer was clinging to a wooden post, half-crazed from the anxiety and the fact that he hadn't slept in two days. The man had been smoking nonstop now for hours.

The rest of the men in the room were huddled over their dials and gauges, or stood at banks of electrical switches. All Groves could do was watch. And wait.

A small man with glasses stared at a clock and then shouted "Five minutes" into a microphone. Loudspeakers in similar bunkers spread over several dozen square miles of New Mexico desert reverberated with his words.

Another man said they'd better take their places outside if they wanted to see the show. Reluctantly, Oppenheimer let go of his support and shakily started out the door. This was it.

Groves felt around in his pockets for the special welder's glasses he'd been given earlier. Once the initial flash of light from the explosion faded, he would be able to look directly at the remaining fireball through the heavy dark glasses.

He found them. And he also felt the strange cable he'd been handed in Albuquerque shortly before driving south to the test site.

It was from Gilbert in Washington. Something muddled, something about Cavanaugh. The man wanted to talk right away or something.

Groves sighed. There was nothing he could do about Cavanaugh right now, not here in the middle of the desert. He'd just have to deal with him when he got back to Washington tomorrow.

He joined the others in the trench outside the control shelter. The outside loudspeaker announced "One minute and counting."

Groves took his crouched position in the trench, his back to the bomb and the expected blast. Once he felt the heat pass he knew he could turn around and look.

Oh, Lord, he prayed, *let there be something to look at.*

He heard the loudspeaker say "Ten seconds," then "Nine," and after that he lost count. His mind went absolutely blank. His body tensed. *This was it. This was it.*

Five miles away it was perfectly dark and still. And then, a millionth of a second later, it was suddenly daylight!

Chapter Twenty-nine

*T*he hospital sat on the edge of the Potomac, with a broad lawn behind it that swept down to the river. During the day the ambulatory patients, or those in wheelchairs, could wander or be pushed down to the bank on manicured trails. At night, however, none of this was visible; instead, the large building loomed in the darkness like a massive, featureless block lit from within by hundreds of small square windows.

Cavanaugh felt the uneasiness grow in his stomach and tighten his chest. The Navy hospital was different at night, far more murky and sinister as it lay cloaked in shadows. And yet, he was drawn to it because within the building was a man who might be able to put his fears to rest.

Earlier, Christine had made several calls. The first had been to Gilbert at the Manhattan offices; he wasn't in but she left a message to call ASAP at her apartment. Then she had tried him at home. Nothing. The next call had been to the Swiss Embassy to check out the Red Cross representatives. Her inquiry had been referred to the Ambassador's aide-de-camp, who was out of the office until tomorrow. She reported all of this to Cavanaugh, who listened but said nothing. He just shook his head when she mentioned Gilbert's name.

Gilbert was a lying son of a bitch. It bothered Cavanaugh to miss the Test. Fat Man was two thousand miles away, scheduled to blow sometime in the next twenty-four hours or so. But Trinity and Fat Man might as well be on the moon. There was no chance he could make it. And his anger had faded just enough to make him want only this last stab at talking with the German sailor.

Christine had agreed to come—she was here, next to him in the car—but not before she had expressed her reservations. They were risking causing an incident that would focus unwanted attention on the Manhattan Project. Groves would react violently to that. Both of them could pay heavily. She told Phil that Groves had reassigned men overnight to Alaska for lesser transgressions.

She had watched his face as she said this, knowing all the while that he believed there was no choice.

"Okay," she said finally, "what's your plan?"

His plan, if one could call it that, was simple. A new shift of doctors and nurses would be on duty this late at night; with any luck, the two of them could talk their way back into the sailor's room, wake him if he was still asleep, and ask three or four key questions. They might not have much time before they were discovered, or thrown out, but a few minutes would be enough. Hopefully. It was worth a reprimand if they were caught; even Christine agreed, and Cavanaugh felt his affection for her grow even more.

The lethargic elevator door opened to a hallway that appeared more dimly lit than earlier in the day. That was good, thought Cavanaugh; they needed every advantage. In fact, the hallway seemed peculiarly empty. The two of them crept down the hallway to the point where it joined with another corridor; to the right, down the hall and half the building's length, was the German's room.

Suddenly, behind them, Cavanaugh heard footsteps. Someone running. He suppressed his inclination to turn around and look; that might reveal fear, some criminal intent. Seconds later a nurse passed them and hurriedly turned into the corridor to the right. Simultaneously, he heard the floor's PA system announce an emergency. The message was garbled, or in the everyday code that nurses used to announce things, he couldn't tell which. He felt his heart beat faster just as Christine's hand touched his arm.

"Something's happened," she whispered.

He nodded but kept walking. At the juncture of the two corridors he stopped and peered around the corner. The nurse who had just run past them was talking with a male orderly; another nurse and orderly came out of a stairwell. Standing by himself and looking totally confused was a member of the Navy's shore patrol. All of them were standing outside the German's room.

"Oh my God," mumbled Cavanaugh. He felt a chill. Christine was right; something *had* happened!

He felt a tug on his arm and turned slightly to see Christine pulling him back. Her eyes seemed to say, "Run!"

"No," he said, "I've got to check it out." As calmly as he could, he walked up to the small group and asked what had happened. For a moment, no one answered; their collective eyes seemed to assess him, asking silently who the hell he was. At last the nearest of the male orderlies spoke.

"The German guy's dead."

Cavanaugh stared back, stunned. "What?" he finally asked. He felt as if something very precious, very personal had just irretrievably slipped away from him. Without thinking, he pushed open the door to the room and walked in. The SP, still confused, did nothing.

Inside, a doctor was bent over the German's body; next to him was a nurse holding a clipboard.

"What happened?" Cavanaugh asked.

The doctor slowly looked up. "Are you the police?" His face was young and pimply.

"No. Army Intelligence. What happened?"

"Coronary arrest." The young man's face revealed no emotion.

Cavanaugh walked closer and peered at the dead man. Out of the corner of his eye he saw Christine move to the other side of the room. The sailor's eyes were wide open, with a ghastly, frozen stare. It looked as if he had been frightened to death. The man's face was pale and drawn, hardly the look of a young man. His hands were gripped together on his chest. He couldn't have been dead long.

"Did it just happen?"

The doctor shook his head. "Five minutes maybe. Ten. Not more than that."

Cavanaugh just stared. Now there would never be answers to his questions.

"I thought he was getting better?" It was a question as much as a statement.

The young doctor took the chart from the nurse's hand and began to scribble something on it. "He was. But this heart attack wasn't related to his condition."

"What do you mean?"

The doctor leaned over and picked something off the edge of the bed and held it up. It was a hypodermic syringe. "I think this man was murdered."

The words hit Cavanaugh like a blow to the body. He grabbed the metal end of the bed.

In a voice as emotionless as his face, the doctor explained. "I think someone injected an air bubble into his vein. It went straight to his heart and stopped it. Dead."

Cavanaugh looked at the syringe and then the body. "But how?"

"Simple. Whoever did this found a vein and stuck a needle in it and fired away. Look. The syringe has no fluid in it, not a trace. That's never the case. And look here." He pointed to a tiny spot on the dead man's arm.

Both Cavanaugh and Christine looked closer. The tiny dark circle was actually a bubble of blood.

"That's where the needle went in. The blood hasn't even fully co-agulated yet. We found the syringe on the floor. Right here." The doctor made some additional notes on the pad. "An autopsy will tell for sure."

Cavanaugh was still too shocked to speak. Instead, Christine asked a question. "Have you alerted the police?" she asked.

The doctor nodded. "Navy police, I think."

It took a moment for Cavanaugh to realize the importance of what the doctor had said. Soon, the military would be here in force. Perhaps even the D.C. police. He and Christine couldn't afford to stay around.

But there was the question of who killed the sailor. "Do you have any idea who did it?" he asked.

The doctor shook his head. "I'm on duty tonight, but I've got the whole floor to cover." He turned to the nurse. "You see anybody?"

"Nope. There was a doctor in here. That's all I know."

"A doctor?" asked Cavanaugh. "Is there another doctor on the floor?"

"There's doctors in and out of here. The Navy guy outside saw him."

Cavanaugh turned and looked at Christine. Was she thinking the same thing? The nurse was pulling the sheet over the dead man's head. Cavanaugh could bet that the dead man never expected to die in an American hospital.

He motioned to Christine and nodded toward the door. "Thanks."

By now, a small crowd was milling in the hallway. Cavanaugh walked over to the nervous SP, who dropped his cigarette on the floor and stamped it out with his boot. "At ease, sailor," he said.

The young man was barely out of his teens. He shifted nervously from foot to foot and stared at the ground. His face told Cavanaugh that he knew he was going to get hell for this. Especially if it was true that the German had been murdered.

"You told the nurse you saw a doctor come in here?"

The young man nodded. "Yes, sir."

"You see anyone else? A nurse? Orderly? Anyone else?"

"No, sir. Just that doctor fella."

Cavanaugh tried to put the man at ease by smiling. "You were here, right? Not in the john, maybe?"

"No, sir. I was right here for the last hour or so, straight through. That's the truth." His accent said he was from somewhere in the South. Georgia, maybe.

Cavanaugh nodded. More nurses were gathering; it looked as if soon the whole hospital staff might be in this small hallway. He was going to take a chance and ask the guard a leading question.

"What did the doctor look like?"

"Tall fella. Thin, you know?"

"You remember anything else?"

"Whattaya mean?"

"Color of his hair, eyes. Anything peculiar about him. Did he have anything with him when he went in the room, for example?"

"He was blond, I think. Yeah, he was. But I didn't notice his eyes. But his hair was short and blond." He started to pull a cigarette from his pack but changed his mind.

Tall and blond, thought Cavanaugh. That described one or both of the Swiss Red Cross men. "How tall?" he asked.

"Your height. Maybe taller."

Christine tugged at his arm and silently motioned with her head down the corridor. Two shore patrol men had appeared at the juncture of the two hallways.

Cavanaugh had to hurry. "Did the man have anything with him? Equipment? Anything?"

The young man shook his head. "I didn't see nothing. Maybe one of those things you listen with." He just caught sight of the others down the hall. He shifted back and forth on his feet again.

Cavanaugh was desperate. "Did he say anything? The doctor?"

"Nope. Just good evening."

Cavanaugh was running out of time. The two patrol men were less than a dozen yards away.

"Did the guy have an accent? You know, did he sound like he was foreign?"

The young man shook his head.

"Okay. When the doctor left, which way did he go?"

"Uh, over there, I think. Down that stairwell."

Christine pulled harder now. "We really must go," she said in a low but urgent voice.

He nodded. "Thanks, sailor. Good luck." The man was going to need it.

Cavanauagh pushed open the door to the stairwell and hesitated. It was empty. Their footsteps echoed with each step, any spoken word reverberating up and down the length of the stairwell. At each floor there was a landing with a heavy metal fire door door leading into the interior hallway. That meant three possible exit points for the mysterious doctor. But which one had he taken? The answer lay crumpled on the floor partially hidden under the stairs at level 1. It was a white doctor's tunic. Wrapped inside was a stethoscope.

Cavanaugh pushed open the heavy door and looked in both directions. The hallway had a dozen people in it, a mix of nurses and individuals in civilian dress, but no one tall and blond. He looked at his watch. Fifteen, maybe twenty minutes had passed since the murder, maybe more. There was no reason to believe that the murderer would still be around. Certainly not if he had his wits together.

The two of them stepped in the hallway and stood by the door.

"What do you think?" Christine asked. "One of the Swiss Red Cross men?"

"I have no proof, but I'd bet on it." He grabbed her arm. "Let's go." He walked briskly, almost pulling her with him toward the central corridor. He stopped at the information desk. A young woman dressed in civilian clothes sat behind the desk reading a magazine called *Screen World*.

316

"Excuse me," he said.

The woman looked slowly up and smiled.

"Have you been here long?"

"Why?"

"Well, I'm looking for someone. He might have passed by here fifteen, maybe twenty minutes ago. Tall guy, thin, with blond hair?"

"Wearing a suit?"

Cavanaugh thought of the two Swiss men in suits. "Yeah, maybe."

"Well, a tall man went out of here a while back. He wore a dark suit and he was tall. Good-looking guy. But he looked like he had just gotten bad news."

"Why?"

"He didn't smile. Sorta grim-looking face. I thought maybe it was just bad news."

Cavanaugh shrugged. Nothing definite, just another maybe. But it sounded right. He said good night and he and Christine walked out to the parking lot.

"What now?" she asked.

He sighed. "I don't know exactly. But I think I should tell Gilbert what's going on. He can call in the Washington police."

He took one last look at the hospital. Someone would no doubt report to the authorities that two Army officers had been on the scene moments after the murder. That would mean questions. But right now, as far as Cavanaugh was concerned, it didn't matter. They could be looking at something far worse than a breach of security.

It was almost midnight. From the hospital they drove downtown to the Manhattan Project offices in the War Department Building where a late-night contingent was at work. The corridors were busy, the inner offices humming with typewriters and voices. After Europe, Cavanaugh had to remind himself that the war was still on in the Pacific.

Gilbert wasn't in but had checked for messages. That probably meant he had tried to reach them at Christine's. General Groves's night secretary, Mrs. McDonald, was in her office. Cavanaugh thought that that could mean only one thing: she was waiting for word from Trinity.

Cavanaugh suddenly felt a combination of anger and disappointment again. By all rights, he should be in New Mexico right now. In fact, he would be at a concrete-and-dirt bunker nicknamed the South 10,000, because it was ten thousand feet—almost six miles—away from Ground Zero. His experiments were placed roughly halfway between the bunker and Zero. Right now, he probably would be checking his equipment one last time. No one would be sleeping. No one would be thinking about a murdered German sailor.

"We need to contact General Groves immediately," said Christine. This was her turf, so she took the lead.

Mrs. McDonald looked puzzled. Then she looked at her watch. "Why?"

"Something has come up. Something very important. I think the General would want to know about it as soon as possible."

"Have you talked with Captain Gilbert?" she asked. Without her glasses, the shadows under her eyes were more visible. Like everyone else, she had been working overtime.

"We've tried reaching him, but I don't think we can wait any more." Christine's face looked pale and tight under the artificial light.

The older woman studied the two of them. She couldn't mistake the looks on their faces. "I don't think we can reach him. Not now."

Cavanaugh started to drill his fingers on the edge of her desk. He—they—had to operate on the assumption that the Germans had a team right there in Washington. Probably with a bomb. Time was running out.

"I can't tell you how important this could be," he blurted out. "Look . . ." Then he stopped. What could he say that anyone would believe?

"Can you authorize a telegram to be sent as soon as it's possible?" asked Christine. "In the meantime, we'll try to get in touch with Captain Gilbert."

Mrs. McDonald looked confused. "What's all this about?"

Christine cut Cavanaugh off before he started to talk. "I don't think we should discuss this. Only that the information we have might require immediate action. And at a level that only General Groves can authorize."

Cavanaugh realized that the secretary had never mentioned where Groves was. No doubt, she had been instructed not to say.

"All right, I'll call Communications. But I don't think anything can go out until early tomorrow morning."

Cavanaugh stared at the ceiling and sighed.

"It's the best I can do. Really."

Later, in the hallway, Cavanaugh stopped for a drink of water at the wall fountain. For the first time in hours, he realized he hadn't eaten anything since lunch. He was hungry, but the uneasy feeling in his stomach wouldn't go away.

Christine looked at him and forced a small smile. "We'll try Gilbert again when we get home, okay?"

"Sure." He smiled back at her. "Are you gonna lose your job over this?"

She shrugged. "Not if you're right."

"I don't know, Christine. I just don't know." He looked both ways down the hall. "There's something else. Something I haven't told you. But it fits into this business of the sailor. At least, I think it does. And that's why I'm scared."

Cavanaugh visualized the pit in Mühlhausen and the modified gun barrels. The cylinders of uranium in London.

"I'll tell you about it. Not just yet. But I will, I promise."

They didn't speak on the drive to Christine's apartment. Instead, Cavanaugh slid down in the seat and laid his head back against the top and closed his eyes. Washington, with its broad boulevards and streetlights, disappeared behind a veil of inner darkness.

It was after midnight when they arrived at Christine's apartment. It was dark; in their haste to get to the hospital, they had failed to leave a light on.

She had barely unlocked the door and stumbled into the living room for the table light when she heard the telephone ringing. She headed toward the hallway, hit the edge of a chair, cursed, and picked up the receiver.

"Hello?"

There was no voice. The caller had just hung up.

"Was it Gilbert?" asked Cavanaugh from the other room. In the darkness, Christine couldn't see him, only hear his voice from somewhere in the living room.

"I don't know. They hung up when I answered. What about a drink?"

Cavanaugh walked to the kitchen, picking his way carefully as he went. He flipped a switch and the tiny room was suddenly flooded with harsh incandescent light. The telephone rang again as he was mixing their drinks. He leaned out of the doorway and listened. It was Gilbert; he could tell by Christine's conversation. A moment later, she walked into the room.

"It's Gilbert. He wants to know where we've been."

Cavanaugh put the bourbon down and walked to the phone. "Gilbert?"

"Where the hell have you been all night?"

"What about you?"

"I've been calling every ten minutes for hours. What's this 'urgent' message?"

"Something's happened. Something big. We can't talk about it on the phone."

There was a pause on the other end. "Look," Gilbert began, "if it's about you getting back to New Mexico, I'm sorry. I was just doing what I was told."

Lying son of a bitch, thought Cavanaugh. "It's not that. This is a hell of a lot more important."

Another pause. "Does it have anything to do with that German guy? The sailor they found?"

Cavanaugh hesitated. "Yeah. But it's more than that. Where can we talk?" He wasn't sure, but he thought he heard a woman's voice in the background.

"I'll come there. To Christine's."

"Okay. When?"

"Now. In ten minutes." Gilbert hesitated again; there was a sound as if he was putting his hand on the mouthpiece. "Make that fifteen."

Each time they passed under a street lamp, the light flooded the inside of their car. Simon's first inclination was to drop down in the seat, obscure his profile. Then he had to remind himself that no one was looking for them. Yet.

But they could be if he and Ernest didn't act immediately.

He had given instructions to Ernest to drive around the block, slowly, to give the American couple a chance to get inside their flat. He needed a few extra minutes to decide what to do. No. He knew what to do; it was a question of how.

This evening had been a matter of luck. Or a sign that their mission was destined to succeed.

Ernest had waited in the car while he went up to kill Josef. That had been unbelievably easy. A simple injection of air had killed the stupid man in seconds. Simon had been in the hospital less than ten minutes. When he returned to the car, Ernest had been terribly excited: the American couple from that afternoon had returned. They had parked their car not ten meters away!

It was impossible to know if the Americans were on to them. If so, their disguise had been compromised. But it no longer mattered. The Americans would be eliminated. Tonight.

Simon had taken a great risk in going to the hospital and an even greater one in choosing to remain in the parking lot waiting for the Americans to return. Almost certainly, they were there to see Josef. He was betting that they would discover the man dead from a heart attack and eventually leave. That would give him and Ernest the opportunity to follow them to their home. And he had been right. They had discreetly followed the American couple from the hospital to a building downtown and finally to this house.

"What do we do?" asked Ernest.

"Wait." He looked at his new watch as they passed underneath a streetlight. "Give them some time. They will go to bed soon."

"And then?"

"We go back."

Chapter Thirty

*C*hristine slipped off her uniform and hung it in the closet. There was a clean one for tomorrow, but soon she would have to do some washing. She sifted through her dresses and picked out a casual one to wear for the next hour or so. Hopefully, Phil wouldn't talk all night with Gilbert because what she really wanted to do was to go to sleep.

It had been a long and tiring day. Even frightening. And it wasn't over yet. Leaning against the doorjamb, she rested her forehead on her arm and closed her eyes. Inexplicably, she had been drawn into a dark, mysterious affair that she only half understood but which frightened her. Phil—poor Phil—was sitting in the living room right now, obviously exhausted, and yet driven by some knowledge that he couldn't fully share with her.

She had guessed enough to know that he wasn't crazy. And tonight seemed to bear his fears out.

God! She had never done anything like this before. Never acted so crazily, so utterly without regard for her own life. Or for her career. She laughed nervously. How had Phil talked her into this? He had asked her for help, begged, maybe, but still . . . What was making her put her neck out like this? She looked in the mirror and straightened her hair. Her makeup had long since disappeared. Mrs. McDonald must have thought her a strange sight to appear at midnight looking like that.

She was looking for her lipstick on the dressing table when she heard it the first time: a rustling sound, like someone stepping very deliberately, right outside her window. Or was she mistaken? When she listened again, she heard nothing. She looked at the ceiling and saw that the fan wasn't on. Maybe it was nothing.

As she was carefully applying her lipstick, she heard it again. This time she was *sure*: it was footsteps. Someone *was* outside her window. She started toward the window to pull up one of the Venetian blinds but then changed her mind. Suddenly she was frightened.

The footsteps stopped. Whoever or whatever it was was still there.

Thinking as fast as she could, she leaned over and turned off the lights in her bedroom. The room fell into darkness except for the small lamp next to the bed. She walked over and turned it off as well. Quietly, almost tiptoeing, she walked to the living room. Cavanaugh was sitting on the couch holding a drink.

"Phil?" she said softly.

He didn't answer.

"Phil?" she said louder.

He jumped lightly and turned quickly in her direction. "Yeah?"

"I think there's someone outside."

"What?"

"Outside my bedroom window. I heard footsteps." Even saying it made her more frightened.

Cavanaugh stood up and put his drink down on the end table. "Stay here," he said quietly. Then he walked into her room, stopping for a moment at the doorway. The room was empty and dark; he could only barely make out the window from where he stood.

For a moment he hesitated, not really knowing what to do next. He hoped like hell that Christine only *thought* she had heard someone outside. But what was he going do if she was right? Go out and confront them? Call the police?

As carefully as he could, he walked over to the window and very slowly pulled the Venetian blinds away from the frame. There was only more blackness on the other side. He stood there for a long moment, listening for even the smallest sound. There was none.

Relieved, he let the blinds fall back and started to walk away when he heard a movement, a crunching sound on the dirt outside. Footsteps moving quickly away. "Oh, God!" he whispered.

Throwing away all caution, he ran back to the living room. Christine was huddled in the hallway near the telephone. She didn't say anything. She didn't have to.

Cavanaugh nodded and pulled her close. "I heard someone too." She gasped and opened her eyes wider.

His mind was racing. What were they going to do now? The car was outside, several dozen feet away, in case they wanted to make a run for it. It would take a minute or more before they were safely inside the car. And another minute to get the damn car started and out of the driveway.

"Front door locked?" he whispered.

"I don't know. You were the last one in."

"Oh, shit," he mumbled. He had no idea if he had locked it. "Stay here."

He quickly walked to the door and flipped the dead bolt. Then he ran the chain across. What else? The lights! he thought. He ran over to the lamp in the living room and flipped it off. Now the entire apartment was dark. There was only the faint illumination on the front porch from the streetlight. At least, they could see anyone coming from that direction.

"Phil!" Christine's voice wasn't loud but Cavanaugh could feel the terror in it.

He rushed over. "What?" His heart was pounding now.

"The kitchen door. The outside one. Someone was turning the knob." She pointed with a shaky finger toward the kitchen.

They both stood there, immobile, barely breathing. Very faintly, he could hear the doorknob turning. Or was it? At this point, he couldn't trust himself or what he was hearing.

They needed something, a gun, anything. Then he remembered his pistol, the .38 that Gilbert had given him. He raced back into the bedroom, pausing at the door to listen for a sound outside the window before going for his duffel bag. He dug around and pulled out the black revolver. His hand was shaking. In the darkness, he couldn't tell if the damn thing was loaded. With his finger he felt the chamber and the rear end of a shell. Thank God! he thought. He flipped off the safety.

"Call the police," he whispered.

She held the receiver and shook her head.

"Call the police, for God's sake!"

"I can't. The line's dead."

Cavanaugh took the phone from her and listened. Nothing. Christine grabbed his arm.

"There's a car outside," she said. "I just heard it pull up."

Cavanaugh went to the living-room window and peered out. The blinds were open and the lace curtains let in the view. She was right! A car had pulled up and stopped immediately outside. A single figure hidden by the shadows started to emerge.

"It's Gilbert!" he whispered loudly. "Thank God!"

Then just as quickly he realized that whoever was outside was still there. Would Gilbert's arrival scare them away? Or force them to act?

"Oh, God," he said, his voice laden with fear.

"What?" Christine asked. "What are you doing?"

Cavanaugh pulled back the chain and fumbled around for the dead bolt. He had to warn Gilbert before something happened!

"Phil, no!" she cried.

Slowly, holding the .38 in one hand, he opened the door. First just a crack, then wider. He could see Gilbert clearly now, walking up to the front porch. He opened the door wider.

"Gilbert!" he shouted. "Hold it! Go back!"

"Cavanaugh!" The man had a smile on his face.

Oh God, go back! But he wasn't stopping. Oh, Jesus! Cavanaugh stepped out onto the porch and waved wildly. "Hurry up!"

"What?"

"Come on! There's someone out there."

Gilbert looked strangely at Cavanaugh, then turned to his left slightly as if something had caught his attention. Out of the corner of Cavanaugh's vision, somewhere at the edge of the porch in the shrubbery, he'd seen a movement, or a shadow of some kind. He glanced back at Gilbert, who had paused, then back to the movement in the shadows. Then everything happened at once.

First Cavanaugh heard a strange, hollow pop and felt something fly by his face, disturbing the air as it did. Almost simultaneously it hit

325

the wall of the porch next to him with a dull thud, sending a small shower of wood splinters into his face. Jesus Christ! someone was shooting at him. Instinctively, he crouched down.

Gilbert saw it too, but froze. "What the hell!" he shouted. For a moment he hesitated at the bottom of the steps, unsure if he should run inside the house or back to his car. His eyes seemed transfixed on something in the shrubbery.

Cavanaugh saw it all in slow motion. Gilbert suddenly stepped down like an athlete preparing for a jump, and then leapt onto the porch, taking all three steps in one motion. He took another step or two toward Cavanaugh when there was another dull pop. Gilbert seemed to stop briefly in midstep; then he stumbled and fell forward, clutching his chest with one hand. There was just enough light from the street lamp to make out a dark patch under Gilbert's hand. For a moment, just before he hit the porch, he locked eyes with Cavanaugh; his face was a macabre mix of pain and confusion.

From inside the house Cavanaugh heard Christine cry out. "Oh, God!"

"Stay back!" he shouted. He whirled to his right and lifted his gun. There was another pop and Cavanaugh felt a splattering of warm liquid and pulpy matter on his face. I've been hit! he screamed in his head. Without thinking, he fired three shots in the direction of the shrubbery. One. Two. Three. He didn't even see what he was firing at. The noise was deafening!

But then, from the shadows at the side of the house, there was a sound, a deep human voice that said simply, "uhh," and then a dark form fell over backward, crashing down on the chest-high bushes.

Cavanaugh didn't move. His arm was still outstretched, the gun in his hand shaking slightly as the extension of his trembling body. In front of him, silent and heaped like a large bag of potatoes, was Gilbert.

"Phil?" It was Christine, her voice a shrill whisper.

From the other side of the shrubbery, hidden by darkness, came the sound of someone running. Cavanaugh jumped up quickly and tried to focus on the figure running down the sidewalk. House lights were coming on all around them. Unconsciously he wiped his face with his other hand. When he pulled it away it was smeared with blood and small pieces of skin and human hair. Stunned, Cavanaugh didn't know where he had been hit. Then he realized that this was Gilbert's blood.

He looked down and saw that the top portion of the man's skull had been blown away. In his hand, reflecting the street lamp like small jewels, were the keys to his car.

Cavanaugh staggered back a little and covered his mouth. He wanted to throw up. Nearby, he heard a car being started.

"What happened?" He felt Christine's hand on his shoulder.

"Gilbert," he croaked. "He's dead."

Christine only gasped and covered her mouth with her hands.

There was no time to lose! Cavanaugh bent down and grabbed the keys to Gilbert's car from the dead man's hands. "I'm going after him," he said.

"What? Where are you going?" Christine was shaking.

Cavanaugh was already down the steps. He turned briefly around. "After the other one. Find a phone and call the police. And the Project offices. Tell them what I'm doing."

"Phil!" she screamed. One of her neighbors was already crossing the street.

"Call the police *now*!" he shouted from Gilbert's car.

Oh Jesus! he thought. What *am* I doing? He turned the key, pumped the accelerator a few times and barely had the car running before he hit the gear and jerked forward. Down the street, rapidly disappearing from view, were two small red dots that he prayed belonged to the car he wanted to follow.

As he passed under a streetlight he noticed tiny drops of blood and skull splattered across his uniform. As best he could, with one hand, he wiped his face.

His heart was pumping wildly. Running through his head, fueled by fear and adrenaline, were the memories of running through the forest at Mühlhausen. He gripped the steering wheel so tightly that his hands started to go numb.

The car in front of him was too far away, too much in the darkness to be seen clearly. Cavanaugh could only hope that he was following the right one. It wasn't until the other car unexpectedly turned that he recognized it as the dark sedan he had seen in the hospital parking lot. He felt another rush of adrenaline.

A taxi pulled in front of him from a side street. Cavanaugh honked and passed him by breaking out into the other lane. The cabbie veered to the right and honked loudly.

He tried to think out the possibilities as he sped down the street and then turned where the sedan had turned moments before. The same pair of red taillights glowed in the distance. Surely the son of a bitch had to know he was being followed! The man was speeding but not making much of an effort to lose him. But that could mean anything: that it was intentional, maybe; or that the driver was careless.

The driver wasn't Swiss, of course; he was German. And he could be leading Cavanaugh into a trap. Or to an ambush somewhere where more Germans were waiting. Maybe where the goddamn bomb was!

Cavanaugh's mind raced. There was something deep down in his memory, some fact that he knew he needed now. Then he remembered. It was the river! Almost certainly the Germans had come by water. From the Chesapeake up the Potomac to somewhere here in Washington. That's probably what they planned for London.

If they had a bomb, it would probably still be on a boat docked somewhere, or maybe hiding in one of the tributaries of the Potomac. But to be effective—really to fire the *parting shot*—the bomb needed to be brought as close to the Capitol and the White House as possible, and then detonated. Then Hitler would have his last laugh.

But then another, more immediate question came to mind: was the car in front of him going to the boat? Or to a trap? Or to both?

Simon alternated between fear and excitement. Things had gone wrong, disastrously wrong, but curiously his whole body was alive with a strange kind of energy, a power that made all his thoughts perfectly clear to him. It would all work out; he would not fail.

Ernest was dead. Or Simon hoped he was dead. That way he couldn't be made to talk. It was too bad, but perhaps inevitable. But it was he, Simon, after all, who had been chosen.

There was no time now. He could see the American's headlights a half-block, sometimes a block, behind him. At first that had scared him. But now he had incorporated the American into his new plan.

The weapon was ready. Fully assembled on the large pleasure boat they had rented several days ago. Herman was with it right now. They only needed to maneuver the boat into position—they had been given strict instructions about that: three preferable locations along the Potomac, two secondary choices in an emergency—and then set the timer. They had an hour to get away.

They had followed the couple to their house to kill them and had

328

failed, but now the American was coming to them. That would do. Simon reminded himself to be sure not to drive so fast, or so cannily, that he lost his follower or was stopped by the police.

If he did everything right, and didn't lose the American, he would have a five-minute edge. Just enough time to prepare for him.

Chapter Thirty-one

avanaugh had only the vaguest sense of where he was going. The sedan he was following had initially driven east, out of Georgetown, and turned right on Pennsylvania Avenue. He almost lost sight of it when the car made a turn around Washington Circle and then turned off on Twenty-third Street. Some inner sense of direction told Cavanaugh that he was now heading toward the Potomac River.

Goddamn it! He cursed himself for not having studied the map of the river more closely. He had a dim recollection of a private boat dock somewhere near one of the memorials, but he couldn't remember if it was the Lincoln or Jefferson Memorial. It wasn't until he broke out of the downtown buildings on twenty-third that he saw the graceful lines of the Lincoln Memorial in the distance. Cavanaugh knew that the river wasn't far beyond that.

There were other cars on the street, moving in both directions, even at this late hour. Cavanaugh had to force himself to focus on the single pair of taillights in the distance.

330

The Lincoln Memorial produced a bowl of light that made the square, elegant building stand out on the otherwise dark shoreline. A mile or two away, roughly parallel with Cavanaugh's car, was the Washington Monument; at this distance, it appeared as a tall, slender shaft of dazzling white light. The moon was waning, at three-quarters, but it lay behind a series of drifting clouds, much like that evening several days ago in Mühlhausen.·

He briefly looked up through his side window to check the sky: he desperately needed the moonlight.

When he looked back at the road he was by himself: the taillights had disappeared! Cavanaugh instantly took his foot off the gas pedal, scared that he might have lost the sedan altogether. Could the German somehow have turned off by the Lincoln Memorial? Cavanaugh made a sharp U-turn on Ohio Drive. He raced back to the memorial and made a full circle around it: there wasn't a single other car.

Desperate now, he raced back down Ohio, which ran parallel with the Potomac. In the distance he could see the dark shape of a bridge across the river, and the circular form of the Jefferson Memorial. He remembered enough from the map to know that the memorial sat on the edge of the Tidal Basin, but he couldn't remember if the entrance to the basin was large enough to accommodate a boat or barge. Jesus! he cursed again, why hadn't he studied the goddamn map?

He retraced his steps and spotted a small turnoff to the right; a small sign read "Private Drive: Potomac Boat Dock." Was this it? He had to take the chance.

Cavanaugh hit the brakes and turned off as quickly as he could, hitting the edge of the curb with the right wheel and bouncing hard onto the gravel road. At least, Gilbert wouldn't care about his car. He cut the lights as soon as he could free one hand.

There was just enough moonlight to get him the half-block to the dock. Or so he prayed. Gradually, he could make out the curved forms of several cars; beyond them were a few buildings, and, farther still, the tops of dozens of barely visible masts rocking gently in the water. Cavanaugh pulled the car over and cut the engine; he was maybe fifty feet away from the other cars.

For a moment he just sat there in the dark, trying to decide what to do next. He picked up the .38 from the seat and looked at it; his hand was trembling slightly. His heart was beating hard and he felt strangely light-headed, as if he had been standing on his head and then suddenly stood up straight. Deep inside, Cavanaugh knew this

331

was it. It wasn't a series of unanswered questions anymore, of intelligence memos or translated interviews: somewhere on the other side of the buildings was the German atomic bomb. He *knew* it. And unlike a bad dream, he wouldn't wake up and make it go away.

Why had he come here by himself? In fact, why had he done everything himself, only confiding in Christine at the last moment?

And when he had finally involved Gilbert, it cost the man his goddamn life! And all out of some misplaced loyalty to a son of a bitch General who wouldn't let him go home. To Los Alamos. To Trinity. Cavanaugh kept thinking how there ought to be police here, or MPs. Or someone else at least. There was no guessing how many Germans were out there.

He stared at the sky. Between clouds, the moon was just bright enough to let him find his way to the dock. Of course the same light favored the Germans.

Inhaling deeply, he darted to the left, to the line of low shrubs that followed the driveway; they might just be enough to make it difficult for someone to see him. Then, cautiously, every sense on edge, he ran to the parked cars. All of them looked remarkably similar, especially at night. Then he had an idea. He touched the hood of the car closest to him, then the second one: both were cold. Then he touched the third: it was still warm. This car had just arrived.

Cavanaugh was close enough to the river to hear the water lapping against the boats and docks; there were a rhythmic series of low thumps each time a wooden hull hit a pier.

As quietly as he could, he walked to the rear wall of the nearest building, which looked like a clubhouse of some kind. Tiny nautical pennants flew from a mast mounted on the roof, each one flapping noisily in the river breeze. Then he worked his way around the side to the front and stopped within the deeper shadow under the eaves. A series of wooden steps led down to a ramp that ran parallel to the shore. Off it ran four other vertical ramps divided into dozens of individual boat slips. Most were occupied.

Son of a bitch! There could easily be seventy or eighty boats out there. How in the hell was he going to find the one he was looking for?

Taking another deep breath to calm himself, he reasoned that the Germans weren't likely to use anything without a cabin. The sailboats were too small. The largest boats were probably too conspicuous and not very maneuverable. That eliminated perhaps two-thirds of the boats docked and left inboards with cabins just large enough to hide an eight- or ten-foot weapon. But boats matching this general description were scattered in slips throughout all four ramps; there was no choice but to check ramp by ramp, even though he would be an easy target at all times.

As soon as he started down the steps he knew he would be even more conspicuous. His hard leather Army shoes made a *clop-clop* sound on the uneven wooden planks of the pier. It was as good as shouting his arrival!

He slowed his pace and tried to ease his feet down slowly on his toes, which was awkward and time-consuming. He knew he didn't have much time. If the Germans were still here, they would be preparing to cast off as soon as possible, probably to move the boat—and the bomb—into position somewhere. Or maybe they were preparing to detonate it.

It was also possible that they were waiting for him.

He was halfway down the first ramp, glancing right and left for a boat large enough and with any sign of activity. With any luck, there would be noise, or maybe lights. There was no way he could physically search each boat he suspected.

As he neared the end of the first ramp he heard a sound like a scuffling motion. Cavanaugh stopped dead in his tracks and felt for his gun in the pocket of his pants. Then he saw something move, something small on the roof of a cabin to the right of him. A cat scrambled off and disappeared through a partially open porthole.

Cavanaugh clenched his fists to stop shaking. He hurried back down the ramp and headed for the second. Something caught his attention just as he passed the first couple of boats—a dull-yellow glow from the window of a medium-size cabin cruiser parked at the end of the dock. When Cavanaugh looked again, the light was gone. At first, he guessed it might have only been a reflection of some kind, the sort of thing he could check out when he got there. But then it reappeared: its source was from inside the boat itself.

He remembered that there were three cars in the parking lot. The owner of any one of them could be the occupant of the boat with the light. It was too dark to read his watch, but Cavanaugh guessed that it was one, maybe two in the morning. Then, from the boat with the light, he heard an engine turn over. Once, twice, then nothing. Oh, Christ! they're leaving, he moaned. Frantic for time, he ran down the dock, his shoes noisily hitting the planks at each step. He had to get there before they pulled away!

There was movement inside the cabin; Cavanaugh could tell by the way dark forms moved back and forth. But it was impossible to tell if each shadow that passed across the porthole was a different individual, or a single person moving. He still had no idea of how many Germans he faced. As he neared the boat he picked out the pungent smell of gasoline.

Cavanaugh arrived just as a man in dark clothing was closing the motor hatch on the rear deck. For an instant, both men just stared at one another, frozen where they stood. Cavanaugh felt paralyzed, unable to move or make a decision. In fact, he was confused. The man he saw was blond all right, or had light-colored hair, but he wasn't one of the two men from the hospital. Cavanaugh was just about to pull his gun, whatever the consequences, when he heard a movement behind him. Startled, Cavanaugh jerked slightly and began to turn around.

"Stand still!" said a deep, powerful voice.

At the same moment, Cavanaugh felt a hard metal object hit firmly against the back of his head; it wasn't enough to knock him out, but enough to hurt and let him know its wielder had a gun and meant business.

The light-headedness crept back into his skull, leaving him dazed and frightened at the same time. He did nothing but stand there and let his hands droop at his sides.

The man behind him suddenly barked an order in German to the man on deck, who scrambled into the cabin. In the brief moment that the door was open, a bolt of yellow light flooded the deck. It was just enough time for Cavanaugh to see something large and cumbersome in the cabin itself. In the yellow light, it seemed as black as death itself.

"Now step down into the boat," the voice behind him said. "Very slowly." The commands were in English but with a foreign accent.

Cavanaugh did as he was told and stepped down into the boat. The gun briefly left the back of his head but returned moments later after Cavanaugh heard the sound of two feet hitting the deck behind him. In front of him, from within the motor cavity, came the sound of the engine turning over again, then sputtering to a start. The exhaust at the water line made a gurgling sound as it escaped from the pipes. Once again, there was the powerful smell of gasoline.

334

"Turn around," the voice ordered. "Slowly, or I will shoot. Your hands up."

Cavanaugh again did as he was told. When he turned around he saw up close the face he had fleetingly seen twice before: at the hospital and in the car in the parking lot. There was just enough moonlight to see that the man was probably in his late twenties or early thirties, thin, with a face that might have been handsome except for a thin, beakish nose. For a moment, they stared silently at each other.

Finally, the German spoke. "Are you alone?"

"Yes," said Cavanaugh. It was unfortunately true.

"Where is the girl?"

"Do you have the bomb here?" Cavanaugh replied.

There was only a flicker of surprise on the other man's thin face before he regained control. "Where is the girl?" he repeated.

"At her apartment." He hoped to God she had already called the police. It was just possible—though hardly likely, he knew—that she would remember their conversation about moving a secret weapon upriver to Washington from the Chesapeake. If Christine remembered that, she might figure out where to lead the police. Dim possibility, he guessed, and probably stupid to wish for. The reality was glum and deadly: he was a captive of desperate men who had no choice but to kill him before he caused any more trouble.

The door to the cabin opened halfway and the second man said something in German. Cavanaugh sensed from the tone and from the few words he thought he recognized that the boat was ready to go.

The blond German nodded and said simply, "*Ja.*"

Cavanaugh looked briefly around. The German had no silencer on his revolver; that might be the only reason why Cavanaugh hadn't been shot yet. There seemed to be only one other man—the one in the cabin. Assuming Cavanaugh could make a run for it, the only direction was the water. Unfortunately, the German's gun made that impossible right now. And his own gun was still in his pants.

What the hell could he do? Involuntarily, he started to shake. At first it was his hands that trembled, then his body. He was literally quaking in his shoes.

Underneath him, the engine began to rumble loudly. The man inside the cabin was giving it gas. Suddenly, the tall German in front of him began to shout in German. Something was wrong.

"*Nein!*" he yelled. "*Anhalten!*"

At first, Cavanaugh didn't know what was going on: the boat had pulled away from the pier, churning up river water as it did so. Then he understood. The boat was still moored to the dock with a rope from the stern cleat.

The tall German made a lunge for it, still pointing his gun in Cavanaugh's direction. He shouted again for the other man to stop. The motor grew louder, the water frothing all around them. Ignorant of the mooring rope, the man inside was compensating for the hesitation by giving the old boat more gas. Cavanaugh looked at the cabin door, with its tiny window lit from within, and then back at the tall German. The man was frantically trying to untie the rope; he alternated between working the rope and checking on Cavanaugh.

This was it! thought Cavanaugh. Under the increasing stress of the straining motor, the boat had begun to rock. Choosing a moment in which the boat was listing heavily, he rushed the German. The man, however, caught Cavanaugh's movement out of the corner of his eye; he rapidly tried to stabilize himself and then pumped off one shot, then another.

Even with the roar of the motor, the noise from the gun was explosively loud. Both shots missed Cavanaugh but hit the rear of the cabin, one directly on the door. The man inside pulled the throttle and cut back the power.

Almost instantly, the boat made an arc in the water and settled down. Cavanaugh felt the deck under him sway like a swing. He bent his knees and steadied himself. The German had been thrown against the rear wall of the deck area, just aft of the cleat. He had been forced to use both hands to steady himself. It was in that instant that Cavanaugh lunged forward again and with all his might kicked the German between his legs. It was the only thing he could think of to do.

The German emitted a loud "uh" and clutched himself with both hands. Even in the darkness, Cavanaugh could see the man's eyes pop; he fell with a dull thud to his knees, still gripping his crotch.

Cavanaugh was briefly startled that his move had succeeded: he just stared at the kneeling man. Then he knew he had to act again. Stepping back and struggling to balance himself in the still rocking boat, he kicked once more, this time aiming for the man's head. U.S. Army issue shoe and skull met in a crushing blow. The German fell over, appeared to blink his eyes several times, and then stopped moving. Cavanaugh rushed forward and grabbed the gun out of the man's hand and threw it into the water.

Almost as soon as he had done it, he regretted it. He should have kept the gun. He could have used it in addition to his own. The sickening realization hit him that he had only a couple of shells left in his .38. One? Two? He didn't even know how many shells a goddamn .38 held!

There was still the other man to contend with. He whirled around and stepped to the cabin door. Stupidly, without even thinking, he started to open it. The door had moved no more than a few inches when simultaneously Cavanaugh heard a loud sound and painfully felt bits of wood sting his face. Stunned, he stepped backward, rushing a hand to his face; he felt tiny bits of wood and warm fluid. Just as he lifted his own gun, the door jerked open: standing there, with a gun aimed at him, was the German pilot. The edge of the door, at the level of Cavanaugh's face, was sheared off.

Cavanaugh had only a second to react. Instinctively, he leaned to one side and fired his gun. The bullet hit harmlessly against the wall. The German was luckier. Cavanaugh heard another shot and at the same moment felt a blow to his arm, just below the shoulder. At first, it was as if he had been hit with a baseball bat; then his arm felt like on fire! He cried out with pain and fell backward, gripping his shoulder. In falling he accidentally pulled the trigger of his pistol; unsteadied, his hand convulsed in the explosion.

As he fell, he saw the door slam shut, then heard noises from behind it. Still dazed from the blow, and in searing pain, he forced himself to sit up, the fire in his arm so intense that when he moved, tears came to his eyes. From underneath the deck he heard the engine rev up: the boat was moving again! This time, the German didn't bother to ease the power. He hit the throttle hard: the huge engine roared, water churned, and the boat lunged forward. It hesitated only a moment under the restraining force of the mooring rope. Then the chrome cleat snapped off like a Tinkertoy and fell with its rope into the water next to the pier. The boat leapt out of its slip and made a sharp turn to the left, then to the right, and headed straight for open water, down the middle of the Potomac.

Despite the pain, Cavanaugh forced himself up, using his one good arm to brace himself. He had to do something to stop the German, to stop the boat! Chances were that the cabin door was locked, or blocked enough to give the man inside a chance to shoot long before Cavanaugh could break through.

He had absolutely no idea if there was another door, or a hatch on the bow of the boat. The tiny catwalk around both sides of the cabin was far too dangerous to navigate while the boat was moving, more so for Cavanaugh, with only one good arm. At any moment the German could reappear, and although he wasn't certain, Cavanaugh guessed that he had at most one shot left in his gun. Whatever he did, he knew he couldn't win a shoot-out.

The illuminated shape of the Lincoln Memorial appeared on the shore. There was no telling what the German intended to do. Or where he intended to stop. It suddenly occurred to Cavanaugh that the man could detonate the bomb by hand. It could already be activated by a timer. That, after all, had been the apparent design of the London bomb.

Cavanaugh desperately looked around the deck. He saw the hatch to the motor compartment; the most obvious thing to do was to kill the motor and then contend with the German. He started for the hatch, then caught sight of a can in a metal frame moored to the wall of the cabin. It looked like a gasoline can. He rushed over and jiggled the screw top, then flipped it open. It took only one sniff to confirm that it was gas.

Without thinking, Cavanaugh lifted the heavy Jerry can from its frame; he had to grit his teeth and fight back the pain that racked his body with every move. Then he studied the cabin door. His plan was deadly, but it was all he could think of.

He rested the gasoline can on the deck in front of the door and kicked it over with his foot. The gas poured out in small waves, splashing against the door and wall and spilling underneath to the cabin itself. Clutching his arm, he kicked the gas against the door with his shoe, making sure that as much of it as possible went underneath. Then he bent down and angled the can, emptying the rest of the contents. The fumes were overpowering, even in the wind created by the moving boat. When the can was spent, he threw it overboard.

The German was easing back on the motor. Cavanaugh knew there were only precious moments left. He fished around in his pockets for his lighter, then remembered he had left it sitting on Christine's coffee table. There was only his .38 left. He dug it out of his pocket and stepped back. As much as it hurt, he grabbed a nearby life preserver and held it with his wounded and bleeding arm. He took aim as best he could and fired.

There was an explosion, more of light and heat than sound, and suddenly the wall of the cabin burst into intense red and yellow flames.

338

Shafts of light shot out of the portholes on either side, indicating the gasoline was burning inside as well.

Cavanaugh was momentarily blinded by the light and felt the heat blast his face and body. Tiny flames flickered on the deck where his shoe had left traces of gasoline. The center of the boat was burning intensely now, flames fed by old wood and years of varnish. The heat was rapidly becoming unbearable. Soon it would reach the temperature necessary to detonate the gasoline in the fuel tank. Or maybe the explosives used in the bomb. If only the boat sank, the explosives would be soaked with water and unable to detonate. He had to count on that!

Choked by the fumes, Cavanaugh looked at the shoreline. The Lincoln Memorial was fading in the distance, although its light still lit up the night sky.

As quickly as he could, Cavanaugh slipped the life preserver over his neck and painfully lifted his left arm over it, then his right. He felt dizzy now, the fumes mixing with the loss of blood to eat away at his consciousness. His shirt was wet with warm blood. He fell backward into the river, thinking as he did so that he needed to put as much distance as possible between himself and the boat when it exploded. *If* it exploded.

Even the shock of cold water didn't revive him. He felt himself bouncing in the wake of the boat, vaguely aware that it was moving away from him.

Oh God, he prayed, please—

Then everything faded and went dark.

Chapter Thirty-two

avanaugh woke up with a headache. It was more like a dull throbbing in the front part of his brain. As if he'd been on an all-night drunk and now was left with a gigantic hangover.

When at last he opened his eyes he had trouble focusing. He knew he was in a strange room, because there were tubes and bottles above his head and a strange but pleasant-looking woman standing nearby. Then he realized he was in a hospital.

"You're awake?" the woman said nonchalantly. Her voice was pleasant too. "Good."

He started to sit up so he could talk when a terrible pain shot through his shoulder. Then he remembered the boat.

The nurse caught the agonizing look on his face and reassuringly took his hand. "You're okay," she said soothingly, "you've had a bad accident, that's all."

He just stared at her and tried to ask where he was. For some reason, he couldn't make any sound. And the only thing he could think about was the last hospital he'd been in and the dead man he'd seen there. Murdered by an injection of air.

"You're in a hospital, Captain, an Army hospital. Take it easy." She smiled and patted his hand one more time before laying it gently back on the bed.

Army. Not Navy. He relaxed and discovered that if he didn't move, the pain in his shoulder slowly ebbed away.

Thank God! he was safe, he thought, and drifted off to sleep again.

When he woke up, the solicitous nurse wasn't there. She'd been replaced by a man, one with a round face and small wire-rim glasses. Academic-looking. Cavanaugh knew that he knew the man, but somehow the name escaped him. Who the hell was it?

"Dr. Cavanaugh?"

The voice was familiar too.

"It's Major Franklyn. General Groves sent me to check on you."

Major Franklyn. Groves. Now he remembered everything.

"Ah," he said, trying to form a word with his lips. They felt as if they were glued together.

"What?"

Finally Cavanaugh was able to whisper it. "The boat?" he rasped.

"The boat? Oh, we have it. No problem."

Then other names and faces flooded his mind. "Christine?" he whispered.

A flicker of disapproval moved across Franklyn's face. "Lieutenant Leiter? She's all right. Gilbert's dead, you know."

Yes, he knew. Thank God Christine was okay.

"There's a lot we want to know, Dr. Cavanaugh. A great deal. The General wants to talk to you as soon as the doctors let him."

Cavanaugh said nothing. Damn right the General would want to talk with him! And he'd want to talk with the General as well.

"We'll be back," said Franklyn.

Right, thought Cavanaugh. Soon.

The conversation with Groves took place the next afternoon. In the meantime, Cavanaugh learned that he was being held incommunicado: no calls in or out. And no visitors.

A series of tough-looking military guards stood outside his door around the clock or nervously inside whenever a nurse or doctor visited. Someone was taking no chances. He also learned that he'd lost a lot of blood and gone into shock while floating in the Potomac. He was going to be okay, everyone said, and the shots they gave him made the pain go away. He even felt mildly good, although he knew it was only the narcotics. When he had the energy, he joked lightly with his nurses. But mostly he slept.

General Groves came by himself. Or, if anyone else was there, they were told to stay outside. Groves stared at him for a long moment, then pulled a chair close to his bed and sat down. There was no "good morning" or "how are you?"

"I want to know what happened," he said directly. His voice was neither warm nor cold, just detached and businesslike.

Cavanaugh told him everything he could remember. Haltingly at first, then in a rush of words. From the first meetings in London to the last events with Brooke and the old man, the British intelligence guy. And all about Mühlhausen and the discoveries there.

Groves listened quietly, his face expressionless, only occasionally interrupting to ask a question. From time to time, he turned and checked the door to be sure it was still closed.

"You're certain the Germans made six of them?" the General asked. He meant the gun barrels.

"Not certain, no. There was a piece of paper, a shipping order of some kind, that said six modified gun barrels had been delivered. And we found only three in Mühlhausen. That's all. I guess the Russians have got those now."

Cavanaugh thought about the shipping order: that and the film, the documentary evidence of his trip to Mühlhausen, were somewhere in a German forest. On the Soviet side.

Groves looked perturbed. Cavanaugh could tell he didn't like hearing the Russians had anything. "And the uranium cylinders?" he asked. "You're convinced they were intended for the gun barrels?"

"I'm as certain as I can be without physically trying to match them."

"Where did the British say they found them?"

"In London." Cavanaugh licked his lips to make talking easier. "That was part of the trouble. They—"

Groves cut him off. All he said was, "British Intelligence, naturally."

Cavanaugh felt his energy draining. It was getting harder to concentrate, and he could feel the pain in his shoulder returning. Soon he would have to have another shot and that always put him out for a while.

"I want to be clear on one point, Doctor," Groves said. He leaned closer than before to Cavanaugh.

"Are you certain that you told the British *nothing* about Mühlhausen? About what you found there?"

Cavanaugh nodded. "Yes. Only you and me. But Conti, the OSS officer, he knows."

"But you never explained what the barrels were? To Conti, I mean."

"No. He knows something, though, I'm sure."

Groves nodded. "And Lieutenant Leiter? What does she know?"

"Only about the German plot, the so-called vengeance plot. I needed her help, I mean, there was no one else, and—" His head was starting to hurt now; the pain was concentrating in his shoulder. "Can I see her?" he blurted out. He wanted so much to see her, to know for himself that she was okay.

Groves just looked at him. "I need you to write all this down. To make a report for me. But not here. Not in the hospital. When you get out, I'll assign you a secure office where you can do it."

Cavanaugh started to ask about Christine again but Groves continued.

"You are to prepare only one copy, do you understand? Don't give the report to anyone but me. And say nothing about any of this when you get back to Los Alamos. Not even to Dr. Oppenheimer."

"But they'll ask me what happened. What I saw."

"Tell them what you did in Germany. With the SHAEF team. But nothing of crossing into the Soviet Zone. And nothing about what you found there."

"What about the boat? And the bomb?"

Groves checked the door again. "We have everything. The press was told it was a boating accident."

"And the Soviets?"

"What about them?"

Cavanaugh shifted, trying to ease the pain in his shoulder. "We need to warn them. About the bomb. The plot. One could be there now, in Moscow, maybe."

Groves briefly looked away from the bed. "We'll take care of that."

Cavanaugh nodded weakly. "What about Christine? Lieutenant Leiter. Can I see her?"

"When the doctor says you can. But I want that report, and I don't want anything to happen to you until then."

Groves stood up and moved the chair back against the wall. He was almost at the door when Cavanaugh suddenly remembered something

343

else. Something that just a few weeks ago had been the most important thing in his life.

"What about the Test?" he asked. His voice was barely louder than a whisper.

Groves stopped and turned around. He smiled. "It's a boy," he said softly, "a great big baby boy!"

It was another two days before Christine visited him. He was reading a magazine when there was a soft knock on the door. Then it opened and she stuck her head in.

"You decent?" she asked. There was a small bouquet of flowers in her hand.

He smiled.

For a moment, they both just looked at one another. Then she walked quickly over and kissed him. Again and again, but very gently. He barely felt her lips on his. A moment later, when they were holding each other, she murmured, "Thank God you're okay."

He pulled apart slightly and felt a sharp stab of pain as he shifted; then he noticed that she had tears in her eyes.

"I'm okay. Really."

She nodded and wiped her eyes with a handkerchief.

"You need a pass to get in here. Did you know that?"

"Yeah. It's like the Tech Area." Then he realized she didn't have any idea what he was talking about. "I don't know if these palookas are here to protect me, or just to be sure I don't run away." He laughed weakly.

She smiled and touched his face. "I was so worried."

"Me too."

She hugged him again. "There's so much to tell you. You can't imagine."

No, he thought, *you* can't imagine. "What?"

"You were in the newspapers. Your name, that is. As the victim of a boating accident."

"An accident?"

"Well, that's what they called it. An unexplainable fire on board a boat. An explosion. That sort of thing."

"My name?" he asked. What about the Germans? Didn't the police find them?

Christine lowered her voice. The door was open and Cavanaugh

344

could see the Army MP standing outside. This visit wouldn't be a private one.

"Major Franklyn arranged it. Yours was the only name that appeared in the press. So far as anyone knows, you were the only one involved in the accident. The police picked you up floating a mile or so down the Potomac from the Lincoln Memorial."

"And Gilbert? And the German shot at your house? What about them?"

"A robbery. It was in the newspapers too, but no one linked it to the boating accident."

Cavanaugh leaned back against his pillow. So that was what they did: made the entire experience a series of small, independent events. Probably caused a mild stir, but nothing to make the press want to waste a lot of time looking deeper, perhaps to connect the events.

He looked at Christine: her face was as beautiful as ever to him, although he could see the stress of the last few days around her eyes.

"And how are you?" he asked. *"Really?"*

She silently nodded her head. "Okay. Better, now that I know you'll live."

The office was very American, thought Christopher Brooke. Plain. Functional. The General's elaborate desk was perhaps the only element in the office out of character. How very different from Lytton-Harte's in London.

Brooke had been with Groves for nearly thirty minutes, during which he had done most of the talking and the General had either listened or read the classified papers that Brooke had carried with him from England.

Groves closed the file he was reading. "Very interesting, Major."

Brooke still found it hard to hear himself called Major. The sudden and unexpected promotion had come through only two days ago, in just enough time to let him arrive in America with a rank that made a secret conversation with a General more palatable. American military officers, he was told, were as sensitive to these matters as their own.

"The Director thought you would find it helpful." He referred to the intelligence report summarizing the interrogation of a captured SS officer. And he deliberately mentioned the *Director* of MI5 instead of Lytton-Harte.

"And what do your people make of it?" asked Groves.

"We have to give it some credence, since we discovered part of a weapon in London. But we have no confirmation that a similar device went to the Soviet Union." Brooke paused; at this point, he was not to bring up the affair with Cavanaugh. "And you would presumably know if a weapon were here in America."

He had been instructed on what to say. Grilled, really, by Lytton-Harte himself. First, he was to present the interrogation summary of Brunig, the captured German; then assess the American reaction. Only finally was he to offer an apology for the manner in which Philip Cavanaugh had been treated.

Brooke remembered asking if that wasn't adding insult to injury—*reminding* the Americans how we used their man to get what we wanted? Lytton-Harte had only smiled. No, he'd said, they were merely sharing information with their closest allies. And, in effect, asking for their forgiveness for less than gentlemanly behavior. Besides, he'd added, they couldn't afford to disagree.

In fact, General Groves had barely reacted. He had listened and he had read what had been given him. So far, that was about it.

Groves responded pointedly, barely acknowledging the report. "Yes," he said, "Dr. Cavanaugh briefed us on this." He'd be cursed if he'd tell the Brits *anything* about the events here in Washington. And if he had anything to do with it, this whole business would stay an *American* secret that no one would ever know about.

"We'd like to know whatever your intelligence people learn, of course," added Brooke. "As part of the continuing Anglo-American work on atomic weapons." Brooke rather doubted they'd hear another word about uranium canisters or a Nazi plot. From the Americans, at least.

"Of course."

Brooke cleared his throat. "The Director wants you to know, personally, how much he regrets the, ah, unfortunate way in which Captain Cavanaugh was treated. It was, I assure you, only because of the *imminent* threat the uranium posed. We had to assume it was for a new weapon of some kind you see."

Groves said nothing at first. "That was unfortunate," he said finally. "And I don't appreciate it. Neither will my government."

Brooke expected this. Instead of reacting, he said nothing. Remain calm, he told himself, no matter what the reputedly stern General Groves said or did. That was the best posture.

346

"So what do you want?" asked Groves. He was growing tired of the conversation. As far as he was concerned, the British could go to blazes.

"To reassure you," replied Brooke, "that this won't happen again. But also to promise you that we plan to share any further developments with you as soon as possible." He pointed to the file folders on Groves's desk. Now all he had to do was raise the final point. The big one.

"And to tell you that we don't intend to go any further with this. Unless, of course, you insist on it."

"What do you mean?"

"As far as the Director is concerned, this matter is closed. The circumstances in Europe are very complex now, one might even say *grave*. One can hardly afford to ignore the Soviets and their substantial armies in Eastern Europe. It wouldn't serve any purpose to involve them, or to let knowledge of these events fall into political hands in *either* of our countries."

Groves stared at the young man in front of him. He'd never planned to tell anyone about this, or, at least, anyone he didn't have to. That would involve revealing the purpose of Cavanaugh's trip to Germany. The *real* purpose.

"No," he said simply. "No need to go further at all."

Brooke felt a rush of relief run through him. Lytton-Harte, that old son of a bitch, had been right: the Americans would buy the plan. They'd have to. Now he understood.

"I'll pass that along to the Director," he said.

"Do that."

Brooke got up and saluted. Groves nominally returned the salute.

"By the way," said Brooke, "I understand Captain Cavanaugh was in a nasty accident. There was something in the paper, I'm told."

Groves hesitated for a moment before responding. "Yes, he was."

"I trust he's all right?"

"Oh, yes. Going back to work soon."

Brooke nodded. "Good. He's an exceptional man."

Cavanaugh smiled at the person next to him. They were alone in the elevator but it made no difference; he would have looked and smiled at her anyway. Christine had never looked better. The last few days, since he'd gotten out of the hospital, had been the best he'd ever had, even though Groves had insisted he billet at a hotel for Army officers.

Cavanaugh smiled again. The hotel management had taken special note of him, especially his comings and goings. Men followed him. He had a car and driver. And yet, he and Christine had managed.

The report was done. It had been hand-delivered to Groves that morning. They had shaken hands and said good-bye. Cavanaugh was finished with Washington and with the Manhattan Project offices. He had this afternoon and tonight left in D.C.: tomorrow he was to take the train back to New Mexico.

And tonight had to be special; there was something very important he wanted to ask Christine. He knew that he couldn't leave Washington without talking seriously about their future. In fact, he wanted to talk about marriage.

She had put him off the last few nights with kindness: laughing, kidding him, showering him with love and affection. But always when the talk turned serious, she had hesitated and pulled back, saying gently, "Not just yet." He wondered about it but decided tonight would be it. He couldn't leave this relationship as he'd left the last.

"I know a place for lunch," she said. "Very quiet. Very romantic."

"Perfect," he said. "Let's go." Maybe he'd just move the discussion up. If lunch went right, well, who knew what he'd say?

"I've got work all afternoon," she said, "but I can be back at the apartment after five."

"And your roommate?" There had only been one brief appearance by the mysterious roommate, and that had been only for a moment, for her to collect some clothes.

She smiled. "Gone for good."

Now Cavanaugh smiled. "She got her man?"

"No, sorry to say. He was married after all. But she's found her own place. Here, in the District."

Cavanaugh grabbed her hand and held it. The elevator doors opened and they stepped out into the lobby of the War Department Building. Moments later, they were outside in brilliant sunshine.

He was just about to ask what kind of food the restaurant served when he saw a tall man with reddish-blond hair leaving the lobby for the street. He was wearing a British Army uniform. Cavanaugh couldn't be certain, but it sure as hell looked like Christopher Brooke! But *what* could he be doing here?

Christine was saying something. "Phil?"

"Sorry. I thought I saw someone."

Her hand gripped his tightly. "Who?"

"Someone named Brooke. From England. Come on!"

348

He rushed forward, pulling Christine behind him, never letting go of her hand.

By the time they reached the door and stepped outside, the man was getting into a taxi and shutting the door.

"Brooke!" shouted Cavanaugh. Could it be? "Brooke! Goddamn it!" He dropped Christine's hand and rushed to the street just as the car was pulling away.

Christine came up and grabbed his arm. "Who was it?"

He shook his head. "I'm not sure."

The taxi disappeared into the noontime traffic.

"Darling?" She took his hand in hers.

Cavanaugh finally turned and looked at her. He forced a smile. "I thought it was someone I knew."

Part Ten

SEPTEMBER 1991

GREAT BRITAIN AND THE UNITED STATES

The only thing new in the world is the history you don't know.

—Harry Truman

Chapter Thirty-three

*R*amsden's meeting with the Home Secretary was in a seldom-used office in the basement of a Whitehall building adjacent to their own. Windowless and austere, the room was dominated by the lingering smell of something stale, decaying. There was no word of explanation about the choice of room from Sir George, except for a brief "More private, I should think."

Ramsden prefaced their conversation with the revelation that his office had been searched.

"Are you certain?" asked Sir George. One eyebrow lifted.

Ramsden searched the man's face for some sense of preknowledge. Or perhaps conspiracy. There was none. "I think so," he said quietly.

"Everything secure? The Archbishop papers?"

"Yes. They're on their way to the PM."

The Minister shook his head but said nothing more. Ramsden dropped the matter but wondered who—if anyone—had searched his office. Was it for the Archbishop files?

From that moment on, for the next quarter hour, the Home Secretary sat quietly through Ramsden's summary, struggling only to find a comfortable position in his ancient chair.

At last, snuffing out a cigarette, he responded. "Let me understand this, Edmund."

Ramsden unconsciously rubbed his neck. His neck hurt like the devil, a condition he attributed to the stress and the long hours of the last few days.

"You have confirmed that our intelligence people found part of a bomb in, ah, when? 1945?"

"Yes. Late June."

The Home Secretary lit another cigarette with a match whose cover read Odin's Restaurant. He looked around, then dropped the used match into a cheap metal ashtray where earlier someone had squashed a small wad of chewing gum.

"And no report was made of this? To other departments. To the PM?"

"Apparently not. MI5 apparently wanted to keep this 'find' to themselves, and somehow they succeeded."

"Yet they confirmed that it was part of a bomb by using, ah, this *ploy* with the American fellow?"

"So it seems." Ramsden thought about the elusive American who appeared to have played an important role in all of this. The CIA still hadn't responded, damn them. All they knew about the man had been gleaned from a *Who's Who* of American scientists.

"Incredible," mumbled Sir George.

The heavy man fell silent, apparently trying to grasp the enormity of what he had been told. He was slumped down in his chair like an inflatable toy that had been suddenly punctured.

"And Lytton-Harte," the Minister asked, "and the man named Brooke? What about them? Are they still alive?"

"Both deceased. Lytton-Harte from cancer in 1949; Brooke apparently from an airplane crash in 1952. And Canning, the man who led us to the so-called Archbishop file, is in poor health. But he may or may not know the full story. Lytton-Harte apparently compartmentalized this operation; only he, and presumably his superior, knew everything."

Ramsden wasn't sure what Canning knew. *Really* knew. But he guessed that a man like that, an accomplished bureaucrat, could well have pieced the story together on his own.

354

"And the American?"

"Alive. Or was, and retired from teaching."

Sir George shook his head again. Something was gnawing at him. He straightened his body. "And that damn gun thing. Where is it now?"

"With the weapons people. Outside of London." Now, wondered Ramsden, would he ask about the uranium canisters?

He did. His eyes opened wider still. "And the bloody uranium?"

Ramsden shook his head. "We don't know."

"You mean to say that several chunks of radioactive material are lying around somewhere?"

"We have to assume so."

"Good God, what do we do?"

"I rather think the PM will have to decide. You see, to undertake a search will necessarily involve large numbers of individuals."

"Can't we do it discreetly?"

"I don't see how."

Sir George fell back into his chair, silent. Ramsden took the opportunity to raise another matter. "I think we should apprise the Americans of our discovery."

The Home Secretary nodded. "Yes. The PM agreed the Americans must be told. Especially if you found, ah, convincing evidence."

"Perhaps," began Ramsden, "I could—"

The Home Secretary cut him off. "The PM is sending Ackersly."

Ramsden was so shocked he could barely speak. When he did, it was little more than a whisper. "Ackersly?"

"Yes. The PM's personal choice, you see."

Ramsden sat there for a moment, trying to comprehend what he'd just heard. But no matter how he considered it, the bottom line was that he was being taken out. The Archbishop files and their future were literally and figuratively in someone else's hands. But that *twit*, Ackersly?

The Home Secretary was preparing to go. He stuffed his pack of Dunhills into his coat.

But there was one other question. "Sir?"

"Yes?"

"Do you intend to make any announcement to the press? We do have a plan, you know, for public disclosure. Everything cast in a historical context, you see."

Sir George was quick to respond. "No, and that's the government's decision, Edmund. And besides, I don't like 'revelations.' They often have the most disconcerting effect on political currents. I couldn't possibly support any public discussion right now. Perhaps for some time, in fact. Until all the implications have been considered."

"Well, in any event—"

Sir George cut him off again. "These are state secrets, Ramsden. I trust you will treat them as such." The voice was more firm than harsh. Then he cautiously added, "A man of your long and distinguished career would certainly appreciate that."

Ramsden suddenly realized that they had never considered releasing the Archbishop files. The Home Secretary. The Prime Minister. Not really. Like Lytton-Harte a generation before, they saw some compelling political reason to keep this rather remarkable historical episode secret.

And although Sir George didn't say it directly, Ramsden recognized a threat when he heard one.

He sighed. Two years until retirement and his pension. At this point, a rather lucrative one if all went well and he played the good civil servant. And then he would have time for architecture and quiet moments in the small country house he and Edith had bought and fixed up.

"I trust we're in agreement on this?"

Ramsden nodded. The meeting was over.

Sir George stood up and extended his hand. He seemed more mellow now, especially since the ax had fallen, the dirty work of silencing Ramsden had been done. The Archbishop papers had once again been dispatched to secrecy, and even if, somehow, the worst happened and the public learned of these ancient events, the PM had made the call. Sir George was even a bit jolly.

"You've done good work, Edmund. Damn good work."

Ramsden forced a small smile and shook Sir George's hand. He was almost out the door when he hesitated, then stepped back to let the Home Secretary exit first.

The man in the blue short-sleeve shirt and regimental tie watched the rain pelt the outside of the window. The huge, lashing waves of rain were interspersed by occasional flashes of lightning that lit up the interior of his gloomy office at the State Department.

Watley got up from the table and walked to the wall switch and flipped it. Fluorescent light flooded the room. He hated fluorescent light, hated the artificial quality it gave to everything it touched. Fortunately, for most of the year, the Washington skies were bright enough to illuminate his office naturally and let him get by with only the table lamp on his desk.

From where he stood, he could vaguely see C Street through the window, although the Academy of Sciences Building on the other side was shrouded in rain.

He sat back down and looked at the two other men at the table: Dobrowski, the senior documents clerk at State, and Boussard, a representative from the White House. Both men were sifting through a small stack of Xeroxed papers recently brought from London.

"What do you think?" Watley asked.

"Extraordinary," replied Boussard. "I can see why you called us."

"Ed?"

Dobrowski shook his head. "I'd give it fifty-fifty. Sounds improbable to me."

"But the documents?" Watley held up and waved a loose sheet.

Dobrowski pursed his lips in a prim smile. "Oh, they look genuine, all right, but the information could be fake."

Watley shook his head. "Say they're genuine. And accurate. Then what?" He stared at Dobrowski. The thin man opposite him was small, with a large, balding head that made him look like exactly what he was: a middle-aged librarian. Only in this case, he was in charge of the State Department Archives and was one of State's resident experts on nuclear history.

"I'd say we fall back on the other documentation. Our own records."

Boussard looked up, confused. "What other records? I thought you said this was all the Brits sent?"

Watley nodded. "This is all we got."

Dobrowski formed his curious little smile again. "I meant the historical records we have." He leaned forward on the table, obviously glad to have this chance to tell what he knew. After all, he had spent a quarter century as librarian, then custodian, of miles of paper history. To his considerable pleasure, it was often said that he knew the contents of every archive in Washington.

"I went back to the Manhattan Project records that are kept in the National Archives. There is absolutely nothing about any Nazi bomb in the collection. In fact, no word of a Nazi plot to use atomic bombs. I checked several other sources. Nothing. I even placed a call to Los Alamos, to the laboratory, to ask them if they'd ever heard of a German

357

bomb. They're adamant that the Germans failed to make one during the last war. And they say the first test of a nuclear weapon in Russia didn't occur until 1949."

Watley raised his eyebrows. "That's it?"

"That's it. They only confirmed that a Dr. Philip A. Cavanaugh worked there briefly during the war. He left in late 1945 to teach somewhere."

"I had him checked out," said Boussard. "He taught at Berkeley until 1963, then at the University of Michigan until he retired in 1983. As far as we can tell, he's still alive and lives in New Mexico."

"Hmm," mumbled Watley. There was still no consensus. And still no answer to several key questions. "Why would the British make this up?" he asked. "It doesn't make sense."

"Well, I'm not saying it didn't happen," said Dobrowski, hedging his bets, "only that it doesn't jibe with the historical record."

Boussard still looked confused. He was in his middle thirties, with a smooth, youthful face that made him look five years younger. "Who is this General Groves, anyway?"

"Wartime director of the Manhattan Project," said Dobrowski. "Died in 1970, so we can't ask him about any of this."

"Could he possibly have kept events like these secret?" asked Watley. "I mean, it would have been such a momentous development and all."

Dobrowksi shrugged. "Possibly. Reportedly, he ran the Manhattan Project like a private fiefdom, so I guess he could have withheld or destroyed any paper history. Pity if he did."

Watley nodded. Another couple of pounds of paper was just what Dobrowski would like.

"Okay. Let's assume that the Nazis had a bomb, maybe two or three. Do you buy this business about a plot? I mean, sending them to Washington and Moscow?"

Both men shrugged.

Watley's frustration was growing. "Okay, do you buy we get in touch with the Russians? Ask them if they had an explosion in, uh"—he looked at his file—"Leningrad?"

Boussard shook his head. "No. The White House wants this kept quiet. Real quiet. The President agrees with the Prime Minister. News like this wouldn't help the Soviet Premier right now. And it would only be used by our enemies against us. *If* any of it happened, that is."

358

Watley thought about the meeting last week with the PM's aide, Ackersly. An impressive young man, bright, well-dressed, the consummate British type. He left no doubt that the Brits were taking these files seriously and that they genuinely wanted the matter kept secret. That was why, as Ackersly reported, they chose to use a direct, personal channel between the two countries. Apparently, they trusted neither their own intelligence arm nor American's Central Intelligence Agency.

"So why do we have to do anything?" asked Dobrowski. "If you think about it, if we don't have a file on this business, it doesn't exist, does it?" He produced his prim smile again.

"Well," argued Boussard, "the White House wants it checked out. Just in case."

"Just in case what?" asked Watley.

"Just in case news of this Nazi A-bomb drops out somewhere."

"It won't come from us." This administration, like all others in Watley's memory, constantly charged the State Department with leaking information.

Boussard was nonplussed. "I don't think that's what the President is worried about."

Watley thought about it a moment. Ackersly had made the same concerned reference to "just in case."

"So what *is* he worried about?"

Boussard suddenly frowned, adding a few years to his otherwise boyish face. "A leak from outside the government. The press, maybe. Someone in England selling the story for a few bucks. You never know."

Odd, thought Watley, Ackersly had expressed the same concern about the American press.

"Well," he said after a moment, "we've checked the records and come up empty. Zero. So it appears that all we can do is find this Cavanaugh guy and talk to him. See what *he* says."

"You think he'll talk?" Boussard wondered out loud.

"Why not? This is a pretty shocking story, after all. Wouldn't you want a chance to tell your part in it?" Watley looked around the table.

Dobrowski's expression didn't change. No, thought Watley, you wouldn't like that. For you, storing history and cataloging it is more important than making it.

Boussard shrugged, then leaned forward on the table. "I think we should check out the law on this. See if we can't hold Cavanaugh liable under the Atomic Energy Act. You know, classified information and all that. We don't want him talking to some goddamn reporter."

Watley nodded his head in agreement. "We'll check it out."

Boussard nervously tapped his finger on the table, his gaze fixed on the point where his finger touched. Then he looked up. "I just don't understand why we didn't tell the Russians about this Nazi business. Back in 1945. Jesus, I mean back then we were Allies and all."

Watley stared at the young man for a moment. Right now he didn't even look thirty. "You wanna know why?" he said. "I'll tell you why. Because we didn't *like* the sons of bitches."

Cavanaugh heard the car pull up before he saw it. When he got up from his chair and looked out the window, he was certain it was the man from Washington: it was a two-door hatchback from Hertz or Avis at the Albuquerque airport. The cheapest car, of course, typical of what the federal government allowed their employees to rent.

The man sat in his car a moment, apparently gathering some papers together, then folding a map, finally checking his hair in the rearview mirror. Only then did he step out of the car and put on the matching jacket to his gray suit.

Over the phone the man's voice had betrayed no particular age, but Cavanaugh could now tell by looking at him, even fifteen yards away, that he was in his early thirties. And very preppy, with a button-down shirt and snappy tie.

Cavanaugh walked back to the chair where he'd been reading and slipped into his shoes. He looked around the living room to be sure the maid had straightened up. She had. Christine had always kept the house neat, tidy, she called it, so that anyone stopping by would find it presentable.

Today, it looked very much like the last time she had been in the room: her objects undisturbed, her art and furniture in place. Only the fresh flowers were missing.

Oh, how he missed her.

The doorbell rang and Cavanaugh walked to the front door and opened it. The man with the youthful face broke into a smile.

"Dr. Cavanaugh?"

"Yes. Mr. Boussard?"

"Please, it's Tom." He stuck out his hand.

"Come in." Cavanaugh led the young man into the living room and waited for him to take a seat before he sat down. Christine would have already offered the man a cup of coffee or something, but somehow Cavanaugh didn't want to encourage Boussard to stay any longer than necessary. Frankly, he wasn't looking forward to this meeting.

He'd been surprised—shocked, really—a few days ago when the call came one morning. A woman's voice saying it was the White House calling for Dr. Philip Cavanaugh. Then a man who introduced himself as an assistant to the President, asking again if he was Cavanaugh.

"Yes," he remembered saying, "that's me."

Then a remarkable conversation had taken place about events almost half a century ago that tapped a deep, half-forgotten well within him of memories and emotions.

"Thank you for seeing me on such short notice, Dr. Cavanaugh. You got my letter?"

"Yes. No problem." Less than twenty-four hours after the telephone call a special courier had arrived with a letter from Boussard on White House stationery and certification that Boussard was cleared to discuss classified matters.

"You want to see my ID?" asked Boussard. He seemed intent on proving he was who he said he was.

"No. Not necessary. I really don't know much that's sensitive these days. You know I haven't worked for Los Alamos for over forty-five years?"

Boussard smiled. "Oh, yes. I know quite a bit about you, really." He smiled again and tapped one of the brown file folders he was holding.

Cavanaugh said nothing. The man probably did know a lot; but then, he didn't know everything or he wouldn't be here.

"Well, I told you briefly on the phone why I wanted to talk with you. Face-to-face." He looked over at Cavanaugh and waited for a reply.

"Yes. About certain events in London in 1945."

Boussard smiled and visibly relaxed. Something in his face seemed now to say, *This won't be as difficult as I thought.*

"Yes, and if it's true, it's an extraordinary story."

Now Cavanaugh smiled. His conversation with Boussard had been brief, out of a concern for telephone security, the young man had said. They would have to meet really to talk. But the gist of it was that the British government had recently made a discovery, about events so remarkable that the United States government felt obliged to check out and verify them.

So what did Boussard know? "What can I tell you?"

"Well, I don't quite know how to begin. Perhaps you can tell me about your involvement with British Intelligence in 1945?"

Cavanaugh sat back in his chair. He wasn't going to play it their way. Not after all these years.

"It was so long ago. Why don't you tell me what you have? As a starting point." By God, at least he'd make them work for it.

"Uh, okay." Boussard withdrew a three-page memo from one of his folders and handed it to Cavanaugh. "This is the summary we prepared for the President. It's a digest, really, of the documents the British Prime Minister provided us. Perhaps you can verify some of this?"

Cavanaugh took it and began reading it.

Oh, yes, he thought, his head swirling, he could tell them a thing or two. First one door opened, then another, then another, to a dozen small rooms in his memory. Images of Brooke, a Nazi SS officer, a dark room, and a ride at night to an air base flooded to the forefront of his consciousness. Finally, after what must have seemed like an eternity to Boussard, Cavanaugh looked up and commented.

"Yes," he said, "this is generally accurate."

Boussard's eyes widened. "My God," he said.

"Of course, it's written from the British perspective. There's a lot missing."

And there was. There was no mention of Cavanaugh's secret trip to Germany, of his "kidnapping" in London, nor of the awful events in Washington, D.C.

"You mean, the Germans really had a bomb? An atomic bomb?"

Cavanaugh grimaced. My God, what did he say to this young man? How much history did Boussard know? And how much history did Cavanaugh want to relive, even now, after all these years?

"Well," he said finally, "they had at least two atomic bombs. Maybe more."

"What?" Boussard was incredulous.

"Yes. I can account for two, and my guess is that they had at least three." Three cities, three bombs: how well he remembered that troika.

Boussard seemed to melt down in his chair, making him look even more like a lanky teenager wearing a suit. "I don't understand. There's no—no mention of more than one bomb in the British files. Only a mention of a silly plot, a plan to destroy three cities."

Cavanaugh took a long time to respond. Finally he said, "That's because the British know only part of the story." He looked at Boussard, who appeared as perplexed as he did uncomfortable, slumped down in the chair. "Maybe you'd like something to drink?"

An hour later, Cavanaugh found himself fatigued and tired of talking. He was seventy-four, he remembered, and he hadn't gone on like this for a long time.

Boussard seemed fatigued as well, perhaps more mellow, certainly less schoolboyish and more somber. He had said very little, except to ask a question here or there, or to mumble "Extraordinary."

"And I assume the Soviets were told about the plot," Cavanaugh concluded.

The young man's face suddenly lightened. "Well, not that we know of."

"What?" Now Cavanaugh was taken aback.

"There's no record anywhere that Groves told the Russians anything. But we do have a British memo that says an agreement was reached, between Groves and, uh, this guy in London, to deliberately *not* tell the Soviets. To keep the atomic bomb a secret, of course."

"My God," Cavanaugh muttered after a time. All these years he'd kept quiet in part because he had a clear conscience: everyone at least knew about the Nazi plot. The Russians at least had had a chance.

It was Boussard who picked up the conversation again. "I just don't understand," he said finally, "how come there's no record on this? Anywhere."

It took Cavanaugh another moment to respond; he was still thinking about the Russians. "I suppose," he began slowly, "that General Groves didn't want one."

"But why? Something so important, so strange . . ." Boussard seemed lost for words.

Strange indeed, thought Cavanaugh. But important? Was history different because these events had been kept secret for so long? Had it made a difference that the Soviets hadn't been told?

"The President just isn't gonna believe this."

"Maybe not."

"But what about the bomb, the one in Washington? Wouldn't it still be around somewhere? That'd be proof."

Cavanaugh shrugged. "I don't know. Groves would have taken it somewhere to be examined. But if it came to Los Alamos, I never saw it."

"But you left Los Alamos in 1945, didn't you?"

"Yes. In October or November."

"Could they have brought it here then? After you left?"

"Maybe. But then, to bring it here would be to involve more people. Less security that way."

Boussard thought about it. "Oh, yeah," he mumbled. Then he looked over at Cavanaugh. He appeared to be choosing his words carefully.

"I'm curious, Doctor. Why haven't you spoken up before? I mean, you knew as much as anyone about this. It's an incredible story."

Cavanaugh had asked himself that from time to time. He and Christine had even talked about it. But something had always held him back. Something about the way he was treated in 1945, mixed with his belief that what had happened was over and done with. And there was something else: his year and a half at Los Alamos during the war had been the most exciting time of his life. Some feeling for that memory had also checked him, perhaps out of loyalty, or maybe just gratitude for that experience.

"I don't know," he said to Boussard. "It just never seemed appropriate."

"Well, I think you know we're all glad you didn't."

We? wondered Cavanaugh. "We?" he asked.

"Well, the President, really. And the Secretary of State. Our relations with the Soviets are very positive right now. Something like this would only open old wounds, you know."

"Yes, maybe."

"I, ah, don't need to remind you, Dr. Cavanaugh," stumbled Boussard, "that the government still holds you to your pledge of secrecy regarding these matters."

"Oh, yes?" After all this time, really?

"Oh, yes, under the Atomic Energy Act of 1947, any work performed under contract, of whatever period, is still regarded as classified." He cleared his throat. "Unless it's been declassified, of course."

Cavanaugh nodded. "But what would you do if I did speak out? Tell my story, as it were."

Boussard grinned awkwardly. "Well, I hope that's not a consideration, Doctor. I mean, we're counting on your cooperation."

Cavanaugh nodded. "Of course."

"If you think about it, for all practical purposes, these events never happened. I mean, there's no record anywhere." He remembered someone in Washington saying that; in fact, the more he thought about it, the more sense it made.

364

"Well, there are the files from London."

"Oh, well, those we can control." Boussard broke into his boyish smile again. "It's kinda funny, you know."

"What is?"

"History. I don't know a lot of history, I guess. But it doesn't seem to me that what you've told me today significantly changes history a whole lot." He smiled. "I mean, here we are today. The Soviets are in a hell of a mess and no one's interested in events fifty years ago."

Cavanaugh couldn't think of anything to say, so he just stared as the man neatly stacked his notes and files. What do you say to someone who says history doesn't matter.

The two men rose, Cavanaugh more slowly, and said good-bye. Boussard promised to be back in touch. When he reached his car he got in and then immediately out again to remove his gray coat. Finally, after unfolding and checking his map, the man backed out of the driveway and drove away.

Cavanaugh stood at the doorway a long time, long after the President's aide had disappeared. He thought of Christine and how much he missed her. She would have loved this morning. Or would she? He felt a mixture of relief and anger. Relief that the man had wanted so little; anger that he seemed to regard the events of 1945 as no more than an interesting historical anecdote. Christine might have reacted the same way.

God, what had become of his own generation? Were they mostly dead? They wouldn't feel the same way as Boussard about history. Not recent history, anyway. And certainly not about the last war.

He returned to the living room and for some reason glanced at the fireplace. On the mantel were photographs of his mother and father. Both dead. And Christine. Dead almost two years now. And his only child, a daughter, and her twin girls. No one to carry on his name, since his own siblings were all girls.

Sometimes he wondered what made him come back to Los Alamos after he retired. Christine never opposed the move, but she let him know that she suspected his motives. So what were they?

For forty years, he had been back to Los Alamos less than a half dozen times. Only once for a reunion of "old-timers," as they called themselves. He remembered saying more than once that he would never return to New Mexico except as a tourist, no matter how much he liked the climate and the landscape. And yet here he was.

The present-day laboratory was only a twenty-minute drive from his home, utterly different from what he had known during the war. And yet, at odd moments, as during a drive to the store, or on a walk, he saw something—or someone—that reminded him of the past. Christine knew the look on his face when it happened; she always broke into a smile and whistled the first few bars of "Memories."

Cavanaugh smiled to himself and then remembered something he'd done the day he got the call from Boussard. He'd walked into his library and bent down to the lowest shelf, the one where he kept an old collection of college textbooks, including the first physics book he'd ever owned. He'd pulled it out, then a few others, and reached to the rear of the shelf to grab an old, faded envelope.

This was only the second time in maybe thirty years that he'd looked at the contents. Today, he pulled them out again.

He carefully unfolded the twenty-odd pages and read first the small piece of faded blue notepaper with Christine's elegant handwriting on it. It said simply,

When this you see/remember me.
Love, C.

The rest of the pages were in his neat, tiny handwriting. He had written them in Washington, in July 1945. It was the draft of his report to General Groves.

Cavanaugh trembled slightly as he looked at the thin pages; they were brown and brittle with age now. He remembered so clearly his surprise when Christine gave them to him, not long after they were married, in this same envelope, tied with a tiny ribbon.

"What the hell?" he remembered saying. *"You're not supposed to have these! They were supposed to be destroyed."*

Yes, she'd said, *she'd been told to destroy them.* But somehow, she believed he needed to keep them. A record, just in case, for some day in the future.

He flipped through a few pages. A diagram of the Mühlhausen gun barrel leapt off the page at him. And then the other drawings, the diagrams of the bomb components he'd seen in London, that night with Brooke and the old man. And all the words, the tiny, precise words ending with his urgent recommendation that the Soviets be briefed immediately.

Odd, but the contents of the report no longer interested him. Not the specifics, anyway. What interested him now, he guessed, was the question of what to do with the report.

Once, perhaps in jest, Christine had encouraged him to write his story, as a book, even as a novel. For history's sake, she argued. Yes, no, he never could decide. Too busy, too many other things to do. Never quite the motivation.

But now?

Well, now there was the time. And just maybe the inclination.

Historical Note

*T*he historical events upon which this novel is based are largely true.

As scientists and technicians, the Germans were enormously imaginative and inventive.

The V-2 rocket was perhaps their most spectacular achievement, but there were many others: the world's first production-line jet aircraft, antiaircraft missiles, faster and more powerful submarines, sophisticated torpedoes, synthetic fuels, poison gases, and the largest and more advanced aircraft wind-test tunnels. Not to mention the industrial techniques and systems to manufacture all these weapons while the nation was at war and under constant aerial bombardment from 1943 onward.

These considerable achievements provided the stage for a postwar battle, a quiet one, between the conquering Allies themselves.

Plans were in place in various degrees by 1944 by all the major

Allies—Britain, Russia, and the United States—to follow military victory with a thorough capture of German science and technology. The various intelligence arms—G-2, MI5 and MI6, for example—were heavily involved at all levels. ALSOS was only one arm of the American effort; Britain had its Red Indians, and the Soviets their own "special" teams. All Allied nations utilized their military forces in whatever ways were helpful in seizing both machinery and personnel.

But the spoils were not evenly divided.

In retrospect, it appears that the Western Allies took possession of large numbers of rockets, jets, and other technological achievements, as well as captured the best of German research laboratories and the cream of their scientists and technicians. The Soviets inherited a substantial portion of German industry, which they promptly dismantled and shipped to Russian sites, as well as aircraft factories, motor-production plants, major electronic laboratories, and a host of smaller but useful industries and programs.

Fortunately, the Germans did not succeed in developing an atomic bomb. Adolf Hitler never grasped the possibilities of nuclear fission, and certainly failed to understand its potential in a weapon. The resources he allocated to nuclear research were minimal compared with other scientific efforts within his Third Reich.

Until April 1945, however, there were reasons for the Allies to believe that the Germans might succeed in making a weapon. Fission, after all, had been discovered by Otto Hahn in 1939. He and Werner Heisenberg, another noted German physicist, were both known to be conducting nuclear research for the Nazis. And physicist Frédéric Joliot continued his atomic research throughout the war in German-occupied Paris.

To ascertain the extent of German success—or failure—the Manhattan Project created its special ALSOS force and sent it to Europe to follow, sometimes even precede, the advancing Allied armies. By May 1945, it was clear from captured scientists, documents, and a small nuclear reactor, that the Germans were years behind their American counterparts. Their prototype reactor, for example, was indeed located in a cave in Haigerloch, Germany, several hundred feet beneath a Roman Catholic church.

In all likelihood, had they succeeded, the Germans would have utilized a bomb similar to the one described in this book. Firing one quantity of fissionable material into another—in the precise quantities, of course, and under the right circumstances—remains the most direct method of achieving a supercritical and, therefore, explosive chain reaction.

Ironically, in the end, Hitler lost the race for the atomic bomb not only because of his lack of vision, but because Europe's best scientists—many Jewish—had either been liquidated or were in America.